You'd look like hell, too, if the Daemon Queen of the Night had hold of you

Lemonade, freshly squeezed, extra sugar added, iced down and watered up, glass in hand, Tina led Wilderwitch to her mother's bedroom.

No matter how much the look-after-yourself travails of the last two-plus months had strengthened her, the Witch was still having some difficulty walking. Consequently, in order to keep up with the girl, she had to levitate herself within a fortunately functional again, metallic-marigold-cast, thought-balloon.

They were in the Zerosses' seaside hideaway on the coast of Fearsome Fobbiat, the Headworld's western ocean. Dr Melina nee Sarpedon Zeross, the High Illuminary of Weir, was in her private quarters, sitting in a chair beside the bed she'd shared with Ringleader, Dr Aristotle Zeross, for the better part of two decades.

Tina's two older sisters, Persephone and Helen, were also there. Looking teary-eyed sad, they were standing behind their mother, hands on her shoulders supportively. Something in the shape of a someone, a child not quite Helen's size, was lying in the bed covered with a sheet doubling as a shroud.

Dispelling the thought-balloon as she did so, Wilderwitch came to ground. She was strong enough to stand on her own but, so struck was she at the High Illuminary's wasted condition, she very nearly lost her balance; thus only just avoided making a remarkably still-pregnant ass on her ass of herself. As it was, she barely registered the boy's apparent corpse.

"Good God, Mel, you look like hell."

"Thanks," Melina said to Wilderwitch. "I needed that."

"You're welcome. What's that?" she asked, finally pointing to the body in the bed.

Suddenly, as if receiving a long-awaited cue, it reared into a sitting position. Already unsteady on her feet, the Witch visibly blanched, sucking air reflexively. The shroud-like sheet slipped off his head. It was Harry Zeross, Kid Ringo, age about ten.

"Fooled you," he said with a big grin on his face.

DAEMONIC DESPERATION

TWO BEINGS, TWO PREGNANCIES, ONLY ONE BODY, CARRYING ON '*WILDERWITCH'S BABIES*'

Copyright © James H McPherson

A *PHANTACEA* MYTHOS PRINT PUBLICATION

Conceived, written and produced by Jim McPherson
Interior Collages, Front and Back Covers by Jim McPherson

Phantacea Publications

(James H McPherson, Publisher)
74689 Kitsilano RPO
2768 West Broadway
Vancouver BC
V6K 4P4 Canada

Phantacea Publications featuring

Jim McPherson's
PHANTACEA Mythos

- ### PHANTACEA One to Six
(1977-80, a series of comic books with artwork by various artists)
- ### Forever & 40 Days – The Genesis of PHANTACEA
(1990, a graphic novel with artwork by Ian Fry, background material and a short story featuring the Damnation Brigade, the Death Dodgers & Signal System)
- ### Feeling Theocidal
(2008, Book One of 'The Thrice-Cursed Godly Glories' trilogy*)
- ### The War of the Apocalyptics
(2009, the first full-length entry in the 'Launch 1980' story cycle*)
- ### The 1000 Days of Disbelief
(2010-11, Book Two of 'The Thrice Cursed Godly Glories' trilogy, consisting of three mini-novels: 'The Death's Head Hellion'*, 'Contagion Collectors'* and 'Janna Fangfingers'*)
- ### Goddess Gambit
(2012, Book Three of 'The Thrice Cursed Godly Glories' trilogy*)
- ### Phantacea Revisited 1: The Damnation Brigade
(2013, graphic novel featuring a complete story sequence primarily excerpted from Phantacea One to Five, various artists*)
- ### Nuclear Dragons
(2013, the second full-length entry in the 'Launch 1980' story cycle*)
- ### Phantacea Revisited 2: Cataclysm Catalyst
(2014, graphic novel featuring a complete story sequence excerpted from Phantacea One to Seven and Phantacea Phase One #1, various artists*)
- ### Helios on the Moon
(2014, the third and final full-length entry in the 'Launch 1980' story cycle*)
- ### Wilderwitch's Babies
(2016, 'Decimation Damnation'*; 2017, 'Hidden Headgames'*; 2019, 'Daemonic Desperation'*)

E-versions also available

DAEMONIC DESPERATION

Auctorial Preamble

****

Did promise in "Hidden Headgames", the 2017 collection of three novellas bridging the prose versions of *PHANTACEA* **Phase One** and **Phase Two**, that "Wilderwitch's Babies" will be back, full-throttle, in "Daemonic Desperation". Well, here it is. No need to guess who the desperate daemon is, either.

Have a quote from the perspective of a onetime perpetual presence (adult, female) trying, and at least momentarily failing, to make a comeback in 5980 Year of the Dome. That'd be thirty years after she was ill-starred for killing the Male Entity (him for the eleventh time according the Entities' own reckoning).

Although some of the events alluded to occurred in "Helios on the Moon", it's taken from '*Pyrame's Progress*', the second novella contained in the aforementioned GAMES collection.

Humanized Memory [the Female Entity], her tremendous visage simultaneously blanking as it reddened both alarmingly and indicatively, hesitated; didn't answer. Something was happening to her, Moon's Angel, on the Moon. Must mean someone, perhaps a devil [Strife], was trying to take her over; to displace the Demon Queen – if it was her – as she did so.

Was that her, walking over her grave, she and Shah's, two in one, their final resting place, moments later? Had to be.

Without going into too many details, in **PHANTACEA** the word 'devil' means, and always has meant, what it did originally: namely, 'little god'. Pyrame's a devil over-coated by Tsishah's demon, whose full name is, or was, Shahiyeda. They, melded, have just been swallowed – more like sucked in – by the accumulated, yet stunningly smooth, Stopstone/Solidium Godcrud of Absudyl, the Subterranean Land of the Mandroids.

Absudyl, sometimes (as in "The Thousand Days of Disbelief") also referred to as Minius, after its only occasionally conscious, primary denizen Magnus Minus, is the westernmost terminus of the Hell-Well of the World. The demon or, more correctly, daemon (as in genius) Pyrame senses walking over her grave subsequently keeps on walking until she reaches the other end of the Hell-Well; until she reaches Satanwyck, Hell on Earth. Whereupon she seizes, howsoever briefly, what she considers her rightful throne, the Highchair of Hell.

Yes, it's Primeval Lilith, the Daemon Queen of the Night; of the Day as well. Her name's generic but, under it, or variations thereof, she's had an exceedingly long history — her-story, if you prefer. And not just in terms of **the Phantacea Mythos**. (Which began in September 1977 with the oversized comic book **Phantacea One**, the first publication in any medium besides a short story written as a teenager in first year university to bear that designation.)

Here's another quote, one taken from an article found on Wikipedia entitled 'Lilith in Popular Culture' …

> *No spirit exerts more fascination over media and popular culture than Lilith. Her appearances are genuinely too numerous to count.*

So, clearly not a character unique to **the Phantacea Mythos**. She's so old she might be preliterate, even prehistoric. This quote was also taken from Wikipedia, albeit in an article specifically about her:

> *Lilith is often envisioned as a dangerous demon of the night, who is sexually wanton, and who … may be linked in part to a historically earlier class of female demons (lilītu) in ancient Mesopotamian religion, found in cuneiform texts of Sumer, the Akkadian Empire, Assyria, and Babylonia.*

All of which works for our purposes. So does the notion that she was the Biblical Adam's first wife, the mother of Cain, Slayer of Abel, whose story made up part of the 1990 graphic novel "Forever & 40 Days – The Genesis of *PHANTACEA*". There, Anti-Patriarch Cain is described as being an incarnation of *'Heliosophos (Helios called Sophos the Wise), the most ancient enemy of devazurkind'*.

Which shouldn't surprise anyone since Cain's father, the Male Entity, Alorus Ptah, the second Biblical Adam and the first patriarch of Golden Age Humankind, was Helios in an unspecified lifetime. (Google up Adam Kadmon sometime. As I've said many times, I didn't make up **the Phantacea Mythos** so much as channel it.)

Indeed, Cain's dwelling place, Enoch City, is shown in 4EVER&40 as being very similar, if perhaps not identical, to Trans-Time Trigon, what follows the Dual Entities across time and space. Has in fact been shown to do so since Helios and Mnemosyne were introduced in 1978's **Phantacea Three**.

What hasn't been shown since those days is that the Female Entity holding onto *pHant*'s Lithesome – or Loathsome, if you prefer – Lily throughout most of that time is how she gets to appear to be a solid being, as opposed to just a holographic projection or a digital face in her computer self's wall.

Come DESPERATION, Luscious Lily isn't hers anymore; isn't Pyrame's either. Have an abbreviated, yet nonetheless pertinent passage from 2016's "Decimation Damnation". It's told from the perspective of a certain Wayfarer in the Wild Weird; takes place on the same day the Witch more that just met Primeval Lilith.

Saladin Devason finished making love to Wilderwitch …. But there was more, he realized, stretching his mental tendrils such that he could read him, Braille-like, without an interpreter. The Master was not altogether himself. He thought he was making love to some sort of darkness-shrouded succubus, a Black Widow woman, one with only two eyes, but one who was not entirely herself either.

The Witch was not possessed, she was coated; rather, her soul-self was. And Saladin was not making love to her, it, the nevertheless effectively possessed spirit. Another horror was. It also had two eyes. Only one of them was in its forehead.

That remains the case at the end of DECDAM. Except, the Demon Queen, who has a brain and concomitant ambitions of her own, no more has hold of Wilderwitch – the last member of the Damnation Brigade in the Weirdom of Cabalarkon, if perhaps not D-Brig's last living member anywhere – than the Witch has hold of her. Hardly the best of situations, I'm sure you'd agree.

Nevertheless, perhaps ironically, Lethal Lily is most of the reason the Witch is healing so quickly. She's also … what? A quarter of the reason the Witch is pregnant; hence, maybe, eventually, our opus's overall title "Wilderwitch's Babies". That quartering of responsibility applies equally to Lascivious Lily, whereas the male half of the equation is the Master of Weir possessed by the Moloch Sedon, the All-Father of Devazurkind, who looks and, as also per pH-4ever&40, may actually be the Devil.

Seems said Devil is after another Sed-son. (In 5980 there are only two left, one on either side of Cathonia.) Needs one, for starters, to retain the Cathonic Zone or Dome in order to shield his Hidden Headworld from the Outer Earth. Seems as well that only the Demon Queen can have Sed-sons.

Rather, only the Demon Queen can conceive a Sed-son. That still leaves her shells to bear them. Or it did when the Demon Queen was solidifying Pyrame Silverstar, and that she-devil was possessing the demon's mortal surrogates. Then again, in the absence of Pyrame she might have to bear him herself on account of the Witch being simultaneously pregnant … with (at least) one girl.

This being **the Phantacea Mythos**, there are plenty of other dynamics at play herein. There are also a few more pages than DECDAM. That's why there's no room for a Character Companion. It's also why there is no teaser at the end of the mini-novel proper. Instead, as you'll see when you get there, there are not one or two, but no less than four (decreasingly brief) epilogues.

Enjoy.

Jim McPherson
Creator/Writer
The *PHANTACEA* Mythos

****

Chapter Titles

- Auctorial Preamble ...   v
- ONE-DEMON: **Panharmonium Begins** ...   1
- TWO-DEMON: **Half-Mama Memory** ...   12
- THREE-DEMON: **Not Half-Mama Pyrame** ...   27
- FOUR-DEMON: **Drawing Contusions** ...   38
- FIVE-DEMON: **Dissembling Daddy's Desiccation** ...   56
- SIX-DEMON: **Arrested Envelopment** ...   66
- SEVEN-DEMON: **Quill Or Be Killed** ...   81
- EIGHT-DEMON: **Sal Misses Mel** ...   94
- NINE-DEMON: **Wilderwitch's Abduction** ...   111
- TEN-DEMON: **Sodom's Gomorrah** ...   123
- ELEVEN-DEMON: **Quaking Cabalarkon** ...   135
- TWELVE-DEMON: **Morgianna's Statuary Remains** ...   147
- THIRTEEN-DEMON: **Skyrise Kills** ...   163
- FOURTEEN-DEMON: **Freespirit Wilderwitch** ...   176

DAEMONIC DESPERATION

— Early Yamana 5980 – The Summer Solstice 5981 —

Jim McPherson

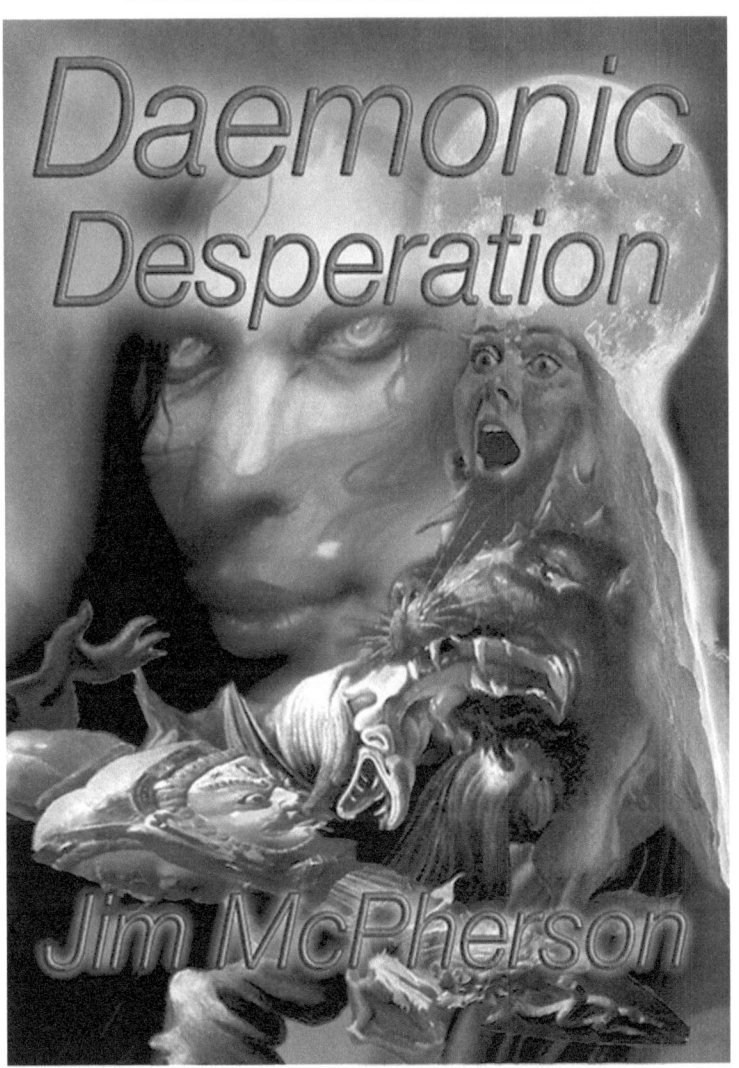

A *PHANTACEA* Mythos Print Publication
James H McPherson, Publisher

ISBN 978-1-927844-21-2
First Published 2019

Daemonic Desperation

One-Demon: **Panharmonium Begins**

========

> So long as you wake up, having a dream, even an awful nightmare, was a sign you were still alive. Sometimes, no matter how sad or scary your dreams were, continuing to dream was infinitely preferable to waking up.
>
> Going to sleep, perchance to dream, was a pretty good strategy. Was certainly better than dying. Except when you were on the Hidden Continent of Sedon's Head. Where, just as often, having dreams meant you were under attack. That being the case, you either wake up right smartly or you die right irrevocably.
>
> For her part, she would rather keep on dreaming.

Devauray, 19 Rudar 5981

Jordan Tethys, white, unshaven, beer smelly, wearing a tattered tweed suit and a checked cap, looked for all the world like the homeless street person he often had been in Aka Godbad City prior to the coming of Panharmonium. An open bottle of pilsner at his side — no cans for him, by personal preference; unless of course neither bottles nor kegs were available — he was sitting in the recently planted garden outside Hope Haven, the converted city hall in New Vancouver, formerly the Fraser Valley township of Hope.

As was often the case he had attracted a large group of children clamouring for him to tell them a story. One of his recent favourites Athena Zeross — he'd been on the heart-shaped island of Shenon the day her mother Melina gave birth to her in Azky of '74 — was sitting on his knee. She took off his cap and squealed at all tee-tee tails attached to his razor-bald pate.

"Which one would you prefer, little one?"

"Begin with mommy and daddy," the seven year old said. "That's where I did."

Tethys chuckled. "So you did, Tina. But isn't that a little inappropriate considering the occasion? How about we begin with your mom's predecessor, Saladin Devason?"

========

The Master of Weir, as black-skinned as all Utopian women were white-skinned, flanked by dozens of Trinondevs, all men and therefore all black, rushed through the Catacombs of the Sleepers. They were horrified by what they saw in the tomb-room of Cabalarkon: devils, four of them. Even allowing for their three eyes only one of them looked relatively normal. That one had blue skin; was wearing a fur garment covering his loins. His skull was mostly shaven; his long topknot glowed with the intensity of Brainrock.

The lone woman was composed entirely of smoky particulates. About the only consistent thing about the third one was a mace, his Brainrock talisman. Otherwise he was changing by the second: an air-strutting centaur, a be-winged Angelyc, a humanoid Saurian, a Simian Sapient, an ebonite demon, a preying mantis ... the variations were endless. The fourth was just a hovering head, completely hairless and with no body in sight.

"Impossible," cried the Master. "Why haven't our orbs activated?" he said to Capputis, his eldest son. The hydrocephalic teenager who, despite his youth, had become his chief adviser could only shrug his shoulders.

"Because I do not wish them to, Saladin. Have you forgotten this is as much my protectorate as this continent is mine to do with as I please? You rule by my sufferance alone!"

A being materialized in front of the four devils. He was as tall as he wanted to be, taller than any of the Trinondevs; far hairier, too. His skin was a fiery red; which made his hairiness seem like sprouting threads of flame. He had horns, a forked goatee and moustache; one of his arms was cut off at the elbow. This was the Moloch Sedon Himself.

"Great Byron has convinced me to leave this world. We have come to pick up my father. Goodbye, Master of Weir. I doubt we shall meet again!"

The date was the 30th of Maruta 5980 Year of the Dome, as we on the Hidden Headworld counted time before the coming of Panharmonium.

========

"Boo," hissed Tina. "I want to hear about my parents."

"And so you shall, child. And your sisters — but you will also hear about many others as well. First, though, since you will grow up hearing different versions of how our Panharmonium came about, you might as well know the truth."

========

Six thousand years ago Xuthros Hor, the Biblical Noah, the tenth and last patriarch of Golden Age Humanity, caused the first Great Flood, the Genesea, that of Genesis, in order to wash the Earth clean of the Moloch Sedon and his equally immortal descendants. Instead they fled to the ancient archipelago of Pacifica, the Places of Peace; call it Mu or Lemuria, if you prefer.

Whereupon, over which, the King of all Demons for something like two hundred fifty years by then, and All-Father of devazurkind, for maybe 200 more, erected the Cathonic Dome out of his own essence. He thereby separated the Inner from the Outer Earth, a condition that persisted, more or less, until he took his leave from the planet aboard the Cosmic Express last November, Maruta.

When Dark Sedon left he collapsed the Dome, causing the Second Great Flood, the inundation of the Pacific coastal regions, as a consequence. In a way, therefore, the devils Hor sought to destroy simply returned the favour — with considerably less loss of land and, quite conceivably, given how prolific humanity was pre-Flood, not all that much more loss of life.

The damage is largely done now. The Earth is on the mend. And, due largely to the superhuman efforts of the Liberation Brigade, many of your Utopian elders and, indeed, sapient beings of all stripes, including Zebranid Lepers like your cousin Andaemyn, we are masters of our own fate once again. But it was a near thing.

The Liberation Brigade were a group of supranormals – call them supras, I do, not so many syllables – who went to the Moon on the UNES Liberty in a futile effort to stop whatever it was that was there. What that was were the Dual Entities: the Male, Heliosophos or Helios called Sophos the Wise, and his companion of a hundred lifetimes, the Female, the Mnemosyne Machine or Miracle Memory, as she likes more than she should. Instead of battling them to the death as they were supposed to do, the Liberators ended up joining them.

Technologically advanced, supremely well-intentioned, Heliosophos was far from omniscient. He was, however, well aware of the existence of Sedon's Head and what would happen if Cathonia – the Cathonic Zone or Dome, celestially speaking then also the Sedon Sphere – ceased to be between it and the rest of the planet. His theory had been to leave it as was while he concentrated on the Outer Earth.

Had been. But Thrygragos Byron, a devil with an enormous head who had lost his body during the pre-Flood Golden Age of Humankind, and never bothered to grow it back, realized that the Entity would turn his attention to the Head and its devils eventually. He determined to leave the planet with all his children, plus those from any of the other two tribes who wished to go with him; Grandfather Sedon, his ever-undying Utopian father Cabalarkon, and all those stuck as sentient stars within the Cathonic Dome as well.

To accomplish that, the Great God caused New Century Enterprises – in effect the Outer Earth parent company of the Head's Centauri Enterprises – to build the Cosmic Express. The original idea had been to use it to scout possible planets where devils could settle. But Bodiless Byron panicked. Jumped the gun, as it were; used this Express to flee the Whole Earth. He deliberately left behind his brother, Thrygragos Lazareme, any who would stay with him, and all the devic and purely daemonic reprobates yet imprisoned within the She-Sphinx, All of Incain.

Sedon had had dealings with Heliosophos before; sooth said, it was Helios who created him many multiple millennia earlier in one of his first lifetimes. He had no intention of leaving him behind such that he could go in pursuit of them. After the Express gathered up the devils in the Cathonic Zone, he had Byron detach two Cosmicars and sent them to the Moon.

Possessing the fourteen aboard the cosmicars were Lord Yajur, the Unity of Order; Pyrame Silverstar, the so-called Pauper Priestess; the Primary Apocalyptics, War, Disease and Disaster; the four-armed Medusa, Mater Matare, Mother Murder, the self-proclaimed Apocalyptic of Death; a lesser Master Deva known as the Vultyrie; and seven fourth generation Thanatoids: Night, Day, Earth, Fire, Spring, Autumn and Winter. It was their task to kill Helios and all those on the Moon with him. Which was why the Liberators joined up with them, the Entities and their fellows. Better your own kind than devils, right? Almost!

Among the Liberation Brigade were the eleven who disappeared on Damnation Island a quarter century earlier. A number of their contemporaries from the days of SOS: the Society of Saints and survivors of both groupings of KOC: the King's Own Crimefighters had also been re-recruited for the journey to the Moon.

They included Mesmer Hent, aka Mr Attraction; his wife, Laodice Atreides, aka both Electrocretan and Elektra Solenoid; Scylla Nereid, aka Fish or Fisherwoman; OJ "Big Max" Maxwell, formerly the first Baron Justice; Tina's Uncle Demios, the Ace of Spades; and her Aunt Morgianna, the White Witch or Morrigan. Already there were the so-called Trigon Spartae, of whom, other than there were five of them, all men, we know very little. Many suspect they were Gypsium-blessed time-tumblers like the Dual Entities, but now's not the time for speculation.

Appreciate that most of these old warriors were approaching sixty, if they hadn't already passed it by then. Even most of the younger supras, Helios, his five Spartae, Romaine Kinesis, whose codename was Doc Defiance, the Liberty's captain, James Aremar, and Ringleader, your father, Tina, were in their forties or close enough. They weren't all old-timers of course. Seventeen of the Liberators, clones of long dead supras who collectively formed the Signal System contingent, were in their late twenties.

Despite the advantages of numbers, and Helios's Utopian technology, the devils were both merciless and formidable foes; Reborn Again Killers, as the saying goes. More than half of the Brigade died there. They included the first Baron Justice, Mr Attraction, Electrocretan-Solenoid, a few of the Signallers, the five Spartae and, as you know, your dear uncle Demios.

Although I understand a number of the survivors intend to write books on their part in that battle, it remains a big secret what actually happened there. What we can say is Helios, Memory, and the Liberators didn't so much win as they came to an accommodation with Yajur, Pyrame and the seven Thanatoids. Why or how, we may never know for sure.

There are rumours aplenty that Mater Matare was pregnant; that she gave birth up there; that her and her offspring accounted for most of the dead. Not only that but that they ate their souls in order to make themselves stronger. One thing is certain. The only devils who did perish were Matare, the three other Primary Apocalyptics, the Vultyrie, and their children, if they in fact existed.

So, while there may have been a victory of sorts on the Moon, it was Pyrrhic. The Moloch Sedon, Bodiless Byron, Phantast the Dreamweaver – the devil, Death Dream, I hate more than any other – and perhaps two hundred more Master Devas had fled the Whole Earth aboard the Cosmic Express; hopefully never to return.

But there were lots left down here: Thrygragos Lazareme, the majority of his spawn – a hundred or so by then – dozens of Mithradites, and even a few Byronics who chose not to join their father on the exodus. The Flood was in the process of wiping out two billion human beings and, on top of all that, the exotics of the Head were now free to spread over the entire planet.

Finally there was the matter of mandroids, Steltsar and the two antediluvian Sphinxes.

========

Very young Athena had been weeping since he mentioned her uncle's demise. Tethys gave her a quick hug. "I'm sorry, Tina. Demios was a brave man. I'm sure he died heroic- ally, but no one on either side of the collapsed Dome escaped without losing someone they loved very much. When you think about it, you did better than most."

"Go ahead," she sniffed. "I'm brave too."

========

In the debacle that swept the Pacific Basin one place remained relatively un- scathed. That was the Outer Earth's Centauri Island. Its survival is not as miraculous as it may seem. Its three peaks, Mounts Kinesis, Zeross and Heliopolis, still contain Gypsium, as does Easter Island in the South Pacific, which also managed to stay afloat. The mostly manmade Centauri and the Inner Earth's island of the same name are now attached to Aka Godbad City, on the formerly hidden continent, what we have agreed to rename Lemuria now that Dark Sedon has departed.

Under the banner of the Empire of Lathakra there came these devils and ar- mies made up of their adherents, hardly all of which were human. Its titular com- mander-in-chief was Thrygragos Lazareme but, as I said, it flew the Labrys, the double-headed, sun-glowing, Brainrock war-axe against the icy blue of the sky, the sea, winter and the freezing cold that made up the Lathakran flag. As such, its real leader was King Cold, Tantal Thanatos, a firstborn of the long gone, still believed dead, third Great God or Thrygragos, Varuna Mithras.

He was supported by his sister-wife, the ever-masked Methandra of Mythland, she of Heat to her breed brother and husband's Cold. Although devils usually re- ferred to her as either the Scarlet Empress or, more simply, Seeress, Illuminaries of old came up with the name Methandra by combining the words Mediterranean and Athena. Mediterranean Athena was how she was named by her original worshippers on the Whole Earth after Master Devas began becoming solid beings four thousand years ago. Thus, in an oblique way, you, Tina, were named after her.

As I just said, or at least implied, the Thanatoids' mother was another of Mith- ras's firstborn — the third being personally despised Phantast the Dreamweaver, who is with Sedon and Byron. Together with her husband, they commanded those Mithradites left on the Whole Earth. They weren't the only firstborns left behind either. Leading the few remaining Byron Spawn were that Great God's Rufous Rudra and Umashakti Silvercloud.

(Parenthetically, his third firstborn – for all Master Devas are born in litters of three – whom Illuminaries named Serathrone Hallow by reputation alone, never made it to the then, as now once again, whole Planet Earth in the first place.)

In charge of by far the most numerous tribe left on the planet, that of Laz- areme, aka Thrygragos Everyman, was none other than Unholy Abaddon. He's a devic suicide, the former Unity of Chaos; more daemon than anything else. Recall his fellow former Unity, Lord Yajur, he of Order, was on the Moon. In case I haven't mentioned it he was possessing Mikelangelo Starrus, the captain of one of the cos- micars that Sedon detached from the Express.

I also know where the third of Lazareme's firstborn, who nowadays calls her- self Freespirit Nihila, but was once Harmony, the onetime Unity of Balance, the Illuminaries' Datong Harmonia, was at the time — also on the Moon, inside the

Female Entity, who's only a machine, the Mother of All Machines as Memory herself would tell you, unless she's humanized by a devil.

How do I know? Because I sent her there!

========

As Jordan Tethys regaled his young audience with his gruesome tale, two of the surviving Liberators, Blind Sundown and Raven's Head, arrived from their Rocky Mountain hideaway. Raven no longer bothered to mask what she was beneath a witch's glamour: a large – very large – raven-headed doe or mare taxonomically related to reindeer, hence also ravendeer, albeit one with a retractable unicorn horn and talarial wings on the upper sides of all four of her fetlock ankles.

When sentient dinosaurs, among many another exotic specie, now roamed the reunited Earth she, Wakinyah (thundercloud) Creature of the Cosmos that they were, seemed almost commonplace.

========

Miracle Memory had only the vaguest connection to Mnemosyne D'Angelo, the supra slain on Sakhalin Island in early 1945. She was much more closely linked to Freespirit Nihila, who looks very much like her, like Memory of the Angels, albeit with three eyes, longer crinklier butterscotch hair, a set of Brainrock chains extending from bracelets on either wrist, and a Brainrock necklace, inspiration for the ill-omened legend of same, for a power focus.

Fifteen hundred years before Christ, the Unity of Balance walked the Outer Earth under the name she'd always favoured, Harmony. (Illuminaries of yore returning to the Inner Earth didn't get around to naming her Datong Harmonia until midway through the next millennium at the earliest.) During that era – at the tail end of the Outer Earth's mostly Mediterranean-centric Goddess Culture to be specific – she married the fabled King Cadmus of Thebes.

(I have no intention of going into the Cadmean Cycle of Minoan Myths, my young ones, but will tell you Cadmus could have been the Heliosophos Entity in who can say what lifetime.)

Just before your daddy joined the Liberators and went to the Moon, Tina, he was on a mission on behalf of Saladin Devason to retrieve the three Sacred Objects, more properly known as the Trigregos Talismans. Others, including the Sarpedons, your uncle, aunt, your cousin Andaemyn and Morgianna's only other child, Tsishah Twilight, were also in pursuit of them. One of them, the Susasword, had been pinning nowadays-Nihila to a slab of Brainrock in the Crystal Mountains for something like five hundred years. She was freed before Sedon collapsed the Dome.

Sensing what was happening on the Moon, she came to see me shortly after the cataclysm began; asked me to draw her there. I was only too happy to oblige. Good thing I did. If there's one hero in all this it's Harmony-Nihila, which is why Panharmonium is named after her Minoan alter ego. But I was talking about what was happening on Centauri Island.

Recall that both the United States and the Soviet Union had dismantled their nuclear, chemical and biological arsenals by the end of last year. They hadn't got as far as disarming their armies, navies and air forces, however. Also, as you might have assumed, if you were old and cynical like me, dismantling didn't mean destroying.

Before the Superpowers could unearth their weapons of mass destruction and rearm their ships and war planes with them, Loxus Abraham Ryne (who was once married to your aunt, Tina, Oriani Zeross) went to the United Nations. He prevailed on governments gathered there to let him send a group of young supras to Centauri. He hoped they could stop the devils and their adherents before they moved onto, and into – since devazurs are possessive spirits – the rest of the world.

Trained mostly by Cerebrus David Ryne, one of Abe Ryne's first set of twins, who had dubbed them the Junior Liberation Brigade, they numbered about fifty. Most were untried and all were horribly inexperienced; students or very recent graduates of Academies of Man then scattered throughout the old Outer Earth.

The JLB was intended to be nothing more than a back-up to the Liberty, its crew of well-trained, well-armed 'normals', and the Liberators: veteran supras, like the remnants of the Crimefighters and the Soviet Supra Supreme, plus the cloned Signallers provided by Simon Lancz's Signal System. Instead they became the vanguard of the Anti-Deva Defense League. ADDLED – as I'm sorry to say, it quickly came to be called – were akin to lambs being led to the slaughter.

And slaughtered all too many of them were.

Fortunately, on the brink of disaster wrought upon cataclysm, what was left of the real Liberators returned from the Moon. Two of them, Aires and Thalassa D'Angelo, had by then learned they were devils; Thanatos-spawned fourth generation ones to be sure, but devils nevertheless. What's more they brought with them their seven previously cathonitized siblings — ones who had been on the missing cosmicars as well as, equally significantly, Pyrame Silverstar and Starrus-Yajur.

Thanks to Nihila's harmonious influence, all nine Thanatoids chose to fight alongside the Liberation Brigade rather than with their parents. The Pauper Priestess and Lord Order made arguably even more important contributions to the eventual victory of sanity. If ever a battle could be called glorious this was it. Many and myriad were the struggles that followed. Great fought small. Both predictably and invariably, the small fell. But the Great also fought the Great.

Although King Cold probably was that now – and even if he was more daemonic than devic by then – the ex-Unity of Chaos, Unholy Abaddon, was once the greatest of devic fighters. During the First War between the Living and the Dead, in what's called the Thousand Days of Disbelief, he (I was but one of many who called him Uncle Abe Chaos, when we were drinking) and his breed brother, Thunder and Lightning Lord Yajur (the Unity of Order, who never drank, smoked or otherwise took anything that might cause impairment) battled each other for almost three years running; hence, roughly, the aforesaid Thousand Days.

Abaddon, though, had committed devic suicide – which is to say he cut out his third eye – after he finally vanquished Yajur, thrusting him into Cathonia. While Order was now decathonitized, he had to possess Cosmicaptain Starrus in order to fully manifest himself. Needless to say, the two litter brothers still hated each other with a passion unmitigated by Nihila-Harmony's return. They went head-to-toe over Centauri Island.

Neither would back down. Would have massacred each other and – no tenths about it – decimated anyone and anything who got in their way in the process. Meanwhile Tantal and Methandra were opposed by all nine of their adult children.

Rather than fight them, first Methandra then, howsoever reluctantly, Tantal joined the Liberators.

This disloyalty drove Abaddon to madness, something he was always on the verge of anyhow. Out of concomitant desperation, he unsheathed the Chaos Blade, slew Starrus the Shell then, with a ghastly last slash, disposed of Lord Yajur forevermore. The Blade had never been fully drawn before; would have gone critical and likely destroyed the planet, had not Thrygragos Lazareme thrust himself upon it.

In what amounted to the supreme sacrifice, the Chaos Blade was annihilated but, needs be, so was Lazareme. It fell to Tantal Thanatos, with his two-headed war-axe, the Labrys of Frozen Lathakra's flag as well as its often volcanic backbone, the island-long mountain range of the same name, to dispatch Abaddon. That should have been an easy task. But Chaos fought on, using the Blade's sheathe.

Abaddon's inspiration rallied the devils. Umashakti Silvercloud squared off with her cross-tribal opposite, fellow firstborn, and occasional friend, Methandra Thanatos. It was Mistress of Lunar Gravity versus Mistress of Vesuvian Mysticism. Nergal Vetala, the Vampire Queen of the Dead, challenged Wilderwitch. One of her adherents, another by then Dead Thing, Kronokronos Mikoto, matched up against OMP, Obadiah Power.

Yet another vampire, one Janna Fangfingers by name as well as power focus, singled out the Untouchable Diver. Radiant Rider was isolated by Zenit 'Blacksun' Suryad, formerly the devic overlord of the Land of Midnight. Cerebrus and Magnifico, his twin brother, had their hands – make that their minds – full with two other Lazaremists, a pair of indefatigable fighters by the name of Ursine Bardol and the North American Indian-looking warrior, Irach Ire (Irache Anger).

========

"I call him Irrational," he said as an aside then, when no one got the cue, added. "That's not entirely a joke by the way."

Kids had no sense of humour he decided, when none of them took it and laughed. It wasn't a wonderment most them couldn't feed themselves with other than cereal or peanut butter and jam sandwiches. He vaguely mused if they could tie their own shoelaces. Probably not. Shoelaces were mostly a thing of the past anyways; replaced by something called Velcro.

Damn the Fatman's CE – Centauri Enterprises – anyhow.

========

Rudra Silvercloud, Storm Lord and Beast Master both, hence Savage Storm, sought out Dervish Furie. No contest, right? Wrong. Something happened. I don't know what. Perhaps Rudra killed Jervis Murray. Anyhow, it quickly became Beast Master against the Ultimate Beast, the full Furie — Lemolo Wildwyck, as antique Illuminaries named him.

Byron's Paladin, a decathonitized Master Deva commonly known as Nevair Neverknight, led the rest of his few remaining brothers and sisters in that Great God against the Frozen Isle's Thanatoids. Lazaremists and Mithradites started going through old Liberators and young Liberators alike, scythes through straw – an apt analogy since they were spearheaded by Underlord Yama Nergal, King Harvest, the devic Grim Reaper, one of them. Looked the part, too.

It had the making of a rout. But I used 'spearheaded' for another reason. Blind Sundown and Raven's Head came out of the sky. They were joined by Golgotha 'Black Skull' Nauroz and his Trinondev Elite. All were wielding both solar spears, copied from Johnny's, and their own eye-staves. All were riding ravendeer, male bucks and female doe cloned from Raven's Head. Each and everyone of them were monoceroses; single-horned devaslayers.

This was Heliosophos's doing, it came out later. When the Liberators attacked the Moon, the first two he co-opted were Sundown and his Beauty. Using Utopian science, he duplicated the spear and cloned her in multiplicity – very quickly and not all that successfully – but they were extremely effective; at least initially. A number of Lazaremists and Mithradites were sucked into their eyeorbs. Still, with their adherents behind them and powers that frankly dwarfed most of the supras, the devils continued to have the upper hand.

Remember that it wasn't just Yajur and the Thanatoids whom Nihila conciliated, if that's the right verb, onto the Liberators' side. There was also the Pauper Priestess. Pyrame – her own name for herself, yet nevertheless one of the most myrionymous Master Devas ever known – considered the Prison Beach of Incain her own private protectorate. In what may be considered a tragic mistake, brought the She-Sphinx, All the Invincible, to Centauri Island to aid her and them.

While her intentions were undoubtedly honourable, All was a Monster Maker, the Mother Machine of all Mandroids. She didn't come alone. With her were mandroids aplenty, including Crystallion, Hell's Horsemen riding their technopomps, their nuclear dragons, and two of Moe Three's Samsarites, Ignatius and Arachne Challenger. At their head was Steltsar.

Seeing, through Raven's Head, the walking horror that, supranormal or not, was far more machine than man was too much for Blind Sundown. In June of 1953 Steltsar, once at least nominally the Baron Tyrtod von Alptraum, led The Rache assault responsible for killing Solace-Sorciere, his beloved, albeit unofficial, childhood bride and eventually official, actual wife.

At the same time The Rache slaughtered most of their fellow villagers, including my old pal and drinking buddy, the Cheyenne Shaman best known as Manitoulin. He was the man who brought them both up – brought up Sedon St Synne and his wife Louise born Riel, a generation – make that two generations – earlier. This Steltsar, by then looking more shark-like than manlike, had also kidnapped their newly born, never-named son the very day he killed Sorciere and the rest all those years previously.

Sundown spurred Raven towards the monstrous mandroid whilst Black Skull and his Trinondev Warriors of Weir veered toward Crystallion and Hell's Horsemen. A number of the other Liberators mistook their actions; went after Pyrame, All, the Samsarites and the rest of the mandroids. The devils hesitated. Mandroids, like demons, were also their mortal enemies.

The demon-loving Hecate-Hellions' Morrigan – Morgianna officially nee Somata (properly Nauroz) become Sarpedon – challenged Pyrame. Fisherwoman, with a fishing gaffe and net she pulled out of the Grey, tried to corral the two Challengers, Nat and the Spider Woman. Romaine Kinesis, aka Doc Defiance, the Gypsium Man, took on All directly.

Appreciate again, Defiance taking on All wasn't entirely accidental. His parents – Alexandros and Roxanne nee Heliopolis Kinesis – were the supranormals respectively codenamed Pluman and Slipper. They had both been on Centauri in 1965; both were killed during WORLD's effort to take over that even then mostly manmade island.

All manifested itself as a Gynosphinx, a diabolical, conglomerate creature with the wings of a demonic pterodactyl, body of a hellcat, tail of a venomous serpent, and viper-haired head of a Gorgon. Although a different Gynosphinx had been responsible for his parents' deaths – and Heliosophos had made him aware of that on the Moon – his actions, unlike Sundown and Raven's, weren't motivated by revenge so much as commonsense.

With an almost professorial detachment, Defiance realized the only way to deal with All was with an overabundance of glowing Gypsium that we also call Brainrock. So he called upon his abilities, sucked Gyps out of Centauri's three peaks, bombarded All with a superfluidity of the miraculous, self-regenerating Godstuff. The Mandroid Mother Machine couldn't handle it. A number of other things happened synchronous to All disintegrating.

Among them, Chaos faltered and Old King Cold sliced off his head. Ringleader teleported Crystallion, Hell's Horsemen and their dragons to the bottom of the Pacific, where they exploded with consequences immediately limited to the unfortunate fish in the vicinity. The sun came out — which accounted for both Fangfingers and the vampiric aspect of Nergal Vetala.

OMP got a shot at Warlord Mikoto that he made count. Thalassa, Aires or one of the other Thanatoids made it rain as if out of nowhere. So much for Vetala's cohort, the Haddazur-animated Dead Things of then old Iraxas, Sedon's Muttonchop, as well as the Reaper's remaining Inglorious Dead, once the Ghostlands' Dead Things. Doc Defiance finished All at the same time Sundown and Raven did in Steltsar. The Challengers disengaged from Fish and went for Defiance.

Not to denigrate everyone else's effort, but the most important result of all this was that, the Gynosphinx being no more, her prisoners were released. Suddenly the devils were reinforced. The arrival of the likes of Abdullah Ziderite, Camorva Freeflight, Pyçonja Volant – who's your slimy Auntie Fish's devic half-mother, Tina, one of them anyhow – Vishnuvita, who may well be Wilderwitch's devic half-mom, Tammuz, the last of the Atomic Twins – Osiraq having gone down with Crystallion and her Horsemen – and a few dozen more Master Devas shifted whatever balance the Liberators had gained back to the devils.

Doc Defiance, who had emptied himself of Gypsium-Godstuff taking care of All of Incain – thus disproving her claim to be All the Invincible – become the dotty Normie Normalman, Professor Romaine Kinesis, again. Ignatius and Arachne, who claimed their templates were the Male and Female Entities from their first lifetimes, promptly killed him.

Although Callion Clones, like many of the still surviving Signallers, they were cloned by Moe Three, not Moe Two. The process Moe III and his primary associate, Aranyani Nightingale, used to make them was radically different from the process his father used to make the Signallers. As a result they amounted a distinct form of life. In fact they considered themselves, with some justification, Samsarites, after the Universal Substance, the dark-grey matter between-space.

Howsoever that may be, the Untouchable Diver and Mr Power were in no mood to feel ecologically correct. Even if they were a distinct life form, an immediate specie-extinction seemed entirely in order to them. Doc Defiance had been a fellow Liberator after all. Consequently, the Diver went into Arachne and hardened her. When he came out, she crumbled into dust. OMP didn't bother with the initial step. With his sceptre, he simply blew Nat Challenger into so mucky-much-dried dick-dildo. Dust, that is.

Pyrame, having lost All, retreated from the field. Her day wasn't done yet. She sought out your eldest sister, Tina. Persephone, like Helen, had some of your father's rings. They were supposed to use them solely for defensive purposes, but the Pauper Priestess had other ideas. One of which was to reclaim the Female Entity; make Miracle Memory her shell again, like she had been throughout much of the Entities' eleventh lifetime.

And not just then. Pyrame had been humanizing the Mnemosyne Machine ...

========

An enormous hullabaloo rose from the crowd in Hope Haven's backyard. Tethys paused to see what it was about. Once he realized just who had shown up, the Dual Entities themselves, Miracle Memory humanized by Freespirit Nihila, not Pyrame Silverstar, he told his audience he'd have to stop. The kids were universal in their jeers and protestations.

"Cool it, will you?" Taking his own advice the legendary Thirty Year Man emptied his bottle of pilsner. "At least give me a chance to get another beer before going on. My throat's dry."

"Lemonade!" cried Athena. She led a charge towards the various refreshment stands dotting the Garden of Hope Haven.

****

Two-Demon: **Half-Mama Memory**

========

Toward The Spring Equinox, 5981

"You killed Cynthia?" disbelieved Saladin Devason.

"Don't need her anymore," Gomorrah-Lilith answered.

Somewhat earlier that same day, in early Yamana 5980, Sal's Cynthia Masterwife wasn't dreaming of dying.

========

With John Sundown and Raven's Head gone, if not definitely dead, and the unloaded, then reloaded, Pani Merchant ship sent on its way south, its skipper carrying Gomez Niarchos's head in a box, the High Illuminary of Weir fulfilled her promise to Wilderwitch. Gathering up her girls, the Witch and their attendants, including a few hand-picked Trinondev guardsmen, she headed out to the coast for some overdue rest and relaxation.

Not even two weeks after leaving the metropolis proper, a blinding snowstorm blew in from Fearsome Fobbiat rendering their immediate world winter wonderland time. A day or two after the blizzard the Witch, in her wheelchair, was rolling toward the edge of the snow and ice-covered, concrete balcony outside her bedroom.

She was wearing a parka and mukluks, with lots of other clothes underneath. Her metallic marigold was in her chair's side pocket. It was cold as the deepest depths of Hell, Dante-version. What she was doing out there, in those conditions, was responding to someone calling her name — her real name; arguably her only name besides Wilderwitch.

It was her mother. Half of her mother anyhow. The other half couldn't be the same other half her mother had when she was conceived. Nor could it be the same half that shared her birth pangs with Machine-Memory. Even for the Headworld, given the time frame of her birth, late Tantalar 5927, both scenarios were quite impossible. What was far less certain was whether she should have celebrated her 53rd birthday or her 28th around Zmas Day.

She chose, instead, not to celebrate anything even resembling a birthday. Was at the time far too preoccupied trying to stay alive for her next one.

========

"Cynthemis Dyana?"

========

Wilderwitch exchanged wary glances with the Female Entity, Miracle Memory as she preferred to be known in fully human form. Which, being otherwise a machine, the Mnemosyne Machine, the innards of Trans-Time Trigon, she could only be when possessing a Master Deva. Unless it was the other way around. And that was a possibility.

Other than possessing or being possessed by a devil who was pinned to a slab of Gypsium-Brainrock-Godstuff in the Crystal Mountains by a Trigregos Talisman, the Susasword, in 1927, 5927 in here – and still was until early Tantalar 5980, December 1980 out there – most anything was when it came to dealing with her.

"Why ask when you already know, Nihila?"

Freespirit Nihila was the devil she and Akbarartha (the Outer Earth's Obadiah Melvin Power, Old Man Power or just plain OMP) encountered in the Faerie Garden of Temporis a little more than a month earlier. As Datong Harmonia, the Unity of Balance, her breed brother, Unholy Abaddon, the Unity of Chaos, pinned her to the aforementioned slab of Godstuff. Devils that they were then, he nevertheless thought he'd killed her

Did so with the aforementioned talisman (the other two being the Crimson Corona and the Amateramirror) toward the end of the 55th Century, Year of the Dome. Utopians of Weir called the Trigregos Talismans, replicates of which Saladin Devason wore on special days, the three Sacred Objects. They called them thus because they were anything except sacred to devils.

Datong Harmonia (or just plain Harmony) changed her name to Nihila, as in nihilism, she told them in the Faerie Garden, because, unless it was nothingness, as a result of her way beyond near-death humiliation she no longer cared about anything, especially harmony. Newly named Nihila, albeit with longer, crinkly butterscotch hair, rather than straight black same, also minus the third eye and broken Brainrock chains on her wrists, looked like Humanized Memory.

Of course, with thick, shoulder-length, dark hair, rather than much longer, yet stringy, partially scalp-baring dark-ditto, a toque, fur gloves, pants, boots and a warm-looking winter overcoat, Wilderwitch also looked much like Human Memory. That'd be Gloriel's aunt, Mnemosyne nee D'Angelo Heliopolis.

Who died in 1945. Who was once the supra codenamed both Circean and the Queen of Spades. Who, as one or the other, had fought both with and against SOS: the Society of Saints. Whom the Witch knew, unfortunately all too briefly. And who never had a third eye that the Witch knew about, let alone could recall.

No surprise there. As the High Illuminary of Weir, Melina nee Sarpedon Zeross, once explained to her, the Female Entity's humanized form was derived from either/or. The first, Harmonia-Nihila, was likely if the Male Entity, Heliosophos, was originally semi-legendary King Cadmus of Thebes, who lived circa 1,500 years before Christ. The second, Memory of the Angels, was conceivable if the Male Entity, Helios called Sophos the Wise, started out as Kadmon Heliopolis, Human Memory's stepson, who was born in 1940 and died in 1968.

Mind you, Mel cautioned her at the time, if he began his existence as Anti-Patriarch Cain, Slayer of Abel, or some unknown other, then all bets were off.

"Not Nihila who knows, Witch. No matter how high up the totem pole she, ex-Harmony, may be in terms of early born Lazaremists, in terms of Master Devas period, her spirit self, her true being, along with her daemonic, subtle matter body, would be automatically imprisoned the moment she entered Cabalarkon's territory.

I was just curious if you'd answer to it. You see, it's a new one on me. I was happy with Witch."

"So was I. Who's humanizing you, Memory … Pyrame or Irisiel?"

"Obviously not Lazareme's female Heliodromus, Witch. Wouldn't be standing here so calmly if I was. The messenger, Angelus, enters Cabalarkon solely at the Master's sufferance. And then not for very long. She slows down, seeks to linger, at her own peril. Myself, I need no one's permission, not even that of the Moloch Himself, to come here.

"The Mnemosyne Machine made eye-staves on New Weirworld, in case you were unaware of that, and I've long since made certain they can't capture me any more than All can or does. Consequently, I go where I please in the Weirdom. With me holding onto her, so does she, Miracle Memory. We're old companions, her and I. Like Siamese twins in one body."

Wilderwitch was about to demand Pyrame – definitely the Master as well as, according to some, Akbarartha's devic half-mother, and an historic enemy of the Weirdom – manifest herself as she most commonly appeared instead of hiding behind Memory's lovely likeness. Was about to, that is, until uncontrollable convulsions began wracking her.

The only other time in living (sorry) memory that she felt anything approximating the sensation was on Damnation Isle, the 30th of November (Maruta) last. She wasn't alone then. Six of the ten members of the comparatively momentarily reconstituted Damnation Brigade, as they'd been freshly deemed by the now, ever-so-regrettably, and relatively recently, late Cerebrus David Ryne, were occupied by demon-devils.

Except for Memory-Pyrame she was alone right now and, to judge from the look of astonishment on Memory's face, it wasn't Pyrame trying to possess her. Which was about it for her memories until she found herself hurtling out of the sky toward the snow-covered forest, way, way below her, howsoever many minutes or hours later.

This was no time to even think 'disconcerting' let alone try to spell it.

========

Toward the end of Balek, February on the Outer Earth, Capputis Masterson, as he was now known, collected Melina born Sarpedon Zeross from her own lower down domicile and brought her to the top floor of a by-then thoroughly restored Skyrise. The hydrocephalic non-clone – he with the gills behind his ears he'd inherited from his Fish of a deviated mother, the Witch's nine years older sister via the Dual Entities – was clearly unhappy about something, but he wouldn't tell her what it was.

All he would say was his father, the Master of Weir, required the immediate presence of his High Illuminary. She was to bring nightclothes. Or not, as she pleased.

She would, however, be staying the night regardless.

========

Quite literally after putting on her stoniest face, Mel packed a small overnight bag then went upstairs with Capputis via the matter transducer the non-clone activated for the first time since the stone gnomes completed their repairs. In addition to her nightgown she filled her bag with some carefully selected medical supplies, including a few, very selectively preloaded syringes, if only for self-protection.

Not quite black-as-midnight Saladin Devason (his mother and maternal grandmother hadn't been purebloods) met them once they arrived. He promptly dismissed his eldest acknowledged offspring and, as she'd been dreading, took her into his bedroom. Wilderwitch and her hadn't been getting on at all well of late. It started about six weeks earlier when middle daughter Helen, following freshly covered tracks in the snow towards the edge of the balcony outside the Witch's room, spotted her wheelchair toppled-over. No Witch, though.

Had she jumped to her death, parka and mukluks, metallic marigold and all? Had she braked, slid off it, then skidded over the edge to her just as terminal end? Maybe yes, but more likely no. They searched everywhere. Still no body. Still no metallic marigold. The Witch couldn't fly, but with it she could air-walk. So that was a hopeful non-discovery.

Finally Melina used her caduceus, her equivalent of the Witch's stunted eye-stave, her oversexed lollipop; tried to contact the Master in Cabalarkon in order to tell him the bad news. Wasn't him she got hold of; was her, the Witch. Only it was: 'Don't call me Witch, High Illuminary; don't even call me Wilderwitch; I am, as you keep deliberately neglecting to recall, Cynthia Masterwife and, as such, I will be accorded the respect due me, from you, and from now on.'

Matters only went downhill from there; so much so Melina caught herself wishing, against her training, the Witch had gone off the balcony, body and all traces of her swept away in Fearsome Fobbiat, that day in mid-Yamana instead of (presumably) using her metallic marigold to levitate herself back to Cabalarkon.

Not only was she no longer answering to Wilderwitch or Witch, she had begun wearing the White Goddess glamour all the time now; what she first put on that distressful Zmas Night, when they laid her Harry in his tub of animation-suspending, but life-preserving Cathonic Fluid. Had changed her hair colour, though. Straightened it, too. Was now the Master's All-White Goddess in actuality rather than artifice.

(Supposedly most personalized witch-seemings were nothing more than auric – as in body aura, not golden colouration – manipulations. Casting them was something else Mel, despite years of howsoever half-hearted, witchy training, on both sides of the Dome, had never come close to mastering.

(Aside from what the Master thought of her, she wasn't much of a witch at all. Certainly not an old-time Anthean like the Witch was born to, hence her being classed a supranormal, as opposed to learning the tricks of the trade, the craft, the same as every other Ant Mel had come across in her sixty years of life.)

Then there was the 2-week tour of the countryside the Master sent her and her daughters on earlier in the month. Although Melina enjoyed being outside the city, she couldn't help but reckon she'd been sent away not so much to show the flag, as it were, and to show off her three wonderful daughters – they were Weir's first family after all – as to get her away from seriously sanity-losing Cynthia. (Some women gorged themselves during pregnancy. The Witch was evidently more into gouging others, starting with their pride.)

They were not only not seeing eye-to-eye by then, the Master must have figured they'd soon be going at each other, stunted eye-stave against stunted eye-stave. Which they might have done. With uncertain results. Melina was good with the things. And she'd had her caduceus for something like forty years longer than the Witch had her metallic marigold. Her gargoyle, not that it was a gargoyle as such (or even a grotesque, as gargoyles were more properly known), may have been the emblem of her medical profession, but sometimes its two snakeheads had fangs that dripped poison.

Although pleasant enough, it wasn't just her and her daughters, with a huge retinue of her Illuminaries and his Trinondevs, including two of Master Kyprian's loyal leftovers, Golgotha Nauroz, who must be 81 by now, or close to it, and Thobruk Grudal, a Summoning Child like Melina, who went on tour. Three others were the cosmicompanions Harry brought back from the Dinq, Doinq, Danq Cavern Tavern the previous Tantalar.

Two of these last were Demonites, his long dead brother's children: Angelica, which didn't sound very Greek or even German (Dem's still living wife Hiliarti was one of those Schroffs), and the even more oddly named Baalbek Schroff Zeross. Which was also pleasant, particularly for her daughters, who enjoyed their cousins' companionship. The third, though, even if she had a pleasant enough personality, wasn't so much so to be around.

Cosmicompanion Carmine Carmichael turned out to be a nymphomaniac; no nicer way to put it. Unless it was 'swinger', although that had the ring of a hangman's noose. Had a tongue on her, too. Which was what might get her hung someday; albeit not in the Weirdom, which didn't do capital punishment, never had.

Liked to tell tales out of bed, did the Outer Earthling. Some of the tales she told, fortunately without her daughters being around to hear them, were about Cynthia Masterwife. According to Carmine, who swung both ways – as (apparently) did the Witch – when the Master was away, the Masterwife would play.

And tie knots; to bedposts, among other places.

========

Mel was a bit of a prude anyhow.

Harry would have called her a bit of a prude anytime. And often did. But, hearing 'C', as she was nicknamed, go on and on about sinful Cynthia – her word, not Melina's – and in such titillating, deliberately tantalizingly lurid detail, almost made her glad she couldn't blush in public. Or even in private, no matter how hard she tried to tint her face pink.

Wilderwitch, she knew, had always been wild. Probably should have been called Wildest Witch. Monogamy, as someone like the Diver might put it – were he here, could anyone locate and then get him, draw him, back here – and Wilderwitch were divorced long before they even tied the knot. Which was only one reason, her total disdain for Christianity's Holy Sacraments, almost everyone was as surprised as Mel was the Witch agreed to marry the Master.

Her own reasons for refusing to marry him, which she'd enunciated well before she became a closet Christian – and not just because of the Fatman's abiding faith in a Celestial God, this despite him being a Thrygragos Brother's shell for by then howsoever long – made a lot more sense. As she told Kyprian Somata in 5950, she finally on her deathbed, after years of ill-health, her attending the then-Master with a consciously, if unconscionably, pre-prepared syringe at the ready: 'Loyalty to the

State does not have to translate into love for it; especially not love when the state's Master is about to become a son of a devil; the son of the Devil.'

Mercy-killings, she rationalized then, as they may well prove again this night, might well prove, well, merciful.

========

It was with huge relief she realized the Master hadn't brought her into their bedroom, as she'd initially feared, for any tripartite, sickeningly kinky sex. It was with shameful relief she realized he'd brought her here to be Dr Melina Zeross. There, in the bed with its mirrored-sidewalls and roof that they had shared since mid-Tantalar last, lay Cynthia Masterwife. She was naked. She was wasted. She was, as the famous Outer Earth song had it, a whiter shade of pale.

"You saved her before," said Sal. "Save her again."

"I saved her leg, not her."

"Sleep with her." On second thought, maybe it was. Quick thinker that she was, she thought thirdly; gasped in horror as much due to outrage as revulsion. Not that her facial expression reflected anything other than outward beneficence.

(Pureblood Utopian women like her put on their face, as it were, before they entered the company of others. This because they couldn't crinkle or wrinkle in front of anyone normally. Proof, one of them, of their extraterrestrial origins — another being that they were as white-as-light whereas Utopian men were the opposite, as black-as-night.)

"What!"

"You're an Althean Witch, a healer," Saladin told her, desperate. "Lay on some hands. Lay on more than just hands if you have to. Save her baby at least."

Relief did not wash over her face only because it couldn't. She did speak much more calmly, however. "A foetus barely two months in uterus does not constitute a baby, Master. Other than potentially I'm not even sure it constitutes an intelligent being. At this point in its existence I don't see how I can save what's inside without saving what's outside first. We'll have to immerse your Cynthia Masterwife in Cathonic Fluid until we can figure out what's killing her."

"Cathonic Fluid's at least partially made up of distilled Brainrock, isn't it? That'd kill her for sure," he added, without explanation.

(Melina didn't ask for one, either. She'd had her suspicious about the Witch for a couple of months now. She'd recovered from the injuries she suffered in Temporis on the Sixth of Tantalar beyond even supranormally quickly, she'd reckoned. And, with a very few exceptions, neither devils, nor their azuras, proven lifesavers both, could last long in Cabalarkon without being detected and automatically captured in myriad Trinondev eyeorbs.)

"Can you transplant the pre-baby? Have someone else bear it? I heard stories about something like that happening when I was growing up."

"You're referring to the Trigon Triplets," she said, knowing he'd probably heard it at the same time she did, and from the same person, Kanin Nauroz (Granny Garuda), one of his proper aunts, also once Kyprian's High Illuminary: "Eden Nightingale, Cybele St Synne and Human Memory, Mnemosyne D'Angelo later Heliopolis. I suppose it'd be possible, if the Witch was a three-thing like her maybe-mother, a machine, a devil and a human, but she isn't."

"Cut it out of her then. Stick pre-baby in a Development Tank so we can bring it to infancy as a clone and have it raised the same way."

"Now you're asking me to do something that's never been tried before. Not that I've ever heard of anyhow. Let me consult with my Illuminaries, scientocrats and fellow physicians. I'll advise you what we can do in the morning." (Cloning was an ages-old technique perfected by extraterrestrial Trinondevs in order to avoid in-breeding. Did so prior to leaving Second Weirworld for the multiple millennia they pursued the Sedonshem in their generational ships, it was that old.)

"Give me a list of those you want to consult; I'll have Capputis fetch them. In the meantime the least you can do is hold her hand."

========

"And she probably did have kids; little Sed-sons, if Pyrame was involved," Mel-Il-luminatus told Wilderwitch the night (Yamana the 1st) they counted themselves exceed-ingly lucky to survive the Master trying to kill Blind Sundown, with all-too-predicable results. "That's her gift; her hold over Sedon. For some reason, heaven and hell come together when she beds Sed on both sides of the Dome. Only she can half-have the deviant little buggers."

"One-third-have … and she didn't."

"No, and how might you know that? You weren't there." The two exchanged glan-ces. The Witch didn't say 'boo' and Mel, who was anything except stupid, didn't say 'oh'.

========

That night atop Skyrise in late Balek 5980 (already 5981 in Satanwyck, where Baaloch Hellblob, the month's namesake, ruled as its Prime Sinistral), the High Illuminary of Weir fell asleep considering why the Master reckoned sticking Cyn-thia-Wilderwitch in a tub of Cathonic Fluid would kill her for sure.

Had to have something – make that everything – to do with the conversation she and the Witch had at the beginning of Yamana, what would have been New Years Day in most places on the Outer Earth, but in here was just the start of the third month in the Mithraic Ternary. (Balek was its fourth and final month. The Lazaremist Ternary started on the first of Surma, the equivalent of March beyond the Dome; their New Year's beginning on its Equinox.)

The Witch couldn't have been there since the events they were discussing took place in 4825 YD. Neither could Master Morgan Abyss, the Death's Head Hellion, who died under the usual mysterious circumstances that same year. However, some-one else could have – someone who could get one-third pregnant – and, if it wasn't Pyrame Silverstar, it could only be her biomorphic, ever-unacknowledged daemon, Primeval Lilith, the just as immortal, or at least undying as well as unaging, Demon Queen of the Night.

Plus, according to seemingly eternal speculation by not just Illuminaries like her, lascivious, also lethal, Lily was the third maternal aspect of Sedon's Dome-preserving Sed-sons. Was she, more so than Pyrame, who'd long denied Lil-ith was her daemon, the one earthborn constant the mighty, as well as mightily masculine, Moloch needed to maintain Cathonia. Had she survived all this time not only to find herself inside Wilderwitch today, but helping to preserve her life since at least early Tantalar?

When she woke up, not all that long later she reckoned, it was no longer an issue. Ding-dong, the wildest, if hardly the wickedest, of witches was dead.

"Burn her," commanded the Master, when roused and come as called by attendants he'd grudgingly allowed stay nearby after his trusted, eldest acknowledged son summoned them. His voice no longer sounded desperate. Now he sounded disgusted, though whether it was with the Witch for dying, or her for failing to save her, Melina didn't feel qualified to determine.

"At least let's have a proper ceremony, sire," pleaded Capputis Masterson, who came with Fish-Mommy's Daddy. "She was Cynthia Masterwife after all."

"And I'd like to do an autopsy before we do anything else," she insisted in her capacity as a Dr Zeross. "If only to find out what happened to her."

"Do as you please, Illuminary. Just make sure you bring me all of their ashes."

========

Wilderwitch opened her eyes.

At the foot of her bed — yes, it was an actual bed, one she'd been in before, more than two months ago now, and not a mat of leaves or furs for a change — she beheld Athena Zeross. Her favourite Silkie the Selkie dolly in hand, Ringleader and Mel-Illuminatus's youngest was in pyjamas; was so excited she was jumping up and down like she needed to go to the bathroom. Which she probably did.

The Witch said: "Huh?"

========

A couple of weeks earlier, maybe a mite more, back in mid-Tantalar anyway, the Witch threatened to throw Jervis Murray off the top of Skyrise. Assuming he could transform to Dervish Furie before he bottomed out, as it were, he'd only be jolted. With the possible exception of OMP-Akbar (Akbarartha, the rightful Kronokronos Supreme, who'd shredded his shape-shifting Cloak of Many Colours in Vancouver), the others would have lived through such a fall as this as well, one way or another.

She wasn't like the others. Couldn't become untouchable or shift states; couldn't levitate, had no telekinetic talents and certainly wasn't a Wakinyah Creature of the Cosmos. Some animals, even some birds, responded to her cajoling, but she couldn't spot any flying beasties big or fast enough to intercept her. For that matter, she couldn't spot any flying beasties anywhere below her. Besides, even if there was something in the vicinity capable of catching her, she was falling far too quickly to cajole anything that could be cajoled.

She didn't stand a snowball's chance in standard Hell, if not Dante's version, of surviving such a drop on her own. A rubber ball had better odds. A thought-balloon didn't need odds and, not that she remembered doing so, she must have grabbed her metallic marigold from her wheelchair's side pocket the moment she felt herself being possessed.

She did not list prescience among her attributes. In her view anyone who did, prophets predominantly, was a charlatan. But, reflexes and a mindset that enabled her to anticipate the worst were definitely some of her strong suits. When she started projecting the floral grotesque she cast out of its topping eyeorb or prison pod, she realized marigolds were the Mexican Flower of the Dead. Seemed today it was more like her Flower of Life. It saved hers.

The eyeorb-conjured sphere it produced slowed her descent sufficient for her to hit the treetops conscious; cushioned her such that she didn't even pop the stitches in her injured leg. Was, nevertheless, a rough landing. The impact sent a shock of agony from thigh to brain and thence from brain to grip, causing her to release her undersexed lollipop, as she also sometimes referred to her metallic marigold. Which meant she had to climb down to the ground. Doing so didn't do her gamey leg any good. The effort was so excruciating she kept having to stop, almost passing out from pain more than once.

Just before beginning her imitation of an aggrieved squirrel, she glanced into the sky from whence she fell. Something very large, an oversized black crow or raven, was barely visible, way up there, flying off northwards toward what she assumed was Cabalarkon City. Its wings weren't very crow-like, however. Dragons had wings like that, didn't they? Probably, she thought to herself.

She made it to the forest floor in more or less one piece; even managed to locate and retrieve her metallic marigold in the tree's branches on her way down. Once safely on the ground instinct took over. She had scrounged a measure of sustenance, and constructed a passable lean-to out of leaves and fallen branches, before the night's darkness settled in and the mental variety claimed her. As she dozed off she had another thought.

Not dragons … demons!

========

"Lemonade!" The little girl repeated. "It's the dawn of the Equinox. You know, 6 a.m. to 6 p.m. Mom says we celebrate it with lemonade."

"Then why doesn't your Mama Mel go get you some?"

"She's in bed with Harry. He's been gone for days and days. He came back in the middle of the night, but Mom says he isn't feeling well. She's afraid to leave him."

"Harry? Your father's out of his tub of Cathonic Fluid?"

"Sort of."

"What do you mean sort of? And why's she afraid to leave him?"

"Because he's Child Harry. Between me and Paree. I'm only six."

"Let's start again shall we, Tina. Huh?"

========

The Witch didn't learn her secret name was Cynthemis Dyana until she met her mother; rather, until she met the Dual Entity who claimed to be her mother. That was in 5939, the year she turned twelve. Until then, she never stayed with anyone long enough for them to give her a name that stuck. Except for the wolves, that is; and they didn't use names. They used marks they chewed into her lower left leg; marks that were still there.

Anyone except wolves included the various branches or stems of the Antediluvian Sisterhood of Flowery Anthea, members of which kept tracking her down after she'd run away from one or another of their Shelters all over the Hidden Headworld. All had tried to adopt her; to 'help her', they said to a one. All had done so with just as much success, too. Which was to say none at all.

All included Mariamnic witches from Twilight, Sedon's Outer Nose, where she may have been born, hence them claiming a next-to-proprietary interest in her; Korant Corn Queens, from comparatively nearby Apple Isle; and often non-human Ophirant snake-sucklers from the Forever Forest of Wildwyck, in the Head's occipital region, the traditional domain of Lazaremist Extremists. (Thunder and Lightning Lord Yajur's unofficial domain until the Thousand Days of Disbelief, circa 5500 YD.)

Reputedly she started running away not long after she started running. Part of her legend – for legend is what she became in her early years – was that she learned to run before she learned to walk. Yet another of her legends was she learned how use Anthean Agates before she could either run or walk, let alone talk. Perhaps even before she learned how to crawl. Had always been good at rolling.

Some said she was a wild child from Day One; that she booted and clawed her way out of the womb, whomever's womb, prematurely. Hence Wildie. Others claimed she was dragged away, as a prepubescent, from an Ant-Shelter in the Forever Forest of Wildwyck by wolves. Unless it was by werewolves — which were and are common enough there. Hence Wolfie.

Which was the name she was using when the likes of Melina and Demios Sarpedon, along with the adults with them, first came across her on Apple Isle as not much more than a toddler, in the late Twenties, early Thirties. Still others said she was a natural-born witch. Hence Witchie. One thing was certain. She was more at home in the wilderness than she was anywhere else. Hence Wilderwitch.

The Witch of the early Eighties, though, was hardly the Witch of the Thirties, most of the Forties and the first half of the Fifties. Not only had she just come back from, in effect, a 25-year hiatus in Limbo; not only was she pregnant; not only had she no bottomless bag, agate-inlaid jewellery, nor cut-anything knife; not only was she suddenly no longer demonized; she only had one functional leg. And God did the non-functional one hurt.

She toughed it out. Wasn't all that difficult in a way. Remembering what foliage was edible; what grubs were a dot-ditto; how to travel by the stars or sun when she could see them, the moss on the trees when the overhang was too dense; all of the above was akin to remembering how to ride a tricycle for anyone else. An atlatl spear-thrower, a sling for rocks, a bow, arrows and, most usefully, a flint knife were just a matter of finding the right bits and pieces to construct them.

There was no need for a splint on her leg either. Not with a metallic marigold to give her a lift. Seems she could levitate after all. Until one morning she couldn't.

========

"Mom thinks he's dying."
The Witch hated repeating herself, especially thrice. So she crawled out of bed.

========

It was splint time. Then it was moose time. Moose were easy to cajole. So long as you weren't trying to cajole them into giving up their meat and, consequently, their lives. This particular moose didn't mind being ridden, but he wouldn't go north. Didn't like civilization. Toward the coast it was then.

Another thing he didn't like was wolves. And wolves weren't easy to cajole. Especially when they were hungry, which they were. Moose meat was a pack-favourite, but witch-meat would do fine, thank you very much. That she wasn't in the best of shape, still pregnant to boot, whereas the moose was big, healthy and had a very impressive rack of antlers, probably had a lot to do with their hunting preferences.

Some people thought Wilderwitch could control animals, order them about, compel them to do her bidding. She couldn't, but she could fight as ferociously as any wild animal. She'd fought a decathonitized devil, Mater Matare, Mother Murder, each intent upon killing the other, to a standstill. She had makeshift weapons, speed, though nowhere near as much as she had pre-Matare – or, more specifically, pre-Flying-Doltaur's harpoon through not just the fleshy bits of her uppermost thigh – and determination.

Which, this last, even if she had hardly been on top of her game once Lilith (must have been the Demon Queen) got hold of her, she was never lacking.

Wolves were just flesh and blood. Weren't particularly smart either. Just crafty. One, two, three beaten back, bloodied but alive, got them rethinking their strategy. The moose's strategy didn't need rethinking. It bolted. The wolves let it go; the Witch looked a far more inviting, if less filling, prey.

She fooled them. Stifling yelps of her own she clambered up the nearest tree. Undeterred the wolves circled beneath it. They could wait. If they'd even noticed the (for her) ancient tooth marks on her leg – more like smelled them, since she was wearing the pants in her two-member family, her and the moose – that made no never mind. Different era, different pack. Besides, hungry is as hungry does, she supposed, worrying about delirium.

The Witch went to sleep. The wolves did as well. The next morning they were still there. Snow anew began to fall. The Witch took a nap. Then came the stampede. About time, too. Moose were loyal. Her moose came back. With friends. The Witch jumped down onto her moose's back; more yelps of pain, grimaces to match. They got away.

She couldn't control animals, but she could communicate with them. In a way. Having a fearsome soul-self to spook a band of moose into stampede-mode helped as well.

The moose and the Witch parted company on Cabalarkon's rugged coastline of Fearsome Fobbiat. Caves were plentiful there. Most didn't have bears or any other beasties hibernating in them. Thinking of Sorciere, years ago, and five members of D-Brig in Hadd, the reputedly (re)conquered Land of the Ambulatory Dead, easily surpassing a month ago by now, she avoided ones with bats in them as well.

Her unborn child foremost in her mind, she was disinclined to go anywhere else. Barring a red tide,   you could live on shellfish and seaweed forever, she decided. Besides, it wasn't as if there was any pressing need to keep moving. Quite the opposite. A demon had tried to kill her. Demons were not known for taking the initiative. And, so far, Witch-hubby Sal hadn't made any effort to locate her. If he had – if Masters were indeed akin to devils in their protectorates – he'd have found and retrieved her by now.

Saladin Devason and Sedon Deva-Father were behind sticking Primeval Lilith into her, she had finally recalled. Before, on the 14th of Tantalar last, he introduced her by name and fame – as Anti-Patriarch Cain, Slayer of Abel's birth mother no less – she'd half-facetiously referred to Sal's dusky companion as Murk Mist, Mad for Mud Magpies. Was she really that old? Far, far older, a product of the primordial ooze, as demonologists claimed? That she couldn't recall. Like Strife to Ants in the past, Lily didn't leave much in the way of her memories behind.

Had Sal and Sed, presumably on lethal Lily's say-so, suddenly made up their minds Witch-she was expendable? Must have. Which-witch was why she never bothered trying to far-speak with anyone via, when it was working, her metallic marigold. Be best to stay away from them. Not that, she suspected, there was much you could do to stay away from Dark Sedon, assuming he was looking for you. (Even stunted eyeorbs had to be charged; worked best in populated areas, not the wilderness.)

Also militating against movement, Pyrame Silverstar was in control of the Memory Entity. Never a friend of hers, the Pauper Priestess was hardly known for having the welfare of the Weirdom high atop her list of priorities. In fact, she'd been cathonitized in 5950 for having the Weirdom at the top of her list of places she wanted to (re)conquer. If the Apocalyptics were any guide, decathonitized devils would kill.

So, had the Pauper Priestess come to the Zerosses' coastal hideaway intent upon killing her? And, if so, why? Because she was carrying Saladin's child? Why bother? He'd had literally dozens of known offspring already. Besides, Half-Conceptive-Mama Memory would never let her kill her. Not even if Maybe-Half-Birth-Mama Pyrame was dominant.

Why had Silverstar come calling anyway? Why hadn't she just had definite Half-Birth-Mama Memory bring her to her? Miracle Memory's Mnemosyne Machine aspect could teleport others as effortlessly as she could herself, whoever was possessing her and, not surprisingly since she comprised a good percentage of its innards, Trans-Time Trigon itself. Worry afterwards, the Witch advised herself. Bear baby first, she kept repeating.

One other thing argued in favour of staying put. She didn't have to go anywhere, not even to scout for food. Had a soul-self to do that. It had mostly recovered from getting scorched by Blind Sundown and his Solar Spear back at the beginning of December 1980 out there on Damnation Isle. Could also range far and wide, all the way to Cabalarkon City if needs be. Many another place as well; including beyond the Weirdom, should she be so inclined.

Could she find Fish (Fisherwoman, Scylla Nereid, Lady Achigan), her sister in more than just Flowery Anthea? They'd nodded to each other back stage on the First of Yamana, just before the Master set into horribly ill-advised motion his effort to slay Blind Sundown after he confiscated his spear. Could she – Fish and her fishisms in mind – fluke upon one of the others, the Diver, Furie, OMP-Akbar, exes all, presuming none of them were, thanks to Johnny, as dead as Cerebrus?

Dare she try for the Frozen Island of Lathakra; where dwelled, Ringleader claimed, the Elemental Twins, Aires and Thalassa once D'Angelo, now and supposedly always Thanatos? They might be devils but, ever-adventurous sorts that they were, they might also be prepared to take a stab at rescuing her.

So might their reputed father, Tantal Thanatos, who thanks to defending it against the Idiot Twins (Tammuz and Osiraq, from Mithras's Eleventh) more than a thousand years ago, apparently had a free pass to enter Cabalarkon's territory. From what she'd heard of King Cold, he was not only the most powerful Master Deva still extant; he was spoiling for a fight. Might he be willing to take on his Grandfather Sedon? Could be!

As much out of curiosity as anything else, she began sending her soul-self south instead of north, toward the city, its outlying townships and decreasingly populated countryside. It didn't have to go very faraway before it spotted something very interesting; some things, make that — some extremely old, planetary-prehistoric, things.

Presumably, as she now understood after speaking with Mel at the seaside villa, to ensure her metallic marigold would run out of oomph, before dropping her the Demon Lilith had taken her much farther away from people than she'd initially thought. It, demonic-her, Miss Ha-ha Murkiness, had let her loose close to the southernmost, coastal extent of the Slopes of the Sleepers, what oddly – make that Sedonically, also sardonically – protected the whole of Devic Eye-Land from the radioactive ravages of the Ghostlands.

Weeks later, with once all-but-ruined leg feeling much better – witches really did heal quickly, just not miraculously – and with a decent percentage of her supra-strength returned, albeit nowhere near pre-Calvary-Cavern level, Wilderwitch had mastered a new trick. She could now release her soul-self without having to slip into a trance to do so.

This proved very useful when she followed it into a very long ago grounded, Utopian millennial, also generational, ship.

The bear did not appreciate being woken up.

========

Lemonade, freshly squeezed, extra sugar added, iced down and watered up, glass in hand, Tina led Wilderwitch to her mother's bedroom.

========

No matter how much the look-after-yourself travails of the last two-plus months had strengthened her, the Witch was still having some difficulty walking. Consequently, in order to keep up with the girl, she had to levitate herself within a fortunately functional again, metallic-marigold-cast, thought-balloon.

They were in the Zerosses' seaside hideaway on the coast of Fearsome Fobbiat, the Headworld's western ocean. Dr Melina nee Sarpedon Zeross, the High Illuminary of Weir, was in her private quarters, sitting in a chair beside the bed she'd shared with Ringleader, Dr Aristotle Zeross, for the better part of two decades.

Tina's two older sisters, Persephone and Helen, were also there. Looking teary-eyed sad, they were standing behind their mother, hands on her shoulders supportively. Something in the shape of a someone, a child not quite Helen's size, was lying in the bed covered with a sheet doubling as a shroud.

Dispelling the thought-balloon as she did so, Wilderwitch came to ground. She was strong enough to stand on her own but, so struck was she at the High Illuminary's wasted condition, she very nearly lost her balance; thus only just avoided making a remarkably still-pregnant ass on her ass of herself. As it was, she barely registered the boy's apparent corpse.

"Good God, Mel, you look like hell."

========

Wilderwitch knew her bears.

========

Knew this one, a massive male, was there long before she dared approach the area of the immense, and immensely long ago abandoned, millennial ship wherein he made his den. It wasn't just because bears mark their territory with various visual and olfactory warding signs. Before getting too close to the massive, but millennia-derelict, spaceship she'd sent her soul-self ahead. Surprisingly, the bear she'd targeted was not the only one to have made his home there. Even more surprisingly, some of the others had seemingly formed a community.

Did that make them sentient, like the Barring Bear Men of the Cattail Peninsula she'd first come across during her wildly wandering, mostly preteen years on the Head? She thought not. Barrings had been developed millennia pre-Flood by the experimental geneticists of old Eden. What some reckoned were the Atlanteans of not just Plato, not platonic, legend; reckoned perhaps not mistakenly as well.

What, by hardly hence-exclusionary contrast, Mel for one believed were Trinondevs come to Earth, and consequently lost, during the Whole Earth's last Ice Age while searching for the Sedonshem. (Mel referred to an era known as the Younger Dryas for some reason. To say the least, climatic events from so long ago were not the Witch's specialty.)

Barrings had intelligible speech whereas she could see via her soul-self that these animals were just that — non-talking, though still somewhat verbally communicative animals. Except their communication methods were mostly growling; not to mention teeth-bared snarling and a kind of sign language that consisted exclusively of whacking and attacking each other. Pups aside, why were these usually solitary beasts living together? More importantly, despite their propensity for spitting, spatting and swatting, why were they so comparatively cooperative?

Had to be because food was plentiful; as in there was plenty to go around. And how was it food was so plentiful in an incredibly ancient leftover from the space-faring yet, to hear Mel-Illuminatus tell it, multi-millennial gone civilization of second Weirsystem? Because the food processors were somehow still working, or working again, after all these thousands of years. And how could that be, besides a source of the Brainrock it would have carried as fuel?

Stone Gnomes, the Witch reckoned. Had to be.

The bear she targeted was likely the clan's alpha male. A loner, he was also the biggest bear she had ever seen; easily bigger than a Grizzly and even bigger than an Alaskan Kodiak. Which, until then, had been the biggest kind of bear she'd ever seen. He was so big she wondered if he was somehow primeval; as in his kind of bear had been extinct on the Outer Earth since long before the last Ice Age ended.

She was no dummy, but neither was she very well educated, not in beyond-the-Dome high school, let alone university, terms. Cave Bear, she mulled. Was that the acceptable term for this kind of ever so enormous beast? The word 'megafauna' also came to mind. There still were huge flightless birds in Wildwyck; survivors of some earthly epoch when mankind wasn't top-of-the-food-chain dominant. Was her targeted bear a leftover from the same time period?

Once thing she wasn't going to do was ask him. Besides, he likely wouldn't have had the vocal chords to answer her even she did get up the nerve to do so.

What he did have in his favour, besides his monstrous size, was his own food replication unit. Which, presumably through trial and error, he'd somehow learned how to use, and which he guarded accordingly, using his size. What he didn't have in his favour, again besides his size, was he was no more hibernating than any of the derelict's other domicile-dependent bears.

Preparing for her next move, the Witch ticked off what her soul-self could do; what she could impart to it in the way of long-distance sensory illusions. Then, one night after the bear slipped into a non-hibernation sleep, she had her soul-self tick it off. True, the bear did not appreciate being woken up. True as well, though, by the time he chased her fearsome soul-self out of his den, and she'd snuck in and sealed the area behind them, he couldn't get back in.

The Witch recalled her soul-self and settled down for the long haul. Here was going to be both home and obstetrics unit.

=========

"Thanks," Melina said to Wilderwitch. "I needed that."

"You're welcome. What's that?" she asked, finally pointing to the body in the bed. Suddenly, as if receiving a long-awaited cue, it reared into a sitting position. Already unsteady on her feet, the Witch visibly blanched, sucking air reflexively. The shroud-like sheet slipped off his head. It was Harry Zeross, Kid Ringo, age about ten.

"Fooled you," he said with a big grin on his face.

****

Three-Demon: **Not Half-Mama Pyrame**

========

Closer to the Spring Equinox, 5981

The girls joined their mother and the boy laughing uproariously at the Witch's expense. "And you needed that," as-much-as-snorted the High Illuminary. "For going wheel-about in a fucking blizzard. We thought you were dead."

Wilderwitch recovered quickly. "So did my mother."

"Your what?"

"At least you didn't say 'huh'."

"Huh?" Melina obliged.

"Tell you at breakfast, a real breakfast. Don't know about you, actually I do, look-ing at you, but I could with some grit. Seems all I've been living on is recycled bear shit."

"Still fay-saying, eh, Witch. Come here, let me give you a big bear hug."

"Be better that than a big bear rug," the Witch rhymed before she obliged possibly the only friend she had left in the entire world, both sides of it.

========

A few days after moving into the derelict generational ship, Wilderwitch didn't appreciate being woken up any more than the Cave Bear had. Fortunately she wasn't awakened by the bear come to reclaim his domain. Sort of fortunately anyhow. Responsive to the tap on her shoulder, the Witch looked up from her fur and clothes-covered pallet on the floor.

"Memory?"

Miracle Memory, in a dark, crewneck sweater, kilted skirt, leggings and sens-ible shoes – exactly the kind of outfit favoured by Human Memory, Mnemosyne born D'Angelo Heliopolis, when she was alive – stood above her. "Been searching for you, Cynthia Masterwife," she acknowledged, with a slight nod.

Whereupon the lovely face of a one-time Lovely Lady, Memory of the Angels, got real grotesque, real triangular, real fast. Scottish-style clothing did a disappearing act as well. Were replaced by a sheath skirt, sandals and, except for straps that ran between her bared breasts and held up the skirt, nothing evidently else. Presumably to ensure there was no question as to who was humanizing the Female Entity, the transformed being spurted a geyser of silver hair from the apex-meeting-points of the three triangular, upper sides of her tetrahedral head.

"Come to kill me, Pyrame?"

"You're mortal, Witch," somehow came a voice back to her out of the grotes-query's now non-visibly be-mouthed head. "You'll die in your own good time. The tragedy of it is, given what you've been through, after I take back what's mine you may not have long to wait. Can't be helped, I'm afraid. Not just me, but the Whole Earth has more need of it than you do."

"I have nothing of yours, devil."

"Don't be melodramatic. Of course you do. You may be a master illusionist, Witch, one of the best ever, but I saw it at the Zerosses six weeks ago. It's what's been keeping you going."

"I've been what's keeping me going."

The derelict ship being somehow heated, the Witch had been using her heavy clothing for bedding. She rolled out of it, directionally away from where Memory-Pyrame appeared to be, and was on her feet in almost the same motion. She may not be as fast as she once was but, inwardly, she felt rather pleased with her speed. Had her makeshift blade in hand. It was never out of reach. Wouldn't be the first time she fought for her life stark-naked.

"Have you indeed? We'll just have to see about that, won't we?" The Pauper Priestess, Pyrame Silverstar, had a solitary eyeball on all three sides of her head from the neck up. Likely all three of said eyeballs lit up simultaneously, but Wilderwitch, unabashed and unafraid, only stared down the one glaring at her.

"Oh, I get it," she told Silverstar, challengingly. "See as in with your three eyes." Then she grew deadly serious. "Too bad you didn't have the foresight to stick one in your asshole, asshole!"

The Witch was prepared for this moment. Had, taking a page out of Saladin Witch-Husband's hospitality manual, already made an accommodation for her accommodations. Hadn't asked for much in the way of trade. Just protection against a certain quadrangular-be-headed devil who could operate in the Weirdom without fear of instantaneous eyeorb-imprisonment in return for a degree of appreciation for what stone gnomes could do.

Although designed to approximate agathodemons, a Greek word that meant good or benevolent spirits, and referred to helpful genii along the lines of a fairy godmother or guardian angel, stone gnomes liked being appreciated. Besides, despite being artificial half-lifers akin to mandroids and the Mantels of Temporis, they were compositionally similar to earthborn, tellurian or chthonic creatures such as faeries and genuine demons. That meant, chances were, they'd enjoy the opportunity to have a devil for dinner.

Pyrame-Memory might have sensed it coming. Probably did, but either there was nothing she-they could do about it, or felt there was no threat. Whatever the case, she-they made no effort to prevent or avoid it, them, coming out of the floor, the walls, the very air itself. Mandroid-mush, Godcrud to not just Master Devas, the Stopstone-stuff of stone gnomes, splattered their shared physical form; began hardening.

In what had to be much the same way the ancients encased their gods – devils that they were – and thereby, howsoever temporarily, manufactured the incredibly lifelike, nowadays almost invariably fractured, or otherwise damaged, statuary of them found in museums all over the world, she had the tripartite being (machine, devil, human) immobilized.

Wilderwitch, though, had no time to gloat. It was happening to her again. Only this time it was Humanized Memory's Pyrame-aspect attempting to take her over. Without an Anthean Agate ensorcelled to shield herself against devic possession, she had to rely on her own considerable mental defences to repel the devil.

Amazingly, it wasn't at all difficult. Even more amazingly, the solidifying, stone gnome statue-making substance found itself with nothing to harden around. As a result it simply melted back into the floor, walls and air. The digitized visage of Machine-Memory grinned out of a sidewall in the millennial ship.

"Very good, Cynthemis. There is something of the like-mother, like-daughter, about you after all."

Wilderwitch had witnessed Machine-Memory manifest herself in just this way before. But that was years ago, decades now, inside Trans-Time Trigon, wherever it was situated at the time. There was, she suddenly realized, a rational reason she could do it here, in a no matter how old and crumbly millennial ship.

"I gather you made these vessels."

"I've made lots of things in my existence. You're one of them, though I had the usual assistance in that regard, including a human body from which to give you birth. Millennial ships were originally constructed by New Weir's Mother Machine. Rather, they were constructed on her specifications."

(New Weir was something of a misnomer. It was dozens of millennia old. Old Weir, though, had probably been hundreds of millennia old by the time it was destroyed, swallowed, by its thereafter equally defunct Solar System's Weir Star going supernova. Was the site of the universe's oldest, non-Celestial civilization.)

"And so were you."

With Pyrame seemingly supplanted by the visage of the non-human Mnemosyne Machine, Wilderwitch sensed the danger passed. She bent down, picked up her clothes, began dressing. Never let go of her makeshift blade, however. It was more her security blanket than the furs she'd been using as actual blankets.

"Bright as well, I see."

"With whose eyes?" wondered the Witch, sitting down to pull on her leggings and mukluks.

"Silverstar's of course. She wasn't trying to possess you, though I wish she had been. Then I might have got rid of her. She was just probing you. Nice try with the stone gnomes, by the way. Wouldn't have held Pyrame any more than they would have me. I may have facilitated manufacturing them, but she's as good with mandroid half-lifers as I am. Wouldn't have been able to make All of Incain her second home if she wasn't."

"Why would she want to probe me?"

"Because we thought you had something of ours."

"Which I didn't."

"Apparently not. Which leaves us with a mystery. What became of the Demon Lilith? It was her, wasn't it?"

"So Sal said. But, in answer, after she tried to kill me I have no idea. If you're so good with millennial ships, how come it took you so long to find me?"

"Because we didn't think you were missing. We thought you were dead."

"Sorry to disappoint."

"That's not what's disappointing. You don't have Lilith, you don't have what we want. You're pregnant, Cynthemis, but it's with a girl. Nice for you, nice for her, assuming you last long enough to have her, but it's back to the drawing board for us — and not just Pyrame and me. Most inconvenient."

"By not just Pyrame and you, I take it you're referring to your non-distaff side, Heliosophos. You two were the Menace on the Moon Cerebrus was so concerned about, weren't you? Harry Zeross, Ringleader, went up there to rescue the decathonitized Thanatoids, the ones other than Demon Land." (Although she presumed Harry was still in a tub of Cathonic Fluid, he had a few days before Xmas, Zmas in Cabalarkon, to tell his astonishing story to his wife, Melina once Sarpedon, and she to her, the Witch.)

"From what Mel-Illuminatus told me, he figured Helios was killed and that therefore you and he, along with Trans-Time Trigon, were thrust back into the time stream." (The Dual Entities were time-tumblers, as opposed to time-travellers, which was impossible. That made them two of most confounding entities in existence anywhere in the cosmic multiverse.) "Don't tell me you're back already, after however many more lifetimes spent in futility?"

"Maintaining the same lifetime in futility actually. My spear side and I sort of got separated. Rather, he got separated. Had his head cut off, truth told. With a sword, not a spear. Except he was possessed by Lord Yajur at the time. So decapitating him didn't prove fatal, just coma-inducing.

"It's fallen to me to keep him, and consequently us, separated. I do otherwise it'll needs be Yajur I reunite and Yajur's the Unity of Order, not Anarchism — though anarchism tends to need extreme orderliness in order to produce a functional society. Besides, until Pyrame got hold of me, I was almost enjoying my independence, partial as it was. Was what you might call a free spirit. Pun intended."

"Pun? Hold on, you're referring to Freespirit Nihila, aren't you?"

"Lord Order's breed sister, ex-Harmony, the onetime Unity of Balance or Datong Harmonia, yes. We were bosom-buddies early on. Fact is my original bosoms – the fleshy ones, not the machine variety – belonged to her as much or more so than they did Memory of the Angels, Mnemosyne D'Angelo, another of your partial sisters.

"Pyrame's are just as nice. Plus, she's far more sexually adventurous than Harmonia ever was, and Nihila isn't at all now that she's found true love; a firstborn, like her, apparently. Except he doesn't exist. And neither does she … again. Not in terms of mobility at any rate; hopefully not in terms of consciousness either.

"Ordinarily that'd suit me fine. Trouble is we're of two minds, pun not intended this time, about what to do about the Moloch Sedon."

"Neither of you are his fans."

"True, but my Love has spent more lives than I care to recall trying to eradicate him. That's rubbed off on me, but Pyrame wants to be Sedon's equal, like she used to be. Or used to think she was, make that, because she's finally realized it isn't her he needs to mate with in order to preserve the Dome. It's her demon.

"That'd be the one she believes I stole from her in 5950, at the termination of Helios's Eleventh, and kept with me for his next eighty-nine lifetimes of living, and dying, throughout the cosmos; more than a few of them here, I might add, when she still had her and got hold of me to boot. And who after thousands of years of disavowing it – as if acknowledging it would somehow diminish her in everyone's eyes, including her own – she has finally accepted is and always has been Primeval Lilith, the Whole Earth's Demon Queen of the Night."

"First among the earthborn; first among the skyborn," appreciated the Witch. "Makes good symmetry. How long have you known about their relationship?"

"Longer than you might suppose, though in my case – and my love's case – I have to admit it was more a suspicion than anything else. You see, the evidence we had indicated there have been sedons, small case, born without any direct involvement that we could detect of either Dark Sedon, large case, possessing their father or Pyrame-Lilith possessing their mother."

"Their children and grandchildren, I'm assuming."

"Just so, though not beyond it seems. Human sedons' bloodlines thin quickly. As near as we could figure when we came back in '75, there was only Saladin Devason on the Inner Earth and Sedon St Synne on the outside left altogether alive." Wilderwitch took a mental note of Memory's qualification, but held back remarking on it. Had more immediate matters on her mind.

"So Sal's definitely a small case sedon?"

"Indubitably. Your ever-so-clever Sisterhood of Anthea, latterly directed by their then superior, Kyprian Somata, and their largely Nightingale hierarchy, deliberately bred Pandora Mannering, Sal's mother, such that she would have the three Great Goddesses Reincarnate. Since she was, of necessity, a mixed-blood, Pyrame had no problem possessing her. End result was that instead of revivifying, if that's the right word, the Trigregos Sisters, she got Saladin Devason. Hence the Simultaneous Summonings of 1920."

"But Sal's father was a full-blooded Utopian, Augustus Nauroz, Master Kyprian's grandson. Devils aren't supposed to be able to possess Utopians."

"Sedon is the Devil, large case; at the very least he's the inspiration for the Devil. More than likely he can possess anyone he bloody well pleases. While the definition of evil varies from person to person, there's no question he's as twisted as he is very, very powerful — near-godlike he'd tell you, emphasis on 'near'.

"He would have taken a demented delight possessing, and perverting, young Augustus in order to impregnate Pandora and thereby thwart the Superior Sisterhood's best efforts to balance the scales. Devils are incapable of disobeying their fathers only because their mothers have been absent damn near forever. Again …"

"Got you. Emphasis on 'near'. I'm aware of the theory behind Panharmonium. Just not so sure it holds any more water than my bladder does these days."

"Believe me, I know the feeling. I've been pregnant more times, in more bodies and in more lifetimes, than just for the three of you."

By that Machine-Memory meant Wilderwitch and her two full sisters, Eden Nightingale, who was born in 5909 and died in late '55 – around the same time the future Damnation Brigade got stuck in Limbo, as it happened – and Fisherwoman (Fish, Scylla Nereid, Lady Achigan, the long deposed marital Queen of Godbad), who was born nine years after Eden and nine years before the Witch.

The three of them were the only mostly human deviants the Female Entity carried to full term during her eleventh lifetime, the one that started in 5908 and ended in 5950. Not so coincidentally their common father, the Male Entity, who may or may not have been possessed when he impregnated Miracle Memory with any of them, was killed around the same time Pyrame was attempting to conquer the Weirdom of Cabalarkon.

For her troubles Dark Sedon rewarded the Pauper Priestess with cathonitization; re-cathonitization in her case. As he had first done in 5916, when she seemingly murdered her own half-daughter, whose name was also Eden Nightingale, he thereby rendered Silverstar a silver star shining out of the night's sky above his Hidden Headworld.

Only this time, because she was threatening Cabalarkon, the undying Utopian he regarded as his father, the Devil as well as Demon King did so with no chance of reprieve. Consequently, on the 30th of Maruta 5980, she had to possess Nehrini Purandar, Cosmicaptain of Cosmicar Six, in order to escape Cathonia. Evidently, sometime between then and now she'd managed to reacquire the Mnemosyne Machine, whom she'd occupied for a good percentage of the Entities' eleventh lifetime.

"Still, as much as the Moloch enjoys his games – his Sedonplay, as your Illuminary pals call them – he's a malicious, calculating bastard. He rarely does anything purely to be mischievous. So there has to be something to be said for the theory." (The Witch's Illuminary pals numbered all of one, Melina nowadays Zeross, whom – as Pyrame would have been well aware – may have been born with the Lazaremist highborn Althea Brand inside her.)

"There's something to be said for shit as well. At least excrement makes decent fertilizer. Ask me the Simultaneous Summonings caused more harm than good. Should have just skipped the 'I-u-m' part of it and called the Panharmonium Project 'pan-harm'. A lot of the resultant Summoning Children were supranormals. Some of them were my friends and most of them died, or had to be neutralized, mostly by us, until our turn came along, just to keep the world safe for regular Norman and Norma Normalmen."

"I am aware of that, Cynthemis. I was around for most of those days, you may recall. Nonetheless, as deleteriously as the Simultaneous Summonings turned out for Master Kyprian, and indeed for your whole Sisterhood's dream of Panharmonium – including the 'I-u-m' part of it – you have to admit there's a delicious irony to the entire episode.

"Utopians of Weir, of Cabalarkon's Weirdom specifically, boast of the purity of their bloodline. Yet, not only is their current Master a hybrid, he's a small case sedon, the half-son of their everlasting, large case enemy as well as – double the irony this – their everlasting benefactor. Have to say I'm surprised you hadn't figured that out until now."

"Johnny did; I didn't. Or didn't want to. I'd convinced myself I loved him."

"Pyrame's remarkably at least partially still be-brained demon loved him; loved his authority, his majesty anyhow. Not Saladin's: his father's; his devic half-father, the Moloch Sedon, I should qualify. Lilith is, even Pyrame accepts that now, and Lilith is the High Queen of the Whole Earth's Demonic Services, Disservices more like, no denying that.

"Dark Sedon is the Demon King; no denying that either. Has been for literally thousands of years. What Norse Mythology identifies as 'Ragnarok' and Richard Wagner reconceived of as 'Gotterdammerung', the Twilight of the Gods, for his operatic Ring Cycle, are variations of events that actually took place years before the Genesea, the Great Flood of Genesis; two hundred and thirty-four of them, to be precise."

"I'll have to take your word for that, Memory. From the sounds of things you're talking about material preserved in the 'Forever & 40 Days' collection of transposed writings I was supposed to study as a child. As you might appreciate from perusing my surroundings, which you seem to be a part of right now, I haven't any copies of the antediluvian Annals of Anthea lying around to confirm it. Besides, I'm hardly a big opera fan. Their composers always seem to take disgusting delight killing off their heroines."

"And you're not one for dying."

"Not so far. You were theorizing … about how Lovely Lips Lily's love for the Sedon Sphere's Sed somehow translated into my love for Sed-son Sal?"

"So I was. I may be mostly a machine – Miracle Memory, as Helios likes to call me, is just Machine-Memory humanized – but I'm such a romantic at heart I still sometimes need some reminding of that. Here's the rest of it. Your subconscious must have picked up on Lilith's devotion to Dark Sedon and transferred it, on your behalf, to Saladin, Sedon's half-son, sometimes host-shell and surrogate sperm-spurter."

"Surrogate sperm-spurter? Now you are sounding like Human Memory." Even if she died a decade before her being thrust into Limbo on the Outer Earth's Damnation Island, the Witch had no problem recalling Memory of the Angel. They weren't really friends, hadn't met all that often, truth be known, but her earthy, often sexually-charged sense of humour was almost as shocking as her own.

"Yet it's the best way to put it. In a way yours was a necessary compromise. The two of you were sharing the same body, hers overlaying yours in true daemonic fashion. So, for the sake of mutual survival, you had to learn to coexist. I know I did, for all those lifetimes I had her. Even the last one, when I reckon I'd ditched her for Future Erebe, then Devic Night. You'd have died, or at the very least lost your leg, if you and Lilith hadn't been meshed."

"If you're right, then why did she quite literally dump me?"

"Upon due reflection the answer to that's pretty obvious, I'd say." Only, as Wilderwitch apprehended right away, it wasn't altogether, if at all, the Mnemosyne Machine doing the saying anymore. It was, once again, Pyrame Silverstar. "Unlike you, who thought ex-Harmonia, self-renamed Freespirit Nowadays-believes-in-nothingness, was humanizing her, seeing Miracle Memory on the High Illuminary's balcony Lilith somehow realized it was me inside her and panicked. Had to have been afraid I'd take her over again."

"And she was right, I would have. We would have, make that. I'm not about to release Memory; especially not with the exceedingly embittered former Unity of Balance waiting in the wings somewhere hoping to expel me and take her over again." If Pyrame knew what Memory had done with Nihila a couple of months back, which she must have, she wasn't about to share it with the Witch.

"Whereupon she'd find a way to kill her breed-brother, Lord Yajur, and thereby promptly kill Helios. Which wouldn't do anyone any good. Least of all Memory, who really hates being continually thrust back into the time stream through no fault of her own. Other thing is, yes, Lilith must have thought she could carry on without you. She was wrong about that."

"Lovely Lips is the one who died."

"Apparently."

"Apparently?"

"Demons may have no souls, but they do have remarkably enduring spirits. What with Sedon's undeniable talents, more so than Sal's, we – that is to say Memory and I – didn't dare do much more than observe you; who we thought was you, rather, from afar. From Trans-Time Trigon, if you have to know. It really is quite amazing that a machine, even one based on Weir's original Mother Machine, has far-sight. Then again she isn't call miraculous because she isn't.

"Anyhow, when you first got ill we wondered if you and Lilith, with the connivance of the Master of Weir and his ever-so-resourceful, if not so reliable, High Illuminary, had managed to pull the proverbial sheep-shedding over our eyes; that you and they had set up a biomorphic doppelganger of some sort – a shape-shifting mandroid or finely tuned stone gnome perhaps – to make it look like you were faring so poorly.

"Then, ever so rapidly, hour by hour, minute by minute, second by second at the end, you deteriorated right before our faraway eyes. Before we knew it, before we could even decide if we should risk teleporting you to Trigon and thence to some proper medical care, in Godbad maybe, not to mention thereby alerting Sedon as to where we were, you were dead.

"We couldn't believe it. A witch of your calibre, after going through so much … twenty-five years in Limbo, facing down a decathonitized Mater Matare, Mother Murder, and coming through a veritable War of the Apocalyptics in relatively one piece … dead just like that. Memory mourned for you, as a mother should. I still thought it was a trick. I had her do some routine scans and guess who eventually turned up in one of the millennial ships?"

"Albeit without demonic Lady Lilith coexisting inside me anymore. How'd she die?"

"Eaten from within by her unborn Sedon of a son-to-be it seems. At the cost of his ever being born, so it also seems. Not surprisingly, given what they are, foeti lack forethought."

"Demon children eat their mothers?"

"You must have missed that class at the same time you were missing the ones on the Annals of Anthea, wife of Noah. Their demon mothers, yes, though usually not until after they're born. It's a common problem amongst both faerie and demon kind. Their offspring feed on them; often quite literally, and I don't mean just by breastfeeding either, devouring them in the process.

"That's why faeries steal human children and demons confine their sexual activity to different species, not all of whom are necessarily human. Nor even sentient, as far as that goes. It wasn't always the case of course. Wouldn't be any demons left if it was. But Lilith's so old – was around seven thousand years ago, maybe more, that she had the Biblical Cain, Slayer of Abel, don't forget – and hasn't been on her own for so much of the last six millennia, she had no appreciation of just how dependent she'd become on others."

"On you, you mean."

"I knew I acquired a topnotch demon while stuck in Andy the Androsphinx for all those hundreds of years pre-Dome, but didn't know it was her; not for sure. But, yes, on me … and on Memory. Due to circumstances beyond my control, I wasn't always the one humanizing Miracle during the Entities' eleventh lifetime together. For the most part she kept Lilith with her, though. Even took our erstwhile Demon Queen of the Night with her into the time stream when her Herr Hel Helios was killed for the eleventh time in '50 and I was cathonitized again."

Wilderwitch considered the implications of Pyrame's assertion. "Does that mean you weren't my devic half-mother?"

"Nor Fish's. Wasn't in either of your half-birthmothers either."

"That's what you meant about you and the Whole Earth having more need of Lovely Lips than I did. Or do. We were both pregnant, weren't we? That's how it works; Lilith only holds onto boys, so I get to keep – and hopefully deliver – the girl. You're afraid that no matter what happens to my baby, the Dome's going to collapse as soon as either Sal, in here, or Sedon St Synne, out there, dies."

"Pretty much got that in a nutshell, albeit not in a baby belly anymore. And now, but for a vampire or two, without Lilith around it seems it will, inevitably, as soon as either/or happens. It wouldn't be too late to buy your seaside property in the Rockies, assuming you could get outside in time."

A vampire or two would explain Pyrame-Memory's earlier comment regarding altogether alive sedons. Didn't necessarily negate their import, wherever they were, Wilderwitch noted additionally. Once again didn't voice her mental notes, not that (conceivably) it would make much difference. Devils were mind-readers.

Voiced instead: "Cerebrus told me St Synne, who has to be well over a hundred by now, was being kept alive in California by some sort of life support machine. Utopian technology?"

"What do you think? Of course it is. So was his headpiece, despite what his poseur cousin Wiccan Warlock, Jesus Mandam, claimed. Other thing is, sorry to say, but you're now an irrelevance. We've already overstayed our Memory-calculated safety margin here. Fare thee well, Witch, Cynthemis Dyana."

That said, the wall of the generational ship went all the way wall-like again. Pyrame-Memory, the joint beings, Pyrame and Memory, were clearly, manifestly, blankly, no longer there. Dark Sedon, even if he was as omnipresent as he was very nearly omnipotent, would not be alerted as to their whereabouts.

Presumably, anyhow.

========

Initially their abandoning her to her own devices, as if they'd never found her, annoyed the beguiling be-Jesus – as the Diver might put it – out of the Witch.

Surely, she reckoned at the time, they could have left some Anthean Agates or other Witch Sisterhood's equivalent behind. That way, on them, she would have had a chance to take herself outside the confines of the Weirdom of Cabalarkon. To take herself to some elsewhere – even if it was to the Thanatoid Death Gods' Frozen Isle of Lathakra – much safer for her to bear her baby in than a derelict, onetime spacecraft.

Her own devices had never fully failed her yet, though. And, a few days later, after venturing deeper into the innards of the enormous, a long time ago, starship, fearsome soul-self first, she came across something that made her realize Mama Memory hadn't altogether abandoned her.

It thereafter became a matter of mastering one of Machine-Memory's other devices.

========

Wilderwitch was no Aires D'Angelo; nowadays no Aires Thanatos. So she'd heard anyhow. Airhead, codenamed Airealist, could damn near fly anything.

Other than Raven's Head, when she was in the mood, the Witch could fly damn near nothing. Had never bothered with a psychopomp either. Was so good with Anthean Agates or other Sisterhood's said equivalencies – was never without some – that they had almost always been her preferred method of travelling long distance.

Had been even after Mel's sister-in-law, Superior Sarpedon (the reportedly late Morgianna or Morg, the White Witch born Nauroz, become Somata, who married Demios decades ago and who'd already become the Hecate Hellions' Morrigan by then), started polluting between-space beyond the Dome with transcendent, devil-eating demons, ones loyal to her alone, in hope of catching the sentient virus, Faceless Strife.

Who the Witch, albeit to herself, had long suspected was actually a malicious, devic Spirit Being; one without a daemonic body or a power focus to call her own. (Even the Witch had trouble retaining her memories of the Hidden Headworld when she was on the Outer Earth. Indeed, because there were so many Mentat-type supras along the line of Magus Maxius, their own Cyborg Cerebrus and the Magnificent Psycho, self-redaction as to its existence was all-but-mandatory for her as well as the likes of Fisherwoman, Lady Lemurian and Sorciere.)

She'd at first recognized the transport for what it did, not what it was. Somewhere in the deep, dark recesses of her own memory she knew that suchlike shuttle crafts were called vimanas in the Vedic tradition. (Not to be confused with Hindu deities' vahanas or vehicles, which were usually depicted as living creatures of fact or fancy; their equivalent of psychopomps. Elephant-headed Ganesha's transportive mouse stood out in this regard, if only for its sheer contrariness.)

Be that as it may, it looked so much like the so-called cosmicar that crashed on Damnation Isle on the 30th of November last year (thus indirectly leading to hers and the rest of D-Brig's escape from Limbo), she reckoned it was just that: an at least partially Brainrock-powered, flying machine.

She intuited a way to get it up and out of there. Either that or, long distance thanks to Machine-Memory, operating with or without Pyrame's support, the vessel intuited it for her. The air itself was nevertheless troublesome. She ended up far to the north of where she was trying to guide her remarkably silent-running, VTOL (vertical take off and landing) aircraft.

Was it Sedonplay she ended up back here? No matter. She landed the vehicle, sort of, and found her way to the Zerosses' door. Whereupon she rang the bell.

An aging, if still fit-looking, bearded, hybrid Utopian – Thobruk Grudal was his name she recalled from last Tantalar, a Summoning Child she'd also heard tell – answered it. His gargoyle, more correctly his grotesque, was a fuzzy puppy dog of some sort. Or a fuzzy baby seal. That would be at Mel's insistence. With tiny Tina around she wouldn't let a Trinondev manifest anything scary atop his eye-stave. The youngster's favourite dolly was Silkie the Selkie, a fuzzy baby seal.

"You are?"

"Wilderwitch."

"Try again." She didn't bother. Went all chalky white, instead. Kept her hair the way it was, though.

"Cynthia Masterwife?" The Trinondev Warrior of Weir looked shocked by her presence. So did the gargoyle atop his eye-stave. In response she half-nodded, despite the passage of weeks' away still used to the despised, unfortunately obligatory honourific. Grudal thereupon confirmed what Pyrame-Memory claimed was the evidentiary reality of the situation.

"You're supposed to be dead."

"Only on my feet, friend. And call me Wilderwitch, please. Cute grotesque by the way. Is Mel here?"

"Sorry," he apologized, mentally recalling the manifest gargoyle into his eye-orb. "The High Illuminary of Weir is, um, indisposed at the moment. Shall I awaken her?"

"Better just show me to a bedroom. I'd like to crash before I have to explain my crash."

Grudal looked over her shoulder. Landings weren't her speciality. He could see that. "You flew that thing? I thought they were just museum pieces."

"Not all of them. Like it? I call it 'Broom', but it's actually a vimana. At least that's what the Vedas – Outer Earth, pre-Hindu, semi-sacred books almost as old as this here Weirdom – called something like it anyhow. Who knows what it runs on, solar or stellar powered batteries maybe, but, yes, unless it flew me, I flew it. Any bedroom will do fine. Fact is so would a manger."

"As you witch, um, Wilderwitch."

"Funny guy, Tobruk."

"That's Thobruk. Tobruk was a battlefield on the Outer Earth during its Second World War. I know. I was there when the Germans took it."

"So was I, a year or so after it fell. SOS: the Society of Saints lost Thalassa D'Angelo around there somewhere. I was one of those called in to try and find her. Did, too, but 'Lassa should have known better. A Sea Goddess and a Desert God, especially given the times a Germanic one, really weren't compatible. You aren't that Thobruk, are you?"

"Only if you aren't that Witch."

"Must have been my mother."

========

The next morning, that of the Spring Equinox, Year of Dome 5981, Wilderwitch opened her eyes. She was alone in bed but, at the foot of it, stood Athena Zeross.

Tiny Tina was wearing pyjamas. The Witch heard her out. Then said again: "Huh?"

****

FOUR-DEMON: **Drawing Contusions**

========

Equinox Eve, 5981

Mostly because of the howsoever sporadic Time Quakes that had started shaking the vast plains of Marutia, Sedon's Cheek, also its Breadbasket, again in 5978, twenty-five years after they'd stopped, the Cheeks were extremely primitive. There were times when dogcarts and horse-drawn buggies, even wheels, didn't function simply because they had yet to be reinvented.

Everyone within the Cathonic Zone or Sedon Sphere knew how to fix that. Eliminate the Moloch Sedon. Beyond the Cathonic Dome, as most of those living on the Hidden Continent somewhat incorrectly thought of the Sed-Sphere, Jesus Mandam, aka Wiccan Warlock, the King Conqueror or, as he preferred by then, the Conquering Christ, reckoned he'd accomplished just that on Christmas Day 1953.

The Dome didn't collapse; ergo Sedon hadn't been eliminated. He'd just been diminished so much so his star, usually so bright it could sometimes be seen during the day, wasn't even visible in the night's sky above his own Headworld for the ensuing quarter century. Jess or Jesse to his friends, not that he had many, if any, of those, never realized how successful he'd been.

He too had been eliminated. Only he never rose again. Not as such anyhow.

========

The west coast regions of the mid-to-upper Head, places like Apple Isle, Crepuscule or Sedon's Outer Nose, the Pristine Isles in Bogey Bay, and the nearby Bloodlands – Sedon's Inner Nose or New Valhalla, as it became more commonly known well over a thousand years earlier – weren't struck by Time Quakes. Which was why Centauri Enterprises and, therefore, the Corporate State of Greater Godbad had been able to make inroads there ever since the conclusion of Godbad's civil war in the late Fifties, early Sixties.

It still took months by ship to go from the exceptionally mountainous subcontinent (Sedon's Lower Jaw, Chin and Goatee) to Cabalarkon (Sedon's Devic Eye-Land). Ship wasn't the only way to go between the two sovereign states, however; not once you got to the northernmost city in Crepuscule (the Land of Twilight, Sedon's Outer Nose), a port called Eventide, it wasn't.

Eventide lay at the bridge of said Outer Nose, just below the Gulf of Corona, Sedon's Human Eye, roughly midway to Godbad from the Weirdom. For the time being airplanes were useless up there because their fuel was too volatile to be trucked that far. However, there was a developing road system suitable for all-terrain vehicles and an even quicker railway run on coal, which was plentiful in Twilight.

Despite using the most rapid transportation methods available, it wasn't until Godbad's traditional New Year's Eve, the night before the Spring Equinox, that the Fatman (Alpha Centauri in here; Alfredo Sentalli out there, where he was born of a Tedesco mother in 1927) was brought the Master of Weir's gruesome gift by Janna St. Peche Montressor. (The Family D'Angelos' Summoning-dispatched matriarch Leonora, the Leonine Superior, mother of the individually renowned Celestine, Dolores, Raphael and Mnemosyne, was a Tedesco as well.)

It wasn't the most pleasant of things to receive on New Year's Eve. Neither was the wooden hat box, though it might have been made in less fabled than missed Samarand, once Sedon's Tongue. The long ago switched, hence difficult to reach, former devic protectorate of Yati, Byron's Dragon, was now on the far eastern coast of the Head.

(As might be expected of someplace once known as Sedon's Tongue, it used to stick out of Sedon's Mouth. Indeed, Samarand City was once Sedon's Tongue Stud. Similarly the Thanatoids' Frozen Isle of Lathakra had once been Sedon's Horn, in the far north, then Sedon's Monocle, off Apple Isle in Fearsome Fobbiat, just beyond the Gulf of Corona, whereas the Grey Lady's Grey Land of Twilight had once been Daybreak, where Samarand was now.)

Janna was the Fatman's daughter-in-law. Was also a Lovely Lady: a highly trained, exquisitely skilled Afrite, as the Sisterhood of the (mostly) lost Byronic, Aphropsyche Morningstar, APM, All-Eyes, was known. Not that APM was lost as such. More correctly she'd been apprehended. Even more correctly she'd been inhumed, along with many of her fellow Byronics, by All of Incain last Tantalar. (Parenthetically 'mostly' because APM fragmented; at least one of her innumerable eyes ending up in SPM.)

It was, nevertheless, a personal loss for him. When they were on the Outer Earth, his regular physician, Connie Lindquist, often acted as APM's willing host. As such her procedures were not necessarily limited to those approved by either the American or Godbadian medical associations. Unfortunately, at least as far as the Fatman was concerned, pregnant again Janna nowadays reserved her own Lovely Lady ministrations for Yataghan nominally Montressor, his son by still much-missed mother, Emeralda Plantagenet Sentalli.

Now in his early thirties, Yataghan remained behind in Aka Godbad City, where he was supervising the rebuilding of Centauri Enterprises' ancillary headquarters. It had been smashed apart by All when she came to capture-consume APM and her fellow Byronics. The vindictive She-Sphinx had done so in retaliation for him ordering the bombing of her Prison Beach. Was a damn shame she hid out mostly between-space because, if that wasn't the case, the bombs would have destroyed her before she got a chance to do a sloppy demolition job on CE's HQ.

Yataghan wouldn't be arriving for a few hours yet, along with the rest of Centauri's guests. They included some of those who fled, alongside him and his son, from the largely manmade (financed by him, albeit through New Century Enterprises, which he controlled) Outer Earth version of Centauri Island, the launch site of the Cosmic Express, last December.

One of them was that selfsame Dr Lindquist. Even though (most of) APM remained in All's between-space prison, along with many another of the Godbadian subcontinent's resultantly absentee deities, he retained some degree of desire Connie might diagnose him as in need of a personally applied prescription.

Faint hope of that, he mused, silently admiring Janna's cleavage as she laid the box on the desk in front of him. Connie was engaged to marry his lawyer, George Hannibal, who would also be arriving with Yataghan. Still, even if he preferred matters at least potentially otherwise, he held a soft spot for her. And it wasn't in his hands, he shuddered to himself, grimace-inducing joke that that was.

So what if her recently late, Summoning Child of a father, Greygreave Translav, the Little Prince, so-called because he'd been a midget – especially when compared to her much longer deceased, approaching-gigantic-in-stature mother Uli Sturlson's Nordic princess – was a founder and mainstay mover within the revived WORLD?

So what if WORLD, the Worldwide Order with the Right to Life and Death, had been revived purely for the purpose of taking out the Cosmic Express before it could even reach atmospheric escape velocity? So what if, in the Forties, Translav devised a serum that rendered terminally ill men and women not only momentarily healthy and active again, it sometimes made them glow?

So what if his consequentially-called Glomen blew up with a really big, as in really dynamite, bang if they didn't ingest an antidote in time? So what if Glows blowing caused extensive damage to the other Centauri Island, in part necessitating his leaving it? So what if the Little Prince, so-called also because he believed he was the rightful Tsar of all the Russians, was relatively recently late because he deserved it for irritating the Fatman so inexcusably?

Centauri was a sentimental sort. Did not believe that the sins of the father necessarily transferred to the son; daughter in her case. Neither was his Buddha-belly his only soft spot. The soft spot he'd been contemplating with respect to Connie Lindquist was in his heart. He liked George almost as much as he did Connie; fine professionals the pair of them. Being as religious as he was romantic, he was all in favour of them getting hitched.

They'd be announcing the date at the party tonight. So, all-in-all – minus All of Incain, please Celestial God – it was going to be quite the blast. Always assuming, not that it was very likely, the dedicated doctor didn't decide to be a deadly doctor and dose up any potential Glomen in her caseload such that they'd to go boom at midnight, accompanied by the fireworks display he'd arranged, as payback for what happened to her father.

He opened the box up. The severed skull of Gomez Niarchos started talking to him.

========

"Intolerable," Centauri blustered when Gomez was finished. "As if I'd ever be a party to restoring the Godbadian monarchy, let alone countenance Godbad entering into any sort of formal union with Cabalarkon that resulted in us remitting tribute to Saladin Devason. Maybe it is time we did something about this objectionable Master of theirs after all."

"Way past time," concurred Demios Sarpedon. The 60-year old, black-as-midnight Utopian Summoning Child, an aspirant to the Mastery of Weir, was completely healed after being wounded when Cloud-General Kronar's fellow, oversized vultures began dropping Hadd's ambulant dead, its Haddazur-animated zombies, onto Sraddha Isle, a stronghold of the Living in the midst of Lake Sedona, the previous Tantalar. "I've been on and on about steps you should be taking against the usurper for months now."

With Janna in her customary place standing behind him, the Fatman (called thus, often to his face, because he was so fat he could barely walk) moved the box with the Sangazur-kept-talking head of one of his greatest supporters such that Niarchos could look at those sitting on the other side of his office desk.

He'd had them come here early, a friend and a small, select group of his closest advisers. Here was his no longer solely holiday home on the shores of the Inner Earth's Centauri Island. It was one of the southernmost Panic Isles, they being a dinky archipelago that dribbled south and westward from peninsular Krachla, which was situated just below Hadd to the northeast of the subcontinent.

Hadd had already been renamed, quite cleverly the Fatman felt, Haas. Its all-but-finalized liberation from the forces of the Undead and their Ambulatory Dead was just one more reason for tonight's gala celebration; one more reason he was determined to make it even more spectacular than usual. Right now, though, the Fatman was all business.

"So you have, Mr Sarpedon. On and on and bloody on some more."

"Not repeatedly enough. I told you what he did to my daughter."

Demios Sarpedon had been more than a mite touchy of late. So much so, like her husband Yataghan, Centauri's son and alternate bodyguard, Janna was wary of him carrying his eye-stave into the Fatman's presence. Before Bodiless Byron became a star in the night's sky, again, that wasn't much of a concern. Eye-staves, even ones as ancient as his, didn't work in devic protectorates, not such that the eyeorbs atop them could capture devils anyhow.

They still had lots of other uses, however, and the one Demios Sarpedon carried was reputedly put together long before Utopians came to the Whole Earth ten years before the Great Flood of Genesis. In some respects there really was no telling what he could do with it. Consequently it, his ever-so-antique eye-stave, was stowed in the umbrella stand just inside the front door.

So was his pouch of eyeorbs. (Not that it needed any. His eye-stave was so old it retained the capacity to make replacements once the previous orb filled up with azuras or one of their devic progenitors.) Demios hadn't objected. He got sufficiently riled he could wreak murderous mayhem with damn near anything. Including, pregnant or not, him being a Summoning-born supernormal possessed of remarkable speed and concomitant strength, old friend Janna herself. Used as a club.

"And I told you Andaemyn went at him first," countered Jordan Tethys, the Legendarian. "Seemed to anyhow. Sal reckoned he was only defending himself."

The Fatman counted the storyteller his friend, one of all too few he sometimes morbidly reflected. Tethys was a deviant, the son of a mortal man or mortal woman, or both, possessed by devils when he was conceived. Like all deviants he thereby acquired abilities that Centauri, who knew of the Outer Earth's Secret War of Supranormals, had participated in them tangentially, classified as supra-special.

Tethys's abilities, though, were more like supra-strange. He never lived longer than thirty years – and them never starting before his latest self turned twenty. Only then he came back, usually in the body of his own, at-the-time-dying offspring, or their offspring, who promptly made a miraculous recovery; albeit for no more than thirty years before he moved on again, likely leaving his host just as sickly, assuming he or she remained alive. As such he had also become known as the Thirty Year Man.

30-Beers was another of his most common epithets. Although it referred to his consumptive habits – not that he drank thirty beers a day, not very often anyhow – he didn't object to it anymore than he did the Legendarian or 30-Years. Tethys wasn't too fond of Author, however, which was how a number of devils he was acquainted with referred to him. He was a storyteller, yes, and, yes as well, he sometimes exaggerated the tales he was telling. But he seldom made anything up. That would be cheating.

The other thing he objected to was this forever-repeated nonsense he began his existence as a devil, namely Rumour of Lazareme. It was calumnious, a slander. Sure, he had a scar in the middle of his forehead where a devil's third eye would be. Sure, all of his incarnations, man or woman, developed the same scar when he came into them. Sure, when they were just his son, daughter or later generational descendant thereof, most of them didn't have a scar in their forehead. And, sure again, he also had a Brainrock quill, what many who knew about devils, and knew about him, suspected might be a devic power focus.

Just wasn't so. Not that he'd ever admit anyways. (Did admit his quill was a Tvasitar Talisman, though. Admitted further that it was forged for the very devil he was supposed to have once been; a devil who also passed his time painting, telling tales or reciting tee-tee tails.) For one thing he was a vastly superior artist than the devil had been. Then again, having been gone upwards to two thousand years now, very little of Rumour's artwork remained.

"And if you hadn't sent Sal back to Cabalarkon," Sarpedon reminded him, "Dervish Furie would have done to him what he was trying to do to Andy."

"From what Young Death has since told me," argued the Legendarian, "The wild man dare not kill. He's terrified of becoming the full Furie, whatever that is; some sort of berserker demon perhaps." (Young Death was Auguste Moirnoir, a perpetually 7-year old faerie trickster who had been residing in a Sraddhite Monastery on an island situated in Lake Sedona, Sedon's Teardrop, for many years now.)

"Bah!" snorted Sarpedon. "I've had it with you devil-lovers. Are you finally ready to do what I recommended months ago, Alpha?"

"I don't do things myself, Mr Sarpedon. I preauthorize what others are to do on behalf of Centauri Enterprises, not the nation." (Which strictly speaking was true enough. However, affairs of state and of his corporation were all but inseparable. Hence why it was commonly called the Corporate State of Greater Godbad.)

"General Anvil?"

The Fatman, an Italian-Canadian born Alfredo Sentalli on the Outer Earth in 1927, but who had gone by the name of Alpha Centauri since first arriving on the Inner Earth in August 1945, Hektor 5945 in here, spent most of his waking life voluntarily confined to a wheelchair. (Saved on the awkward, not mention exhausting, walking.) Manipulating its in-arm controls he rotated to face General Quentin Anvil, the Hero of Hadd, at least as far as Greater Godbad's Centauri-Enterprises-controlled mass media was concerned, for an update.

"Preparations are well under way, sir," said the burly veteran of the Godbadian Civil War, a fighting fit fellow despite being an Inner Earth Summoning Child and hence sixty years old. Everyone there had been through the Civil War, even Demios, though he and late wife Morgianna fought on the losing side of it, with the anti-Byronic, pro-Auranja monarchists. By contrast Tethys was a Japanese-looking nun, Sister Jordan, during a good percentage of it.

"Nonetheless I can't see getting a fleet complete with fuel tankers, helicopters and a few planes up there for at least another year. The logistics are just too daunting." Centauri had read the same reports. Had, just as much so, read into the same reports; with the same conclusions in terms of a massive invasion fleet.

"Of course, to listen to Mr Sarpedon, that wouldn't be necessary had we a friendlier Master on the throne of Weir." He turned to his right hand man on this side of the Dome, Cromwell Necator. "Can you extract the current one, protector?"

(The sadly recently late O'Ryan James Maxwell handled Sentalli's security matter on the Outer Earth's Centauri Island until his reported demise while on the Moon in the service of the Great Man, Abe Ryne's SPACE Council — SPACE being the United Nations supported Society for the Prevention of Alien Control of Earth, a Ryne-rendered acronym like AMERICA, the Alliance of Man for the Extermination of International Criminal Associations.)

Even though he was an army-trained, Special Ops killer like his similar-to-Gomez-Niarchos, long time Sangazur-possessed father Godfrey, he too was a media darling. It was the younger Necator, an albino, also like his father and suggestively, though by no means decisively, like most Sang-symbionts, who led the bombing strikes on the Prison Beach of Incain early the previous Tantalar; on the Ninth, to be precise; more than four months gone now.

Not that it had prevented Incain's resident, between-space She-Sphinx, All the Invincible, from traversing the Grey all the way across the Interior Ocean of Akadan to Aka Godbad City the next day. Aka Godbad City was where Centauri usually resided. Was there the She-Sphinx went on a rampage, ruined Centauri Enterprises' ancillary HQ and seized a dozen or so of Godbad's deities, Byron Spawn the lotus lot of them, including most of APM All-Eyes, in the process.

Crom agreed with the media. As Centauri's enforcer and, therefore, as the Corporate State's designated protector – was named after that Protector, Lord Protector Oliver Cromwell, hero the English Civil War – he felt himself a legitimate liberator. Was proud of it too, even if it was from their lives he liberated most of his targets. What he wasn't was a fool.

"We've all met Saladin Devason, sir. He's been in Godbad before, most recently that I know about in '73, when he was checking out Godbad City, an old Weirdom, among other things." (Godbad City, where Centauri Enterprises' main headquarters, as well as many of its manufactories were based, was All's next target that day. There, though, she (it?) concentrated on trashing its airfields and Godbad's air force.)

"After what I heard happened to him later on that same trip on Shenon, he should have learned his lesson about leaving Cabalarkon. That he didn't might be more of a comment on his intelligence, or lack thereof, than anything else but, after what happened to him at the Sraddhite Monastery a few months ago, he surely must have figured it out by now.

"So, yeah. Once I reach Eventide I can easily arrange passage on a Pani Merchant vessel to go the rest of the way up there. That said, while I've some thoughts in terms of methodology, I don't foresee much hope of either a successful extraction or even, push comes to shove – off a high building, this Skyrise of his for example – a successful extinction. If everything we've learned about him is right, and both Mr Sarpedon and Mr Tethys verify as much, the Master is next to God in the Weirdom."

"What my brother-in-law is," clarified Demios, "Is the equivalent of a devil. Despite what smartasses like my twin, its High Illuminary, claim about it really belonging to Dark Sedon, Cabalarkon amounts to his protectorate. He feeds on the adulation of his people, they empower him, so unless he – heavens forfend – dies, the only way you're going to dislodge him is by having Utopians turn against him."

"Turn in your favour," interpreted Centauri.

"In our favour, Alpha." Demios knew him as Alfredo Sentalli, too. Had in fact been working for him beyond the Dome on the other Centauri Island when the launching of the Cosmic Express took place on November the 30th, the equivalent of Maruta the 30th in here. "His hold on their loyalty is fragile at best. All it'll take is a little nudge to redirect their lemming-like hero worship to someone more worthy, a genuine hero. His sister, my wife, would do for starters."

"Morg's dead!" The Fatman had been over this with Demios many times; loathed having to go over it again. "All that's left of her is some kind of chrysalis-approximating statue you retrieved from what I hear is now called Diminished Dustmound." Actually it was called Demon Mound, a name coined by Demios himself once he regained enough strength to return there not all that long after her reported disgrace as much as her death.

"What's worse, Morgianna died fighting alongside the Dead, which hardly makes her a hero in my books. What's even worse, she was in the process of killing Dervish Furie, whom I knew and liked, when Blind Sundown, whom I also knew but didn't much like, killed her. I'd say that places her amongst the vilest of villains. Ask me, she got what she deserved."

"Good thing I didn't ask you then. But him killing Morg for whatever reason is precisely why the Master sentenced Johnny to Immediate Death." Both the Sarpedons, his wife and her eventual husband, participated in the amazingly kept-secret, so-called Suprawar beyond the Dome. Demios's initial codename was Blackguard, which he earned when he was just Morg's bodyguard. He became the Ace of Spades, which he much preferred, after they married.

"Gomez here figures he did so as a sop to the people. Which indicates to me, as it should to you, just how well-loved my wife remains in the Weirdom."

"Demios may be onto something, sir," Quentin Anvil considered. "The five Outer Earth supras Harry Zeross brought with him to Hadd called themselves the Damnation Brigade. From what I saw of them, they had some mighty impressive abilities. And Gomez just told us they made quite a splash upon their return to Cabalarkon.

"Indeed, from the sounds of things Utopians, to a man or to a woman, looked upon them as definite heroes; maybe even as the answer to their prayers. They certainly regarded Blind Sundown and Raven's Head as devaslayers, which they might have been, and hoped they'd eventually provide the Trinondevs of Weir with the wherewithal to kill, or at least cathonitize, devils rather than just capture them in their prison pods."

"Thanks for the thumbnail review, General," said Centauri, maintaining his formal tone. "You started off saying Mr Sarpedon might be onto something."

"My point, sir, is that despite their extraordinary abilities and undeniable popularity, Saladin had the balls to give four of them the boot, including three of those who were with us in Hadd. For all we know he might have had the Zeross girls send them to their deaths somewhere. The insides of an active volcano comes to mind; Sedon's Peak on the Cattail or Mt Maenalus on Apple Isle perhaps.

"Then, only a few days later, he had as much or more nerve to take on Sundown and Raven directly. To my eyes Sundown looks like an Irache. And from what I heard of him he's much more sympathetic to their plight than ours or even that of the Living. Granted also, he had killed what was left of this D-Brig's leader, Cerebrus David Ryne, whom I gather he'd mistaken for Cabalarkon, the undying Utopian Dark Sedon considers his father.

"Point being Saladin took them on even though, as you've told me yourself, from your dealings with them on the Outer Earth a quarter century and more ago, they're not only accomplished killers, they're virtually invulnerable. Yet, even if he only forced them to flee, he got away with it. Got away with it, at least in part due to the desire of the populace to avenge what happened to his sister, who also went down thanks to this Sundown fellow, one man killing machine that he seems to have been.

"There must be some way we can use their no matter how misguided devotion to ex-Superior Sarpedon to our advantage."

Centauri wasn't persuaded. "In other words, do exactly what he did to his advantage three and a half months ago; more now. It seems to me, General, the Master beat us to the punch. He's already staked out that territory as exclusively his own. His daring to challenge D-Brig, Sundown and Raven in particular, was calculated to cement the then howsoever wavering support of his people. He did what he needed to do in order to do to stay in power. And, if Mr Sarpedon is right about a Master being akin to a devil in his or her own protectorate, I do mean power.

"On top of that, from what Mr Niarchos was saying he's managed to get Wilderwitch on his side. She isn't just sharing his bed, either. She's pregnant with his heir; even went so far as to marry him. From what little I recall of her, she wouldn't have done that if she perceived him as somehow unworthy of her love and loyalty.

"On top of that, she seemed to support the Master's effort to turn on Sundown; to execute him in the coldest of blood in front of dozens, maybe hundreds, of guests gathered to celebrate his wedding to her. Not only that – and this to me verges on the incredible – he did it with the connivance of your twin sister, Mr Sarpedon, her eldest daughter Persephone, and in full view of life-loving Ants like Tsishah Thrae and her own sister, Lady Achigan.

"Has she lost her mind? Have they all lost their minds? As well, and this should trouble everyone who's helped to make Greater Godbad what it is today, a place of peace and ever-increasing prosperity that rivals, if not surpasses, anywhere on the

Outer Earth, she's probably where Devason came up with the absurd notion of restoring the monarchy. I mean, see above."

"How so?" wondered Tethys, obligingly.

"Just told you. Wilderwitch is Lady Achigan's sister. Lady Achigan's husband is Achigan Auranja, Duke of Achigon – despite its funny spelling – and Godbad's last king. You and I know they're with us now: the same as Lady Achigan's foster sister, Amphitrite of Lemuria, is; the same as the undersea Akan and renegade Piscine water-breathers are; the same as you and your late wife were, are in your case, Mr Sarpedon; the same as so many other onetime enemies of Godbad, non-Byronic devils, and nowadays your father, Godfrey Necator's Valhallans included, protector."

"But the Witch has been gone a quarter of a century. She probably has little or no idea how far we've come with respect to realizing what her very own Superior Sisterhood refers to as the goal of Panharmonium. She's as much a spanner in the works as this Master's egomania's making him a nuisance. An ever increasingly dangerous nuisance, I shouldn't have to emphasize, the longer we leave him sitting on what he's got buried in the Slopes of the Sleepers."

Those there knew what he meant: the 6,000 years' leftover, Utopian generational ships, and the space-spanning alien technology that went into them.

"He, or more likely your sister, the female Dr Zeross's Illuminaries and the Weirdom's scientocrats, their techno- and biomages both, are eventually going to pull a King Conqueror and figure out how things work up there. They could make demons, Mr Tethys; the same shape-shifting, man-eating biomorphs the Sraddhites call Indescribables and witches the eldritch earthborn, even if theirs would be more like born out of a test tube.

"And when they do that, we down here, and they out there, on the Outer Earth, are going to be in big bird-splat. He has to be stopped."

"I'm agreeing with you, Alpha," Demios reiterated. "It's the how I'm disagreeing with you about."

"So you are, Mr Sarpedon. Myself, I'd say us finding a way to use your late wife's statuary remains against Saladin Devason are, give or take either a tit or a tat, approximately nil. If, like the General says, a pre-emptive invasion's still a year away – even if it's only half a year away, which I'm sure is what General Anvil meant to say – then extraction's the lone practical option I can foresee. Only now it's two that have to be extracted." The Fatman had clearly made up his preauthorizing mind on this matter.

"Work on that methodology, protector," Centauri instructed Cromwell Necator. "For starters, now that Great Byron's shining out of the night's sky and eyeorbs can work here, you might want to have the Weirdom's ambassadors disarmed. Don't have them locked up, though. Not yet anyhow. We'd have to come up with a better excuse than what their borderline imbecilic Master did to Gomez to justify that."

"So long as it isn't Morg turning traitor in Hadd," tentatively agreed Demios, whose sister was in charge of the Godbadian ambassadorial corps long distance.

"Reading my mind, Mr Sarpedon?"

"My eye-stave's in the umbrella stand, Mr. Centauri."

"See it remains there, Janna," the Fatman instructed his daughter-in-law, only half-humourously, before returning his attention to his guest. "It's no secret I've never liked what you, nor they, Cabalarkon's Illuminaries and Trinondevs, can do with those eye-staves of yours, theirs, even inside a devic protectorate. And I don't mean the way you or they sometimes march around with them as unnerving-looking gargoyle-labarums. Still, I see no reason to overly antagonize the Master right this minute. Nor your sister, the High Illuminary, for that matter."

"Antagonizing them at all might not be the best bargaining ploy, sir," said Necator, evidently already working on his methodology.

"Why not, pray Celestial God tell?"

"Myself or my agents may need an in to the Weirdom itself. Seems to me an opportunity may be presenting itself with the recently announced marriage between … what? Higher-ups in the food chain of the self-declared Hate-Sedon realms of Lemuria-slash-Temporis and the City-State of Cabalarkon; not to mention Mama Amphitrite on Shenon, Witch Isle. It'd be advantageous if you could wangle a couple of us an invite to attend it, as your representatives.

"Might not take much to do so, either. You've already jumped at the chance to have our flag changed from the grey-skies backing the Byronhead to CE's blue-skies backing the Headworld in relation to the Whole Earth's globe. Let's go a step further and declare Godbad a devil-free zone. Give or take a few holdouts scattered around, notably Petrogod, or whatever Illuminaries call him, inside your son, Mr Niarchos."

(Ferdinand Niarchos was the governor of New Iraxas, Godbad's oil-rich, but both super-polluted and super-polluting north-easternmost province. He did live in Petrograd and Petrogod, when he was around, did tend to regard it as his protectorate. Except, Byronics didn't really have protectorates per se. Besides, he wasn't always inside Governor Niarchos any more than Byron, when he was around, was always inside the Fatman.)

"Tzihk-rzrui," said Janna born St Peche, who was brought up in Dukkha, Sedon's Upper Lip-Tip, hence the French-sounding last name. (Outside Subcranial Temporis, Dukkha was the only domain – formally a Duchy or Dukedom like Achigon {with an 'o', not an 'a', hence the Fatman's remark about it having a funny spelling} – where the natives consciously spoke an Outer Earth language. Didn't really matter. Like everywhere else on the Hidden Headworld, you were there you understood what everyone was saying; just took a little while longer was all.)

"Means Alberta crude in some native language in Northern Canada."

"Alberta crud more like," the Fatman said, referring to the bituminous tar-sand gunk found up there since ancient times. "Isn't good for anything except caulking canoes." (Even though he'd been born in Toronto, he'd hardly ever been back to Canada since slipping across the border and joining the American navy in 1943, at the age of 16.)

Turning towards Necator, he proceeded to correct him; something he didn't do very often. His 'protector' – Oliver Cromwell had been no friend of Catholics, which Centauri remained – didn't handle criticism very well. Took offense at All's rampage and wanted to go back to Incain in order to do the job properly: go all Hiroshima, not Dresden, on All's changeling ass. (Centauri stopped him; said she wouldn't be so restrained the next time.)

"Actually All nailed Petrogod. He was inside Benoit Dugas, one the Untouchables Dr Samarand liked having around on the outside's Centauri Island."

"One less lie then. We go devil-free, we can at least purport to demonstrate we're on the same side as this Devason, despite his evident half-parentage, pretends to be."

"The lying bastard," Demios contributed unhelpfully.

"Precisely, Mr Sarpedon, though I believe his non-devic half-parentage was indisputably legitimate. We certainly would never dare to address him as Mr Devason; nor should any of our representatives. Very well, protector, but I will only go halfway with you on this. Because Godbad is a de facto devil-free zone already, please get hold of the president and ensure the following is issued. Or words to its effect:

"'Prior to our entering into any negotiations with the Weirdom of Cabalarkon, said Weirdom's ambassadors may keep their eye-staves only insofar as they retain them in their embassies, or other previously acknowledged residences the sovereign state of Greater Godbad's authorities deigns to allow them do so. However, should they dare to exit said pre-approved areas, they shall not be asked to disarm. Rather, they shall be shot on sight.'

"See to it our police and paramilitary forces are accordingly outfitted with armour-piercing weaponry — or whatever they need to burst their thought-bubbles. Mr Sarpedon, you shall leave your eye-stave, no matter how old it is, with my daughter-in-law until you return to the Cattail or wherever you intend to go next. Janna Montressor, see that it is locked up in a Solidium-reinforced safe prior to tonight's gala."

"Have you gone absolutely insane, Alpha?" Sarpedon exclaimed. "My eye-stave and its orbs can overrule any other eye-stave and its orbs. Ask anyone who was on Sraddha Isle to verify that if you must. I, and them, my eye-stave and its orbs, have been on guard against them and theirs ever since I came back from Hadd."

"Haas, Mr Sarpedon," the Fatman reminded him, still in officious mood. (He did business formally; only dropped the honourifics over meals or when he was drinking.) "Hadd, old Iraxas has been renamed Haas. And so you have, albeit you did not come back here until quite some time after Bodiless Byron was atomized."

"I was hurt."

"So your were … in defense of the Living's right to live and the Dead's to stay dead. Or at least immobile. While it's true Utopian ambassadors made no discernible efforts to harm me or mine while you were, um, indisposed, they could have. And they can, if we let them get too close to us. Let this be the message they send back to their Master and his High Illuminary; to you two as well, Mr Sarpedon, Mr Necator. Neither compulsion nor coercion shall be, ever again, if they ever were, the way of Godbad."

"Hear, hear," said Quentin Anvil.

"Beer, beer," altered Jordan Tethys, cracking open another pilsner.

Janna said nothing. It wasn't her place to say anything. She was in complete agreement with her father-in-law, though. They couldn't afford to lose the little bit of APM All-Eyes they had left to a rogue Trinondev. Or even Demios Sarpedon, should he choose to scan the area for devils. For one thing it, she, her little angel of an eyeball, might be necessary to Centauri, with his medically morbid girth and unsupportable lifestyle, in case of a cardiac event.

"Mr Necator," the Fatman put to the albino, decisively, "Should you truly need an invitation to this wedding our, um, official friends, Lady Achigan and Aortic Amphitrite, are scheduling for their children up there come Midsummer's Day, June, Azky, then approach them yourself. Or, better yet, have an ambassador of your own do it for you.

"Although I shouldn't have to tell you this, just be careful how you deal with them. I don't believe for a moment they're our actual friends. If they were, they never would have been a party to, shall we say, the deflection of the Cosmic Express into Cathonia at the end of Maruta, November. That said, you may want to mention how indulgent we've been of all this Panharmonium Project preposterousness of theirs for what's going on a couple of decades, or more, by now. It's beyond time they rewarded our tolerance.

"So by all means – by any means except All of Incain, make that – send someone to Witch Isle. Have them sent there on behalf of Greater Godbad; have the President or Secretary of State authorize it if you must. If Lady Achigan or the Gynarch isn't there, have Aortic Tsishah or better yet, since Tsishah Thrae's Mr Sarpedon's step-daughter, Ventricular Telepassa, assuming she's back from wherever she went, get hold of either/or. Howsoever you do so, secure you or your agents, or both, an invite to this wedding. Then apply appropriate methodology."

Demios Sarpedon could not conceal his disgust for Centauri's simplistic remedy to the problem of Saladin Devason. Nor did he appreciate him throwing Wilderwitch, whom he'd known nearly all her life, and whom he admired greatly – all the more so since she'd found a way to come back from the dead 25 years' unaged – into the same Machiavellian mix with the hateful Master of Weir.

It was so Outer Earth of him. Was as if the cathonitization of Bodiless Byron, who had used the Fatman as his shell for something like 35 years, until last Tantalar, had robbed him of any semblance of intelligence, let alone cunning. As if, hmm, he was holding something back. Was that something a Master Deva?

"You're not listening to me, none of you are. An assassination attempt on Saladin Devason has no more chance of success than an invasion does. Tidal waves and typhoons are the least of what the Master – any Master, past, present or future – could throw at any Godbadian fleet once it enters Cabalarkon's waters.

"And what Sal could do to you or your agents, Crom, doesn't bear exciting an imagination as sick as yours. Turned inside out, heart still beating outside, in broad daylight no less, comes to mind, from historical records of barely 500 years past. So long as he's in the Weirdom, the only way to get rid of him is to undermine the faith with which Utopians of Weir, the inbred idiots especially, empower him. As for the Witch, yeah, sure, Fish is definitely going to help you kill her last remaining blood-sister."

Necator took predictable offense at that. Deliberately semi-fay-said in order to emphasize his displeasure: "And ... what? Some sort of faerie-cast Stopstone statue's going to be more effective than a blade in the gut or a bomb in a truck?"

"You're forgetting my Morg died attempting to secure the Trigregos Talismans for the Weirdom. They've proven their worth against devils time and time again. By contrast there never was any guarantee that whatever Sundown, Raven and Mel's geniuses, or their stone gnomes, might have come up with – not that they'll come up with anything now – would have proven the slightest bit helpful to Utopians in our everlasting war against devils.

"No matter how imbecilic our parents and grandparents have become, and their parents and grandparents before them – you'd be surprised how many of them are still alive – Utopians don't forget their past. And they won't forget how my wife died. Whether, or whether not, the sanctions he took against D-Brig strengthened his position, and made it that much harder to topple him, his sister's statuary re-mains – as you so callously put it – are all that's necessary to shift the balance of sentiment to me and to our heirs: our daughter Andaemyn and her other child, Tsishah Twilight, as you prefer to Thrae, and whom you seem to distrust so much."

"Because she's a Hecate-Hellion," interrupted the boxed head of Gomez Niar-chos. "A demon-lover, the same as her mother before her. Worse. Her father was that fairy-feller, Tom-Tiddly Taddletale, the blue-skinned troubadour who used to show up around here fay-fairly-frequently, though I haven't seen him in a while. That makes her part demon to start with. On top of that she looks like an Irache, which probably means she's a demon on top of her." (Something about even talking about the eldritch earthborn brings out the fay-saying in just about anyone.)

Gomez was more than just outwardly preserved by a Sangazur Spirit Being; remained his own self, a fully conscious, sentient entity. He was, however, having only lately returned to Godbad, completely unaware of just how important Tsishah Twilight – actually named Thrae at birth, and whose last night as the life-loving Antheans' Aortic of Shenon, Witch Isle, was tonight – had become to the ongoing struggle to fully liberate relatively recently proclaimed Haas from the yoke of once-Hadd's Dead Things and their vampiric overlords.

Demios was too full of vitriol to enlighten him as to his step-daughter's emer-gence as a major player in that regard. Sooth said, he wasn't too sure he approved of her efforts to reconcile living Iraches born and raised in Hadd, old Iraxas, ones who practised a literal form of ancestor worship – they liked nothing better than having their dead relations over for tea and scones, as the saying went – and those born and raised in the northwest Cattail Peninsula's Irache Nation, who reckoned the Ambulatory Dead an abomination.

These last were nominally allies of the Godbadians and the Forces of Living's long-time bulwark, the Sraddhite Warrior Monks, as currently led by Thartarre Holgatson, Demios's friend and in many respects his saviour. Were for the most part also the subjects of Mani-Balam, Jester Jaguar, Tsishah's ex and the father of her four children, one of whom was a vampire … twice over.

Their 'invasion' less so than 'return' (as they had it) from the east, in support of the Godbadians coming in from the west, was supposed to be an easy-peasy reclam-ation project, not the start of an armed conflict with their indigenous cousins of five hundred years gone by, let alone an armed reunion with the Godbadians cast as the enemies. Which is what happened not long after their arrival in Haas.

Thanks to Tsishah's efforts, further bloodshed might yet be avoided, albeit at the cost of Godbadians taking a secondary role in the affairs of what the Cattail Iraches wanted to proclaim anew Iraxas (no 'New' about it) and, maybe, the dis-placement of Thartarre's people, who were mostly descended from Northern Marutians, across the still next to impassable Diluvia Mountain Range that separated the Head's Penile Peninsula from its Cheeklands.

Unless, that is, the remaining vampires – who were holed up primarily in Necropolis, formerly the Gleaming City of Manoa – found a way to re-establish their pre-eminence atop Hadd's food chain in the new state of Haas. (What was nominally New Iraxas was actually a Godbadian province whose current government was led by aforesaid Ferdinand Niarchos, Gomez's often devil-possessed son.)

"Says a talking head yet yapping because of the child of a pair of Master Devas."

Sangazurs, whose primary territory was the Bloodlands, Sedon's Inner Nose, New Valhalla, were indeed the offspring of two devils; ones in possession of no one save themselves. All azuras came about the same way; by themselves, non-possessing Master Devas only ever had Azura Spirit Beings.

Although Sangs had a variety of devic parents, Mater Matare (Mother Murder, the Apocalyptic of Mundane Death) was their most common mother. Their most common father was the Apocalyptic of War, Mars Bellona as ancient Illuminaries of Weir named him. Bellona's star no longer shone in the night's sky, in Constellation Apocalypse; hadn't done so since the 30th of Maruta last. Matare's did; did again, make that. Had done since the 6th of Tantalar, the same day Bodiless Byron and his Primary Nucleoids did, also again.

Sangs were symbiotic. In return for what amounted to a home to call their own, Sangs not only animated, and thereafter maintained, the corpses of otherwise dead men and women, they allowed their initial owners, as it were, to keep their grownup minds, their innate individualism, active for years, decades, potentially even centuries, beyond death.

By comparison, the bodies of Haddit Zombies were enlivened by the Sangs' azura-cousins, the Haddazurs, virtually all of whom were also Vetalazurs, after Nergal Vetala, whom Raven's Head more so than Blind Sundown, took care of, also again, last Tantalar. They continued to corrupt, however. So much so they, the Dead Things Walking who for so long held sway in Hadd, old Iraxas, recently renamed Haas, dissolved in heavy rainfall.

Which, its air force salting the thick, rainless for approaching five hundred years, cloud-covering of Hadd, was primarily how the Corporate State managed to begin asserting its control over the Land of the Dead. (Rain still fell in Haas, just not as much as it had in Tantalar and early Yamana. Hadn't got to the point that Haas was as sky-dry as Hadd had been for 500 years, but there were fears among Godbadian-trained meteorologists that it might suffer from drought come the presumably sunny summer ahead.)

"Like me," contributed Tethys, ostensibly a deviant, the son of mortals possessed by devazurs when he was conceived, draining his beer.

"Gentlemen, please," said Centauri. "We are all working toward a world where everyone gets along. Including devils and demons."

"You may be, Alpha," Demios countered. "But never forget, be they Hellions or just pro-life, Morg, Fish, Tsishah, their Athenan followers and their War Witch predecessors have been battling bats, as they put it, fighting for the Living against the Dead, the Undead, and, yes, against both demons and devils, since long before even your original self was born, Jordy."

"Don't be too sure of that, Dem," said the 30-Year Man. Then, as if catching himself in an improper act, suddenly exclaimed: "Ouch!"

"Did you just bite your tongue?" wondered Centauri, questioning not so much his eyes nor ears as rubbing in the obvious.

"I was thirsty."

"Want some vinegar?"

"This is deathly serious," said Sarpedon, infuriated at the exchange of banter between the two former lovers, albeit when 30-Beers was a woman, Sister Jordan, and the Fatman, only six or seven years newly arrived from the Outer Earth, hence their unfortunate offspring, Kirin, who still lived in the convent wherein she was conceived. (Unfortunate because she suffered from what was now generally known as Foetal Alcohol Syndrome, was prone to fits and often claimed to see Jesus Christ at the bottom of glasses and bottles.)

"Together, my family and I, along with Tsishah's Athenans and Andy's Zebranids, we shall see to it Morg's memory lives forevermore. I don't need your assassins, Crom, nor your precious fleet, Quentin. As useful as they may be otherwise, I don't even need Tsishah, Andy, nor any of their people. Not to take the Weirdom I don't. I can do that by myself, without anyone else. All I really need to do is get there, me and my eye-stave against Devason and his Master's Mace. And all I really need to do that is you, Jordan."

"Then get yourself up to Eventide and take Crom's boat," dismissed Tethys. "Or hire that Dead Thing mercenary Andy and my daughters, Yomikuni and Katatribe, palled up with when they were wandering the Head with Kronokronos Mikoto looking for the Trigregos Talismans. He's Brainrock-blessed. He can teleport you up there. That's how Akbar and some of his buddies in this ridiculously named D-Brig of theirs got back to Cabalarkon."

"Damnation Brigade," Centauri provided. "Though I agree with your assessment as to the ill-advisability of their group-codename. It does seem somewhat portentous, doesn't it?"

"Portentous," scoffed Tethys. "It's a self-fulfilling death-wish if I ever heard one. Might as well have called themselves the 'Please-Condemn-Me-to-Hell-Everlasting' Brigade."

"He's disappeared," Demios put to them.

He and Tethys were referring to Alastor Molorchus, a one-armed Outer Earthling who'd been on the Head since '68. A colleague – some said partner, in the sexual sense – of Professor Romaine Kinesis, who named Brainrock Gypsium in 1948, he was helping to develop the teleportive fuel eventually used in the Cosmic Express on the Outer Earth's Centauri Island when an accident left only his right arm behind out there. The rest of him ended up in here.

As disturbingly demonstrated on Sraddha Isle last Tantalar by Young Death, the perpetually seven year old male trickster most commonly known as Auguste Moirnoir beyond the Dome, he was indeed an ambulatory Dead Thing. As to whether he was possessed of a Sangazur or was simply Godstuff-maintained like the Dual Entities somehow were, no one, not even Molorchus, could say for sure.

"So he can self-teleport," said Tethys. "Good for him. Can't find him, go for a psychopomp. Your Tsishah's a soul-self, Demios. Must have. Most top-drawer witches have. Keep them in their top drawers, along with their underwear; those that wear underwear. Use them to activate their totems, like Fish did her Delphi, among others, years ago. Eden Nightingale had her Medici, her nightingale, not quite so many years ago. What's Tsishah's … a bat?"

"Not funny." Demios knew precisely what – make that who – his step-daughter was using as her psychopomp. So did Tethys. So why was he goading him?

"Precisely what I'm saying, Dem," said the Legendarian, thereby implicitly showing his displeasure for all things Tsishah while, at the same time, circumspectly avoiding any further details in that regard. "None of it's funny. You know my limits. I can't draw Sal out of the Weirdom without his permission and I won't, for reasons non-violent, draw you nor your wife's statue into it. As I've repeated so many times it might as well be my mantra, I may draw the occasional conclusion, but I shy away from drawing contusions.

"I got into enough trouble in Hadd for sticking my pencil-thin nose in where it didn't belong. You want to erect a monument to your Morg in Cabby's central square so you can start a revolution, you do it without me. Same goes for you, Crom. Not that, like Demios says, you'd be able to assassinate Saladin even if I drew you into his back pocket. Not in Cabalarkon anyhow. You persist with this fool-hardiness about all I'll do for either of you is write your epitaphs."

"With your pencil-thin nose, Rudolph?" Even bodiless heads in boxes could attempt to crack wise on the Headworld. It was that kind of Hidden Continent.

"With my Brainrock quill, numbskull."

"No one's asking you to violate your principles, Jordy," interposed Centauri, dropping the formal form of address. Which he rarely used for Tethys anyhow. "But you've convinced Devason to leave Cabalarkon before. I've every confidence you can do it again. You make a living telling tales, so where's the harm making one up? Any-where you draw him outside the Weirdom will be fine with us, though my personal preference would be to Island Leviathan's congealed turd of Whaledreck Island.

"You can even draw him back there, to the Weirdom, afterwards. Just so long as you don't do it until Mr Sarpedon here is ensconced on the Master's throne. Otherwise, well, no matter how impregnable you, Mr Sarpedon, Devason himself, nor anyone else, General Anvil, believes this intolerable Master can render Cabalar-kon, invasions are always messy things. You'd be saving a lot of lives."

"Dem's right, Al," said Tethys, resisting the temptation to open another pils-ner. Centauri, whom he called Al not out of discourtesy but out of friendship, was in a miserable mood. "You have become hard of listening. The only lives I'd be saving are Godbadian. And that's for the, duh, elementary reason Sal can make it impregnable. Besides, there are stories everywhere you go on the Head. I may have missed a few, but I don't have to run around inventing more. Everyday events don't need my input to take care of that."

"What about doing something for me, Jordy?" requested the head of Gomez Niarchos. "Extractions are within the range of your deviant-talents. And I'm more than happy to give you permission to bring the rest of my body here. You do owe me one. I did die saving your hide after all."

"That's true enough," Tethys acknowledged, howsoever reluctantly.

Usually through no fault of his own he rarely made it to his full 30-year life-span-allotment within his latest body. So, even if it lasted only four more years, he was grateful for the reprieve Gomez gave him back in '64. (Gomez wasn't around when Tethys's previous life – the one he took on after Sister Jordan died – ended, but he was on Ap Isle when Tethys came back as George Taurson, his then twenty-some-thing year old son by Miracle Maenad, who was born in the late Forties. Was quite a reunion … by now ambulatory Dead Thing with an only recently alive compara-tively young man from … what? Two of Tethys's lifetimes earlier.)

Besides, he had no sickly offspring, or their offspring, of an appropriate age – twenty being seemingly the minimum – he could move over to at the time, slightly less than 16 years ago. Then, as now, he hated the sometimes decades he spent in an unconscious, Limbo-like state waiting for one to start dying. Missed adding cab-inets of memorable files to his repertoire when that happened.

Another thing he hated was the agony, even when it was combined with the resultant ecstasy, of giving birth. Which was why he preferred coming back in his sons, grandsons, or their male descendants. Was also why he was beholding to Gom-ez for keeping him around as a man in '64. George Taurson, whose body he now kept going, was only 16 in '64 whereas his then next-in-line daughters, Katatribe and Yomikuni, were well into their thirties.

Katatribe and Yomikuni Tethys, both only recently deceased thanks to the Hadd-wars that ended last Tantalar, were among the Temporis-born, then fully alive mercenaries led by Pyrame Silverstar when she attempted to conquer the Weirdom of Cabalarkon in 5950. As such, given the year, and the inherent risks of their profession, Tethys would have been far more likely to have gone into one of them before George even turned twenty, let alone got deathly ill.

"I'll get your body back, but that's as far as I'll go."

"Glad that's settled," said Centauri, raising a glass in his pudgy hand. "Never too early to start a party, is it? Bubbly all around?"

"I'll stick to beer," muttered Tethys, glad to see the Fatman reverting to non-business mode. He was much preferable that way.

Not that he was a bad businessman. The idea of keeping Demios away from his eye-stave was particularly welcome. He didn't object to psychokinetic force shields or the showy little grotesques Trinondevs sometimes manifested atop their staves. He didn't really mind them using their orbs as devic prison pods either. However, he did object to them using them to compel you into doing something you didn't want to do.

Should Sarpedon compel him to draw him to Cabalarkon, which he might have; should things go wrong, which they would have; should Saladin find out of his involvement, which he would have; well, it would hardly be the first time he didn't make it to his full allotment of 30 years because he'd been compelled to do something he didn't want to do. Sal might not be an illegitimate bastard, but he was a vindictive one.

"To a New Year," toasted Centauri, after Janna filled their glasses, except for that of the Legendarian, with genuine French champagne brought in through the now-sealed Nag Gap from the Outer Earth's version of Centauri Island. "To even Better Days."

"So say we all," said Cromwell. Demios Sarpedon, Quentin Anvil and Janna St Peche Montressor echoed him, downing their hatches. Not having anywhere for it to go, the severed head of Gomez Niarchos merely sniffed his while, for once, Jordan Tethys was speechless.

Whereupon Demios disappeared through a teleport-hole in the floor.

========

"Was that what I thought it was?" gasped the Fatman, feeling his pump thumping as dishearteningly as it was 35-years-uncharacteristically for him. Since losing Byron's preservative presence he'd often felt short of breath. "One of Ringleader's teleportals?"

"Looked like it," agreed the Legendarian.

"But who?"

"One of the Zeross girls would be my guess. Looks like Saladin Devason's pre-empting you, Al."

****

Five-Demon: **Dissembling Daddy's Desiccation**

========

Anteal Fools Day 5981

After Child Harry's innocent, yet scarily effective prank the morning of the Equinox, they hugged and kissed and did their best to renew their friendship.
Did Wilderwitch and Melina long Zeross. Succeeded too, from all appearances.

========

The Witch's return certainly had an almost instantaneous effect on Mel's health.

Her appetite came back. She noticeably began putting on weight virtually overnight. Her personal Stone Gnome, as the joke – attributed to Yehudi Cohen, the still missing Untouchable Diver – went, must have been reemployed as well since, within a week, she was looking altogether her usual porcelain beautiful, ambulatory alabaster self. And for someone seemingly in their mid-to-late thirties; not someone who'd turned sixty the previous Tantalar.

As they had both here and in Cabalarkon City prior to their unintended separation in early Yamana, the Witch and Mel-Illuminatus invariably met for meals. Sometimes they got together in the afternoon as well, when Child Harry was having his nap. That an estimated 10-year old needed naps, went to bed so early and stayed in bed until late morning did strike the Witch as odd. Harry had been sick, Mel claimed. He needed rest, lots of it evidently, and that was about all she'd say on the subject. They had plenty of other things to chat about, however.

Mel had been all over the Weirdom, the Headworld's Devic Eye (in silhouette), showing the flag, on the Master's behalf naturally, while they were apart. With her daughters in tow – they were Weir-on-Earth's first family – she'd done a winter tour of Cabalarkon's outlying areas. For a time they'd even drafted a couple more Zerosses to go with them: 'A' and 'B', Angelica and the oddly named Baalbek Schroff Zeross.

Whose name really wasn't all that odd, Mel-Illuminatus illuminated the Witch. Baalbek was the name of an ancient, though still extant town in the Cedar Mountains of Lebanon. It had been called Heliopolis in olden days. Ancient olden days only if one considered the era of Classical Greece and Imperial Rome such, that is to say. Which, coming from a Weirdom whose first cyclopean structures were put in place pre-Flood, Mel didn't.

Ergo, Baalbek Schroff Zeross was named after the Family Heliopolis. At one time their father, Harry's older brother, the 12-years' late Demonites, was the lover of the 16-years just as dead Roxanne 'Hot Rox' Heliopolis Kinesis. A Lovely Lady Summoning Child, Roxanne was a supranormal whose codename was Slipper. Along with Sorciere – Solace Sunrise become Sundown, twice, only once legally

– Slipper was about the only female supra who could regularly boot Wilderwitch's butt about the block.

One of her sons, the one by Demonites, was Cosmicaptain Dmetri Diomad, last Tantalar's Trigregos Titan in Hadd. Her firstborn and only other child, the one by Harry's maternal uncle Alexandros – as dead, to the day, as his wife and a one-time leader of the King's Own Crimefighters codenamed Pluman – was Professor Romaine Kinesis. At the ripe old age of 44, Rom became a latter day supra who codenamed himself Doc Defiance, the Gypsium Man. As such, on the 30th of November last, he was the first Outer Earthling to encounter Devil Wind, Vayu Maelstrom, prior to the Byronic Nucleoid even getting as far as Damnation Isle.

Young as they then were, Rom, Harry Zeross and Roxanne's nephew, Harry's cousin, Kadmon Heliopolis, one possible origin for the Male Entity, gained a measure of notoriety in the Fifties and Sixties as the Gypsium Triumvirate. Rom was also the accredited inventor of the Cosmic Express's teleportive fuel; was Alastor Molorchus's research partner on the Outer Earth's Centauri Island until '68; and was on the Moon when Harry went there to rescue the remaining Thanatoids of Lathakra.

Like Helios and a few others, he was believed to have perished when Lunar Trigon collapsed in on itself after being bombarded by those on the UNES Liberty. And Mel knew all this how? Not from 'A' and 'B', that was for sure. They were in here as of the 30th of Maruta last. Still, she had her sources; had lived, albeit mostly in a nunnery, in Aka Godbad, recall, and kept up contacts long distance.

Couldn't get to the Outer Earth herself, not without Harry pre-Tub, but knew people who could; notably Jordan 'Q for Quill' Tethys, the Legendarian, albeit only through All on Incain. In other words, ask me no questions and I'll tell you no lies, to quote Li'l Abner's Mammy Yokum. (Whose creator, Al Capp, had only died a couple of years earlier, if that, she further advised.)

'A' and 'B' were born within a year or two of the Witch getting lost. Their mother, Hiliarti nee Schroff, was not only still alive but – Wilderwitch might recall Mel mentioning previously – was nowadays the Outer Earth's version of the Superior Sisterhood's Sister Superior. They, she should further recollect, were cosmicompanions; hence their arrival date; the same as the Witch's return from Limbo date.

With 'C', Carmine Carmichael – whom Baal called 'Hot Box' for the same more like rude than just insensitive reasons an earlier generation called Roxanne 'Hot Rox' – and some help from 30-Beers (the aforesaid Legendarian), adult Harry dispossessed them of the only briefly decathonitized devils, Amateram (Ama-Tera), Susal and Crinsom, last December, Tantalar. He subsequently brought them to the Weirdom from the watering hole cum whore house where he found them. That would be the Dinq, Doinq, Danq Tavern Cavern, Cheek-side of the ever-rain-soaked Diluvian Mountains, the wettest area on the Whole Earth.

Harry and Jordy had been frequenting the Dinq since the Sixties. Being the 30-Year Man, hence also 30-Beers, but whom the Witch had likely last encountered as a nun, Sister Jordan (his daughter, the consequently re-enlivened Ukemoshi Tethys), the recurring, story-telling deviant had probably been frequenting it since it opened, a thousand years and maybe many centuries more by now. From most reports, that is to say from reports mostly his own, Jordan Tethys had been around for at least two millennia.

The Witch had no problem recalling Tethys. Although he wasn't the only deviant in her pre-Limbo acquaintance who had been around that long, he was a memorable character. Had been in Hadd with Harry, Golgotha Nauroz, hundreds of his Trinondevs, all too many of whom didn't make it back, and five members of D-Brig. Had drawn Saladin Devason there as well. He'd done so with his Brainrock quill, what some believed was once a devic power focus.

Even if it was with his permission – the Master enjoyed acting Masterly, not that he was so much so beyond the Weirdom – that turned out to be a big mistake. Fortunately he got Sal back here before Wildman Dervish Furie had a chance to do him any serious damage. Besides to his pride, it went without saying; as it should have gone without happening. Despite the timely rescue, Saladin told her before she came out to the coast at the beginning of Yamana that, as useful as his abilities were, meaning his quill, he no longer approved of 30-Beers.

As for 'A', 'B' and 'C', the Witch said: 'Yes, of course I remember them.' She was lying. Rather, she was being forgetful. Melina recognized her failing. But, other than they were making marvellous contributions to the life ordinary Utopians, often with hybrid dependants, led in the countryside, she didn't offer any further insights about them.

Wilderwitch figured there had to be more to it than that. Otherwise, why would Mel have mentioned them? She chose not to press the issue. Neither did Mel comment on the Witch's forgetfulness. She'd had similar blanks prior to her disappearance and, for reasons of her own recovery, the High Illuminary of Weir didn't want to remind her of them right this moment.

Among the things Mel did expand upon – not that she was under any obligation to do so – was she had also been beyond the confines of the Weirdom. Went, via a long range Master Transducer, an ancient but remarkably still functioning teleportation device, she said, less to Wilderwitch's astonishment than it would have been prior to Yamana the 1st, to Subcranial Temporis. There she met with the Thousand Caverns' usurper.

Not that Mel used that term; used instead Kronokronos Supreme. That'd be Lakshmi of Lemuria, all of 18 and already the Witch's best-kept-private enemy.

Wilderwitch didn't say that last to Mel any more than the High Illuminary called the mandroid-guard-body-wearing, half-daughter of Dand Tariqartha, hence Arthadot, a usurper. A girl, even one born in 5927, and who had lost a quarter century in Limbo, had to retain some secrets, even from her supposed best friend. She had no doubt Mel was selectively keeping as much from her. What was so important about 'A' and 'B' anyhow?

Lakshmi Arthadot, yes, confirmed Mel-Illuminatus. And her mother, Aortic Amphitrite, she of Shenon, Witch Isle. Fish's altogether unrelated Summoning Child of a stepsister, once the Outer Earth supernormal (mostly for what her guard-body could do) codenamed Lady Lemurian, was now staying in Centurium, Replicated Versailles, full time with her daughter. She was, after All, upper and lower case 'A', far more experienced at ruling anything than the teenager.

(Wilderwitch had no trouble reading into the upper and lower case inclusion the fact that Amphitrite was very familiar with All of Incain. The She-Sphinx, Mandroid Monster Maker that she also was, was probably the most reliable way through the Cathonic Dome since the Nag Gap from the Inner Earth's Aka Godbad City to the Outer Earth's Centauri Island shut down in mid-December last.

(What she perhaps should have read into it was Temporis might well have another way out. After all, OMP-Akbar came through the Dome both ways, once in August 1945 and again last December, apparently under his own power, small case. Had she been a mite more with it she might also recall that the caverns of Temporis were full of replicas, some of them actually alive rather than just programmed Mantels. It wasn't as if her first time there was the last time she was there; just the first time since Limbo.)

The wedding between Lakshmi and Fish's son by the Master, Capputis Masterson as the hydrocephalic non-clone (brought up as an actual clone) was deemed the moment Sal recognized him as legitimate, was still scheduled for Cabalarkon City on the Summer Solstice. It was only its announcement that went by the wayside when Saladin sought to slay Sundown at the beginning of Yamana, for killing his 'beloved' sister Morgianna on Hadd's by then drenched Dustmound back in the second week of Tantalar just past.

Equinoxes and solstices, Mel added unnecessarily, were considered auspicious occasions everywhere you went on the Hidden Headworld. Weren't just considered thus; were as well. Look who fell out of the night's sky – rather, who made a relatively controlled descent out of it – on Equinox Eve. You, Witch.

How nice for them, Wilderwitch condescended, verbally recollecting what happened the last time Arthadot deigned to enter the Weirdom; accompanied as she was, besides her Kronokronos Supreme's due entourage, by Morg's other daughter. That'd be the one besides Andy (Andaemyn), the one whom the Witch did recall, namely Tsishah Thrae, commonly called Twilight. With them, too, were the recurring fauna, past pal Pusan Wanderlust, and, yes, her very own middle sister Scylla Nereid (Fish, Fisherwoman, long nowadays Lady Achigan), her-stories all of them. Likely the weather wouldn't be all that was hot come Midsummer.

It was a lazy-headed statement. Hardly her first – the Witch had all but given away her then current 'occupation' by a leg-saving demon back on the 1st of Yamana – but, hey, maybe prescience was one of her attributes after all. Perspicaciously, Mel made a mental note. Not prescience; foreshadowing in the form of a forewarning.

Wilderwitch didn't have to be sleeping with anyone to make matters hot.

========

As the days went by the Witch, being Wilderwitch, grew increasingly restless; antsy as she referred to it, making a joke at her Sisterhood's expense.

========

Short of going for a very long walk, a not-yet-waddling limp in her case, there wasn't much she could do about it, either. She didn't think she'd damaged the vimana too badly when she crash-landed it on Equinox Eve. But its controls wouldn't respond to her touch as they had when she first piloted it from the Southern Slopes of the Sleepers to here, the Weirdom's mid-coastal region of Fearsome Fobbiat.

As if akin to her VTOL's immobility, Mel and her family showed no inclination to return to Cabalarkon City. Just as tellingly, no one volunteered to drive her there in one of the somehow rechargeable, electronic ground-cars still sane and relatively competent Utopians used for standard transport over any distance in the

Weirdom. It was almost as if the powers-that-be, be they the Moloch Sedon, up there in his night's sky, the Master, over in Cabalarkon City, or – and this was a disconcerting thought – Pyrame-Memory, in wherever Trans-Time Trigon was located, didn't want her going anywhere.

Were they conspiring to keep her from leaving the Zerosses' hideaway? Unlikely. Pyrame-Memory was/were afraid of being detected by Sedon; would know that, whatever Saladin agreed to, he would do so only with the knowledge and at least tacit approval of his devic half-father. Hardly for the first time she wondered why she headed north instead of south.

Was it, as she told Melina, because she wanted to get her bottomless bag, weaponry and agates back from Saladin born both Nauroz and Devason? So she wouldn't have to go through just this sort of brain- and body-sapping hanging around waiting on others to do something? Not hardly, though she did hate dependence. Far worse, she hated being a slave to her own emotions. But that was the truth of it, wasn't it?

She'd come north, she finally acknowledged, if only to herself, primarily because she still loved Sal. Boy, was she a boob with boobs belonging in a booby hatch.

At least fay-saying was fun.

========

One of the oddest things Wilderwitch observed over their days together was Child Harry, when he addressed her at all, called Mel 'Illuminatus'. 'Mel' she could understand, that's what he always called her as an adult. In a way 'Mom' might have been more appropriate, given his apparent age and undeniable reliance on her. Illuminatus, though, struck her strangely.

Perhaps only slightly less peculiarly, the Witch couldn't help noticing that even once he started joining them outside the Zerosses' villa, within a week of her reappearance there, young Harry never strayed far from Mel or her daughters. Sooth said, Mel never let Harry play alone. If she wasn't with him, one of her daughters was — and they in turn were never left unsupervised.

Which must have annoyed the oldest two, Helen, 12, and especially Persephone, 16, no end. Good thing it wasn't beach weather. They were of an age for bikinis – the skimpier the better in Helen's case, not that she had much of anything to show off as yet – and boys, in that order. Tina, 6, could care less about either/or. All she really wanted, and didn't get as much of, thanks to Child Harry – 10, they'd decided – was attention.

Be it indoors or outdoors, in the family room or in his own bedroom, not that he slept there, on the fenced-in grounds or on the shale and pebbly beach walking beside her, one or another of Mel's Illuminaries was always there with him. Equally always Thobruk Grudal or one of his trusted Trinondevs was never out of earshot, if not necessarily sight.

Just as worrisomely, Mel herself, the High Illuminary of Weir, second only to the Master and perhaps Golgotha Nauroz, Ubris's clone, Weir-on-Earth's chief Trinondev, in terms of the Weirdom's hierarchy, rarely left the house. And then only when accompanied by Grudal, her fellow Summoning Child and long-time shadow.

Another thing the Witch noticed was the Illuminaries Mel left with Harry were just that, fully trained. Apparently none of her apprentices could be so assigned. Similarly, while some of Grudal's Trinondevs were recently admitted women, the only ones he left in charge when he was off-duty or body-guarding Mel were men, veterans of Hadd for the most part, and therefore the most experienced members of Weir's Warrior Elite on the premises. All very interesting, she thought. Clearly all was not well on the Cabalarkon coast of Fearsome Fobbiat.

Curiosity, and perhaps not just curiosity, was eating at her. She finally got up the nerve to ask Melina how Hubby Harry came to be Child Harry. Mel, back to her statuesque self by then, a rainy 1st of Antheal, April, was surprised Wilderwitch couldn't figure it out herself. Rather than answering she got up, left the room. Wasn't annoyed. Or didn't seem to be. Disappointed came closer.

When she returned she handed the Witch a spare copy of the 'Forever & 40 Days' aspect of the transposed, antediluvian Annals of Anthea she happened to have lying around, as she put it. (Her library was nowhere near as large as the one Illuminaries kept in Cabalarkon City's Citadel of the Thinkers. It didn't even take up a whole wing of the house; just most of one. A guest house took care of any overflow of same, library books; as well as excess guests.)

She bid her read the section she'd earmarked while she went back to check on Child Harry, whom she'd left playing with Tina under the supervision of her Illuminaries and Grudal's elite guardsmen. The Witch did as bade, cringing as she reacquainted herself with what became of old King Kad's wriggly wiggles.

It was almost as if she was reading about the death of a brother she never had.

========

Cathonic Fluid was the invention of the Male Entity. At least he claimed credit for it.

========

More than likely it was something else the Dual Entities came across in one of their earliest lives together. The Female Entity had merely stored its recipe in her memory circuits. Meaning Trans-Time Trigon's remnant, Mother Machine innards. Which she, Machine-Memory, carried with her from lifetime to lifetime; his lifetime to his lifetime — she seemingly didn't have independent ones of her own.

As was well-known, in his Fifth Heliosophos plucked out Cabalarkon's left eye; plopped it into a tub of the stuff. Or a variant thereof. Cabby was only a typically long-lived Utopian scientocrat specializing in genetics, the building blocks of life and full sentience, back then, in the first Weirsystem. (This happened on a tri-peaked asteroid therein known as … what else? Trigon.) His eye was everything in the way of additional raw material Helios required in order to concoct what became, twenty standard years later, Dark Sedon.

To this day the All-Father of Devazurkind believed 'Call-Me-Cabby' gave him life. Which is why he regarded the now undying Utopian – not Helios – as his father. Was also why he turned the geneticist into what amounted to a psychic vampire. He, Dark Sedon, believed that should he-who-gave-him-life die the true death then he, the Moloch, would die, too. Or, more precisely, become susceptible to dying; become mortal, in other words.

That probably wasn't true. As a god, devil that he was, chances were he would persist as long as folks worshipped him. Nonetheless, he and those he took with him on his self-generated Sedonshem — namely, the by then only hundreds of devils who escaped Helios causing the original Weir Star to go supernova – survived many multiple millennia traversing the cosmos without having any adherents along for the ride.

They did so, survived, Illuminaries like Mel were sure, because devils enjoyed never-ending stellar empowerment, as she put it; were nourished by starlight, put more simply, not 'adulation made alimentary', to quote her again, echoing the Diver. Be that as it may, the lone non-devil Sedon carried with him all that time, preserved in an ever-renewing tub of Cathonic Fluid, was his Cabby of a thought-father.

Proof of the theory Cabby's survival ensured Sedon's survival? Maybe. Which was why killing said Cabby the Daddy, undying Cabalarkon, or at least holding him prisoner, with the ultimate option of killing him, seemed such an obvious effort to make for so many. Among those many count Pyrame Silverstar and her demon – had to be Primeval Lilith, the arguably wholly sentient, as well as seemingly indestructible, Queen of All Daemons.

As for devic blood being a catalyst to turning enhanced Cathonic Fluid into an equivalent of the Fountain of Youth, that was Cabalarkon's idea; one-eyed Cabby then being a still ordinary, albeit exceedingly, if not precisely impossibly, long-living – and regularly breathing – Utopian scientocrat.

Prior to having the Mnemosyne Machine destroy Weir Star in hopes of destroying devils in their thousands, three generations of them, and simultaneously their adherents, multiple millions, even billions, of them, Helios took Cabby and many another with him to a neighbouring planetary system. There he set up New Weirworld, a three-peaked part of which – called Trigon, naturally – he ruled as King Kad.

Among those he took with him, on millennial ships, besides Cabby, whom he made his chancellor, and indeed millions of non-devil-worshipping Utopians, were the Trigregos Sisters. They were the mothers of the third generation of devazurkind, the Master Devas — the Thrygragos Brothers, with no doubt judicious input from lone Numero Uno, Sedon Himself, being the third generation's fathers.

The Great Goddesses, whose Entity-given names were Demeter, Devaura and Sapiendev, body, soul and mind, were three-in-one deities who only separated when they were giving birth. As such, three-as-one, they humanized Machine-Memory. Which endeared them no-end to Heliosophos, whom she in that lifetime – as well as more than a few subsequent ones – came to call King Kad, Helios the Horny.

All in all their lives way back when verged on perfection; approached happily-ever-after, fairytale stuff. New Weirworld Trigon approximated an undeniable Utopia. Not one set up, howsoever unintentionally, presided over and thoroughly regulated in approaching Orwellian fashion, Big Mama-like, by Weir's original Mother Machine. Until, that is, the no-end aspect of it started ending. King Kad began dying of old age.

Chancellor Cabby – even then Utopians were by nature very long-lived – tinkered with Cathonic Fluid. Rendered it, at least potentially, a form of Cleopatra's Bath. He reckoned the re-jiggered formula lacked only one ingredient: devic blood. Being mostly insubstantial beings when not humanizing Machine-Memory, the Trigregos Sisters couldn't provide it. And there were no other devils left.

Ah, but there were ...

Self-named Sedon survived Memory nuking Weir Star. As remarkably, had somehow managed to preserve his three, second-generational sons along with hundreds of their third-generational offspring. As severely radiation-damaged as they were – so much so they were thereafter, by themselves, unable to impregnate female devils with anything except Azura Spirit Beings no different from what every other male Master Deva could accomplish – Sedon and his three sons arrived in New Weir's Trigon territory.

With Sed's thought-Daddy Cabby as its chancellor handling negotiations in Helios's decrepitude, deals were struck; devils being to this day incapable of violating their oaths. Sedon would donate his blood to the tub of Cabby's specialized fluid. King Kad would rejuvenate. Dark Sedon – today called thus because his star was usually only visible at night – would then form his Sedonshem and, taking his sons, though not his traitorous daughters, and all their remaining offspring with him, leave New Weirsystem forevermore.

The one proviso the Devil made was that 'don't-have-to-call-me-Cabalarkon' agree to accompany them. He did. Whereupon Sedon did as promised. He bled into the tub of mostly animation-suspending Cathonic Fluid in which King Kad was already submerged, for purposes primarily of preservation. Worked as well. King Kad began rejuvenating. Only he, King Kad, opening his eyes and seeing who his benefactor was, leapt out of the tub and attacked the Devil.

It was too soon. The fluid didn't have time to fix. He kept rejuvenating. Not-yet-altogether-Dark, in terms of the night's sky, Sedon didn't have to repel a baby. He just stepped back and watched as Helios reduced to a pre-foetal droplet of wriggly wiggle then dried up before his very eyes.

Thus he, Helios, died. And when Helios dies …

========

"Devic blood?" wondered the Witch later on that afternoon, once she and Mel were together again.

========

"Whose?" she wanted to know. "Pyrame didn't say anything about donating any blood to rejuvenate your husband. And, from what you told me before, only two other Master Devas can come here: Tantal Thanatos, King Cold of Lathakra, and Irisiel Mercherm, the Messenger of the Gods, devils that they are."

"You do try me sometimes, Wilderwitch. It wasn't any of them. Couldn't have been." Although she stopped short of scold-mode, Mel did sound exasperated. It was as if she found the Witch's expressed lack of comprehension a sign of unacceptable mental lassitude for someone she deigned call friend. Still, she never could resist an opportunity to illuminate dimwits.

"Pyrame's known as the Pauper Priestess for a number of reasons. One of them is she hasn't got a Brainrock talisman to call her own. Another is she hasn't got a devic protectorate to call her home. Mostly, though, it's because she hasn't got a body to call her baby. Never has had. Hasn't needed one, sooth said, because for most of her time on the Whole Earth, either side of it, she's been occupying a high-level daemon in not just my view; no matter how often she tries to deny it, none other than that of Demon Queen Lilith."

"So she is, and always has been, a Spirit Being," Wilderwitch began to understand. "She must have been possessing another of these cosmicompanions ever since she was decathonitized. Someone like 'A', 'B' and 'C'. Or the ones your Harry came across on the Moon and brought down to Frozen Lathakra."

"Not necessarily," Melina felt obliged to point out. "While that'd be true initially, on the 30th of Maruta last she could have body-bounced into any number of sentient beings, any number of times, until whenever she got hold of Machine-Memory. The only other thing we can say with some degree of certainty is she couldn't have got hold of Lilith-Gomorrah because first Memory then you had her."

"Gomorrah, as in Sodom and Gomorrah, as in the Wandering SAG Gap?"

"And the Stationary SAG Gap. That one story you do remember?"

"Tell it to me anyway." Mel did. When she was done, the Witch had this to say: "In other words, even if she had thought to give her blood to Harry in his tub it wouldn't have done any good because her blood is actually Memory's. Rather, it needs be comes from the body Memory somehow automatically manufactures when she's humanized."

"Just so. You can eliminate King Cold from your list of potential blood donors as well. The Master insists the Thanatoid can no longer enter the Weirdom without being hit by every prison pod there is up here. Of course he still has trouble accepting the Thanatoid entered the Weirdom unmolested in the first place. He'd never come up before, with or without permission, according to Illuminary records.

"Fact is he was only declared a welcome devil when he saved the Weirdom from the ravages of the Idiot Twin going nuclear in 4825, whereupon both he and his sister-wife, Methandra of Mythland, who was then still Mithras's Virgin, fell into a thousand year sleep. For a time the Master couldn't accept he, Thanatos, kidnapped me and my daughters from right here; from right here right from under the noses of his precious Trinondevs."

"Who else could have done it? Surely not Irisiel. She's just a messenger."

Melina prefaced her response with one of her famous shrugs. "Doesn't matter anymore, does it? The whole episode's moot, irrelevant, nowadays. The Master used his Speaking Stick on us and seems satisfied that, whosoever took us there, we were held against our will in Lathakra while Harry, in order to guarantee our safety, went to the Moon and rescued the Thanatoids' remaining children. And the cosmicompanions, as you just mentioned, they were occupying.

"It's arguable his blood would have done the trick in any case. Same holds true for Irisiel or any other Master Deva who might have slipped through his defences. Or those of his half-father, which would have taken a whole lot more doing. Third generational devils like the Thanatoid and Angelus, the devils' 'keryx', have the subtle matter bodies of debrained demons they acquired here on the Inner Earth starting about four thousand years ago."

"You're saying their blood's as useless as Pyrame's; all the more so since that's another reason why devils call her the Pauper Priestess? She doesn't really have any blood of her own."

"At least your hearing still works."

"And the rest of my head doesn't?"

"Not as well as it should, I'd agree. With respect to Irisiel, her primary attribute is speed. While it's true she can come here, and has, as late as last Tantalar, December, she only stays long enough to deliver her message, whatever that is. Otherwise, if she stood still even for the time it took her to remove the top of Harry's sepulchre, cut herself and drip blood into his tub, her third eye would have been sucked out of her skull and she would have been imprisoned in an eyeorb, demonic body and Tvasitar-talisman both. Which in her case is a herald's staff very much like my caduceus, albeit minus the twinned snakes.

"By the way, the word 'caduceus' comes from ..."

"I remember, the Greek for herald's staff."

"Doric Greek, 'karykion'. While Illuminaries made up her last name by combining Mercury and Hermes, the heralds of the Roman and Greek pantheons. As for her first name ..."

"After Iris, the Rainbow. Remember that too. Who then?"

"Oh, come on, Witch. Get real. King Kad was rejuvenated, irretrievably, multiple millennia before the Sedonshem came to the Whole Earth. Only four devils had bodies altogether their own back then. Three of them were the Thrygragos Brothers. Varuna Mithras is dead whereas, thanks to you, your D-Brig and mostly Mother Murder's Quadrang Nucleus, Unmoving Byron's star in the Sedon Sphere.

"As for Thrygragos Lazareme, he's been asleep on the Isle of the Undying One for decades. And centuries before that, as you should also remember. Ever since Chaos killed his favourite child, Datong Harmonia, the Unity of Balance, your Freespirit Nihila. Mind you he'd been none too lively since he helped extirpate his brother, Thrygragos Mithras, on Thrygragon near the end of the 44th Century of the Dome.

"Have I ever told you we Illuminaries believe Lazareme's pillow is Mithras's head pulverized for softness?"

"Oh, probably. Who can remember everything you tell anyone anyways?"

"Other than me, you mean?"

"Then why ask?" Melina seemed momentarily flummoxed so the Witch took advantage of her hesitation to ask her a different question.

"Forget it, Mel. Answer this one instead: Why would the Moloch Sedon give his blood to rejuvenate Aristotle Zeross?"

========

"Because I asked him to!" The speaker was not Mel-Illuminatus.
It was Saladin Devason.

****

SIX-DEMON: **Arrested Envelopment**

========
The First and Second of Antheal 5981
About the same time ...

========

Saladin Devason was away, at play. Before leaving he rather boastfully told Cabby of the new denizen in the depths. Cabby was of course the still one-eyed, black-as-midnight, thus-far-forever undying Utopian the Moloch Sedon considered his father. Plus, he whose body he – the Devil and Demon King both – kept preserved in a tub of Cathonic Fluid between-space in the Weirdom named after him.

Disregarding the Master's warning to stay put, that there were those out there, damn near everywhere, who wanted to remove the 'un' from 'undying', the Ghost of Cabalarkon decided to go for a haunting. He thought it might be interesting to have converse with the recent arrival. It had been quite some time since they'd done that — always assuming, him being so non-ghostlike and not submerged, him being altogether alive in other words, he could see him.

As call-me-Cabby's spectral self wafted round the corner and neared the crypt, which contained a cage rather than a sepulchre, the two Trinondevs on guard outside were reacting to something. There was, the spook on psychic walkabout perceived, a sudden blur inside the cell with the newcomer. The blur said: 'Special delivery.'

Then the Trinondevs were encased in thought-bubbles generated from eyeorbs atop their own eye-staves; started to suffocate. As they collapsed, the air beyond their force shields came alive. The blur ran away, almost as if it had never been there. Stuff came out of the catacomb's walls, floor and ceiling.

Cabby lingered long enough to see said-stuff take on humanoid forms, to kneel before the denizen. Godbadian or Outer Earth garden gnomes, albeit not ones made of painted wood or coloured plastic, seemed their shape of choice. Beat the Easter Island (Rapa Nui) Golems – Moai, they were called he remembered from someone, maybe one of the Warlocks who used to come around years ago now – whose likeness they used to take on until he complained about what he perceived as their cultural appropriation.

The denizen certainly had a fine old eye-stave, thought the spectre, as he wisely decided to take himself back to his tub between-space. Who knew what else it could capture besides devic and azura Spirit Beings? Was there much difference between devazur ghosts and human or, in his case, Utopian ones? Was hardly the first time he'd wondered that. Probably wouldn't be the last either.

From the way things were looking they'd have plenty of time for conversation in the days, weeks, months, even years ahead.

========

Wilderwitch did not move. Neither did Melina Zeross.

Both were stunned by the Master's sudden appearance and, frankly, the Witch had been dreading this moment ever since she (must have) decided to take her vimana toward Cabalarkon City rather than use it to escape the Weirdom altogether. Consequently, it fell to Saladin Devason to make the opening gesture.

Which was to open his arms and say: "Welcome home, Cynthia Masterwife."

========

The Witch still did not move. Saladin and Melina exchanged glances. Mel nodded. Saladin did not close his arms. He did, however, rephrase his greeting.

"Welcome back, Wilderwitch. I understand you brought me something."

"Besides me, my love for the renewed offering, our daughter for the birthing?"

"No," said Saladin, condescendingly, "You, your love and our daughter for the birthing. The vimana is only icing on the cake of humble pie you just force-fed me."

In terms of affection their embrace was a far cry from what the Witch and Mel exchanged that first morning of her return to civilization. In truth it was somewhat akin to the weather outside. Lukewarm at best. It was Spring, however, and only a matter of time before everything got more pleasant.

Midsummer's Day remained a long way off.

========

'Caducity' looked somewhat similar to 'caduceus'. It mostly meant impermanence, transitoriness, perishableness; usually referred to the weakness of old age.

King Kad's terminal caducity just went the other way.

========

According to what Saladin Devason said that night after dinner, when the three of them, alone again, got to discussing Child Harry's remarkable reversal of life expectancy and why his finally acknowledged – for their ears only – devic half-father never dared repeat the procedure that led to King Kad's opposite-direction death. The reason for that was Sedon, bordering on omnipotent in many respects, lacked anything approaching omniscience. He couldn't be sure if, say, he spilt some of his blood into a tub of the stuff containing Cabalarkon, that his thought-father wouldn't rejuvenate all the way to a promptly desiccated spermatozoon himself.

That happened, well, Sal muttered, not wanting to overly commit, to thereby in effect complicit himself, let's just say Sedon wasn't one for wriggly wiggles and leave it at that. Even the Mighty Mooch of a Moloch had to resort to possessing sentient beings in order to father anyone non-devic. As well, everyone he half-fathered was mortal. He, the King of Devils as well as the latter day King of Demons, had no intention of sharing the inevitability of their fate.

So why, the Witch demanded to know, did Sedon agree to try it on Harry, besides as a favour to his half-son? Because it wasn't Cabalarkon, Sal obliged; perhaps a mite by pre-practised rote, she suspected. Then why did you, Mel, let him try it on your husband? Harry (Rings, once Kid Ringo, long Ringleader, the second of two, after father Angelo who died in 1968) might have emerged just fine after a year or so within the miraculous liquid.

How did he know it would work? Sedon didn't, Sal claimed. And the Master never asked me, said Melina. I needed him, Sal insisted. Why?, required the Witch.

"In order to save our Weirdom. I needed his rings. More, I needed him to wield them."

"Because," grasped the Witch, at last figuring out something that had been bothering her for a while now, "'A' and 'B', Angelica and Baalbek Schroff Zeross, couldn't get them to work for them." (Although Mel claimed both Harry's half-broth-er Demonites and blood-brother Kadmon Heliopolis had used them in the past, it seemed the ability to use them came with actual blood-transference and the cousins, despite their paternity, did not get enough of it being born.)

"Not well enough for my needs, no," Saladin confirmed, eyeing Mel-Il-luminatus as if she'd betrayed a confidence. Which she hadn't. "Maybe, over time, they could have but, no matter how bright they are, no matter how much potential they may have, they're no naturals. Circumstances being what they are, I had no time to train them properly. Wouldn't know how for one thing. Wouldn't have the patience for another."

Even though the sun had gone down, not that they'd seen much of it these last couple of drizzly, early Spring days, Wilderwitch had finally seen the light.

She turned to Mel. "And each of us knows who are naturals, don't we?"

"Only I wouldn't let my daughters use them," Melina provided, uncharacteris-tically defiantly for her. "Not after what happened to Harry. And especially not after what happened when Percy got hold of three of them, then tried to use them against Blind Sundown at the beginning of last Yamana."

They'd used them before that, too, though Mel didn't feel the need to add to her declaration. Said this instead: "You were there, Witch. You know you don't take on one without taking on the other; no matter how far away they are when you try." She was still referring to the two, not just self-pronounced Wakinyah Creatures of the Cosmos: the first of whom the old, then-blind Cheyenne Medicine Man named Manitoulin raised; the second of which he traded to Sundown, along with his Solar Spear, for his eyes, such that – miraculously – he went to his death, some ten years later, able to see again.

"You saw what became of her afterwards." In this she was referring to eldest daughter Persephone. "As if the injuries she suffered when Raven rode out of the air itself and head-butted her onto the floor weren't bad enough, she very nearly died of Gypsium Sickness. And for that, for being a mother, I'm branded a traitor. "

Saladin coloured, visibly disliking her tone. "Not a traitor. If you were a traitor I would have you tried and, if found guilty, duly executed. I rely on you as much as I ever have. I merely keep you on a shorter leash than previously. And don't look so shocked either of you. I'm well aware the Weirdom doesn't practise capital punish-ment. But I'm the Master. I can do as I please.'"

Somewhat thoughtlessly Wilderwitch looked to Melina for elaboration. As was her wont, the female Dr Zeross, Althean healer that she was – and no doubt mindful of how much damage she could do to herself and her family by carrying on as she had been – simply shrugged. It fell to Saladin to fill in the details.

"My sister-in-law continues to perform her assigned duties as High Illuminary of Weir. In fact, while you were, um, gone, she very successfully smoothed over our differences with Lakshmi Arthadot, the Kronokronos Supreme of Temporis, she also of Lemuria, and her mother, Aortic Amphitrite, once the Outer Earth supranormal Lady Lemurian, she of Shenon. These differences, you might recall, were a direct result of regrettable events you were party to at the beginning of Yamana last."

"You were supposed to exile Johnny, not sentence him to death."

"So you advised. I, however, as is my right as Master of Weir, determined differently." (While he had the right as Master to order executions, had he succeeded it would have been the first time in beyond living memory that anyone – let alone any Master – ordered capital punishment for anyone in the Weirdom. And ordinary Utopians, imbeciles included, lived for a very long time.)

"I should have dealt with Sedon. Devils keep their promises."

"Unlike witches."

"I better go check on Child Harry," said Melina, attempting to excuse herself.

No fool she – not for very long anyhow – she recognized the underlying tension between the two of them, the Master and the Witch. The first, at least in the Weirdom, Sedon's sizable Devic Eye-Land, was approaching all-powerful. By contrast the second, as witness the not very well-veiled threats she'd been making against Lakshmi of Lemuria, was prone to powerfully violent reactions. Even an accomplished healer and diplomat, which Mel was, knew better than to try and sort out these differences. That was for them to do.

"You shall stay exactly where you are, High Illuminary." Saladin insisted, brooking no disrespect from his evidently deemed lackey.

A voice as compulsive as his might have made him a supranormal beyond the Dome. Might have, if he'd stayed out there once the original Amsterdam Academy of Man dissolved just at the Second World War was about to break out in bloody earnest came the Spring of 1940. He hadn't. The Sarpedon Twins had, as had Sal's year younger sister Morgianna. At least she didn't think he had since he wasn't out there when 15-year-old she got there, in '43.

"You shall stay right there, your seat glued to the chair, until I dismiss you. Something I as yet am not prepared to do." Melina bristled, but neither moved nor objected.

Wilderwitch had experienced devic eyefire before. Both Freespirit Nihila, in the Faerie Garden of Temporis, and Mater Matare, in its adjacent Calvary Cavern, had subjected her to it back on the 6th of Tantalar last. In neither case had it harmed her overly much. However, looking at Melina's eyes, was she a devil (instead of, arguably, just born with one, Amal-Althea Brand, insider her), had she unleashed hers right that moment, the High Illuminary would have melted the Master into so much Saladin-slag.

What the hell, considered the Witch. It's Antheal Fools Day. Plus, thinking of the imbeciles of Weir in particular, it didn't seem likely the Master killed fools. Not so figuratively putting her life on the line, she therefore chose to stick up for her fellow be-bosomed buddy, the supremely talented physician-cum-surgeon who as much saved her leg, if perhaps not her life, until Miss Murk – Primeval Lilith, the ages-old, somehow indestructible, Demon Queen of the Night – showed up, arm-in-arm, with Sal-Sedon to complete the job most of a week later.

"Surely looking out for the best interests of your children doesn't – can't – amount to treachery."

"Fortunately for you," said Saladin, managing to retain his comparative cool, even if he couldn't do so without issuing an implicit warning to the effect he was approaching the end of his tether, "I feel in an expansive mood. As my sister-in-law is so fond of pointing out, until I declared Capputis my heir apparent, my people – in the majority's idiocy – looked upon the Zerosses as Weir's First Family. It seems that misapprehension has carried abroad."

"I'm becoming apprehensive as to where this is heading," the Witch couldn't resist wisecracking. She was no Diver; no Furie, nor even a Sundown, when it came to making with the wit. Was, in fact, more like Cerebrus or his father, Loxus Abraham Ryne. No one ever laughed at their attempts at humour, feeble as they invariably were.

'I must be just hoping to crack the ice', she smiled to herself, feeling immune to Sal-son's wrath. Reaped a blizzard in response.

"Belatedly," Melina agreed, finding her tongue again; making it spout acid. "You were all in favour of it a month ago."

Wilderwitch did an abrupt about-face in terms of humour appreciation; started to object when Saladin, end-tether nearly reached, held up his hand. For once the Witch shut up. "I have already expressed my sorrow that I mistook the Demonic Dominatrix for you, Wilderwitch. Please do not make me do so again."

And so he had, though his sincerity was another thing she wasn't convinced of as yet. Still, if she herself didn't realize – unless a more appropriate word was 'recall' – Lilith was inside her until being dumped over top the forest, it was at least conceivable Sedon had blanked his half-son as to that reality as well.

She let him continue. Which he did: "The fact of the matter is, while we in Weir do not subscribe to the notion of dynasty, others do. As a consequence the three Zeross daughters are highly desired amongst those with whom we would consider allying. And in these troubling times judicious alliances may be the only way we can maintain the Weirdom's integrity in the face of unwanted, if not unwarranted, interest expressed in our mostly unworkable, but undeniably extraterrestrial technology by the devil-lovers of Godbad.

"In my view and indeed, as my sister-in-law has just observed, in the view of – let's call her Cynthia Masterwife, shall we? – by exploiting this misapprehension we might attain certain advantages for the Weirdom. The High Illuminary, however, did not see it our way. She refused to sanction the proposed marriage of her daughter Persephone to Solomon Taurson, grandson of Miracle Maenad, matriarch of Apple Isle.

"This refusal has had the predictable repercussions. It has driven Miracle's Korants and their male counterparts, the Mithrant Military Brotherhood that has controlled not only Ap Isle, but most of the vast plains of Marutia, Sedon's Cheek or Breadbasket, for countless centuries, in the direction of the Corporate State of Greater Godbad, Centauri Enterprises and its perfidious Fatman, Alpha Centauri."

"And my twin brother, the late, officially state-beloved, Morgianna's own beloved, incidentally," enlarged Mel-Illuminatus, despite her better judgement risking anew Saladin's retaliatory tendencies, just in case the Witch had missed the import of Sal's statement. She, Wilderwitch, hadn't. She knew all about Miracle Maenad; knew all about her prior to late 19/5955 anyhow.

Knew her real name, Cybele St Synne. Knew who her father was, the not-yet-dead Outer Earth centenarian Sedon St Synne, Gloriel's maternal grandfather, who'd also been raised, albeit a generation earlier than the Sundowns – make that more like two generations earlier – by Shaman Manitoulin. Which of course made Cybele Gloriel's generation of D'Angelos' aunt. Knew Solomon Taurson had a twin sister and who their parents were: Meroudys Maenad and Wiccan Warlock, aka Jesus Mandam, the Conquering Christ.

Furthermore, she had come across Alpha Centauri, albeit mostly as Alfredo Sentalli, his Outer Earth birth name, many times pre-Limbo. If memory served he, Sentalli, was Papa Rafe's (Gloriel's father, Raphael D'Angelo) godson. Since she looked a little like Human Memory, Papa Rafe's youngest sister, that almost made them relations. Of course, assuming Celeste Mannering was Hush's mother, and Hush was Pandora, Saladin's mother, then he, Sal, might be related, too; albeit by religion, not blood.

"Who has been," Saladin led, as if out of the blue, "With your carefully kept covert compliance, conspiring to take over the Weirdom for thirty years."

"So says you!" Melina reacted angrily. Angrily the only way she immediately could, that is, in terms of voice, the look in her eyes and her bodily gesticulation. As disturbingly as ever her facial expression remained completely composed. (Having a stone face might have been useful diplomatically but, the Witch knew, as did Saladin, she didn't have a stone heart to go with it.)

"So say any number of others as well, High Illuminary." The Master of Weir liked to hear himself speak. Particularly when he was being hurtful. "Although, as I've also said, repeatedly, approaching ad nauseam, I should have said, I'm delighted to see you back in the land of the living, as it were, Wilderwitch, that's why I transported myself here today. To tell my ever faithful sister-in-law that any restrictions I placed on her have been lifted. Your short lease has been rescinded. You and your daughters are free to do whatever you please from now on."

"Mel?" Wilderwitch queried.

"We've in effect been under house arrest, Witch. Whenever I go somewhere on the Master's behalf, be it via Matter Transducer to Cabalarkon or Centurium in the Thousand Caverns; by ship to Apple Isle, where I risked life and limb explaining to Miracle Maenad why I didn't want Persephone involved in an arranged marriage; even by electric golf cart on our old, millennia pre-Roman roads into the countryside outside the city, my daughters stay behind. Under the Master's care, as it were.

"Or, if they didn't, as when we went on our tour with their cousins, 'A' and 'B', we travel with such a huge honour guard it's a wonderment anyone sees us, let alone gets a chance to shake our hands." She didn't need an invitation from the Witch to go into the reasons why that was. Did need a pause to determine if she wanted to go on. Decided she did.

"Part of that had to do with my relationship to you; to Demon Queen Lilith morphing about as you, make that. As I told you, also approaching ad nauseam, it wasn't good. Some of it has to do with my onetime relationship to Gomez Niarchos and his even after-death, Sangazur-preserved loyalty to Alpha Centauri; Al Sentalli, as you probably knew him best. I've known him as both. Known him as both my friend and my enemy, truth told. Most of it, though, is because of my twin brother.

"The Master's right. Demios has been plotting to take over the Weirdom for thirty odd years. Longer if you have to know; which was why the Master issued the Challenge of Weir when he turned thirty rather than wait until Demios and I did a year later. But I haven't been helping him. Who has been helping him all these years, and a lot longer before that, before the Master even became Master, was his 'beloved' sister, my sister-in-law, Morgianna born Nauroz, but become, at Master Kyprian's insistence, Somata.

"Among many another thing, Superior Sarpedon for one, whom you hated, Morg was also known as the Morrigan. In case you've forgotten, Witch, it's an honourific, like Miracle Maenad is to the Korant Sisterhood. It refers to the fact that she was once a demonic War Queen. Wrested it decades ago – as you might recall if Eden Nightingale hadn't tampered with your memory – from the Ararat side of Harry's family."

The events Mel-Illuminatus was referring to occurred in the mid-to-late Forties, when the Witch often travelled with Master Kyprian's successor as the Antheans' rightful Superior (their top-of-the-food-chain Nightingale, David-Cerebrus and Saul-Psycho's mother) and Eden's darling daughter Aranyani — officially by Loxus Abraham Ryne, though equally likely by the old satyr, Cybele-Miracle's father Sedon (or Satan) St Synne.

The Ararats were maritally related to the Zeross family through Harry's mother Megaera, herself the daughter of Olympias (officially Sangati become Kinesis, but always of the Ararats), who died giving birth nine months after the Simultaneous Summonings of 1920. Died, as it happened, giving birth to … well, it was a long convoluted story that also involved Fisherwoman and Laodice born Atreides, whose mother Clymene nee Catreus had once been a Morrigan herself.

(Both of whom made no secret they believed she died giving birth to Barsine Mandam, who was brought up as Jesse's twin sister when the real twin was eventual Headmistress Virginia 'Ginny' Mannering, Abe Ryne's long time, actual mistress.)

"Was so," Melina finished up, relying on second or third hand reports, since she was then currently a prisoner of the Family Thanatos of Frozen Lathakra when it happened, "From the sounds of things the Morrigan once and again, briefly, on Haunted Dustmound in Hadd back in Tantalar — as Furie and the rest of your comrades who were there, were any of them still around, could testify. Save Golgotha, Black Skullface, I should say, but he and his crew may have come back too late to have caught all of it."

Or been otherwise occupied staying alive, she could have added but didn't. He and his Trinondevs, Janna St Peche-Montressor and her Athenan War Witches, Thartarre Holgatson and his brown-robed, shave-skulled Sraddhite priests and priestesses, all of whom had their hands full with much more than just who and what Morgianna brought in that day, at least in part thanks to her one-armed man, the teleportist Alastor Molorchus, whom most everyone realized was a Sangazur-animated Dead Thing by then.

"To be more accurate," Saladin qualified, "Like her Hellion of a daughter Tsishah Twilight – who was here with Pusan Wanderlust at the beginning of Yamana, you might recall – she was coated with a demon. Other than it makes her look like an Irache, which had a lot to do with why she was able to marry the one she did, I don't know about Tsishah's. But my sister's was a demonic War Queen. Her name was Mara Nighe, I believe, as in Nightmare. And it ill-becomes you, or anyone else, to speak ill of the dead, High Illuminary."

"I wasn't speaking ill of anyone, Master, dead or alive. As I thought I made clear, I was stating a certainty."

"As was I, when I stated you were covertly conspiring with your brother to dethrone me." He was leading up to something big, the Witch sensed. Was the real reason he was here, in all likelihood; to stick it to Melina, at least figuratively. "Deny it to your heart's content, but I have it from the proverbial horse's ass. Surely you're not going to call your precious twin a liar."

Once again her eyeballs betrayed what her face couldn't. This time, though, they didn't light up incandescently, like torches, as if she was about unleash something ghastly; fiery daggers, if not eyefire. If anything they became weepy. Melina was absolutely appalled by his assertion and, from her reaction, Wilderwitch was sure she knew why. He wasn't making it up.

"In order to save our Weirdom, you said," the Witch said, before Mel could insert her foot deeper into her own mouth and truly infuriate Saladin. "In order to save your Weirdom is what you meant to say. You needed Harry to wield his Gypsium rings. I've seen what he can do with those things. And it isn't just to teleport himself and anyone else he so desires. Even when he was a kid about the same age he appears to be now he could use them to far-see.

"Thanks to Magus Maxius, Mel's charge during the Outer Earth's Second World War in the Forties, Homer Skullian had that ability. So does Gloriel D'Angelo with her Little Angels; at least I hope she does, wherever she is. And so too do I in a way, when I send my soul-self out ahead of me. You had Sedon rejuvenate Harry, on whatever pretext. Then you had him use his rings to scout out Demios's whereabouts and remove him, bring him here."

"To Cabalarkon City, yes," Saladin admitted. Sounded thoroughly chuffed, even more full of himself than usual.

"That's why Child Harry was so sick when he came back Equinox morning," Melina finally spoke; taking it all rather well, Wilderwitch reckoned.

Then again, with his Master's Mace always in hand or lap, likely nothing she threw would get through to him. Nothing she shot either — and, as Codename Illuminatus, Mel had been known to wear guns on the Outer Earth. Had also been known to wield her caduceus as what it actually was: not as a stunted eye-stave, as a product of the Olympian Tantalus.

(Sundown and Raven's Head, when they were together, had a knack like that too. Called it, somewhat unimaginatively, their cosmic aura. As if a backup, Johnny also had his 'exclusion zone'; had had since before he traded his eyesight for Raven's reins, she'd heard more so than witnessed. Fish's bellybutton bauble was similar, albeit even more useful — could elongate as well as expand, both impenetrably. So was OPM's regalia, except he destroyed it, all three pieces of it, in Hideaway Damnation at the very beginning of December-Tantalar, when he was possessed, unbeknownst to the rest of them, by the Apocalyptics.)

"We figured he'd just grown restless and run away."

"For days and days?" Saladin scoffed, taking delight in denigrating his High Illuminary's intelligence. "Hardly. You know how much Harry, teenager, man, then boy again, misses his Mama Mel. He is obedient, however. When I summoned him, through Grudal, he came as called. It took to Equinox Eve before we managed to locate your brother but, after that, well, we overheard him telling the debauched Fatman how much he wanted to come back to the Weirdom, so we obliged.

"It's too bad he didn't have his ages-old, pre-Earth eye-stave with him at the time. I would have enjoyed demonstrating the superiority of the Master's Mace again. But I'm not complaining. We've been having such fabulously, um, illuminating discussions ever since his return, him and I. Which is why I was so late consummating our reunion."

"Awfully confident, aren't you?" said the Witch, getting antsy again. Although not quite four months pregnant, she'd been feeling much more heavily laden, as it were, since her return to 'civilization', also as it were, on Equinox Eve via vimana. (Coastal gravity, perhaps? Recharged Metallic Marigold overburdening her?) Nevertheless, she'd had enough delays.

"Shouldn't I be?" Saladin's smugness was akin to smog. It permeated the room so much so even the Witch was getting misty-eyed. "It was your idea of course. Rather – I'm forgetting myself again – it was Cynthia Masterwife's idea. She even interceded with Sedon, on my behalf. On the Weirdom's behalf, I should say. Before she passed away, I should add."

"You've still got me," said the Witch, shamelessly. She'd shed no tears when Mel told her about Lethal Lily's demise. "And our daughter. If you'll have us."

"You'll have her. Even I won't go that far."

========

That night, in the room at the Zerosses' coastal hideaway that the Witch had taken for her own even before her disappearance, they went further than usual. Which for them was saying something. It was nice to have her back again, the Master thought afterwards, the third or fourth time afterwards. So accomplished; so enthusiastic.

Nice to have both of them, two-in-one, back, he corrected himself. Was better than Melina, either two-in-one or singly, as they had been years and years ago, again at hateful Master Kyprian's insistence. Even with Lilith-Gomorrah enveloping her, together with an equally entering-second-trimester Sed-son underneath her skin, in her baby belly, the High Illuminary was disappointingly unadventurous.

Was a good idea at the time, though.

========

Hours later ...

========

Their day began innocently enough, albeit after some additional, strenuous, anything but innocent, sexual exertions on the part of both sides of the bed's occupants. Atop it, to either side of it, on the floor beside it, everywhere except underneath it, though they tried that too; didn't enjoy the concomitant head-banging that resulted. (During pregnancy is the best time for that sort of thing, the Witch only now recalled. As for Saladin, he had so many kids – all of whom, oodles of oddly, under 20 – he was, he claimed, an anytime is the best time sort of guy.)

It wasn't Antheal Fools Day anymore. Was, however, the first chance they had to speak at any length since their reunion. And Lilith-Gomorrah's with Wilder-witch. Who was a far better host for a Demon Queen than a full-blooded Utopian prude by the name of Melina nee Sarpedon Zeross. (He'd made an ash of her after 'death' then re-sprinkled her, dead foetus and all, over Melina shortly thereafter. Remarkable creatures, demons.)

For one thing the Witch was a deviant in that at least one of her parents had been devil-possessed when she was conceived and given birth. Perhaps counter-intuitively, that meant she was largely human, earthborn like Lilith and not extra-terrestrial like devazurs or even Utopians, as far as that goes.

For another, her fearsome soul-self was approaching demonic in many respects. Which, since she was demonic in every respect, served Lilith's purposes admirably. Most importantly she didn't get eaten away like the High Illuminary did; hence the dilapidated condition the Witch found her in when she returned to the Zerosses' coastal getaway. Was, non-sexually-speaking, somewhat harder to control, however.

It was a fair day, cloudy but not raining, neither too cool nor particularly warm. They dressed accordingly. He pulled a woollen vest over his long-sleeved caftan, she put on a heavy linen chemise with a fur shawl and comfortable leggings. They ordered an early morning breakfast and, when it arrived, went to eat it on the balcony outside the Witch's room at the spacious villa.

Mel-Illuminatus wasn't with them. Was, presumably, sleeping in, with Child Harry beside her. (She was enough of an Alt that contact with her was conducive to healing.)

"So," Wilderwitch wondered, "How are you going explain my comeback after all that flummery Melina tells me she spewed at my state funeral?"

"You're an illusionist. How else do you think I was going to explain it? And it's the truth. You certainly had me fooled. I was sure you were dead."

"Yet you knew enough to sprinkle her ashes over Melina. And they weren't illusionary. Have to admit I was surprised to discover the Sed-son inside her went with her as well."

"You shouldn't speak of yourself in the third person. I find it very confusing."

"Not half as much as I do, believe both halves of me. Got an answer?"

"It's what Cynthia wanted. I merely honoured her death wish."

"Stop sounding the dumbbell dingdong with me, Sal-bell. You honoured her life-wish."

"All right. I succumb. Drag it out of me. Yes, even I, dumb-ass Master that I am, and have too often been, knew sprinkling the ashes of cremated demons and faeries over top another sentient being gives them, the demons or faeries, a new host and, therefore, a renewed lease on life. It's been done in the Land of Twilight since it was the Land of Daybreak. Probably long before that; before there ever was a Hidden Continent in all likelihood."

"So you knew she was a demon."

"I didn't say that, goddamn it. I knew Cynthia Masterwife was you and you have to admit you're not normal, not even for a witch. Ask me that soul-self of yours is awfully demonic, especially when it comes to looks; its looks, not yours. I didn't realize it was magnetically so; that it attracted demons.

"Now that you mention it, though; now that we both realize who you were and who you are again, both halves of you, doubly pregnant; I have to admit I'm as impressed as you seem to be with the pre-baby business. Lilith must have taken care of that herself. The night she died, the night Cynthia Masterwife died, she had me summon the High Illuminary to her deathbed. She must have accomplished the exchange then."

"How?"

"Speculatively speaking?" She graciously allowed him that option. "The same way she transferred both her and the foetus back to you, I imagine. They kissed. Although I wasn't there, I can just picture it. Open mouths, lips sealing to create a tunnel, tongues tangling into a corkscrew roadway, dying demon mother, unborn half-devilish son inside her, creeping along the roadway of hell from one shell to another in the form of, I don't know, a juicy scarab beetle maybe. Unless it was a pregnant ant. Demons can shift size as well as shape; draw stuff into or out of Samsara, the universal substance, and vice versa, as needed."

"Thanks for the image, Sal. I'll treasure it in my mind forever."

"Always happy to oblige."

"I gather Lilith left a husk behind, like a snake sloughs its skin. You had to pyre-afire something, so she would have the ability to externalize her soul. Check that. Demons don't have souls; externalize her mind then." (Demons were notoriously all body, albeit without much of a mind, whereas devils were by nature fully bebrained, but bodiless, Spirit Beings.) "Then, once you sprinkled her over Melina, she redacted Mel's memories and clipped in the notion she'd done an autopsy."

"The High Illuminary did do an autopsy. Rather, she supervised it. Had quite the crew there as well: senior Illuminaries, pathologists, some of her fellow physicians and handpicked scientocrats; biomages she likes to call them. She even had it videotaped. You can order it from the Citadel of Thinkers, if you're so inclined. She never twigged, not until you came back anyhow, if then, it was a demonic husk containing the … what? Another husk, I suppose; of an unborn boy baby. Neither did I. For the same reason."

"Which side of the mouth are you talking out of now?"

"You think Sedon's inside me? He isn't or, if he is, I can't sense him."

"Funny about that. You see, I can't sense Lilith inside of me, either. Then again I never could, could I? Nonetheless, I don't think she is. Sorry to disappoint."

Her assertion bothered him. Whereupon she shadowed, eyes concomitantly darkening and, skin lightening like someone afflicted with an all-over pallor, simultaneously beamed, dazzlingly so. Bloody tricksters he must have thought, though relief was as evident on his face as it was in his voice.

"You're good, Cynthia."

She disillusioned him immediately. Face-dancers could do that sort of thing. One second he was speaking to Wilderwitch, slender – lean, more like, considering her pregnancy – even buff after six weeks in the rough; unkempt rat's nest hair; gypsy gorgeous. The next second he was speaking to Fey Woman, plump, facially as well as bodily, clearly unfit but nowhere near unattractive, Rubenesque. Which for some made her extremely attractive; an A-plus-size, she'd told him when they were together all those years ago.

Coiffed hair, not a strand out of place presumably thanks to hairspray; professional-looking, Outer Earth businesswoman's haut-couture-clothing instead of the Witch's furs and untailored smock. Was all business as well: "Cynthia Masterwife is dead, Sal." She face-danced some more. Was, to his Black God, the White Goddess complete with hair-hiding skull cap she had appeared to be on Zmas Night last year.

Then her skin sucked in on itself like drying-up, yet still bleached parchment. Became ghastly white instead of goddess white. Her eyes less fell out, then drizzled down her cheek like something out of a Thirties horror flick. She stuck out her tongue. There was an improvisation of a pregnant ant on it. She swallowed it: "Wilderwitch lives."

"Stop that," he demanded. She did; was herself again.

"Only I can't, can I?" she said, pre-epiphany. "I'm dead, burned and ashes-scattered." Then she had it, her epiphany. "Wait, I was born near the end of Tantalar 5927. I lost 25-years in Limbo. That makes me 28, if my math skills haven't atrophied. Say I didn't. Say I was born 28-years ago. That'd be 5953 and, admittedly as 1953, that was a highly significant year in terms of the Secret War of Supranormals.

"Many a supra-female gave birth in '53. Most, if not all of them, did so around the traditional Midsummer Day in the Northern Hemisphere. Gloriel, Radiant Rider, was definitely one. She had Estrella, Star Dark, who grew up to be a tactless, over-the-top Lovely Lady wannabe I had to, um, discipline in Vancouver the night the Byronic Nucleus brought us inside. Sorciere, Johnny Sundown's Solace Sunrise, would have been another, except she was killed giving birth.

"Barbara become Ryne, the thorniest of the Plantagenets – part porcupine, that woman, if you got her riled up – would have too. Except she committed suicide awhile before her due-date. Some say Saul-Psycho drove her to it; others say she did it because she was carrying his child, not his father's, her husband's, not Abe Ryne's.

"Electrocretan, Laodice Atreides, Hent by then, had Zenobia, who doubtless grew up to become as, um, electrifyingly gorgeous as her mother. Corona Power, Rachel Cohen, and Thorns' baby sister, the youngest of the Plantagenets, Polyanna become Mayhew, all of them were pregnant and had children. Girls the lot of them, I seem to recall. And that's only the ones I can remember off the top of my pointy pinhead. There were more; too many to count really."

"My beloved sister and thoroughly unloved brother-in-law had my even less affectionate niece on Midsummer's Day 1953. Had her out there as well."

"Andy, Andrea Sarpedon, that's right. Her parents actually called her Andaemyn, didn't they? As in 'without a demon'. Which raised more than a few eyebrows in Outer Earth witch circles, hence Andrea; hence also a pretty speedy splendour to hide her stripes. So that's when I was born. June 1953. God, I'm brilliant. Say hello to Wilderwitch Two."

"You're nuts."

"No, that was one of the other Plantagenets, Anjou, Mandasoma or Emeralda, the one who married Al Sentalli, your Alpha Centauri, and had his Yataghan. Whichever one it was, Mandasoma I think, was really good with nuts. Hell, it must have been her. She married one: Boris Gagarin, the Sleeping Giant, in a way the Soviet Supra Supreme's equivalent of Mel and the Skullians' Magus Maxius. Had

I not been with Jervis Murray nine months beforehand, I would have had a child around then myself. I wonder who my father was?"

"Me?"

"Not if we're to stay lovers, which I'd like. How about your delusional pal Jesse, Jesus Mandam, the self-proclaimed Conquering Christ? He was always after me; got hold of me a couple of times as well, the disgusting prick. Except his kids by Meroudys Maenad were born around then, weren't they?"

"A few months earlier, I believe. Not that that would have made any difference. It's women who can't become pregnant again, not if they're already pregnant. Men don't have the same restrictions. All they need is another woman to get pregnant. Elementary birds and bees stuff that, Witch. Want to borrow the book or would you prefer Helen or maybe Tina Zeross recite some of it to you?"

"I'll take your word for it, Sal, though it does seem rather farfetched. Whatever happened to the stork, evil creatures that they are? Ask me Christians buggered up when they started depicting their sort of Satanic, as opposed to Sedonic, devils as horned humanoids."

"Could be it ran off with one of Miss Murk, Mad-For-Mud-Pies' magpies. Their names are Solomon and Balkis, by the way, but you're probably aware of that. You'd have to ask the High Illuminary for the details, but their grandmother, Miracle Maenad, was forced to foster them out when they weren't very old. The girl was brought up in the court of Queen Godda, God-Devil, the somehow everlasting ruler of Twilight's feeorin faerie folk, whereas the boy was trained in the Bloodlands, New Valhalla, by Sangazur-possessed warlords.

"Point being they've grown up to become, at least potentially, major players on the Head: Balkis is the Korant-slash-Mariamnic Ventricular of Shenon, while Sol's in line to become the new Taurus, head of the Mithrant Brotherhood. They're no fans of Godbad, are like grandmother, like grandchildren, in that respect. So I'd like to keep them on my side as much as possible.

"Of course that it isn't very likely anymore, is it? My High Illuminary, in her ever-so-exceptional enlightenment, rejected Sol; claimed he was an inappropriate suitor for her precious Percy of a daughter. Then again, the fact they're stuck on the Outer Earth with no apparent way to get back, unless I send Harry for them, might have had something to do with it."

"That isn't quite accurate, Sal. Mel's a romantic. She reckons marriage should be based on mutual love, not political or financial convenience. That's probably why she didn't get pregnant back in '53, that and the fact she was a nun then. Could be Persephone thinks the same way – not about becoming a nun – but, even if she doesn't, Mel says times have changed since our youth. So much so Percy's considered awfully young to get married nowadays.

"Not that anyone's ever old enough to get married as far as I'm concerned. Don't believe in it myself, as you know. And neither do you. Except for political or financial convenience it seems. Besides, how would I know what Percy thinks? I take the nub of your gist, the thrust of your crust, though. Wouldn't want to scuttle any of your grand schemes through sheer caprice. The Witch, my mother, was always a bit of a bed-bouncer, so I'll pick someone otherwise unknown for my father. Tell me, have you announced Child Harry's rejuvenation to the Weirdom yet?"

"And admit it was Dark Sedon's blood that brought him back? The boy would be lynched on the spot. So, no. I haven't given much consideration as to how we're going to reintroduce him to the populace, truth told. As you may have noticed, he hasn't been very well. While we think we got to him in time to arrest his development backwards, so to speak, we're not sure how long he'll survive.

"That's another part of the reason the High Illuminary and her children have been staying, somewhat against their wishes, on the coast: to keep him out of the prying public's eye. Tongues will wag as easily as eyelids will blink, don't you see. It's also why she never lets him venture very faraway from her. Her life-force, her Althean healing ability, her supra-normalness if you will – she's a Summoning Child, don't forget – might be all that's keeping him going."

"So I'm Child Harry's mother. By Adult Harry. That's why he's a natural. Mel's going to be pissed. Hubby Harry had a son between Helen and Tina she didn't know anything about."

"She'll get over it."

"Because she's a pragmatist or because you've her twin brother?"

"Bit of both; mostly the latter. In a state of Arrested Envelopment."

"Score one for the Master," Wilderwitch made an invisible tick in the air. "You've Demios encased by a stone gnome?"

"Close enough. Quite literally. They're between-space, but they're always within reach of him. He's too dangerous to just be left under just lock and key like any common miscreant."

"Too popular is what you mean to say, but I understand your reticence to come clean. Especially, if only in case of fire, you're likely not the only one with a key. What've we missed? Oh, Wilderwitch Two and Child Harry came here, via some rings Adult Harry left in my keeping, as a token of our brief fling a decade ago, when I wasn't much older than Percy is now, in order to reunite with my mother, his grandmother. Only she died before we got here.

"Oh, and you didn't believe we were who we said were. So we had to prove ourselves by capturing Demios Sarpedon. Which we did. That about cover it?"

"I like it. No, I love it; love you. You're as devious as you are daemonic, in the additional sense of being possessed by genius."

"No, I'm as devious as I am a deviant. Let's emphasize everything by making a grand re-entrance. I'll fly you back to Cabalarkon City. In my vimana."

"You crashed it. Thobruk Grudal notified me as much Equinox Eve. The scientocrats I sent out that very night, the ones you probably thought were just Grudal's Trinondevs looking it over, as a kind of curiosity, have verified it doesn't work anymore. And they're technomages. You don't argue with technomages; not even when they call it a cosmicar."

"Seriously?"

"A, B and C left Earth in a cosmicar; yours, I'm to gather. Rather, theirs ended up on your Damnation Isle and they came back without it, thanks to Brainrock. But, yeah, so I'm told."

"Not work for them then. It wouldn't have. It only works for me."

"Then why hasn't it?"

"Oh, come on, Sal. Get real, to quote Mel. I haven't been altogether myself since I came back to civilization, have I?"

"You don't say ouch as much when we frolic but, otherwise, how so?"

"I've had company. And I don't mean my fearsome soul-self. Have had ever since I gave Mel a hug and caught Lily again. Never occurred to me I should have worn a sheathe. Or a condom, if you prefer. Anyhow, I hope it'll work without it. It is part of me after all. Still, I've a feeling the vimana won't recognize I've had to relinquish it howsoever temporarily."

"It – your soul-self – has Lilith?"

"I told you I couldn't sense her inside me anymore."

"I thought you were having me on."

"Again? So soon after breakfast? You are insatiable, Sal."

========

Sometime after the Master left the city the night before ...

****

Seven-Demon: **Quill Or Be Killed**

========

Antheal 2, 5981

"What's that light coming from your desk, Illuminatus?"

Tricky question that. Answer was: The glow coming from the until-then-blank pad of ordinary paper on the High Illuminary's writing desk was letters formed of and by, long-distance, via between-space, Brainrock-Gypsium ink, aka Godstuff Guck. Which was a fuck of a lot better than got stuck fucking. Which was what happened to his devic half-father two millennia earlier in what was then the Land of Daybreak.

He'd never learned the rule about fucking faeries: Never fuck them in fairyland.

========

He – the same he whose devic father got lost fucking faeries coming up to two thousand years earlier – had forgotten just how vast the catacombs were.

Underground, their hewed stone uprights, and even more impressively engineered ceiling, patched as it sometimes was these days with concrete or cement blocks, formed the foundation for the vast central courtyard of Cabalarkon City. Around it stood a few of the omnipresent, firestone-capped obelisks that somehow provided power to the metropolis.

They porcupine-spiked Cabalarkon's sparsely populated countryside as well, though outside the city proper they were more likely to have fallen down; been left to lie uselessly about, almost as if they were inanimate imbeciles of Weir.

A lot more than obelisks fringed the plaza. There also stood perhaps the best preserved architectural testaments to the Utopians of Weir on Earth's former glory to be found anywhere on the planet, on either side of the Cathonic Dome. The oldest was the Citadel of the Thinkers, where Illuminaries continued to do most of their work.

Not quite so old, nor quite as high, but much deeper and wider, hence much more voluminous, the rectangular Masters' Palace was yet another impressively massive, cyclopean structure. (Cyclopean simply referred to the notion that it was so huge and seamlessly constructed, out of colossal, yet nevertheless precisely honed, stones many reckoned it could only have been built by one-eyed Cyclopes.)

While its planning stages may well have begun pre-Dome, work on it probably didn't get underway until well after Dark Sedon raised Cathonia, his Headworld's interior sky, out of his own essence and thereby separated the Inner from the Outer Earth. Constructed in still recognizable segments, it took centuries to finish, if it could ever be said to be truly finished.

Indeed, the spectacular Hate-Sedon Sphere in its interior central courtyard was comparatively recent, only a few hundred years, whereas the laboratory biomages used and continue to use to try and clone, in her absence, maybe even death on the 1ˢᵗ of Yamana, was a matter of mere months old.

While it served as the official residence for Masters of Weir and their entourage right up to the 25ᵗʰ year of Saladin's reign, these days its best housing went to the likes of Golgotha Nauroz, his family, clones the lot of them, many of the highest ranking members of his Trinondev Elite and, sometimes, guests of the Weirdom.

Among these last, Carmine Carmichael and her two fellow, rescued-by-Ring-leader, cosmicompanions, Angelica and Baalbek Schroff Zeross, stayed in the Masters' Palace when they weren't out in the countryside doing their good works. (Which mostly consisted of increasing the supply of fresh victuals for the benefit of those within and without the city who, like them – even if it did prolong life quite dramatically, a claim they found suspect – refused to eat the slop that spilled out of the stone gnomes' food processing units.)

The Grand Cathedral, with its three suggestively familiar spires, was arguably the most fabulous pile of cyclopean stonework still standing in Cabalarkon. Ironic-ally, given that it was called a cathedral, it was mostly built by (arguably) demonic Angelycs, with a 'y', and technomages using extraterrestrial lifting equipment most of which now languished inside it. As such, while it wasn't dedicated to any deity or deities it did contain, as if a museum full of retrieved artefacts from extremely distant – pre-Earth distant – days, remnants of technology no one seemed to know what to do with anymore.

When he was around, decades ago now, Sal's Outer Earth friend, Wiccan War-lock (Jesus Mandam) and his (adoptive) father the Judge (Sedon, once also Satan, St Synne, Miracle Maenad's father as well as that of Sophia long D'Angelo, Gloriel's mother) spent endless hours inside the cathedral tinkering with is exhibits. (Despite its appearance and lack of deities, it was pretty clear what the cathedral was dedicat-ed to — Science!)

There was absolutely no question Alpha Centauri knew what he wanted to do with them. Presumably it was the same Wiccan and Judge Warlock had in their day … get them working again. For the Good of All and the Greater Glory of Human-kind. Rather, if only for starters, the Greater Glory of Centauri Enterprises and the Corporate State of Greater Godbad. In other words, Jordan Tethys was under no delusions, the Fatman himself.

Not that the legendary 30-Year Man cared a whit for any of that crap. He was here for the sole purpose of retrieving the decapitated body of a burbling buddy, a Sangazur-kept-lively friend and fellow good-deed-doer by the name of Gomez Niarchos. Found it, too. Replaced it with a manikin he'd specially prepared for just that purpose. Drew the real body home to daddy — by a personally illustrated, between-space postcard.

Found dozens of other bodies as well. All had heads. With one exception all were submerged in a tub of Cathonic Fluid, in a state of suspended animation. That one's animation wasn't suspended, either. He was, however, so agitated hanging might not have been out of place, if only to calm him down for a while. Unfortu-nately there was little doubt the Master of Weir was saving him for just that … hanging. From the neck until dead.

Even though, as Tethys saw it, and put to him – after drawing his guards asleep, which they next-door-to-immediately were – that from his point of view it was quill or be killed, Demios Sarpedon didn't want to be retrieved the same as Gomez Niarchos's body. He wanted his approaching impossibly old eye-stave.

He'd come to it via Ubris Nauroz: Auguste Moirnoir, aka the Black Death's father; Celestine D'Angelo, aka the Celestial Superior's Nubian, co-caller of the Simultaneous Summonings of 19/5920; and in every respect quite the his-story in his own right. Even way back then, Sal's consequential grandfather was under no illusions as to who had half-sired Saladin therefore Devason.

His was better than any old Master's Mace any old day of the week.

========

Wilderwitch and Saladin were hardly the only ones bed-bouncing later that same night of Antheal Fools Day. Much to Mel's annoyance, Child Harry was too; bouncing on their bed.

"What's that light coming from your desk, Illuminatus?"

Sometimes postcards weren't delivered by either mail or messenger devils. They just appeared on an until-then-blank pad of paper atop the High Illuminary's writing desk.

========

Put together, which they already were, the words read:

> 'Sal has your brother, Mel. Don't ask how. Still can't figure it my-self. Dem's being a dipstick. I can get him out, but he'd rather be killed than quilled. Wants his eye-stave so he can go at Sal man-to-man; imbe-cile to imbecile, more like. Thinks the people's love for Morgianna will translate as support for him; make it stronger than the Master's Mace.
>
> 'I've had it with the pair of them, so I'm going to do what he wants and draw it to him. Let them kill each other. Or try. Give you one guess who the winner will be. Won't be a guess, will it? I'll cover my tracks so Sal can't trace anything back to me, but you better grab your children and get away while you can.
>
> 'Both of Morg's kids and the fauna are in the Whiplash Mountains. You know where. You'll be safer there than anywhere else. Stay away from Shenon, Apple Isle and Godbad. There are those in those places you can't call friend anymore.
>
> The Fatman's the most prominent, in all respects, but I'd be par-ticularly wary of Sheba Faerieflight if I were you. She feels as slighted as her grandmother was insulted by the way you ever-so-cavalierly, High and mightily Illuminary of you, dismissed her twin brother's suit for your daughter's hand in marriage. Not to mention the rest of her body.
>
> C.U. soon. Sister Jordan.'

Child Harry could read as well as any decently educated, non-anorexic 10-year old could; looked quizzical. "Don't tell me you've got another name, Illuminatus."

"It's from Jordan Tethys," Melina nee Sarpedon Zeross told him; once again more surprised than disappointed he hadn't been able to figure that out for him-self. "His abilities are a little like that 'Ghostwriter' fellow from the Saints and first version of the Crimefighters. You know, Diego Rivera, the Diego Rivera married to Dolores D'Angelo, Superior Sorrow, not the other one, the famous muralist."

Child Harry inclined his head, significantly eyeballed the letter and gestured at the signature. Gave her one of those pathetic looks of his that said, howsoever silently sarcastically, 'I'm so helpless without you.' "Sister Jordan was how I knew him best," she responded to his unspoken question.

"Knew her best, on second thought," she corrected herself. "Make that knew her longest, on third thought. He was a nun then. A female nun," she added unnecessarily. "So was I, for a while. An exceptionally, um, chubby devic shell by the name of Alpha Centauri – that's the Fatman Jordy's warning me about – thought I'd look good wearing a crucifix and a penguin suit. I still have the crucifix. But that was both before and after your time."

Mel thought some more, said some more, more urgently this time.

"Listen, Ringo," she instructed him, employing his childhood codename. "Use your rings. Get my daughters. Bring them here. Quietly. We won't be staying long."

Child Harry did as bade. By the time he returned with her girls, Illuminatus, as he referred to Melina when he bothered to talk, had already opened her Solidium safe — Solidium, or Stopstone, being the counteractive to Gypsium-Brainrock. She handed each of her daughters one of their father's rings. She also had a photograph album from the family archives open.

"This is where we're going," she said, pointing at prints Hubby Harry took of them the last time they saw her, on-a starless-night, dark-as-midnight, twin brother, Dem's wife, her sister-in-law, their Zebranid-striped daughter Andy, Andrea or Andaemyn, and then, maybe-still, Aortic Tsishah, Morg's other daughter, who was also visiting the Sarpedons at the time.

"Tina, you're taking me. Don't worry, I'll hold your hand, tell you what to do. Helen, you've the boy. He's good with rings, but he hasn't been well and already took enough of a chance at worsening his condition by bringing the three of you here. Persephone, a lot depends on you. But you're the oldest, so it should.

"These are desperate moments, children. My brother's in the catacombs. At least he was a few minutes ago. He's having some cranial cramps at the moment; needs his doctor's attention directly. Have a look-see before you get him, Percy. And don't take no for an answer. In fact you're no Jordy, so don't even ask him if he wants to go anywhere. Just grab him and go. Wherever he is!"

Mel gave them each a different photo of their target destination. Then, realizing Saladin would have their coastal hideaway ransacked looking for clues as to their whereabouts as soon as he discovered they'd absconded, decided to take the entire album with her. Took the pad of paper upon which the Legendarian sent his letters, in the form a letter, with her as well. No telling what Sal, with his Speaking Stick, his Master's Mace, could turn up after an unhurried perusal.

"You'll all be a little sick afterwards," she forewarned them. "But don't be afraid. You especially, Percy, since you've the most to do. Your cousins are in the Whiplash Range, girls, Andy and Tsishah. We've lots of other friends there; many of whom you've met. One of them is Pusan Wanderlust. You'll recall her. She's exceedingly hard to forget; looks kind of funny for a girl, has hooves and a goatee. Doesn't wear many clothes either. And they're usually made of wool. What little of them there are."

"The goat-girl," Athena squealed with delight.

"Kind of like Uncle Monster," Helen said. Paree was referring to Wildman Dervish Furie; how he appeared after he came back from Hadd last Tantalar.

She didn't say it with delight. Didn't say it with regret. Said it with perplexity. He was long gone, thanks mainly to her and Persephone, but she had no more idea now than she had then as to where they sent him, pretty – but pretty skinny – Gloriel, Glory of the Angels, who sometimes had silver hair and sometimes had rainbow hair, and the Santa Claus with the big shillelagh, his Homeworld Sceptre, OMP-Akbar.

"Kind of capric, I'd say," did say Persephone, somewhat haughtily showing off her superior vocabulary. "Carries around a shepherd's crook. Was here with Auntie Tsishah in Yamana, when Raven's Head almost killed me. Has a scar in her forehead. Crook glows in the dark. Daddy thought she was once a devil, like Mr Tethys."

"He did?" said Child Harry.

"You did," confirmed Melina. While she couldn't look jittery, she did glance from one daughter to another in a jittery fashion. "But, whatever Pusan may be, or may have been, she'll sort you out quickly enough. She's a genuine healer; has, unlike me, truly supra-talents in that regard. Right, any questions?"

"Who's Tsishah?" Tina was so young, so high-energy, so non-retentive.

========

Tsishah Thrae (Utopian, faerie, Dukkhan), she of Twilight, Tsishah Twilight then, was a thoroughly trained witch. Only death could take that away from her. Neither was she just trained in the rites of the Superior Sisterhood, that of Flowery Anthea. (If then, assuming she acquired similar knacks to Morgianna, her late mother the Morrigan.)

Flowers had branches; so did the Anthean Sisterhood. One was that of the Mariamnics, they of Crepuscule, the Land of Twilight; hence again Tsishah Twilight. Morg, who had her in the Thirties, when she wasn't much older than Helen was now, had some of the same training. Never got as far as her daughter did, which was to the top.

Tsishah not only rose as high as you could go in the Mariamnic Sisterhood, she managed to find a way to get back down again, as herself, and human enough to bear children without having them eat her alive. No mean feat that, considering the heights of fairyland she reached. It had rarely been done before. Indeed, no one in Cabalarkon – whose residents rarely ventured to Twilight anymore – was sure if it had been done since, at least to that degree.

(Dukkhans were altogether human; just grew up speaking French as their first language instead of Sedon Speak. Not that that made much difference to anyone else. Not after a few seconds or minutes adjustment. They didn't have blue skin, either; that was her conceptive father, Tom-Tiddly Taddletale, after his ashes were sprinkled over Tammuz Rhymer, her residual father.)

The reason for her good fortune must have had something to do with her mixed-up paternity. A Summoning Child like her mother Morgianna, Rhymer was born in time-retarded Dukkha. The Dukedom of Dukkha was a seldom visited city state across Bogy Bay from the Pristine Isles, once the devic protectorate of Plague (Carcinogen the Leper, the Apocalyptic of Disease) and Crepuscule-Twilight, Sedon's Outer Nose; the Bloodlands or New Valhalla being Sedon's Inner Nose.

(Alongside the imported Lazaremist, Morrigu Badhbh, Battle Babe, its former ruler and devic mother of many of its Sangazurs, Godfrey Necator was currently leading the Dead Thing faction of Godbadian supporters against the still leaderless Sangs. Interestingly, the majority of these last once worshipped Mars Bellona and his fellow Apocalyptic, Mother Murder.

(Back in Tantalar, not all that long after the Apocalyptics and their two allies {Catastrophe's Vultyrie and Antaeor 'Demon Land' Thanatos} were decathonitized on the Outer Earth's Damnation Isle, Golgotha and his Wyvern of Weir Trinondevs shredded War, by then an imbecile animated by Guardian Angel Tyrtod. Shredded that Tyrtod, too — azuras being easy-peasy to suck out of shells and into prison pods compared to their devic progenitors.)

That made Dukkha as much inside as it was outside the Sedon's Upper Lip area of the Forbidden Forest of Kala Tal, Sedon's Moustache. (Kala Tal was the brood sister of Nergal Vetala, the Vampire Queen of the Dead, though probably not of Mater Matare, Mother Murder, the Apocalyptic of Mundane Death. Her Talazurs, by a variety of mostly Mithradite, male Master Devas, brought madness to whomever they possessed, hence the Forbidden Forest bit.)

Its location was the main reason the Dukedom, which as often had a duchess leading it as it did a duke, was both time-retarded and seldom visited. Said Tal – the forest thereof, not the arachnid Mithradite whose protectorate it was – was as frightful as it was, for sanity's sake, just that, forbidden. Madness was the only prerequisite for taking a hike in those weirdling woods. It was also the next-to-inevitable result of such a hike.

His birth name was Tammuz Rhymer, yes, but, by the time he impregnated an almost identically barely teenage Morgianna, he had already become the faerie type known as Tom-Tiddly Taddletale. The former, Rhymer, wasn't around anymore. The latter, Taddletale, probably was — cremation, so long as there was no big wind around to blow away their ashes, only gave faerie types, like their daemonic cousins, another shot at remaining vital.

(His fairy-blue skin was reminiscent of another set of Terrible Twins, Aires and Thalassa D'Angelo, apparently always Thanatos, albeit solely when they were using their elemental attributes. Of note to some, when Thrygragos Lazareme – who may or may not be still around – looked at himself in the mirror he saw himself as having blue skin as well. When other people laid eyes on him they reckoned him their idea of God, hence Thrygragos Everyman.)

Even though she didn't have her first child, a daughter, until she was thirty, Tsishah spent years as the Antheans' designated Aortic on the heart-shaped Island of Shenon, which lay off the west coast of the Cattail Peninsula in the Head's Interior Ocean of Akadan. As the ruler of the Ants' atrium or auricle there, she was like Amphitrite of Lemuria and two others, currently an Anthean-Althean-Afrite, in reverse order, Ventricular and a Mariamnic-Korant, dot-ditto, in that she was a Quarter Queen of what many a male, and more than a few females, referred to, negatively, even nastily, as Witch Isle.

Since her recent retirement – her attempt to retire, rather – she'd set up house and home in the Cattail's Whiplash Mountains, overlooking the Prison Beach of Incain at the southernmost coast of the Head's eastern ocean of Tempestuous Psychron. Zebranid Lepers – one of whom she wasn't, but half-sister Andy was – had maintained a colony there since the Fifties.

A veritable stronghold, it was founded, made and kept strong, with their presence, by Tsishah's mother Morg (Morgianna born Nauroz, become Somata then Sarpedon), alongside her renowned husband Demios, he with the incredibly ancient eye-stave. (Morg had many claims to fame. The Hecate-Hellions' formerly formidable Morrigan was also a former Quarter Queen of Witch Isle, an Outer Earth Anthean Superior and commander-in-chief of Inner Earth's Athenan War Witch Sisterhood. Now, though, she was just dead; albeit famously so.)

They and a band of then relatively young Utopian followers, many of whom were Summoning Children like the Sarpedons, established it some years after Morg's year older brother Saladin Devason, the then newly confirmed Master of Weir, exiled them as a group in 5950. A large percentage of the male and female Zebranids who lived in the Whiplash Range – about as faraway as one could get on the Hidden Headworld from Cabalarkon – were the children and grandchildren of these exiles.

As might be expected by their descriptive appellation, they had black and white striped skin. Their pigmentation only visibly set them apart from the rest of humanity. Otherwise they seemed perfectly ordinary; as ordinary as orange-skinned, and orange skin-textured, Bandradins such as Achigan Auranja, the former king of Godbad, were anyhow. Unlike pureblood females from Cabalarkon, whose faces couldn't wrinkle or crinkle when they were speaking to you, their stripes did not mark them as obvious extraterrestrials.

Yet they were; at least their ancestors were. Their distinguishing characteristic was a product of the same peculiar genetics pureblood and near-pureblood Utopians possessed. That the men weren't all-black and the women weren't all-white; that all the members of both sexes were varying degrees of zebra-striped; at least in theory that was because, though purebloods or near-purebloods themselves, they were born outside the Weirdom of Cabalarkon.

And why did where they were born make a difference as to whether their skin's pigmentation was either one colour or another, dependent on their sex, or striped?

Could have to do with Cabalarkon's air or the fact the Moloch Sedon privately regarded it as his protectorate and the effect that had on purebloods, inbred idiots that most of them were. More than likely, though, it was because nowhere other than in the Weirdom of Cabalarkon were there either stone gnomes or stone-gnome-made-to-work food replication units. Denied access to the spume that came out of these units, Zebranids simply reverted to their natural state, which was black and white simultaneously.

Tsishah's sons and daughters, the three who were still alive, the Zeross girls' other set of cousins on the Inner Earth besides Andy and the Schroff Zerosses, did not stay with their mother. Except for her first born, still teenage daughter, who lived in an Anthill, a Sisterhood Shelter, with her firstborn daughter, they resided with their father and his extended family in the Free Iraches' secondary homeland in the northwest corner of the Cattail Peninsula.

This was hardly surprisingly given he was a militant Irache who desired nothing less than to return his people to the Iraches' undisputed, first homeland, across the Strait of Jaag from where they lived now, and had done for approaching five hundred years. Namely old Iraxas, ex-Hadd, renamed Haas.

They didn't see eye-to-eye, Tsishah and the father of her four children. Especially hadn't since he gave over their first born son, the one who wasn't alive anymore, to Fangfingers, born Janna Somata, the by-default mistress of Manoa, the once again Gleaming City. (As for Second Fangs, as she was called after being turned by First Fangs, a Lazaremist christened Vladuca by ancient Illuminaries of Weir in ages long past, she wasn't alive either. Might not even exist anymore, though she'd been like that a few times since becoming a vamp circa 4500 YD.)

The capital of a onetime Weirdom, one of a perhaps surprising number that once dotted the Hidden Headworld, Manoa had been built over so many times it was mostly underground. That, other than in torchlight, its top level gleamed anew had little to do with its gold casing and most everything else to do with why the land was renamed Haas, as in 'has' rain; has also sunlight. Has also had its walls and the rest of its outer surfaces cleaned.

Manoa was the last bastion of ex-Hadd's Ambulatory Dead and Fangs' own, presumably once-more-to-command Undead; hence its alternative name of Necropolis, the City of the Dead. Even if she hadn't been seen since last Tantalar, Janna Fangfingers was its by-default mistress because, in that selfsame month, the tenth in the Mithradic Ternary, the Iraches' deity, their long-time, albeit only then-recently revitalized, fertility goddess, Nergal Vetala, the Vampire Queen of the Dead, came in contact with the devitalizing end of Raven's Head's unicorn horn. Endgame Vetala, this time hopefully forever.

He'd been known to visit his mother once in awhile; he being Toothy Teoti (Teotihuacan) Tsishah's again now Undead Son. Probably wouldn't be doing that anymore. As Mel-Illuminatus, strangely delighted by the news, had already heard from old friends far-speaking to her in confidence via their eye-staves, the boy's half-sister Andaemyn had recently taken up with an Irache militant of her own.

Only he hated bats.

========

The next day …

========

Wilderwitch, realizing there was no point trying to keep something secret from someone who carried around a Speaking Sick, his Master's Mace, confessed the vimana she'd indulgently, if not so much wittily, named Broom, was a gift from her humanized birth mother, Miracle Memory. Being mostly a machine, Machine-Memory, she must have somehow configured Broom's controls for her use only. As a result of her confession, Saladin Devason knew exactly what he was doing when he got into it. Knew it would work and knew why as well.

Only one person – one thing, more like – was there to send them on their merry way that early morning, the 2nd of Antheal, 5981 Year of the Dome. Wilderwitch's fearsome soul-self – barely visible, thank devic half-father Sedon for small mercies – waved at them as they took off. It (she?) looked somewhat, albeit moderately, not to mention, because it was so horrifying to behold at the best of times, very much disconcertingly, pregnant.

Was of course far too early to determine if either/or or both, separately or back together again, would stay that way.

========

Broom was not shaped along the lines of a flying-saucer-type discoid like some of the unworkable vimanas stored in Cabalarkon's tri-towered Grand Cathedral. Instead, it most closely resembled a squat, partially squashed, cylindrical cigar-tube consequently bulging at the sides. It was nowhere near as large as a cosmicar; nowhere near the size of a bus. Which was how Cosmicompanions 'A', 'B' and 'C' had previously described their cosmicar to him.

At which point the High Illuminary provided, out of her family's meticulously kept archives, photographs Harry or her had taken on the Outer Earth of standard buses such that he could make an informed comparison. Even so, the technomages he summoned to examine it were persuaded it was much closer to the former than latter. Big duh that. Even Melina had to admit Outer Earth buses couldn't fly; except in movies, that is.

Saladin Devason estimated probably only a half dozen men, with not very much equipment, could fit comfortably into it. Figured further that, initially, the Witch's vessel must have been some sort of shuttle craft. Utopians aboard the now thousands of years' derelict generational ship would have used it whenever they had to leave the ship in order to explore nearby planetoids or recently detected phenomena. Overall, it reminded him most of a rocket boat, a covered speedboat the likes of which he'd seen lake-racing in Godbad and the Cattail Peninsula during his trips to those places years ago.

He didn't realize how speedy it was, however. In fact they were over Fearsome Fobbiat, the Head's western ocean, before he even noticed he was beyond the confines of the Weirdom's traditional twenty-mile sea-limit. When the Godbadian submarine surfaced, let loose its missiles at the VTOL, he once again thanked his lucky star, half-father that it was, as well as his heart and the fitness regime he'd maintained over the decades, for his continued longevity.

Then again that was after the missiles missed — Wilderwitch thus, thankfully, demonstrating how good a skipper she was ...

At which point it suddenly occurred to him that the submarine and its missiles were more of the Witch's illusions. His little mother used to pull similarly perverse psychological pranks on him, too. That wasn't why her banned her, Young Life, prohibitively Pandora 'Hush' Mannering, along with his little father, Young Death, prohibitively born Augustus Nauroz, from the Weirdom.

Acknowledging his parents were fucking faeries would diminish imbecilic confidence. Which was no good for anyone; save perhaps the devils who still wanted to control it.

And, with it, the Moloch Sedon's Daddy Cabby.

========

Despite his howsoever backhanded (hence only sort of) efforts at reconciliation the day before, Saladin Devason hadn't really expected his High Illuminary, Mel-Illuminatus, to see them off that morning. Regardless of her subsequent, no doubt sincere affirmation of loyalty to the Weirdom, she'd have hated him using Child Harry to take her brother prisoner. So why would she be there?

He wouldn't have known about the far-sent letter she'd received from the Legendarian the night before. Might have recognized the letters making up the thing atop Skyrise. Sure, the handwriting might not be unmistakable, all the more so since it was printing, but there couldn't be much doubt how it got there.
   Or could there?

========

"What's that?" Saladin Devason queried in evident astonishment.

He did so as Wilderwitch piloted Broom towards his, after-Sundown, completely repaired and refurbished, glass and metal architectural monstrosity.

And Skyrise was an architectural monstrosity. In a huge, proud, in-part-antediluvian city, one fashioned exclusively, other than it, out of highly crafted stonework, even stone gnomes must have blushed themselves into quickly crumbling fired-clay with embarrassment when they were forced to finish it.

"On the Outer Earth it's called a billboard."

"There was nothing there when I left yesterday afternoon," Sal insisted.

There was now: a billboard atop Skyrise, where they'd been intending to land. Beside the glowing wording was a graphic of a very scary mare's head. You'd definitely never find something with such big, frighteningly large teeth on a hobby horse. Did once in awhile find something like it manifested on the end of an eye-stave, however. Was a Night Mare's head.

The wording read, Godstuff-glowingly-so: 'Morg lives!'

"Guess I'm not the only one who resents being played for a fool, Sal. Even if it was on Antheal Fools Day."

"I'll let that ride for the time being. Not that I've much choice in the matter since you're driving. Is it solid?"

"It isn't one of my glamours, if that's what you're asking. Isn't anyone else's either, I wouldn't wager ... I'd know. I'm no Sorciere, but I'm good with illusions. (Sorciere, Solace born Sunrise become, twice, once officially, Sundown, may not have been the best witch ever, but not many were better than her when it came to casting glamours.)

"I'll fly through it if you don't believe me, but it looks pretty solid to me."

"A simple yes or no would have been sufficient, Witch"

"Where's the fun in that?"

"What's this?"

"I told you what I think it is. If I wasn't so busy dodging the Godbadians' missiles, I'd have proved it."

"You got the markings wrong."

"Huh?"

"I guess the High Illuminary never got around to telling you that, virtually from the moment Bodiless Byron's star was positively identified in the night's sky last Tantalar, Greater Godbad switched its flag from the cloud-grey Byronhead Pennant to the banner of Centauri Enterprises. That'd be, against a sky-blue background, a pair of curved swords and ploughshares bracketing the Globe of the Whole Earth with the Hidden Continent of Sedon's Head in its centre. The Byronhead was part of the sub's markings.

"I don't hold it against you, though. My Little Mother fancies herself something of a trickster. Don't worry. I won't ban you. Not until you give me a proper heir, anyhow."

Was he teasing? No matter.

Recalling what he and year-younger pal Wiccan Warlock (whom he'd first met as Jesus Mandam on the Outer Earth in the very late Thirties, when they both attended the Amsterdam Academy of Man, the first version thereof) determined it was for, years ago, Saladin pressed the button he was indicating. A minimum of six thousand years since one was last fired in anger – at least on that particular aerial speedboat – a particle beam shot out of Broom's side, blew the billboard into smithereens.

"Now you can fly through it." She did. Flew Broom over the city, two or three times, just to show off.

Then, at the Master's insistence, she landed in the Great Central Plaza. She'd learned her lesson. And not just how to land properly. Even if there may have been a real one somewhere off the coast, Saladin hadn't been fooled by the illusory submarine. Hadn't been worried she'd haul him off southwards, to turn him over to his enemies, Godbadian nor anyone else. They were not equals. He was the boss.

As if to emphasize that, the eyeorb atop his Speaking Stick opened. Out of it came Wilderwitch's fearsome soul-self, complete with Demon Queen Lilith, and she as pregnant as she, or it, had been when they left the coast that morning. He could have stuck it, them, back inside her anytime he pleased.

Wouldn't, as he'd already noted a few times on their journey here, have anyone to fly the vimana then. Rather, since it didn't work with Lilith inside her, the vimana plain wouldn't fly. Not that either would have made any difference. He'd had Sedon inside himself all along. She was sure of that now. And, chances were, the Moloch would have protected his hybrid-Utopian half-son no matter what.

Chances weren't, maybe she should have crashed instead of landed. One thing was certain, she wouldn't be having a similar opportunity again anytime soon.

Saladin had called Lilith-Gomorrah the Demon Dominatrix for a reason.

========

Wilderwitch's touching Broom down on Cabalarkon's central plaza, midday Antheal the Second, attracted ample attention. What attracted even more, sent eyelids fluttering, eyeballs double-taking and tongues a-wagging, was their emergence, evidently a couple again, from the Witch's vimana moments thereafter.

Even in the Weirdom of Cabalarkon, set as it was on a hidden continent where, from the perspective of an Outer Earthling, the miraculous was relatively commonplace, someone having seemingly risen from the dead was practically unheard of. And then usually only heard of second hand. From Pani Merchants or folks like Jordan Tethys who occasionally visited Cabalarkon, where he traded tales told for non-stone-gnome-slop, as bad as it was.

(Was getting better, even Saladin, who'd been to the Outer Earth as well as most places on the Head, had to admit. This was due in large measure to Cosmicompanions A, B and C, who must have some peasant blood in them. Ever since Harry Zeross brought them up here back in Tantalar they'd spearheaded the increased delivery of countryside crops, albeit as yet mostly from last year, to the conurbation of Cabalarkon City.)

The main exception were firsthand accounts from survivors of the Trinondevs' campaign, as led by Golgotha-Skullface, the 80-year old clone of Ubris Nauroz, Sal's grandfather, in Hadd the previous year. There, in what was now Haas, folks, often comrades-in-arms who, mere minutes or seconds earlier, were fighting at their side, definitely did rise from the dead — whereupon they promptly became the ambulatory Dead.

Identical, or near enough, to the ones they'd dreamed about Tantalar the Four-teenth last out on the Slopes of the Sleepers.

========

It wasn't just in Cabalarkon that eyeballs did double-takes either. One set had three eyeballs on overlapping heads. Another set had one of two in his forehead. When it wasn't just one of one, the biggest star in the night's sky, and with a mouth for a pupil. So often the antics of offspring, partial offspring in their case, bewildered parents. The Moloch Sedon only cut out his right eye in solidarity with his thought-father, Cabby the Daddy.

That he rarely appeared without his right arm cut off at the elbow. Well, that was in homage to the Male Entity.

========

In some respects it was a good thing Sal's Speaking Stick was also a Hearing Stick, as was Wilderwitch's approximate equivalent, her stunted eye-stave, Metallic Marigold; once again fully recharged as it was. Was a better thing the Master's Mace, his mike-on-a-spike, did not amplify Capputis Masterson's cry of concern as much as warning. Would have restricted their options if it had.

"Hold off coming out, father. Uncle Dem-Wit got away. He's out there some-where, waiting to waste you!"

Lofting up from Broom, side by side with the black god, Saladin Devason, the Master of Weir, rose his very much pregnant White Goddess. They were envel-oped in the Master's impervious thought-bubble as ameliorated by her own Metallic Marigold. Well, they trusted it would be impervious.

Their weaponry might fail, but Sedon wouldn't let them down, would he?

"Let all be revealed," Saladin brazenly proclaimed via his mike-on-a-spike, which did self-amplify, albeit only by the Master's will. So much for the notion of Wilderwitch Two. "My beloved sister, Morgianna Somata, does not live. My belov-ed spouse, Cynthia Masterwife, does live. Long live Cynthia Masterwife!"

Impervious or not, he was expecting Demios Sarpedon, from wherever he was hiding, to attack him anyways. If he could get out of his cage, he could get into the Master's armoury; could thereupon get hold of a sniper's rifle, complete with anti-tank ammunition imported from Ap Isle. Could get hold of a lot of things, though thankfully not his antique eye-stave. That was in Godbad. Or had been Equinox Eve. He had made a point of telling Child Harry to leave it there. Despite what he said to the High Illuminary and the Witch the night before, he was afraid it might actually be a match for his Master's Mace.

That Sarpedon didn't attack them might have been because he didn't want to endanger old pal Wilderwitch, whom he would have heard was Cynthia Master-wife. Or had been when Gomez Niarchos was wholly here end-Tantalar, begin-

Yamana last. He might believe her dead, though. His sister had eulogized her as Wilderwitch, not Cynthia Masterwife.

Was more likely Sarpedon got cold feet. Had no way out of the Weirdom. Should only be a matter of time before he was recaptured.

========

Once Saladin and Cynthia, Master and Masterwife, made their dramatic, boldly visual and loudly announced re-entry into the mindset of Utopians throughout the Weirdom — and a certain, suddenly recalculating three-thing a fair distance below it; once Demios Sarpedon refused to come out and die like the fool he was; they withdrew to Skyrise. Capputis Masterson and Golgotha Nauroz attended them as soon as they could.

As difficult as it no doubt was for them to imagine, that truthfully wicked witch, Wilderwitch, last of the self-cursed Damnation Brigade, deceived the Master. In a nefarious play for his throne and access to our extraterrestrial technology, she kidnapped the real Cynthia, who was already pregnant, got hold of her metallic marigold, hid her away then, using her despicable talents of delusion, took her place in his bed and at his side.

A Master does not stay deceived for long, however, and once he learned of it he exercised his right as Master and summarily executed her. The High Illuminary was there. She'll confirm everything once she comes back from the coast with her daughters, and someone else. Made it look like her death was a result of a wasting sickness, even did an autopsy to prove it, but it wasn't. The Master had sucked the life right out of her. With his Master's Mace.

Didn't realize it could do that, did you, did either of you? Too bad about the son she was carrying, but he thought her pregnancy was as make-believe as the glamour of White Goddess Cynthia she was wearing. Nothing for it now. Wasn't like the pre-baby was even into its second trimester, was it?

In case she had allies, which she must have had, more weedy witches working their wiles after infiltrating the Weirdom, he had the High Illuminary eulogize her. Figuring that would lull her snake-suckling sisters, who had to be connected to the slime that freed Demios Sarpedon, into a false sense of security, he secretly went in search of the real Cynthia.

It's not that he didn't trust them, but he dare not give away any more details of his quest. Extirpate one cancerous coven, they should understand, another external bag of hags will want to know how you did it, so they don't go out the same way. Never underestimate witches, he advised them.

Suffice it to say, he didn't just find her. He brought her back to Cabalarkon.

========

By the Master's will, Capputis and Golgotha left their presence, set about spreading the good news of Cynthia Masterwife's return around the city.

Return with a working vimana no less.

****

EIGHT-DEMON: **Sal Misses Mel**

========

Towards The Summer Solstice 5981
Months passed ...

========

On Golgotha's orders Trinondevs used their eye-staves to levitate, to thereby cart Broom into the bowels of the Grand Cathedral seemingly effortlessly. Which really did look like a miniature version of the Entities' Trans-Time Trigon. So much so it was no wonder they were as close as the Weirdom came to worshipping anyone.

Indeed, if anyone knew the real Trans-Time Trigon currently lay in Absudyl-Minius, deep beneath their feet, they would marvel at how accurate the up-top replica looked. Was almost as if the Grand Cathedral was it shrunk. Which it might have been — albeit six thousand years earlier when Cabalarkon the place, not the Undying Utopian, was still an island.

Within it the scientocrats of Weir put the Witch's vimana through extensive tests. Came up with further proof that Outer Earth cosmicars were almost certainly Utopian design. Not only that, it might have been the name they used pre-Earth; vimanas being a term coined by Subcontinental Indians that meant, not surprisingly, 'chariots of the gods'. Discovered all this minus the guiding light of their long-serving High Illuminary, it had to be said.

Melina nee Sarpedon did not return from the coast. Nor did her daughters or that one other, whomever he or she was, the Master had mentioned. Plain disappeared, hadn't they. Were they victims of an external bag of hags taking revenge for what the Master did to Wilderwitch? Had they been kidnapped by Master Devas again? No one, especially not the Master, nor his pregnant wife, was saying.

Not that anyone asked. Wasn't as if either/or, let alone both, went walking around the streets answering anyone anything. That was Mel's job; hers and her underlings, one of them. Might not have known of course. Nevertheless, it didn't look good on the Master in particular. That was for sure. Even if no one was saying it; not out loud anyhow. The streetlights did start flickering more often, however. Bad sign that.

Without their inspirational High Illuminary, the scientocrats were forced to rely upon between-space stone gnomes and their analytical, original Mother Machine technology even more heavily than usual. As also usual, it had to be said, they were getting nowhere. Then, within a week of her return, Cynthia Masterwife deigned to work with them. A stunningly short period of time thereafter, once he'd given his sister-in-law up for lost, Saladin bestowed upon her the title of High Illuminary. She was that helpful. And they were that successful.

As she demonstrated, time and time again, she had the ability to activate Broom immediately albeit, just as significantly, not always. At first some sciento-crats argued there had to be two Cynthia Master-wives; two besides that truly evil, fortunately truly dead one called Wilderwitch masquerading as the original.

A few – ones whose loved ones, despairing for their sanity, felt should have known better – even claimed they saw them together once in a while. That is to say sometimes it appeared the Master's white-as-light wife was accompanied by a white-as-a-sheet doppelganger; what some, recalling an obscure Outer Earth term, dubbed a tulpa or thought-form, though not a phantasm given actual flesh. Turned out the scientocrats weren't losing their minds.

Masterwife sometimes did have a ghost, a very frightening-looking ghost, ac-companying her. What was even spookier, both of them were just as pregnant. In any event, when the ghost and the wife were seen together, that is to say when they were together as visibly separate entities, the vimana activated. When they weren't, when Masterwife showed up without her ghost visibly beside her, Broom didn't.

All very mysterious but, because of it, by careful observation of both situa-tions, the scientocrats were able to pinpoint where the vimana's activation triggering system was located. It then became a matter of discovering how it managed to iden-tify Cynthia Masterwife to the exclusion of anyone else.

Waste of time that, she advised them. The trick is to get it to activate for anyone. Even an alpha-male Cave Bear. Come on, Golgotha. Pick three or four of the best and brightest of Cabby's scientocrats. Let's go for a ride. Which he did, the black-skull-faced leader of Weir's Warrior Elite being her other regular accompanist those days. Which they thereupon did, scintillating Cynthia piloting Broom.

Capputis Masterson, whose enlarged cranium did seem to contain more than just the standard allotment of snapping synapses, demanded to go along. His fath-er agreed. A few days later they returned from the south-easternmost edge of the Slopes with gargantuan grins on their faces.

They'd been to the derelict generational ship where wicked Wilderwitch and her now extirpated coven of snickering snakes lurking in the weeds, whomever they were, kept Cynthia after the Witch displaced her. Remarkably not just Cynthia Master-wives and Cave Bears could now get vimanas to work for them.

When they had a chance to speak together alone, Capputis was nowhere near as ebullient; as full of glee and concomitant good cheer. Was, contrarily, glum and gloomy as he reported to his father, the Master of Weir, just how disturbing they found it, Golgotha Nauroz, the scientocrats and him, looking out Broom's cockpit window and seeing Cynthia's horrifying ghost – as they'd come to prefer to terrify-ing tulpa – flying at the same pace alongside them.

What were they in league with? Where did Cynthia's familiar, her shadow crea-ture, get those really big, really black and ever-so-awful, as in awesome, wings that sprouted out of her shoulder blades. Where did she hide them ordinarily? Where did she hide, period, when she wasn't visibly beside Cynthia? Inside her? Was she a demon? Wasn't all that exercise bad for her unborn baby? Or was it a demon too?

To which Saladin replied: "We are in league with anyone, and anything, that is not in league with devils."

========

The Cave Bear's millennial ship was hardly the only one abandoned in Cabalarkon, the territory. Many of the other long pre-Earth, asteroid-sized vessels held reclaimable cosmicars. Reclaimable quickly became reclaimed such that by early Vanalal, May on the Outer Earth, there existed a small Utopian Air Force made up of vimanas any trained Trinondev could operate.

(Vanalal was named after a sixth-born Lazaremist, Vanalana Wheatstalk. Oddly given it was the third month in his Ternary and, as on the Outer Earth, either late Spring or early Summer, she was that Great God's Harvest. Her power focus was a cornucopia, however; not a scythe like that of the fifth-born Mithradites' King Harvest, Underlord Yama Nergal, one of all too many Deva Deaths, one howsoever fortuitously cathonitized since last Tantalar.)

There was a corollary result; one that perhaps should have been expected. In order to service this Air Force of theirs and, indeed, to stay with the vimanas when the Trinondevs were sent by the Master on their ambitious, more and more far-ranging training missions, the Weirdom's between-space stone gnomes, a finite number apparently, had to be in effect reassigned.

As more and more stone gnomes were reassigned, by the Master's will, the streetlights didn't just flicker more often; they began blinking on a nightly basis. More and more repairs weren't done; more and more food replication units broke down; and more and more of the food that came out them was not just piss-poor, it was piss-pure. Consequently, Capputis, not yet twenty, but who now had charge of keeping his thumb on the pulse of the people, warned his father, more and more of the imbeciles of Weir were, put plainly, getting pissed off.

Tragically, at least as far as Capputis was concerned, the Master seemed completely indifferent – worse, entirely insensitive – to the growing displeasure of the populace, the source of his Masterly might. He was obsessed to the onset of monomania with the Family Zeross's altogether discourteous, dynastic disloyalty, as he termed it; their evident abandonment of the Weirdom the night of Antheal the 1st, the morning of the 2nd at the latest.

How dare they? How dare she, more to the point? After all he'd done for her and her, clearly, congenitally ungrateful children.

Saladin properly Nauroz, except when in sardonic mode, a mood to ridicule, never referred to Melina by her given name. Sure, he would have had her twin brother hung, or otherwise disposed of, but only after he was found guilty of conspiring with the devil-lovers of Godbad to overthrow his rule. Since, as Child Harry would confirm, if they hadn't absconded with him, he was in the process of doing just that before his apprehension, there could be no doubt of that.

They'd both overheard Sarpedon betraying his star-born nation to the allies of those their ancestors dedicated their existence to eradicating multiple multi-millennia ago. Said momentous event – when they left the Second Weir System in order to pursue the Sedonshem – occurred roughly two hundred thousand light years, by most reckonings.

(Said Second Weirworld was where, until then just recently, the ill-fated King Kad once ruled. Ruled, as it also happened, alongside Miracle Maenad {humanized as she often was at the time by the Trigregos Sisters} and their long-serving chancellor, a biogeneticist by the solitary given name of Cabalarkon.

(At his "son" Sedon's insistence, history had it, the even then not yet undying Utopian left on the Sedonshem. This would have been shortly after King Kad's no longer wiggly expiration, whereupon Miracle Maenad would have vanished back into the time stream along with Trans-Time Trigon. As history, often disputed, also had it, they, Sedonshem and Trigon, would cross paths, howsoever non-chrono-logically, many times afterwards.)

Sarpedon had admitted his disloyalty too — albeit not to the Weirdom, he claimed, just to its illegitimate master. Did so freely, with no hint of shame, no taint of coercion either, on Sal's part, in their discourses together; their diatribes, more like. Before he got away; before (presumably) the devil, Irisiel Mercherm, got him away. And Child Harry, with his precious rings, his, Sal's, lookout onto the rest of the Head. And his, Sarpedon's, nieces, so eminently valuable on the marriage market. And, most intolerably of all, Dem-Wit's duplicitous twin sister.

High Illuminary, no. She was the lowest of the low, the vilest of witches, the most bilious of bitches. Why did he ever let her back into Cabalarkon? Why did teenage Harry, back in 5960, have to fall in love with her: a hard-headed, hard-hided mass of machinating marble more than two decades his senior? To make matters even more inexplicable, her and Harry's mother, Megaera born Kinesis, had been enemies in the late Thirties, years before young Zeross came along. And he had that from the miserable Mel-mare's mouth firsthand.

She was at least as bad as her twin brother. And Demios Sarpedon was the most heinous, the most absolutely non-absolvable of traitors. He could provide confirmatory witnesses. No question of it. Assuming some of those he'd allowed her invite to the wedding of Capputis Masterson and Lakshmi Arthadot, she of Temporis, mostly on their mothers' recommendation, bothered to show up.

Hell, he told Cynthia Masterwife during one of his increasingly frequent tirades on the subject, even though he wanted to see him he didn't need Jordan Tethys, who may or may not have saved his life in Hadd back in Tantalar, to verify it. Nor did he need any Godbadian corroboration. Cromwell Necator or Quentin Anvil, for example, both of whom were there when he, thanks to Child Harry overheard Demios's declarations of intent to overthrow his Mastery. They were old, albeit long ago publicly reconciled, enemies of Lady Achigan and Aortic Amphitrite, so they'd be believed.

Not that they could lie under the influence his Speaking Stick, his Master's Mace. No one could. Sarpedon had tried to suffocate two Trinondevs with his eye-stave. They'd testify to that; no ifs ands or buts about that. And who had brought him up here in the first place? Speedy, Irisiel Mercherm, Thrygragos Lazareme's Heliodromos or sun-runner, devic messenger of the gods, devils that they were, Sarpedon's allies that they are.

Speedy's involvement sealed the verdict. And it had to have been her. He'd convince the court of that as soon as he got them back. The blur Cabalarkon described couldn't have been anyone else. Irisiel dare not stand still in the Weirdom. She did, the Trinondevs' eyeorbs, the prison pods atop their eye-staves, would activate even if the Trinondevs themselves had fallen asleep on the job. Which they had, and which, even if Sarpedon tried to suffocate them the moment they woke up, they've been punished for already.

Harshly. With albeit recallable guard duty on the outermost Slopes of the Sleeps, on the U-for-Utopian shaped border of the Ghostlands. They better nab the missing miscreants pretty damn soon, though, because after a few months out there they'll be underneath them, in a tub of Cathonic Fluid, awaiting a cure for radiation sickness.

(The border wasn't a closed 'O' because it ended at the edge of Fearsome Fobbiat, the Hidden Headworld's western ocean. That the radiation zone didn't penetrate either the Mystic Mountains, to the distant north, and the Flood or Lakelands to the south was because they were already devic protectorates in 4825 when the Idiot Twins blew themselves up, thus bringing the century old expansion of the Empire of Lathakra to an ignoble termination.)

But Demios Sarpedon's execution would only come after an open trial, he assured her, knowing capital punishment was anathema to the Witch, life-loving Anthean that she purported to be. An open trial in the courtroom of a proper Visionary, one trained in the ways of Old Weir, with a duly constituted sentencing jury, and only if that was their recommendation. Surely she, the fled High Illuminary, could appreciate that.

He couldn't very well exile her brother again, could he? Of course not. He'd just come back, again and again and again, until one of them breathed their last.

========

"Am I not an adequate replacement?"

========

"In many ways, yes. In other ways, more than adequate. But she knew everyone. Had been most everywhere, on both sides of the Dome. Had a mind like a steel trap, as the saying goes out there. Though why steel needs a trap I never could figure out. It isn't a rat. Doesn't carry diseases. Unless it's progress." He waited for a response. Got a slight grin, which was better than usual for him. From her anyhow. Or anyone else, for that matter.

Carried on regardless: "She didn't just have ambassadors she could far-speak with via eye-staves like you do. She had spies, informants, all over the Head. She had other ways of communicating with them, too. Radios, birds, who knew what else. Learned all sorts of shit out there besides medicine. That old bastard, the seventh son who thought he was a fucking faerie love god, Angus Dre'Ath, really was a master spy."

(For a number of years, roughly from 1938 until 1946 or 47, Melina still Sarpedon looked after a quadriplegic by the name of Maxwell Dre'Ath. He, a supranormal fellow Summoning Child who codenamed himself Magus Maxius, was the seventh son of said seventh son. And yes his father Angus did fancy himself a faerie potentate; the hereditary High King of the Seelie Court, which held sway over Crepuscule, the Land of Twilight, from Beltane {May Eve} to Samhain {Halloween}.

(Which – a faerie potentate – it turned out he was, by dusting at birth, if not necessarily by birth. Likely would have been again, had he ever moved back here full time. Instead he stayed on the Outer Earth where, yes again, he acted at the top level of British Military Intelligence for much of the Second World War; this despite him being resolutely Scottish.)

"She passed only a fraction of her tricks onto the other Illuminaries. We know that, we interviewed them, me with my Speaking Stick, you with your metallic marigold, as you call it."

"I'd have got more out of them with agates."

"You'd also have got away. Or had that option."

"I already had that option, remember? On Equinox Eve. With Broom and without Lily or her Sed-son-to-come inside me. I chose to come back here instead. Come back to you."

"Did you? I wish I could be so sure. You ended up at the Zerosses, not Skyrise. Don't tell me you still can't accept why that happened?"

"You sound like an old phonograph record skipping, Sal. I was new at flying. The weather was lousy. I couldn't see very well. Didn't know how to read the instruments. Still don't. Still fly by dead reckoning. Can't go where I can't see. You say it was Sedonplay and maybe it was. The Moloch realized Mel couldn't handle Lily and her baby, his unborn Sed-son. He needed me back. Maybe Machine-Memory conjoined with Silverstar did, too. I can't say; won't speculate. Leave it be. There's nothing more we can do."

"That isn't like you, Cynthia. But it might be like the Witch. How can I trust anyone I can't compel?"

"You might be able to compel me."

"And you'd resent it. So I don't. What useful thing could I compel you to do for me anyhow?"

"Find Mel and her family. Compel me to do that. Compel me to bring them back, Mel and her brother anyhow, to face trial. The others are innocents. Give me my agates, I'll do it without compulsion. Might take me awhile but, one way or another, I'll be back before Big Brain's big day. Wouldn't want to miss that. Fish and Lemurian will be here; maybe they'll know where the others are. I haven't forgotten them, you know."

(Big Brain was Capputis Masterson, whereas Lady Lemurian was the codename his future mother-in-law, Aortic Amphitrite, used when she was on the Outer Earth during the Secret War of Supranormals. Fact is, besides being able to breathe underwater like Fisherwoman, Sea Goddess, Oannes Atlantean – who Fish killed before Thalassa apparently always Thanatos thought she'd killed Fish – and the Diver, among others, who didn't actually need to breathe, her guard-body was the most supra thing about her.

(Being a mandroid, one she now supposed – more like remembered – fashioned by the inhuman Monster Maker, All of Incain, it was mutable. Couldn't change shapes, not with her pressed within it, so much as extend stuff. Made her bulletproof and mechanically strong. Also made her somewhat her akin to Steltsar, who first appeared toward the end of the Second World War out there. Except, of course, Steltsar seemed to be all-mandroid; not one controlled by whom it contained howsoever protectively.)

"Neither have I. And that's another reason I can't trust you to come back. How can I trust someone who still doesn't trust me? I didn't have the two Zeross girls send them away."

"No, that was the Magnificent Psycho, Saul Ryne, Cerebrus's twin, and my daughter, Fey Woman, wasn't it? We've established that, haven't we?"

"Why the constant questions then? Henpecking ill-becomes you, my little chickadee."

"Touché. Not to mention touchy. Here's another one. Why does Lily shield her thoughts from me? There are times she's in ascendancy; when I think I'm asleep. Only I wake up as tired as I was when I went to bed. It isn't because of our dual pregnancies. She comes out and talks to you. Or your half-father, doesn't she? What do you say to each other?"

"Funny you should ask. I've been wondering about that myself."

"How convenient. Is that the real reason you won't let me have my agates back? For fear I'll use them not to get away; that I'll use them on you instead? I could, you know? Or you could just let me use your Speaking Stick. To force you to soothsay? This is not a relationship being built on mutual respect, Sal."

"No, it's built on sex and mutual potential parenthood. You want me to soothsay, how about this? If it were up to me I might be tempted to return you your agates. So long as you agree never to come back to Cabalarkon. I might even be persuaded to ship your bottomless bag and the rest of your witch-paraphernalia somewhere outside the Weirdom where you could pick it up.

"But you wouldn't swear never to come back, because you're not all you, are you, Witch? You're perfect for Lilith-Gomorrah and Sedon-Sodom wants Lilith-Gomorrah to have his Sed-son. It'll be the first time that's ever happened. Did you know that? She giving being birth all by herself, without coating anyone. Even if it's more like undercoating. So it's not up to me any more than it's up to you. Sedon wouldn't let you go, Lilith wouldn't want to go, and I do love my Cynthia Masterwife."

"Because Cynthia's an amalgam of the two of us. I got you. Yet we separate all the time. Why couldn't I leave her in my soul-self and my soul-self in someone else? Not a pureblood like Mel. That was killing them both. One of your hybrid daughters, maybe. Heard you had a couple by Outer Earth supras going back almost as long as Big Brain."

(Evidently, as per usual according to Mel-Illuminatus, who didn't mind talking out of school, as it were, two of them were the absolute stunner, Laodice by then Hent, and none other than Headmistress Virginia 'Ginny' Mannering. Apparently, neither of them remembered having his daughter, remembered ever being on the Hidden Headworld and, most remarkably in Ginny's case, having any children whatsoever.)

"Or one of the female Cosmicompanions, Angelica Schroff Zeross or this Carmine Carmichael I hear so much about. Is Hot Box really such hot stuff?"

"No point asking me. You're all the heat I can take, though I'd prefer you restricting yours to the bedroom, where it belongs. We shouldn't be arguing so much, you know. It upsets me. And you know how rash I can get when I'm upset. I did kill the Wicked Witch of the Wilderness, didn't I?"

"Sucked the life right out of her. At least, logic aside, so you've managed to convince most everyone. Including a great many I'd have thought weren't imbeciles of Weir."

"By the Master's Will, so I have. As for Carmichael, I'm saving her for Jordan Tethys. They hit it off in the Dinq, Doinq, Danq last Tantalar, before Harry brought them, 'A', 'B' and 'C', here, He's been back since; mostly to see her, I understand. She's Jordy's enticement for coming to the wedding. Goes without saying I'll leave it entirely up to them as to whether they're each other's reward for attending the wretched thing."

"I gather she's another one you've Speaking Stick stuck it to."

"Only in terms of Master's Mace sooth-speaking," he countered.

"Too bad he won't come."

"Now that really is a bad pun," he complained.

========

"Wasn't meant to be a pun," she told him. "He won't come, to the wedding I meant, because he's most responsible for freeing Demios and warning Mel to abandon ship."

========

The Master gaped at her.

He relaxed only slightly when her complexion grew even more pallid and those discomforting, always approaching feral, eyes of hers weren't quite so human-looking anymore. Were, as they sometimes struck him – which they sometimes did, strike him, mentally speaking – probing, ocular daggers.

A pincushion he wasn't; didn't appreciate her trying to change that. Hadn't she heard the only time a woman can change a man is when he's an infant in swaddling?

"And you know this ..."

"Because Cynthia Masterwife is your new High Illuminary of Weir, Master. The Witch has been thinking quite a lot about this Legendarian fellow of late. Ever since your previous High Illuminary mentioned his name in a conversation they had some while ago with respect to Hot Box and the Schroff Zerosses. I know him as well as anyone does, maybe more, and like her I know what he's capable of doing with that Brainrock quill of his. Or hers, as may be. It occurred to her ..."

"That he might be able to draw her missing fellows in this D-Brig of theirs where they are. And then draw her to them."

"As it has already occurred to you, obviously. What has additionally occurred to me, however, is Tethys, with that quill of his, could have, um, occurred everything that occurred the night of Antheal Fools Day. He was among those with your enemies in Godbad, Morg's twin and Centauri Enterprises' Fatman, when you were listening in thanks to Child Harry's rings."

"Doing more than just listening in. Extracting Dem-Wit, minus his ancient eye-stave, like the rotten tooth he is."

"Just so. Shall I tell you how he's responsible for all that happened that night? Or, and here's a better idea ... why don't you do it for me? You're not very good at keeping secrets."

Saladin shrugged, sighed to go with it, then did: "He did. Most of it anyhow. Drew the Trinondevs asleep, drew Sarpedon's eye-stave to him from Centauri Island, drew the blur Cabby the Daddy saw that delivered it, making it seem like it was Speedy doing the delivery. He probably also drew a warning for the female Dr Zeross to get her family away from the Weirdom before I could retaliate.

"Which I could still forgive her for. I've rescued hapless women from covetous covens of wretched witches before. I just wish she hadn't taken Child Harry with her. Barring Jordy's return, Kid Ringo provided the only far-sight I had access to, and I need far-sight if only to find out where they went."

"So you can get her back; get Mel back. Sister-in-law, the High Illuminary, the female Dr Zeross. Oh, Sal, silly Sal, for once just say it. You're in love with her, aren't you? With Melina Sarpedon. Master Kyprian always pictured you with garter-socks underneath your starchiest haik and Mel right there beside you, all in white, to match her skin complexion, backless back to the crowd, tossing her wedding bouquet over her head to a bunch of Illuminary bridesmaids."

"Nice try, Witch," he evaded. "You almost had me fooled. Coupling bunch with bouquet gave you away; backless back only confirmed it. Wild as you were as a kid, you were a regular fashionista when you stayed here with the liminal Nightingales, mother and daughter, and Fish back in the late Forties while attending great-grandma Copperhead."

(Master Kyprian often referred to upper level witches as liminal, meaning they walked around as good as accompanied by between-space. As for why Sal often called her Copperhead, the word 'Cyprian' on the Outer Earth referred to the metal, yes, but Copperhead – as in a Northerner snake who supported the Southern Confederacy – also came to mean 'traitor' during her lifetime.)

Saladin first encountered Wilderwitch as Wild Child Wolfie in the Thirties, but her going to the Outer Earth at the age of 15 or so – to attend to "big sister" Sorciere, Solace Sunrise by then officially Sundown, during a difficult pregnancy – tamed her. Although an inveterate face-dancer, whatever guises she assumed while in the services of SOS: the Society of Saints, then KOC: the King's Own Crimefighters, were as well-dressed as the situation allowed.

The Nightingales were not Ant Nightingales, though they were Ants; mother Eden was anyhow. Daughter Aranyani was about 6 years the Witch's junior, 5933 v/s 5927, so was still in the midst of her earliest training. By the time Sal's predecessor as Master of Weir was dying, Eden was Kyprian's designated successor as Mother Superior of the Whole Earth's Superior Sisterhood, that of the life-loving Antheans.

Had, to say the least, come a long way since arriving on the Head in 19/5939 at the age of thirty; arriving, it should be added, evidently completely unaware the Hidden Continent of Sedon's Head even existed. Was almost as if she was a natural born Ant, the same as the Witch herself was, albeit eighteen years later.

Indeed, Eden may well have been just that, a natural. Came with her parentage they believed; their parentage. Even though Eden was long gone by then, not for nothing was their similarly endowed middle sister (Fisherwoman, Scylla Neried, Lady Achigan), considered the best witch left on the Whole Earth, either side of it, before Wilderwitch escaped Limbo.

Fish was Kyprian's champion during 5950's Challenge of Weir. As they'd known for a number of years before the eldest died and the youngest disappeared, Eden and Fish were Wilderwitch's half-sisters via the Dual Entitles, Heliosophos and Miracle Memory. Half-sisters in the sense that Memory was being humanized by different Master Devas – possibly three at once in Fish's case, to judge by the three power foci then Aortic Merthetis found infantile her with, and that she still carried, or wore, in the case of her Vesica Piscis – when they were conceived.

By then, the late Forties, the Witch had her own daughter Fey in tow. Fey was conceived out there, but born in here in 5946. As for Fish, she was still mourning the death of her third child (of six, Mel told her) and second daughter, who's name was Melusine. Ever so ironically, if tragically, this Melusine, a water-breather like her parents – dad being the aforementioned Oannes Atlantean – had drowned in the Gulf of Aka in 5946.

(The Gunk of Aka, as fishism-prone Fish had already began referring to the vast, but heavily polluted, waterway south the Godbadian province of New Iraxas, as currently overseen by Governor Ferdinand Niarchos, son of dead Gomez. Indeed, it was the absolutely filthy condition of the Gulf – and her abiding desire to clean it up – that first estranged Fish from her Bandrad-descended husband, then King Achigan Auranja, whose long-ruling family owned most its oil wells and attendant industries, shortly after their teenage wedding in the mid-Thirties.)

Kyprian's attending physician in 5950, the glue that joined them all together besides Kyprian herself, was Melina still Sarpedon. As Summoning Children she, along with twin brother Demios and Sal's sister Morgianna, were a year too young to contest the Challenge, which of course was why Saladin, as was his right, called it for that year, instead of the next.

"I didn't deliberately couple bunch with bouquet, so consider yourself still fooled. Tethys didn't, though. Have you fooled. Did he? Not ever. You just weren't in the mood for sharing; not out loud, because then you'd have to condemn him too. He came here to retrieve the headless body of Gomez Niarchos. The rest of it just sort of happened."

"Don't know about 'not ever'. And the word you're looking for is 'occurred'."

"That too."

"I overheard him. We overheard him, Child Harry and I, just before Ringo rang Sarpedon up here. Jordy said he'd bring Gomez's body back to him, to his head, on the Head, in Godbad. That whatever you called it ... billboard ... just confirmed it. He's pulled the same writing in the sky stunt before; notably at the end of the Thousand Days of Disbelief, if you know your history. Which you probably don't.

"I've been expecting him to draw himself up here ever since. The High Illuminary, though – the former High Illuminary, make that – she'd been expecting him to come by as soon as Gomez's head made it to the Subcontinent. That's probably why she insisted I have Golgotha behead him in the first place. To draw him up here."

"For the same reason I just mentioned, so he could find my D-Brig friends, our friends?"

"Secondarily, maybe ... generously, at best. As the Diver may have told you, my dream, fever dream, Phantast folly, last Tantalar: it wasn't altogether just that. There was a genuine assault upon the Weirdom. One led by my half-mother, Pyrame Silverstar, yes. The proof of its genuineness was Underlord Yama Nergal's star shining in the Sedon Sphere that very night. Daddy Moloch cathonitized him for his effrontery. He'd have gone after the Pauper Priestess as well, almost certainly did, but she eluded him. We both know how, don't we?"

"She got hold of Machine-Memory; unless it was the other way around. Humanized her. And Memory's hidden Trans-Time Trigon somewhere even the Mighty Mooch can't reach. Somewhere on the Outer Earth presumably. As loathsome Lily would tell you from firsthand experience, thousands of years of it, Pyrame has always had a way out there, through All of Incain. The She-Sphinx is a good as her pet. Incain is as close to a protectorate as a pauper priestess ever gets. Is that who Mel wanted Tethys to find, Pyrame Silverstar?"

"Might have been, thirdly, after your pals. But firstly, for both of us, we want the Trigregos Talismans."

"The Diver said he destroyed them; threw them into the caldera of Sedon's Peak. Lilith saw him there, after she got herself tossed out of Hell. Somehow got into his mind; found out what had happened in Hadd, specifically to Vetala's Soldier, who had all three of the things. Was around the right time too."

"Said. You're hardly the only witch on this continent, aren't even the only one whose parents are the Dual Entities; and I doubt very much you're the only one with a soul-self. Cerebrus wasn't the last mentalist. Neither is this Psycho of yours; ours, since his actions have called into disrepute my own, even though – as hard as you still find it to accept – I did nothing."

"There's plenty of eye-staves beyond the Weirdom. Sarpedon only has the oldest one. It manufactures its own eyeorbs. They'd fit his followers', the ones I exiled thirty years ago, if the ones atop the eye-stave they left with got filled up. Plus, when it comes to mind-work compulsion's second nature for devils. As for memories, well, that's someone's name, isn't it? Chances are as a baby you learned to say it before mommy."

"So you're saying he only thought he destroyed them."

"Made to think it, might be a better way to put it. All I'm saying is it's just as possible as he did. Both the High Illuminary and I – her there, me dreaming – recognized the three girls he split into on the Slopes. They're Telepassa of Godbad's triplets. Reputedly they're hers by the Male Entity from his first lifetime, before he became the Male Entity."

"Telepassa's a highly skilled witch in her own right. Has to be in order to be selected a Ventricular of Shenon. She's not just an Althean witch-healer either. Like Harry and my sister-in-law she had training as a medical doctor in Godbad; went through an Ant Shelter, if only for the first seven years of Anthean indoctrination after her triplets were born; and started out as a Lovely Lady Afrite; the same as her mother did, I understand."

"We find them, we find the devils' thrice-cursed Godly Glories. At least that was how we had it reckoned."

"You understand?"

"Telepassa's not her real name. So the former High Illuminary claimed anyhow. Claimed as well her mother was Human Memory, Mnemosyne D'Angelo Heliopolis. Your predecessor knew her. So did you, I imagine. Whichever one of you is ascendant right this moment, I expect. Both halves of you then. She was born on the Outer Earth in the early Forties and Pyrame still had Lilith for at least part of the time in those days."

"Telepassa of Godbad is Europa Heliopolis," the Witch snapped, albeit without going crazier that she already was, two-in-one. "That's a statement. And her daughters might be her half-brother Kadmon's kids? That's a question. I'll have to file both away for future reference. And clarification. We could be related."

"You do that."

"They're not on Shenon?"

"Not anymore. The previous High Illuminary was able to ascertain that."

"Thanks to her spies."

"No, thanks to our ambassador to Witch Isle; one of her Illuminaries. And from talking to Aortic Amphitrite, among others, in Temporis and elsewhere. She's tight with my niece, the older one, the one who didn't try to kill me in Hadd. She told you she'd been busy travelling about on my behalf."

"So no one we know knows where they went."

"Not that we know. But Tethys could draw them; could draw my Trinondevs to them and draw them back here, once they're captured. They don't even need to capture them; they just need to get hold of the terrible talismans, if they still have them. Always assuming they're still inside. If they're beyond the Dome, well ..."

"Of course Tethys could also draw Child Harry and the rest of the Zerosses."

"And a Trinondev to him. Doesn't even need to be Golgotha, though they're friends; have been for decades; for however many of Tethys's lives he's had since they first met. I am too, his friend, though he does strain my patience sometimes. In any event, all a Trinondev needs do is to get close enough to rascally Ringo for him to hear my voice. He does that he'd be back here lickety-split. I told you he's an obedient boy."

"Because you've preconditioned him to obey you unconditionally."

"A Master's Mace has multiple purposes, Witch."

"Lily. The Witch doesn't know I saw the Diver on Sedon's Peak. Not unless he told her and she figured an alligator with a memory-sucking snout was me." (Truth was, being daemonic, she more like covered him long enough to seep into his mind in order to glean his relevant memories. Of course, being a demon, not a devil, she was under no obligation to tell just that, the truth.)

"Please yourself. I say the word, he hears the word, he brings back the rest of the Zerosses and Sarpedons too, with or without their consent. All Jordy has to do is draw himself up here and we'd have him." (Lilith's adventures after Machine Memory ejected her on the Moon were well known to the Master. Taking a lead from her once again current host, she often regaled him with stories about not just them at bedtime. Needless to say, with or without Pyrame Silverstar holding onto her, she had quite the her-story.)

"Stone gnomes?"

"And Trinondevs. But mostly me. Jordy comes here, he's spotted, I find out, he can't get out without my say-so. While compulsion's always an option with me, it might not work on a deviant like him. Still, he doesn't cooperate, he stays here, drinks the Naurozes' rotgut homebrew until he does cooperate. I reckon it would take maybe one bottle, two at the most, before he's begging for his quill back."

"He wasn't spotted."

"I wasn't here, that's the damnedest thing of all. You'd been at the Zerosses for over a week, I'd had Demios Sarpedon for almost precisely as long, and I chose that night of all nights for our reunion."

"So you're saying it was a fluke he came for Niarchos's body the one night you're not in the city?"

"You and I don't believe in flukes, Cynthia."

"Wilderwitch again. When we're so nice and private like now. Was it Sedon-play then?"

"Hardly. His blood brought Child Harry to me. Why would he conspire with 30-Beers to take him away from me? And it wasn't the High Illuminary, otherwise she never would have had me cut off Gomez's head. No, he may be a drunk, but he isn't an excessively stupid drunk. I suspect he knew what we were up to and did a drawing. Of me.

"His drawings fill in, you know. He can pan them backwards, like a God-badian or Outer Earth movie camera on a crane. I've seen him do it, many times. In a variety of different incarnations as well. The moment my background wasn't of Cabalarkon City anymore, he drew himself up here. Had the headless manikin of Gomez Niarchos all prepared; must have. The clothing, everything about it, was perfect. And who'd have noticed? Wasn't like anyone would give blood to a headless Sleeper. Be an awfully one-sided conversation if they did, wouldn't it?"

"But he didn't draw Demios away. Everyone we interviewed who saw him vanish said it was in a ring."

"Tethys could have faked that as well but, more than likely, no, you're right. Sarpedon was atop Skyrise. He'd already used his antique eye-stave to command stone gnomes to build that billboard thing and I wasn't around to countermand him. He'd used it to wake most everyone up. Was waiting for my return.

"Like Capputis said when he warned us, Sarpedon must have intended to take me on directly, as soon as I returned, only I was delayed by your little show of pique over Fobbiat. Child Harry or one the Zeross girls ringed him away, involuntarily, because if he had wanted to get away earlier Tethys would have happily obliged. He's a wuss that way. Knows he's the only one who comes back besides Pusan Wander-lust; much prefers his friends altogether alive and unpossessed, even by a Sangazur."

"So he obliged him the other way, by bringing him his eye-stave. That's how I figure it too. Great minds and all that."

"For which I intend to congratulate him."

"Before or after he cooperates."

"Probably before. As a further incentive for him to cooperate."

"Maybe it's a good thing he won't come then. Playing a Trigregos Gambit only results in losers. Look what happened to Vetala's Soldier, Cosmicaptain Dmetri Dio-mad, Demonites' son by Hot Rox, once he got hold of all three of them. Even the scent of them, according to the Diver anyways, drove the last three firstborn devic goddesses, Umashakti Silvercloud, Methandra Thanatos and Freespirit Nihila, who thinks I'm her incarnation, completely insane."

"Because you born with her inside you, like Barsine Mandam was with Ner-gal Vetala inside her and Copperhead reckoned the previous High Illuminary with Amalthea Brand, Lazareme's Female Healer, inside her. That her getting hold of the devil's caduceus when she was outside in the Thirties and Forties brought her abilities to the fore."

Wilderwitch had heard all that before. "The first two had to be rescued by their brood brothers, Byron's Savage Storm and Varuna Mithras's King Cold. Then the four of them just left Nihila dangling, as good as dead again, on the back of Vetala's Brainrock throne. Hell's Rotting Teeth, look what happened to the Female Unity, both pre-Nihila and post-Harmonia.

"Damnation, look what happened to us, to me; look what happened to the Byronic Nucleus, look what happened to the Damnation Brigade, Cerebrus for sure, all because I put on the Crimson Corona back in Vancouver, then insisted the Nucleoids let me wear it when they brought us inside. And I didn't even have it after midway through the Faerie Garden."

"You haven't done too badly."

"Maybe not so much so lately, but my morning conversations with the bottom of a toilet bowl haven't exactly been a piece of cake. Unless I'd indulged in one the night before."

"Were you as gross prior to being so daemonic?" (Saladin preferred daemonic, meaning genius, to demonic, meaning – basically – man-eating monster.)

"You'd have to ask my friends that; if we could find any of them."

"Oh, we will. Eventually. Half the Headworld knows we're looking for the Zerosses by now. Pretty soon half the Headworld's going to know we have the wherewithal to fetch them, too. Or punish whomever's harbouring them. Tethys will come up here for sure then. It'd be too good a story to miss. What'll be the spin he puts on it, I wonder. Extraterrestrial technology versus that of the Outer Earth, in the form of Centauri Enterprises? Wouldn't be much of a spin if he did. Because that's what it'll be."

"Boys and their toys, eh? Same old, same old; shame old, shame old, dick dildo. It comes down to that we'll have to fire an entire ambassadorial corps. Which I've – or should I say we've? – been urging you to do anyways, since most of them are probably at least as loyal to Mel as they are to you."

"Duly noted. Again. I told you I've taken it under advisement. Got anything more concrete to offer? Because if you don't, I do."

"Concrete as in hard, I got you." Wilderwitch, whichever witch it was, didn't snicker; didn't titter, either. "Really, Master, one of these days you're going to have to grow up; in terms of maturation, not masturbation. Since you're in offering mode, though, I think I'll take you up on the offer you intended to make."

"Which was?"

"Is. In order to demonstrate I'm more than an adequate replacement for Melina in all respects – except when it comes to performing wedding ceremonies, which I'll always refuse to do – you're sending me back to the Zerosses' hideaway. Once there I'm to poke around some more. Mel's fallible, you're persuaded. She must have left something behind to give us an idea where she went. We just haven't found it yet. Besides, you sniffle, while I love you lying on your butt, I hate seeing you sitting on it. You say there's nothing you like better than a challenge, take this one and do us both proud. Do both halves of both of us proud."

"She's Child Harry and her daughters. They've Harry's rings. She's smart she's gone to the Outer Earth."

"Then I'll go to the Outer Earth. Harry's rings aren't the only way out there. Fey got through somehow, somewhere. The Stationary SAG Gap, the pathway we Ants use off to the side of the main caldera on Sedon's Peak, comes to mind. You're supposed to be pregnant in order to access it and, while Fey might only be fat, I'm definitely that. So is my soul-self.

"The Kore Gap on Apple Isle might be open again; Al Sentalli's NAG Gap, after Nagasaki, the link-way from Aka Godbad City to the Outer Earth's Centauri Island, might not be as shut down as everyone thinks. Probably isn't if you're right and this Europa-slash-Telepassa fled outside with her triplets and the Trigregos Talismans. Stands to reason it'd be the easiest one for a Godbadian to access."

"Except the Fatman blew it up, though not before All's whelp, Sharkczar, the mandroid monstrosity that almost got me and Jordy stewed alive seven years ago, came through it."

"All the more challenge, then. All of Incain is Pyrame's way through the Dome. The She-Sphinx is linked to its Egyptian counterpart and Pyrame's way isn't just Pyrame's way. Although I'll grant you it's dependent on All's mood, I've used it before, and not just as Lilith-Pyrame. OMP-Akbar got back to Temporis by himself last Tantalar, which suggests there's at least one there, too.

"You're my High Illuminary now. Best stay away from Lakshmi of Lemuria."

"Point taken. Trans-Time Trigon is another obvious way out, assuming it isn't there already. Europa-Telepassa might be Human Memory's daughter. Memory of the Angels may or may not be the basis for Machine-Memory. But Wilderwitch definitely is Miracle Memory's half-daughter. Mothers have been known to do daughters favours."

"Not at the risk of revealing where they're hiding their Trigon. Sedon's primary concern is his unborn Sed-son. He's keeping an eye on him full time, in case you haven't figured that out yet. How else do you think the foetus survived after you, your Lily aspect, died and I burned your husk to ash? Pyrame wants to take Lilith back; wants to mesh her, mesh them both, Sed-son inside them, with Machine-Memory, like they were before, probably dozens of times.

"That'd free up the Witch and her soul-self, but if you think Sedon's going to let that happen, you're just not thinking. He knows Machine-Memory's still around, knows she and Pyrame are a unit again, and now knows, if he hadn't already, that Heliosophos is being preserved, as a bifurcated being, by Lord Yajur."

"Because you told him."

"Because he learns from osmosis. But also because *you* told me, yes; though, like I said, he probably knew everything anyhow. Machine-Memory's as much his mortal enemy as her male counterpart; like staff, like distaff. You think he's going to give her control over the reproductive processes leading up to Sed-sons now that she's finally figured out that whoever has Lilith alone, not Lilith-Pyrame together, gains the key to keeping up the Dome?"

"That's why he agreed to take a chance on rejuvenating Harry. He wanted to farm her out. Have Child Harry bring in new potential mamas from both sides of the Dome, stick lithesome Lily in them, and let you play surrogate Sal-Stud-Stallion over and over again, just like you did before, when you were trying to singlehanded-ly revitalize the Utopian race."

"Lithesome certainly sounds better than loathsome."

"Does to me, too. Care to comment?"

"Wasn't a matter of singlehandedly then. Not after we established that, with the proper mates, any fertile Utopian man and any fertile Utopian woman could just close their eyes and think of Utopia. Was, boiled down to the bare bones of it, just a matter of the High Illuminary picking out the right pairs. Which was another reason she was so invaluable."

"Will be now, though, won't it. There's only one fertile you. There always has been only one Demon Queen. Except, her Demon King can't start doing it until my Sed-son is born and ludicrous Lily's ready for another roll in the heaving hay of his heavenly hotel for star-stuck devils."

"Preferred lithesome. Heaving hay isn't bad. Never thought of Skyrise as a heavenly hotel for devils, so congrats on that, too."

"Thanks. But even you should agree the situation is ludicrous, Sal. Even if he sets Lily up in a different body, leaving me to do the heavy birthing, he won't be able to do it again, not with the same guarantee of success. Not so long as the Dual Entities are out there and Memory knows what she does now. They, even if it's just she, will find a way to thwart him."

"First of all, while you're right about there being only one Demon Queen, he doesn't need me, never has, just someone fertile to possess. Second of all ..."

"You shouldn't be saying All so much. It's like saying 'here, kitty, kitty,' in an African game farm. The cubs might come, but so might Mr and Mrs Man-eating Lion." She was playing on Sal's fear that All of Incain would eventually kill him. Also the twin facts that Memory made All, albeit as Ginny the Gynosphinx, and that Pyrame was at home in her; in both of them, come to that: All and Memory.

"And you're like a little kid who keeps interrupting because they're afraid of being left out of the conversation."

"Mine was funnier."

"In your opinion. Anyhow Sedon is as stuck as they are; Pyrame-Memory teleports you to them, he finds out where they are. But he still has to find a way to get rid of them without losing Lilith like he did in '50. All the more reason ... sorry. And that's another reason you can't leave the Weirdom. Sedon's in control here. He doesn't want to give the Entities the opportunity to take him on at a place or time of their choosing."

"Entity," she corrected him, almost reflexively. Then brightened up, slipped back into teasing mode. "Seems I'm doubly privileged. I may not have a guardian angel protecting me like Gloriel used to think she had. I've got a guardian devil instead, the Guardian Devil, the All-Father of All Devils, to go along with being occupied by a demon, the Mother of All Demons."

"Now you're saying 'All' too much. Deliberately too, I'm thinking. You'll be saying it all night if I don't let you go. So, all right, you can go. Just don't go too far. If you can stick your soul-self in a hybrid I'm betting your Guardian Devil can as well. Intriguing notion, though. I wonder how Carmine would feel waking up being six months pregnant."

"Fat, I'm not altogether guessing. But don't worry, Sal. I'll be a good gal pal. I'll even take Golgotha and a couple of his bravos with me just to make sure I don't stray. Maybe I'll ask Thobruk Grudal, Mel's shadow. He's been down in the dumps ever since he lost her again; albeit possibly not due to devils this time. We won't be long, a week at the most."

"Take Grudal, but leave Nauroz behind. I may have need of him here. Not just because he's popular with the people, either. Practise makes perfect and he's a natural, albeit non-born trainer. He's also proficient at flying vimanas. And we do want to provide our incoming guests with an entertaining fanfare, don't we?"

"Even beyond the twenty-mile sea-limit."

"If necessary way beyond it. Besides, it'll be good for Grudal to get away. Even if I am a year older than him, he and I grew up together. Boy-palled around as kids. I hate leaving him on guard duty out on the Slopes just because the invidious healer he was supposed to be body-guarding befuddled him."

"Boy-palled around because, being both hybrids, no pureblood would pal around with either of you, I'm to understand. Including the Sarpedons, I'm to take that as a given."

"So you are, Miss Perceptiveness."

"That'd be Mrs Perceptiveness, Mr Perceptive. Grudal it is then. Do me one further favour. Besides tempting fate and saying All, all too much. Stay away from Carmine Carmichael if you start missing me too much."

"Not a chance of that."

"Um, Sal. You might want to rephrase that."

"So I might. Sorry. I will and I won't. Will miss you and there's not a chance I'll go anywhere near Hot Box. Do me a favour of your own, though. Bring back some salt."

"Huh?"

"For all the humble pie you keep making me eat." He felt good jokes should always be recycled. Even if no one laughed at them.

========

For a vimana Broom was a cheap hussy with a sleek chassis. She'd now fly for any-one with the proper training. So it was Cynthia Masterwife flew her up the coast, but Thobruk Grudal flew her back, with sinful Cynthia sitting in the co-pilot's seat. Saladin Devason might have wondered about that, if he ever found about it. Which he might have, eventually.

He did wonder why, after weeks of refusing to do anything more than act as his hostess and, with him beside her, participate at the wedding as an approving observer only, she'd finally decided to do the High Illuminary's duty and perform the ceremony itself. When he asked her she simply shrugged, disturbingly Mel-like; said she'd changed her mind. She could have been more forthcoming; said she changed half her mind.

Had it exchanged, rather.

****

NINE-DEMON: **Wilderwitch's Abduction**

========

Towards The Summer Solstice 5981

Midsummer's Day was rapidly approaching.

It wouldn't be just the marriage between Capputis Masterson and the usurper Lakshmi Arthadot – she as much of Temporis as Lemuria these days – that would make it memorable. Even after nearly three decades, certain supras, former supras, and not just supranormals, found midsummer days memorable. So did at least one of their daughters.

So too would Wilderwitch Two, if she existed. Which-witch she didn't. Was hoping for a comeback. Her 28th birthday was supposed to be on or about Midsummer.

Too bad she was, perhaps understandably, if not necessarily forgivably, so forgetful.

========

Most shooting stars shot downwards, toward a planet's surface. One star shot upwards first, toward heaven, Sedon Sphere that the Hidden Headworld's immediately beyond atmospheric heaven was. By the time she did come down, which she always did, eventually, all too close to All and hers, the She-Sphinx's, and therefore Pyrame Silverstar's, Prison Beach of Incain, which she virtually never did – Irisiel Mercherm wasn't stupid – Tsishah Twilight had already resigned herself to her graveyard fate.

Then, after Irisiel delivered her message to Tsishah and her remaining Panharmonium Project pushers, a nearly top of the totem pole devil – in terms of sheer, albeit perhaps not unmatched, abilities – having taken the place of an azura most of half a year earlier, things suddenly started looking up.

Weren't looking quite so high as where the devils' Angelus or 'Keryx' had just been. Tsishah wouldn't be taking Herr Hel's place in the She-Sphinx's Stopstone saddle; wouldn't be riding All through the night's sky, chasing down the night's – sometimes also the day's – biggest eye. No one would. But chances were she wouldn't be dying either.

Her new job, the assignment she'd accepted, was to get Fisherwoman's Mighty Mollusc in the semi-celestial sky to stand still long enough to get swamped then solidified big time – Stopstone Shit big time – should that chance present itself. Which, while it still might, probably wouldn't needs be taken anymore. It was all a matter of establishing equality, a balance, between everyone: devil, faerie, any sort of azura, any human, daemon genii and, yes, even man-eating demons, plus any other sentient being you cared to mention.

Which was the whole point of the Panharmonium Project, the Pauper Priestess put to her. And if Freespirit Nihila – ex-Harmony, formerly Datong Harmonia, the one-time Unity of Balance, due to circumstances she could have controlled, but head-strongly chose not to – was no longer capable of performing said-task, well then, someone else would have to do it for her. Harmony's peculiarly post-Summoning-Child-incarnation, for example.

Freespirit Wilderwitch, for a fact.

========

So much of her life had been so hectic of late she forgot it was approaching the 28th anniversary of Sorciere's murder, and consequential mutilation, while she was giving birth to an obviously never-named girl-child. So much of both halves of her life since the morning of the Spring Equinox had been so hectic she'd also forgotten Shaman Manitoulin, who had helped raise both her, Solace born Sunrise, and her eventually legal husband, John Sundown, had died that same day.

Truth told, their entire village had been massacred on the 22nd of June 1953, on or about that year's Midsummer's Day. Truth told also, the massacre was carried out by The Rache under the leadership of Grave's Head and Man-Monster Machine, as Shamanitoulin identified them, howsoever equivocally, with his final breath.

The former, Grave's Head, turned out not to be Will Tombstone, the Summoning-aged, Texas-raised, supranormal once codenamed the Solidium Kid, among other things: Kid Cemetery for one; Straight Shooter as he, being an American patriot, preferred. The latter, nonetheless, did turn out to be Steltsar, a supra-cyborg by then more machine than man.

John Sundown and Raven's Head killed them both during his – more so than her – Vengeance Quest throughout late '53 and early '54. Killed most of The Rache as well. And most of the Warriors of the Writhing Moon. Even managed to kill Grave's Head, though he turned out to be Jesus Mandam, Wiccan Warlock, the Boulder-Brain Conqueror, King Conqueror or Conquering Christ, rather than Crackshot, yet another of Kid Cemetery's noms de guerre.

Only went to prove that bit about stuff happening. Stuff did.

What neither Sundown nor Raven's Head knew – mostly because they either didn't know, or didn't remember, anything about Sedon's Head – was that Sorciere did not die having a girl-child. She died having a boy-child. This boy-child might have been a small case sedon, one of potentially dozens of Sed-sons conceived in Vancouver City the previous autumnal equinox. Could be, even if there was just the one, he would grow up to become the last one left on the Outer Earth besides Sedon St Synne, who was locked up as a war criminal in Spandau Prison at the time and, approaching 80, wasn't expected to last too much longer anyways.

Jesse realized this. He had a list of supras and their spouses or bed-bouncing partners, be they other supras or just normal men and women, who'd been in the city when Wilderwitch did her ecdysiast routine in the Hotel Vancouver's ballroom and thereby got the balls rolling, mostly in the sack; her with Jervis Murray, a reproductive dead-end if there was one. Had this list because he'd been the one who invited most of them.

Did not invite anyone to possess them, however. Didn't need to; not once large case Sedon brought not just Lady Lust with him from the Inner Earth's night sky.

The Rache raiding party Jesse led that day as the Boulder Brain Conqueror (hence the Grave's Head misidentification), led that day in the Rocky Mountains' early summer season, was only one of many. They were harvesting boy-babies, leaving specially prepared Stopstone, mantel or homunculus replicates of stillborns – even if sometimes they were of the wrong sex – behind to take their place.

The Rache, a Nazi Revenge Squad made up mostly of surviving European Axis supranormals, and their allies, including the Warriors of the Writhing Moon, their Japanese equivalent, intended to raise them as a favour to their god, the Devil, capitalized. The idea of course was to reap his – said Devil's, not Jesse's – favours in return. It didn't quite work out that way. Wasn't supposed to; not that he, Jess, was one for sharing.

Wasn't much for nurture, either. He had figured out how to up the ante far beyond anything allowed in Monte Carlo or Las Vegas; to turn what was until then a typical Sedonplay along the lines of the birth of Saladin Devason in 5919, and the next year's Summoning, into a Godsend. Had found a way to get the Moloch Sedon out of Cathonia physically.

To force him to come out in order to retrieve (reap?) his potential Sed-sons, in their diapered-dozens, before the often undeniably powerful, but even more often, disappointingly so, dark-arts-duped charlatans and fools in The Rache could sacrifice them. And, in doing so, to stand still long enough to be dumped upon by a Sundown-dropped-from-above-Salvation-Island, Soviet-constructed H-bomb.

What need had they of spies when they had Jesus Mandam and he, as Wiccan Warlock, not only had access to Utopian technology on the Hidden Headworld, he understood much of it?

========

Cynthia Masterwife, her Wilderwitch half anyhow, was reminded of Sorciere's death in an only momentarily startling, but nonetheless brain-boggling manner.

Thobruk Grudal and her, with her flying Broom, arrived at the Zerosses' unexpectedly heavily guarded hideaway on the coast of Fearsome Fobbiat without incident. (Apparently Saladin had detached a lance of Trinondevs to the estate just in case Mel et al returned. Hadn't bothered telling her, however.) Two frustratingly clueless days later, she walked into the room Melina long Zeross, in her capacity as the High Illuminary of Weir, called her study and everyone else called off-limits.

There, at Mel-Illuminatus's work table, flipping through old photograph albums, sat Sorciere.

As usual Thobruk Grudal and a couple of Trinondev veterans around the same age as him – which might make them Summoning Children or near enough – were shadowing her. Seeing the evident newcomer they reacted protectively, throwing up mental force shields around the Master's six months' pregnant wife.

Cynthia raised her own metallic marigold, her Mexican Flower of the Dead, albeit only on the 1st and 2nd of November beyond the Dome, eyeorb open. "It's okay, boys. You can drop the thought-bubbles. I can see through illusions. Badly aging witches about to break their noses dropping dead on the table in front of them scare me even less than regular ones do. Even if she's gone stark raving I'll have no problem hastening the process to the degree it's required."

Grudal hesitated. To his eyes the sitting witch looked like an attractive Irache no older than her early-to-mid thirties. And that in ordinary human, as opposed to ordinary, not even necessarily fully pureblood Utopian, terms. He'd met her a number of times over the last couple of decades; seen her not even six months previously in Skyrise, accompanied by the recurring Traveller, Pusan Wanderlust, an unmistak-able, always female faun or fauna.

And, while it was true she usually did look much the same, he understood that wasn't because she wore a glamour. Ostensibly she wore a debrained demon. Which, since it did, was why she always looked much the same. Suspicious sort that he was, the bearded Summoning Child often wondered if she was instead already dead.

He'd spent a great deal of his adult life as Mel's minder; notwithstanding his own marriage, over twenty-five years earlier and – as they say – counting, spent vir-tually all of it, virtually his entire life, being her admirer. While that last was never to be more than just that, an unrequited infatuation, he'd been all over both sides of the Cathonic Zone with Melina nee Sarpedon Zeross.

So, even if he hadn't been in Hadd with Golgotha Nauroz and the rest of his there, tragically decimated, squadron this last time – and the contingent's survivors included a couple of the men standing beside him right this minute – he knew about all there was to know about Dead Things. Had encountered more than a few in his 60+ years of life. Many were Iraches; were born, bred and all too often died, as in were sacrificed, Iraches.

(Decades ago, down Godbad way, an Irache rabble-rouser by the unlikely name of Reilly Haddeus – who'd been back in Aka Godbad again, briefly, at the end of Maruta according to the High Illuminary's 'sources' there – tried to put a stop to that by sacrificing Godbadians in their stead. Was quite the his-story, was Haddeus. Couldn't have been him in Godbad, though.

(After a long hunt, Second Fangs, Janna Fangfingers, tracked him down. Didn't so much sacrifice as tore him into shreds; shreds she proceeded to feed to her oversized vultures' chicks.)

Some Dead Things, be they Irache or non-Irache, didn't even smell bad. Occa-sionally a few did bite ... and not in the sense of the defiant Outer Earth term 'Bite me!' either.

========

Three more Trinondevs, albeit ones not in the usual Arabic or Middle Eastern style robes of regular Warriors Elite like Thobruk and his confrères, came into the study from off the balcony. They were dressed in basic denim, pants and shirts, along with sturdy boots. Steel toes? Combat boots? Had, it seemed to her, been outside taking in the glorious view of the ocean afforded from there. Had, Cynthia Masterwife finally perceived, dulled sort that she was, been waiting for her.

The two Trinondevs flanking their all-too-familiar leader were manifesting identical gargoyles (grotesques): a white mare's head; were horse heads with big, frighteningly large teeth. Were Night Mare's heads. And Grudal was waiting for the lead one's orders. And the youngest of the three entering was striped. And ...

"Oh, I see," both read and said Cynthia, somehow maintaining her non-La-thakran cool, in the late springtime's heat — no air-conditioning in Cabalarkon; at least not in that part of it. "Nightmares?" she deliberately misinterpreted, knowing bloody well whose symbol they once were; whose psychopomp one once was equal-ly so. "Don't tell me you're afraid of witches."

"Only in the sense they're so unpredictable," said the lead one, the one she recognized.

"Been a while, Ace."

========

Demios Sarpedon, once the supranormal codenamed Blackguard, then the Ace of Spades, hadn't aged very much in 25½ years. As a pureblood Utopian, he wouldn't have. Did look somewhat haggard; had clearly led a rough life. Cynthia didn't approve of the way he'd entirely shaved his head but, hey, when you're in a state of evidently arrested envelopment, as the Master once described a condition similar to the one she found herself in this minute, it wasn't her place to criticize.

The irony of it was, when Sal used that ever-so-clever, for him, term, he was referring to the very man standing so cockily in the door frame.

Anytime would be fine, Guardian Devil.

"Not sure how I should address you, woman."

"Given the precariousness of your situation," Cynthia provoked, she hoped convincingly, reversing the field, "I'd recommend deferential politeness. Start with 'your highness' then follow it with abasement and a suitably grovelling apology." The Irache witch, the one who looked scarily like Sorciere, smiled at that.

"Release her, Grudal," Sarpedon ordered. So much for the notion they'd raised their thought-shields protectively.

"You sure that's wise, sir?" said the Trinondev, Mel's long time minder, Cynthia silently reminded herself.

"No. What I am is sure of is that's what I said." Not waiting for compliance, Sarpedon opened the eyeorb atop his eye-stave.

His was oldest left in the world — any world, always assuming Second Weir-world, where it was reputedly manufactured, and where may yet dwell the Trigregos Sisters, no longer existed. (Which may or may not be true.) Seniority counted. Its thus revealed, extruded eyeball emitted what must have been akin to devic eyefire, only its colouration was more like that of a fireworks display than a flame.

The force fields surrounding her dissipated under its kaleidoscopic influence. So did the one she'd cast about herself. Her Metallic Marigold abruptly started to heat up, becoming too hot to handle. The false Sorciere shot Demios a glance. He quit smiling. Her stunted eye-staff equally all of sudden felt normal again.

Cynthia Masterwife was feeling her weight, wanted to sit down. Didn't want to give him the satisfaction of showing her babies' belly-wrought weakness. Or unleashing her fearsome soul-self, though that was next. Once she sat down of course. Might lose her ability to stand once she loosed it. Wouldn't be the first time; would be the first time in six months of being baby-bellied, though.

"I'm waiting for the grovelling, Dem-wit."

Ignoring her entirely, he turned to the witch at the table. "You sure she's salvageable, Tsishah?" (Name confirmed her suspicions. Had why she looked so much like Sorciere, too.)

The apparent Irache regarded her, over under sideways down, from her place behind the table. She seemed entirely unflustered. "You know me, daddy Dem. I'm not sure of much of anything anymore. Your sister, though, thought they both were; both halves of her. I'm just hoping they're as separable as they are salvageable."

"I've seen them together, Aortic," said Grudal. "Seen them together separately, I mean. So they are."

"Thobruk Grudal," snorted Cynthia, still standing, regally defiant. "Traitor to the state."

Like Mata Hari before the firing squad, she supposed, though that Mata (there'd been a Mata in the Suprawar as well, on the Axis side — the Witch's perhaps exact contemporary, Ramona Avar, was her daughter by Count Viper) was no proper witch. For reasons having nothing to do with sitting down – reasons Tsishah's words had just emphatically warned against, howsoever unintentionally – she decided to hold off on releasing her soul-self.

They want us separate, let them separate us. It was a bargaining chip anyway. Such were her thoughts. These were her words, first to Grudal: "The Master will be sorely disappointed to have to have you executed. Not you, though, daddy Dem. He'd be so delighted he might even do it himself. That's cute by the way. A witch hiding under a glamour of being our friend Sorciere calling you daddy. Why don't you just dispel it, Tsishah. Show Daddy Dimwit how much older and sicker you look than he does."

"I'm not liking you," said this Tsishah, not dispelling the glamour. "Not liking much of anything right now, but not liking you most of all. Or have I mentioned that already?"

"Cynthia Masterwife is not a likable person," Grudal confirmed. "One hopes you will be more pleasant to get along with, after the exchange is made."

"There will be no more Cynthia Masterwife when that happens, Thobruk," said the sitting witch. "There may be a Cynthia Master's Daughter, though. We just haven't got that far yet."

"Whoa," demanded the standing witch, not that she was all witch. This had just gone beyond gamesmanship, not that there was much chance of either of them, this Tsishah either, backing down. "What exchange? What are you playing at, Demios. And why's your non-daughter, if I recall her-story correctly, playing at being Sorciere?"

"Deals have been struck, whatever you are," Sarpedon responded, neither taking his eyes off Cynthia, nor letting the eye sticking out of his eye-stave's eyeorb lose its focus on her. "My twin sister, the soon-to-be-again High Illuminary of Weir, will be happy to explain everything to you, or at least to your Witch-half, once she arrives. As for your demon-half, I'll let her milk Tsishah's brain for it."

Tsishah folded the photo album shut. Even more meaningfully-eyed Cynthia Masterwife. "Shouldn't you be sitting down?" she said, echoing her thoughts, "Bloody Mary, Mother of Celestial Blob, you look about ready to topple over. My part of the deal, part of it anyhow, is to make sure your Sed-son isn't damaged."

"Your part of the deal?"

"I'm good with demons. Or I was. Used to wear one as a matter of fact more so than necessity. At least so I thought."

"You needed it. That's why you look so lousy under your glamour. How'd you lose it. Or did it lose you?"

"For all of Mel's Christian cant about demons being confined to the hell-fires of eternal damnation, they're extremely flammable. Unfortunately mine didn't leave enough ash behind for me to be re-sprinkled with it. As for why I'm wearing a glamour, call it cosmetic. I prefer those who see me now, see me as I was rather than as I am."

"How about I call it vanity? Because that's what it is."

"As you say. As for what it was, it did look like this Sorciere of yours, not that I ever met her. Not as such. Did meet her daughter. She was a Shah, too; a Shahiyeda, not a Tsishah. We were born on the same day, in the same place and at the same time. I became a Faerie Queen, she became a Demon Queen. It's a long story. Sit down and I'll tell it to you."

Cynthia Masterwife was severely tempted. She had many a question to ask; in both voices, if it got that far. With her Guardian Devil showing no signs of being divinely intercessory, she felt she should at least be comfortable.

One thing was immediately bothering her: "Cynthia Master's Daughter?"

Before Tsishah, nor anyone else there, could respond, something fluttered through the left-open, sliding door to the balcony. It had wings coming out of its back, angel-like, a serpent entwining either arm and a bubble-like head with no hair on it, but possessed of some very recognizable features.

Was also very white. Everything about it was white: skin, wings, serpents, even its outfit, which seemed to have been inspired by a man's tuxedo. With flared tails, yes, but also with its own kind of stick-like tail extending out of its spine or tail bone between them. Not that this thing was male, unless it was a male with big bosoms. Everything except its features was white. They looked pasted on the bulbous head. Were of a lemonade-yellow lollipop-top, with a happy face sketched upon it.

That was enough for Cynthia Masterwife. "I think I will have a chair."

========

Together with Grudal and Trinondevs she left with, Cynthia Masterwife, the Weirdom's by now familiar, six months pregnant White Goddess and recently appointed official (if not in the hearts of the majority of its people) High Illuminary, returned from the vanished Zerosses' former hideaway on the coast of Fobbiat a couple of days before Midsummer's Eve. Was full of news.

Well, half of her familiar self was full of it anyhow.

========

"You were brilliant," she told Saladin Devason triumphantly, careful to plump his ego. "Sending Thobruk along instead of Golgotha was positively brilliant, even prescient. He knew the lay of the land, as it were. Twigged me as to just how anal Mel was; how meticulous, I should say. Seems one of hers and Harry's photo albums wasn't with the rest of them. We found the negatives, though. They're in the Whiplash Range, just above Incain. Positively."

"I know," said Sal. "I've already sent Golgotha and a few of his men there in one of your vimanas. Given how fast they fly they should have arrived already. All I'm waiting for now is for them to get close enough to Child Harry for me to order him, through their eye-staves, to fetch them home. I've always felt the father of the groom deserves a wedding present too."

Saladin smiled; thought that approaching aphoristic. She didn't.

"How ... who told you?"

He caught himself frowning. Somehow or other Cynthia didn't seem herself. Was that the best she could do? Ordinarily she would have reposted with some snappy comeback. Just as he was about to answer, she stiffened. Sal had seen the likes of it before, coming out of her as well as going into her. Coming over her was a more accurate way of putting it this time.

It was licentious Lilith. Couldn't call her Lilith-Gomorrah anymore. As she'd told him during one of their private conversations together while the Witch thought she, both halves of her, was asleep, Gomorrah was only a name she acquired a very, very long time ago, albeit perhaps not by her standards; acquired well over 4000 years ago, to be more precise, and then only after Pyrame Silverstar had possession of her.

As pregnant as Cynthia, which wasn't odd, she was in complete Haunted Dustmound, Black Widow guise; her Miss Murkiness raiment enlarged to accommodate the pregnancy. And that was a bit odd. Of late, Lily's Dark Lady likeness (aka Olivia Tenebrous) – which he found quite attractive – had been subsumed within the Witch's soul-self. Which he found as loathsome as it was fearsome. So this was a decided improvement. Then it wasn't.

She transmogrified into something even worse. It was reminiscent of a crocodile-headed pterodactyl, a terrifying baby-belly-bloated reptilian with really big, black and ever-so-traditional wings – traditional for a demon – forming from her gown and expanding out of her upper back. Had a fabulously long tongue; forked of course.

It caught something between-space, pulled it out. Whereupon she, whatever she'd become, devoured it. Wasn't a pregnant ant, though it did crunch as she chewed. Wasn't an illusion either. Not unless the sound of it crunching was illusory. Then she was back to her still six months pregnant, white goddess self.

He didn't swallow his tongue. Was quite proud of that. Instead he used it. To answer her: "I think you just ate her."

========

"All is in readiness, Priestess?"

"Of course All is in readiness. She always is."

"I didn't mean the She-Sphinx. I meant, you know, is everything ready."

"It will be, once we hear from your brother, Traveller."

========

Like a spider's web the catacombs spread throughout the underside of the city. Tendrils of it, in the form of transportation tunnels leftover from bygone centuries when everything functioned the way they were built to function, some of them presumably still open, led to the Slopes of the Sleepers.

There were no rails or tracks in these tendril-tunnels. So they weren't meant for anything approximating the bullet-trains found on today's Outer Earth. Or even in bigger cities on the Godbadian subcontinent. As for what they were meant for, that was anyone's guess. Well, not anyone's — there were many apparent vehicles on display in the Grand Cathedral. Some might have been used down here.

For the most part, the tunnels were as sturdy as ever. Dependent how clear, and for how far the one you chose remained uncluttered by detritus left behind, as opposed to collapsing floors, walls or ceilings, you could walk, run, hitch a lift on one of those glorified golf-carts stone gnomes somehow managed to keep working, ride a donkey or be a pallbearer on a horse-drawn dray hearse through them to the Slopes of the Sleepers anytime one was available.

Which, remarkably, was fairly often. Remarkably because it was a rare month any of the imbeciles of Weir were even diagnosed as suffering from Imminent Death; was a rarer year any of them died before they were placed in a tub of Cathonic Fluid and thereafter transported to the Slopes of the Sleepers for entombment.

Never less than two hundred and fifty miles (400 km) from the pupil-port of Cabalarkon City, the Slopes were a vast ovular area, the orbit of Sedon's Devic Eye, that somehow formed an effective buffer separating the Weirdom from the more than a thousand years' uninhabitable Ghostlands, formerly the Elysian Fields, containing as it did then old Valhalla.

It was from the Ghosts, shortly after four members of the Damnation Brigade (John Sundown, Raven's Head, OMP-Akbar and Dervish Furie) returned from Hadd over six months ago now, that Underlord Yama Nergal, the devic Grim Reaper, with Trigregos Diver and the freakish-looking Pauper Priestess (Pyrame Silverstar) – her upper head had three triangular sides to it; peering out of each was a single eye, that of Providence, like the one on the American dollar bill – launched what was almost universally perceived to be the Master's fever dream made manifest.

The Slopes were called such because there, in caves and culverts cut into the faraway-from-here, barrow-like hills or mounds, some of which contained covered-over millennial ships, 'slept' almost all the Trinondevs who had come to Earth nearly six thousand years earlier. Their mission then, what remained that of the Utopians of Weir on Earth now, their reason-for-being, was to destroy the Moloch Sedon, the mighty eye-mouth not always in sky. Rather, the mighty eye-mouth not always in the sky simultaneously.

(Some devils – APM All-Eyes being a notable other one – could be in two places at the same time.)

Not only him of course. Just as much their target were his three sons, the Thrygragos Brothers — one of whom, from all evidence, was dead already, had been since 4376 YD; another of whom shone out of the night's sky nowadays; and a third … well, no one was too sure what had become of Thrygragos Lazareme. Them and their Master Deva sons and daughters, the true devils, the third generation of devazurkind.

(Presumably Nihila-Harmony's Great God of a father – also Thrygragos Everyman, whom Cabalarkon's Sarpedon underclass once actually worshipped, albeit most of 1500 years ago during the reign of the fabled Death's Head Hellion, Morgan Abyss, the Melusine Master of Weir – remained asleep between-space somewhere on Tympani, Sedon's Eardrum, aka the Isle of the Undying One. That was certainly the last place anyone sentient, man, devil or deviant, as in Jordan Tethys, had seen him.)

Indeed, most of the Utopian men, women and children who ever lived in Cabalarkon's Weirdom were entombed within the Slopes. Here, in the catacombs themselves, 'slept' virtually every former Master of Weir on Earth. An exception was the last Master, Kyprian Somata. She didn't sleep; only those who could be awakened could be considered Sleepers.

Kyprian, whom Saladin sometimes referred to as Copperhead, an American Civil War term for traitor, was dead. Good and dead; unless it was bad and dead.

Her last resting place was a carefully kept secret. He knew where it was; he was in the same place. Make that a previous him was — the same previous him, father of the current him, whom two of his daughters killed when their triplet sister, Ukemoshi to their Yomikuni and Katatribe, needed not dying.

He supposed they were just happy to see her still breathing. Even if suddenly she, eventual Sister Jordan, had a scar in the centre of her forehead.

In the catacombs slept a few honoured others. One of them should have been Cabalarkon, a sort of psychic vampire the visitor had known far longer than he dared admit. Only he wasn't. A second was Ringleader, Rings, Aristotle Zeross. Only he shouldn't have been. It was his understanding, ocular proof obviously deceiving him, that Harry had been dispersed as a ten year old not so very long ago in the Cattail Peninsula. His ashes had been, rather.

He didn't have to die. Could have avoided getting involved in any of that misguided Irache mysticism he did get involved in, poor sod. Was a family affair, wasn't it? And you definitely want to stay away from certain families. However, like all too many children, and teenagers – who are just overgrown children after all – he thought himself immortal. Just head-strongly chose not to do so and paid the premature price for being mortal.

Being clay-like, mantels were cousins to eldritch demons. Were earthborn; consequential chthonic cousins to faeries and mandroids as well.

That made them, perhaps counter-intuitively, highly flammable.

========

It was Midsummer's Eve, Year of the Dome 5981.

========

Tomorrow was the wedding day of Capputis Masterson and Lakshmi Arthadot, who was named after Shri Lakshmi, the Hindu goddess of beauty, wealth and abundance. Tomorrow was also Athena, Tina, the youngest of the Zeross girls' seventh birthday. He'd promised to tell her some tee-tee-tails of her choosing. Would deliver as well, in due course.

Was an anniversary of his own, too; one not nearly so pleasant nor worthy of celebration as being wed was for the bride and groom. Or their families and friends. Or having a birthday party was for a child. Not that Tina needed an excuse to celebrate anything other than being awake. To say the least the girl was, not always enjoyably, hyperactive.

Seven years ago tomorrow, on the heart-shaped island of Shenon, where, not coincidentally, Tina was being born at about the same time he and the Master of Weir narrowly avoided being stewed alive by Aortic Amphitrite's man-eating, waste-not, want-not, Lemurian frogwomen. They, he and the Master, were somewhere they shouldn't have been, the Lemurian atrium or auricle, true. True too, they'd seen something they shouldn't have seen. True as well, that something was nothing they'd ever want to see again.

They'd seen All of Incain, in her solid semblance of a She-Sphinx, giving live birth to a monstrosity who eventually became known as Sharkczar, a now more mandroid than machine variation on the recurring Steltsar template. Had been captured by the self-same horror, who evidently had no need of an infancy, and given over to the frogwomen for disposal.

He still sneezed at the memory of their spicing.

========

Many of the dignitaries invited to attend the wedding were already in Cabalar-kon City. Others, including those in his own party, were waiting slightly more than twenty miles offshore in the Valprey, a Pani merchant ship named after Greygreave Valprey, an amphibious Summoning Child who, to some, was a hero of the God-badian Civil War. Among them was Aortic Amphitrite, who'd severely scolded her frogwomen just after Ringleader saved them, he and the Master, from an even worse scalding seven years ago. They, him with them, would be arriving in the morning.

He'd drawn himself hither for purposes both preparatory and reportorial. It was always nice to have permission before one in effect took over someone's Weirdom.

Right now, if only to clear his mind of its cobwebs, amidst the cobwebs of the catacombs, he was just taking a walk. As he did so, he heard many a whisper, many an enticement. All a Sleeper needed was a droplet or two of blood in order to regain consciousness; to thereafter speak to you. But, he knew, many a Sleeper wanted more like a pail full of plasma in order to revive such that he or she could walk about long enough to die an immediate death, as opposed to a lingering, ever after only imminent one.

Jordan Tethys ignored them. This was not his realm, not that he had a realm of his own, other than quarters at the DDD (the Dinq Doinq Danq Cavern Tavern), Marutian side of the Dilluvian Mountain Range, and his tent, which he'd left in the Whiplash Range along with one of his sketchpads. He would not presume to play God here. Not that he ever played God. Well, not since becoming the Thirty Year Man anyways. No Sleeper had ever harmed him. He would only act, react, if he was attacked. And then all he'd do was flee.

He was troubled. Albeit not at all from Cabalarkon's perceptive absence and hardly at all by Ringleader's apparent presence. Had been troubled for months now, ever since he'd drawn himself here, to this very place, the Catacombs of the Sleepers, in order to retrieve the decapitated body of his Sangazur-kept-lively, burbling buddy Gomez Niarchos and ended up doing far more than just that.

Rather than interfering in the running and, potentially, though it hadn't as yet come that, in the ruling of the Weirdom, he should have fled then. Notwithstanding Saladin Devason's invitation to attend the wedding, relayed to him, intriguingly, at Aortic Amphitrite's insistence, via the deviated (like him) faun Pusan Wanderlust – who wasn't really his sister in any way, shape or form, other than they both recurred – he probably shouldn't have come back now.

Sal was a vindictive Master. Was – as even he, Tethys, had finally been per-suaded – long overdue for a howsoever non-deadly takedown. As if it hadn't been previously, that was apparent from his treatment of John Sundown and Raven's Head on Yamana the 1st of last year, Headworld time. (Yamana, January out there, was the eleventh month of the Sedonic Year, the third in the Mithradic Ternary that ended it on most of the Head.)

As it – his at times purely petulant vindictiveness – may or may not have been apparent from the way he had, if he had, got rid of the rest of the Damnation Brigade, including Cerebrus David Ryne, terminally, shortly before that. And Fish's sister in more than just Flowery Anthea, Wilderwitch, six weeks or so after it, reputedly just as terminally. Still, flight was only a quick flourish of the pen away, his signature made with his Brainrock quill, and he didn't need to sign anything except the air itself to get away.

He was a tale-teller, a collector of stories worth repeating. He wanted to be where the action was; it was in his blood, his self-inherited blood. And here was where the action was going to be over the next few days. First, like any good reporter, he had to set the scene; put things into perspective. And that required interviews. The first person he intended to interview was the Sleeper Cabalarkon, which was yet another thing about his blood. Before he could become a blood donor, though, he had to draw himself to him, to call-me-Cabby.

Which, walk done and seated on a bench outside the crypt wherein non-dead, but not exactly lively either, Rings, Adult Harry, severely Gypsium-sick as he probably still was, lay in his tub of Cathonic Fluid, he was in the process of doing when his Brainrock quill, as if with a mind not his own, drew him somewhere else.

========

Cynthia Masterwife did not have a chair. Neither did either half of her, Wilderwitch or Demon Queen Lilith – can't call her Gomorrah anymore – have a chair. It was still three months before either of them, if either one of them were to have one, could even have a baby. They did sit in one, though.

Whereupon what had come fluttering through the left-open, sliding door to the balcony had a joke.

========

"About time you got here, Mel," said her twin brother, Demios Sarpedon. "Where've you been?"

"Where I said I was going, Dem." You definitely want to stay away from certain families; ones who can't even bother to be nice to each when they weren't alone.

"Wipe that stupid grin off your face."

"And disappoint your littlest niece. Tina put it there."

"Tina isn't here. Wipe it off."

"Wait. I've been saving this up for weeks now. Where's the Witch?"

As if in answer Tsishah Twilight began to materialize stuff out of her jewels, bangles and even more circular things. Most of it glowed. Most of it Cynthia Masterwife recognized as originally belonging to Wilderwitch. "Those are my enchantments," she said, "The Witch's enchantments. How'd you get hold of them?"

"By learning how to be a self-psychopomp," said the human, make that Utopian, caduceus. "Again, after all these years. Ready for it yet?

Cynthia sighed.

========

"If Capputis Masterson can be call-me-Cabby's Cappy, call me Cabby's Caddy."
****

Ten-Demon: **Sodom's Gomorrah**

========

Eve Of The Summer Solstice 5981

While Pandemonium may not be the Abode of All Demons it once was, it was still the capital of Satanwyck, the devic protectorate (since the Outer Earth's French Revolution) of Baaloch Hellblob. Sometimes it was all of Satanwyck: what was less formally, but perhaps more aptly, known as Sedon's Temple.

Was definitely where Pyrame Silverstar began her latest march toward realizing her long-held dream of mutually acknowledged, and respected, equality with the King of All Demons, the All-Father of Devazurkind. If aka Sinistral Sloth of Satanwyck could have a capital called Pandemonium, then she and her like-minded female Master Devas could have one called Panharmonium.

Right now she was heading toward exactly where she wanted it to be.

========

Along with dozens of other third generational devils, as well as a few fourth generation Thanatoids, Pyrame escaped the Cathonic Zone on the last day of Maruta 5980, November 1980. In a way her progress – or lack thereof – since was a series of mini her-stories featuring her successive shells as much as they did her.

Her first, Nehrini Purandar, Cosmicaptain of Cosmicar Six, the transit bus-sized 'vimana' she came to ground on, had been perfect for Pyrame's purposes. Unfortunately for the one, more so than the other, due to the fact that, shortly after her escape from Cathonia, aka also Lord Lazy sent her, the two of them, one in the other, to Pettivisaya, the City of Wailing Souls, their relationship didn't last.

For four millennia, maybe more, Pettivisaya had been Grand Elysium, the heavenly capital of Valhalla, the Elysian Fields, the Laughing Lands of the Glorious Dead; a veritable afterlife paradise not just of mythology. Then, thanks in no small measure to Pyrame herself, in the 49th Century of the Dome the entire realm became the Ghostlands.

To this day the Ghosts remained a radioactive wasteland. The Living could not do so, live, within their boundaries for more than a week or two at the most. Even if they managed to find a way out, exposure to the realm's air especially rendered them so diseased they invariably died within a matter of a few more weeks or slight months of their escape.

Not for nothing were Death's Angels, the once glorified, now bodily corrupted, mostly Nergalazur-made-ambulatory Dead Things who still subsisted, somehow persisted, within the Ghosts, commonly known as the Inglorious Dead. They were as unapproachable as they were unpleasant to behold and, except in old legends, essentially forgotten. Even less endearingly, their touch could kill.

The Japanese notion of 'Hungry Ghosts' didn't do justice to suchlike abominations. They preyed on just about anything alive. Not surprisingly this proved largely self-defeating. Nothing lived, they'd have to survive on nothing, which wasn't possible. Fortunately the azuras animating could go to sleep, albeit not before digging themselves, in their corpse shells, well under ground, where they could get stay dry — rain and running water being a big problem for the vast majority of these ambulatory Dead Things.

Ostensibly he, Sinistral Sloth, Lord Lazy, sent them there, they two in one, because she, Silverstar, wanted to discover how word reached stars in the Sedon Sphere to be ready for the incursion of the Cosmic Express; it with its much needed and very much welcomed potential shells aboard.

Most commonly Baaloch claimed Underlord Yama Nergal, one of the comparatively highborn Mithradite 'Earthlings', the Ghosts' overlord and after whom the Sedonic month of Yamana was named, would be able to accurately assign responsibility, solo or shared, for that daring and indeed almost impossible to accomplish act of, as far as Pyrame was concerned, ballsy brilliance.

Although he'd plausibly deny the allegation, the Pauper was convinced Lord Lazy sent her to the Ghosts knowing full well its rampant radioactivity would wreck her shell. Purandar died, Hellblob must have figured she, Silverstar, would recathonitize. Which she would have, had Purandar died. Which she did not, though she did become perhaps still terminally ill.

What saved her-Pyrame, if not necessarily her-Purandar, was the Nergalids' Harvester – the devils' second Grim Reaper, the first being a Byronic by the name of Vanthysces Vastness, whose star was only briefly out of the night's sky back in Tantalar – showed up in time to send her-them, Pyrame still inside the Cosmicaptain, to the Prison Beach of Incain.

The idea, the promise she made to this consequential King Harvest, was Silverstar would convince All, its resident, self-proclaimed invincible She-Sphinx, to release one or both of the idiotic Atomic Twins. (Interestingly enough, although ancient Illuminaries named one Osiraq, they named the other Tammuz, the same first name as Tsishah Twilight's Summoning-aged, eventual faerie fart of a father.) Once released he, or they, one Atomic Twin or both, could return to the Ghosts.

There, they – also known as Cautes and Cautoprates until the events of Thrygragon, in the Gregarian Fields, Sedon's Head, on Mithramas 4376 YD, next door to forever their father Thrygragos Varuna Mithras's torchbearers – having caused it, could clear it of the enervating and ultimately deadly radiation that had been deva-devastating the area for well over a millennium.

It was a sensible proposition. The twins exploding had turned the Laughing Lands of Radiant Elysium radioactive in the first place. They did so, it must be admitted, thinking it was on her direction. (It wasn't; Pyrame, missing her demon, had already been taken out inside a ringot by the Death's Head Hellion – herself, aka Morgan Abyss, the Melusine Master of Weir, holding onto said demon – but they weren't to know that. And she hated admitting it.) Be that as it may, presumably other than the Moloch Sedon only they could undo the damage they caused.

So she had gone to Incain. There, with the antediluvian construct's acquiescence, which would have taken no longer than a short walk along the All-swept beach to secure, would have fulfilled her bargain with the Nergalid. In and of itself this was to be expected. Devic oaths were inviolable. Then again they weren't supposed to kill lesser beings either. Pyrame, though, had been decathonitized. So had the Primary Apocalyptics and Mater Matare. As witnessed by their outrages in Temporis last Tantalar, their oaths didn't forestall anything anymore.

Pyrame was old-fashioned in that respect. Sure, it took her a while, the better part of two weeks and more than a few missteps – she was even eaten by a whale, one who fortunately didn't bear grudges – but she eventually made it back to the Ghosts. Made it there with only one of the Idiot Twins in tow, it had to be said, and he, whichever one it was, Tammuz or Osiraq, was empowering All of Incain at the same time.

She made it there nonetheless. Felt good about that. Devic oaths were supposed to be inviolable; even oaths made by decathonitized devils. At least, notwithstanding the activities of others, notably the Apocalyptics in Temporis during the first week of Tantalar, so Pyrame had predetermined hers would be, then as now. Was a matter of credibility, wasn't it?

She was minus Purandar by the 14th. The Cosmicaptain had deteriorated so quickly – not to mention so badly – from exposure to the air in Pettivisaya that, upon arriving in Incain, she, Pyrame, had to insist the She-Sphinx get her another sentient shell right smartly. Which turned out to be the first of her missteps.

No matter now. Fact of the matter was she was quite pleased with her present situation. Yama Nergal wasn't of course. Wasn't then – one Twin, especially one who also had to power All, wasn't enough to clear the Ghosts of its radioactivity – and certainly wouldn't be now, shining out of the night's sky as he had been since the selfsame 14th of Tantalar last year.

What pleased her the most, all in all, was she wasn't all in All anymore. Hadn't been since she popped into Tsishah Twilight, who was then still the life-loving Anthean Sisterhood's official Aortic of Shenon, never to look back, on the 13th. She'd agreed to go into Tsishah for purposes purely amatory. Whereupon either Lady Luck or just plain serendipity, which in devic terms was much the same devil, albeit with a capital-S for Serendipity, presented a combination of circumstances that were so irresistible she never even considered looking back.

They, this combination of irresistible circumstances, came in the form of an Outer Earth supranormal, one who should have been dead a quarter century earlier, carrying three not exactly sacred objects, especially not to devils like her. They also came in the form of three Lovely Lady blood-sisters Tsishah knew about because, among other things, they lived in the Ventricle next door to her atrium or aorta on Witch Isle.

Although in the Pauper's case it was more a matter of great-grand-parentage, the lovely triplets, who were not yet twenty, had a mother with much the same grand-parentage she did. So Pyrame popped over to her – Telepassa of Godbad being the name she'd been using for something like 20 years by then – for purposes coercive. As she was well aware, even anarchistic-oriented Afrites tend to obey their mothers and that, after yet another combination of circumstances, was what led to Pyrame's currently happy situation.

The Pauper Priestess was now in complete control of one better than All of Incain; had been, though not completely, since the 14th of that tenth month of the last Sedonic Year, the one named after King Cold, Tantal Thanatos. She was all in All's mother, as the She-Sphinx thought of her. Was in the Mnemosyne Machine, Machine-Memory more familiarly, none other than the Female Entity. Was humanizing her; making her, their joint being, Miracle Memory.

Facially and physically she wasn't just thirtyish Human Memory's doppelganger either. Although the third eye shining out of their shared forehead was her own, she could have as easily passed for Freespirit Nihila, albeit with shorter, much darker hair, and without the Gypsium-glowing necklace, chainmail surcoat and eminently extendable, actual chains — Nihila being ex-Harmony, Datong Harmonia, the now (once again) perhaps permanently late, former Unity of Balance.

She was wearing a stylish, non-breasts-baring – non-nipples-baring, anyhow – gown; one suitable for someone about to attend a wedding. Designed specifically for her, she in Miracle Memory's miraculously manufactured body, by none other than Human Memory's niece, Anna Maria nee D'Angelo Dre'Ath, who nowadays ran Radiant Rainbows Fashion Emporium in Paris, France, she'd acquired it during a relatively recent trip to the Outer Earth.

Cost a pretty penny too, buckets of them; silver doubloons in her case — silver being one of her calling cards. (She'd given herself the last name of Silverstar primarily to at least put herself on a pedestal figuratively standing beside Star Sedon, undeniably the brightest star in the Hidden Headworld's night sky.) Not that, Pyrame knew, money was a problem for a Female Entity that could conjure up a body of her own simply by possessing, or being possessed by, a devil who didn't have one to call her home.

As Pyrame further knew, anticipated more like, she would soon be acquiring something even more valuable than just a body and a fancy dress to go with it. Would soon be reuniting the rest of her, the rest of them, become three-in-one them. Would soon be in, over, have control of, Primeval Lilith, the Demon Queen of the Night. Whom she'd next door to always disavowed having, if only because her having her, her needing her to keep Sedon hers, felt somehow degrading.

Always from not long after Year of the Dome Zero (0 YD) until 5950, that is. Which was when Miracle Memory stole her from her just as she, Pyrame, killed the time-tumbler (time-bumbler?) Herr Hel Helios. Did so, as Sedon should have appreciated, in order to prevent him killing Kadmon Heliopolis, age 10, nearly two decades prior to him becoming, yes, Herr Hel Helios, the Male Entity. (No Helios called Sophos the Wise, no Moloch Sedon; no Sedon, no devils. No devils, no Master Devas, no her.)

She got libidinous Lily back, all would be right with Pyrame's world again. Be right with the whole world; not just both sides of it. Because there would no longer be two sides to it.

There'd only be the one world left. For the first time in nearly 6000 years.

========

She paused her pacing of the Valprey's main cabin.

Like her audience, whom she'd been regaling with her-story and the her-stories of her shells over the past six months, she was awaiting word from Cabalarkon, the place and the undying Utopian both. Was awaiting, more than anything else, for their collectively designated ambassador, Jordan 'Q for Quill' Tethys, to return to the Valprey with call-me-Cabby's blessing for what they were about to do with his Weirdom.

She stretched, so did they, briefly, then once again settled back to hear the rest of her-story, of Pyrame's Progress. She spoke as if possessed. Which she was. Unless it was the other way around. Albeit not so much so by Machine-Memory as her own memories, unreliable as they no longer were … mostly thanks to their relatively recent acquisition.

Also due to the fact that she'd vowed never to lie to herself again.

=========

"Nearly sixty centuries ago, I had no chance to flee the Great Flood of Genesis, the Genesea, to the comparative safety of the archipelago of Pacifica, the Places of Peace; Mu or Lemuria as the majority of Outer Earthlings continue to think of it. Couldn't do so because I was already imprisoned within Andy the Androsphinx, the by then moribund one that still stands in Egypt, on the outskirts of Cairo not far from, yes, Heliopolis, Sun City, the Biblical On.

"I'd been stuck there something like seven hundred years prior to Xuthros Hor causing the Flood. Even though the Debacle damaged it, him, it wasn't until months, maybe years, decades even, later that I finally managed to break loose. Not only did I get out of the Egyptian Sphinx, with an undying body to boot – one a recent shell of mine now controls, howsoever temporarily – I discovered how to master him.

"Believing all except those on Hor's ark drowned in the Genesea, I scoured the steadily repopulating world for others of my possessive ilk. It seemed a futile effort until I came across a remarkable being. He was solid, like I was now, so I initially thought he was a demon, an earthborn elemental. I was only half wrong.

"While he was an immortal he wasn't earthborn. He was the King of All Demons by then, though. And I soon learned he was much more than merely that. Should have realized it right away, sooth said, but most of a millennia had passed since our last meeting and so much had changed for both of us. Although we would acquire many different names in time, I was Gomorrah to his Sodom — the Moloch Sedon, the God-King and Father-Creator of All Devils.

"As I just indicated, the Outer Earth was a desolate, only sparsely populated place in the centuries immediately after the Flood's waters receded. Sodom, as I shall call him, took me through the Cathonic Zone, as the Dome is most correctly called; showed me what he had preserved on this, his Hidden Headworld. Then, as now, albeit with the exception of the Ghostlands, the Inner Earth was teeming with life. Especially in terms of sentient beings that life was much more varied than on the outside; still is. But there was a problem.

"Cathonia would collapse, he seduced me, if we did not mate and have children; both beneath the Dome and beyond it. If that didn't happen the Inner Earth would be inundated just as it should have been by the Flood. All that life would be lost. These children had to be male. Additionally, they would be mortal, which we were not. That meant we had to keep on having children, at least one a generation

– though the more the merrier, due to this not at all minor matter of their mortality – and on either side of the Dome.

"Our first offspring was a girl. Sodom was horrified. More, mortified. And, in the old sense of that word, he died. The Dome did not collapse, however. A year later there was another Sodom. We tried again; this time with success. He still died. Stayed dead as well, until our daughter reached the age of seven, a somehow significant age and one she has remained to this day. But there would be more Sodoms. And we would have more children, boys for the most part, though I kept having to change bodies to have them; my host shells being as mortal as his.

"In time our relationship, which we'd carried on from multiple millennia traversing the stars, stabilized. Every year we took on a different body. Every other year I would go through the Egyptian Androsphinx to its Sister Sphinx on the Head, Ginny the Gynosphinx, by now calling herself All of Incain.

"Sometimes I – rather my shells, since I didn't have to the do birthing myself – would have daughters, sometimes I wouldn't conceive at all, but every time I had a child he, Sodom, would die. On both sides of the Dome our relationship became ritualized. We became identified with the seasons. I was the constant, the Mother Goddess. He was my Year King, called the Moloch or the Judge. Bad years we were infertile, myself and the planet. Better years I had a daughter; best years a son.

"No matter what the result of our passion plays, many of which we had to perform in public, he had to die every year; more often than not deliberately sacrificed by our adherents. However, unlike in the refined Rites of Spring celebrated as Easter on much of the Outer Earth – and under various names here on the Head – that initially happened in winter, either after the harvest or around the solstice, in the dead of the year, when I gave birth anew.

"When I did give birth in order to renew the year, that is to say. Which I already have. Regardless of results, every year I had to find another body, though generally speaking my former shells ruled on wherever they were — possession by me, not him, was extremely healthful, hence why I had already become known additionally as Providence. And every year, every spring, he found me, in another body of his own.

"Needless to say I grew weary of the endlessness of the process. Despairing for my existence, another Judge came into my life. This one I believe was a demon, Daemonicus, the original Demon King, the one supplanted by our All-Father during what has come down to us as Ragnarok, the Twilight of the Gods.

"This Daemonicus may also have been a dusted devil like the Grey Lady of Crepuscule allows herself to be whenever Twilight's Queen Godda, God-Devil, dies. If so then he was the first of our kind besides Sedon, the Thrygragos Brothers and myself to gain solidity. He was happy to call himself Sodom, however, and for all I know he may well have been our Sedon.

"Oh, we liked being young adults, him and I. I even came to like bearing our children since it made them sturdier, more longer lasting over time. Still, we switched bodies every generation or so, but only when we wished. Similarly, free as we were now, we nonetheless continued to have children. Albeit, mostly because I'd lapse into a prolonged coma after every birth, rarely more than one or two per body. In short, except for that, we were happy.

"For many centuries my man-demon Sodom and I, as Gomorrah, ruled huge swaths of territory on the Outer Earth; areas not just in and about what we had come to conceive of as our sea, its eventual Mediterranean, but far away from there as well. Together, in the vicinity of what, for reasons I shall shortly detail, is now known as the Dead Sea, we built a pair of magnificent metropolises we named after ourselves.

"Tragically, some two thousand years after the Great Flood of Genesis, Golden Age nostalgic, so-called after the Golden Apples their racially-varied ruling classes ate in order to give themselves extraordinarily long lives by mortal standards; these very much patriarchally-inclined human tribes learned not only of our existence, but of the wondrous joys we provided those who would follow us.

"These Edenites, as they styled themselves; Atlanteans, as they're commonly recalled beyond the Dome; Xuthrodites or Horrites as we thought of them, the descendants of Xuthros Hor, the Biblical Noah, his primary wife Anthea, and those of their family, sons and daughters, cousins, those who'd survived the Genesea in this Ark of theirs – don't ask me what it was, neither of us saw it – howsoever you call them; they became jealous of our various wealthy, as well as healthy, domains.

"What they were most envious of was of course our success, Sodom's and mine, and the adulation we were duly accorded because of it. What these inter-lopers wrongly termed my absolute matriarchy, these men and their female subjects – for subjected these Ants were to their men's will – determined to destroy. Using unearthed Edenite technology, they caused an asteroid to shoot out of the sky. It obliterated our adjacent cities. Indeed, the impact crater it left behind eventually filled in with water but, so salty and mineralized was it, virtually nothing could live within it. Hence, as promised, the Outer Earth has had a Dead Sea ever since.

"I survived, but my Judge was lost forevermore. Tralalorn, the immortal abom-ination that was my first child, was taken to the Inner Earth by the Demon Sedon. Immortals can die, he claimed. If you knew how to kill them, which he did. And he would kill her, he promised me, if I didn't lay with him; if I didn't bear more of his sons on a regular basis. We came to an accommodation, he and I. I no longer had to hold onto the mother until the boy was born. Nor did I have to do it every year.

"Really, all I had to do was endure having my shells have a few nights of baby-belly-begetting sex with him – he in his shell, to be precise – two or three times every generation or so. Having another Sedon Incarnate in order to preserve the Cathonic Zone wasn't an unbearable bane, I supposed, pun intended … Bane? Bairn? Forget it.

"Then, not even forty years past, an Outer Earthling, a Summoning Child like you, Aortic, discovered what was going on. Many of you here will recall him; Solo-mon and Sheba less so than the rest I'd imagine, though no doubt not for lack of trying. He was a damnable Celestial, a Horrite, an Edenite; a deviated partial-grand-son of mine no less.

"He was your father, Taurson, Ventricular; your son-in-law, Corn Queen: be-come Wiccan Warlock in here, born Jesus Mandam out there. Learning what he had learned from whomever, he thereupon went out of his way to kill every still alive half-son I had conceived with Sedon on either side of the Dome.

"What did he want, this homicidal, latter day Jesus of yours? Not peace and brotherly or, Heaven forbid, sisterly love, this self-proclaimed Saviour of Supranormalkind, that's for certain. No Panharmonium enthusiast he, this Mithraic Messiah so despised by even his own father, a genuine, and genuinely good-hearted, Mithraic Magus if ever there was one. He wanted to wipe out devils; nothing more, nothing less. The murderous maniac cared zilch about the Head, the diversity of life contained herein, or what would happen if the Dome collapsed.

"Give him credit, Sedon fought back but, no matter how many times he found and had him killed, this astounding Summoning Child rose from the dead, to kill more and more of our half-children. Who, despite their half-parentage, weren't capable of pulling off the same stunt. No wonder, as I've since heard, he began calling himself the Conquering Christ. Resurrection, presumably the skill to hide his soul somewhere, and the Machine-Memory-like ability to manufacture homunculi to house his ever-returning spirit self, was his supra-attribute.

"Frustrated beyond measure, the Moloch could do little except come out of Cathonia and rape me, me in my shells, he in his shells, over and over again. What else could he do? He, Sedon, demanded of me. What else could I do, as much as I hated it? We had to keep procreating more and more living sedons, small case, to replace those being systematically wiped out by this immediately recurring mass murderer; this Mandam madman who couldn't be stopped, yet would stop at nothing himself, not even at killing pregnant women whose unborn babies might – only might, mind you – have been Sed-sons. It was too much for me.

"Thus, after literally thousands of years, my own All-Father became my enemy. As a result, if only to save my shells from such unconscionable, yet inexplicably unpreventable slaughter, I determined to stop him violating me, us. Wiccan-Jesse – more like Wicked, even evil, Jesse – couldn't read minds. Neither mine nor Sedon's; not that I'd ever heard anyhow. So I reckoned there was only one way he could learn who as Sedon impregnated me; whomever I was in, ditto that dot.

"He, the Moloch, must have boasted about it to his thought-father. Since I only ever picked the most gorgeous of women for his most handsome of men, might have shared photos of them, whoever they were, together. Whereupon he, Cabby the Daddy, must have passed on the information to Wiccan-Jesse. Couldn't be any other explanation, I figured. Ergo the key to any success I will have comes with controlling the Weirdom, with controlling Sedon's actual father, after whom it's named.

"I knew how to do that. It was simple really. Invade the idiots. Non-Conqueror conquer them. I tried it thirty years ago, hardly for the first time, but Dark Sedon got rid of me. Last Tantalar, within a scant fortnight of my return, I tried it again, via the Ghostlands. Once again though, the demon-devil proved too much for us.

"He cathonitized my devic ally, Underlord Yama Nergal, whose only desire was to force the Moloch to clear what had once been the Elysian Fields of radioactivity. Scattered what was left of his forces, Death's Angels, throughout the Ghosts; perhaps even outside them, for all I know.

"He would have recathonitized me as well, except I abandoned the field. I didn't go into All; didn't flee back to Incain. No, even if I would have been safe inside All, I would never have made it. Travelling between-space, Sedon would have intercepted me long before I got to the Prison Beach.

"Far better was what I did do. Which was to retain possession of the natural-born healer, Ventricular Telepassa, she of not just Godbad. So it was I in effect followed the Godstuff-trail then sending Telepassa, Telepassa's triplets, Ino, Agave and Autonoe, and Telepassa's other daughter, young Semele, beyond the Dome. Only I followed it the other way, backwards, toward its source. Fled not so much away from the Weirdom as below it.

"Fled to where Sedon dare never go; to Absudyl, the Subterranean Land of the Mandroids; to Minius, formerly the daemonic domain of the self-proclaimed Mighty Minotaurus Magnus Minus, a debauched dissolute who nevertheless had, and could have again, if you know how to rise him up, his uses. Fled ultimately to where the Godstuff-trail led me. To where I knew it would, to Trans-Time Trigon. Whereupon I eventually reasserted my prior mastery of the Mnemosyne Machine.

"Memory's now mine. Plus, due in large measure to you, Irisiel, and for which we all thank you, Sedon is finally convinced that isn't going to change. Deals have been struck. Deals we devils especially make cannot be broken. That includes deals made with the Devil himself, our All-Father. Within a matter of mere hours we shall even have a capital city; the first capital city in its history, its her-story, the first capital city in the existence of the whole Head.

"We shall have our Panharmonium."

========

Ventricular Balkis Mandam, Sheba Faerieflight, slapped her head.

========

The faerie she slapped, a Tinkerbell, didn't scrunch or squelch. Didn't even complain like the ones Cynthia Masterwife had been eating before, morning sickness kicking in prematurely, puking them up again. It wasn't so much slapped against her head as slapped into her head. Faerie Flights were like that; were composed of often flying faeries.

"Cousin-Uncle Jordy's had an aneurysm," she announced, tears in her eyes, once the message was received and parsed through her hive-like brain.

"My Georgie's dead!" gasped the two-toned redhead born Cybele St Synne, in 1909 on the Outer Earth, but who had been using the honourific, Miracle Maenad, since the late Thirties.

Miracle-Cybele wasn't any old Korant Corn Queen, though at 72 she was getting on in years. As Miracle Maenad, she was the Korants' Corn Queen, had been since '38, when she succeeded none other than Pyrame-Liltih-Memory. She was also a Trigon Triplet; which meant that, like Eden Nightingale and Mnemosyne born D'Angelo, become Heliopolis, both of whom were long gone, there were those who believed she was an incarnation of one of the Three Great Goddesses (Demeter?), the collective, second generational mothers of devazurkind.

Mind you, there were those who believed Cybele-Miracle was also, bodily, the current residence of Divine Coueranna. She, aka Kore-Concord, arguably the initial Myrionymous Kore, Kore of the Many Names, was a highborn Mithradite. Her protectorate had been most of Apple Isle until she vanished, presumably never to return, in the mid 59th Century of the Dome, well over a hundred years ago now.

George Taurson, the most recent embodiment of Jordan Tethys, was her son; her son born in '48. He was where the legendary 30-Year Man went to revivify, as well as rehabilitate, in '68 after all that beastly business on Apple-Ape-Apis Isle. Evidently, even though, technically speaking, George Taurson no longer lived in any meaningful way the moment Jordy's spirit went into him, Cybele-Miracle still regarded George's physical husk as George himself.

(She knew her Headworld history, did Miracle-Cybele. There had been cases of 'husks' coming back to life, as it were, once the Legendarian exhausted his thirty-year lifespan within them. One of the most famous of these so-called Quit-Quills, Q for Quibble, unless it was Squab, which did have a 'q' in it, figured in the early stages of the Thousand Days of Disbelief. So she was right to have hope her Georgie might be all hers again in the unlikely event she lasted until 5998.)

"Fin-fucking-caustic-soda," exclaimed one of the non-possessed ones there.

Had a pearl-like, iridescent as well as opalescent Vesica Piscis effectively glued to her navel; had had at birth. As a consequence Fisherwoman (Scylla Nereid, Lady Achigan, the ex-Queen of Godbad) couldn't be possessed. (Or touched, as far as that went, not if she didn't want to be. Fish, though, liked to be touched; for an aquatic was quite the Earth Mother. Wouldn't have had so many Fish-fry if she didn't.) Rather, she couldn't be possessed while it was undamaged. Which it hadn't been back in mid Tantalar when Freespirit Nihila got hold of her howsoever briefly.

Truth told – something else devils always did prior to being ill-starred (cathon-itized) – it hadn't taken all that long to re-strengthen, if that was a word. Less than a few days after Nihila and her had a mutually agreed upon parting of the ways. This within hours of the Living claiming their fabulous victory over Nergal Vetala, her Soldier (the self-proclaimed Trigregos Titan) and her Dead Things Walking, on by then Drenched Dustmound.

Hence how she reclaimed her soul-self, presumably from Nihila; how she thereupon managed to turn her latest psychopomp, an actual batoid, Eagle Ray Revenant, so soon after her preceding one, her psycho-bicycle, ceased functioning at the Sraddhite Monastery. This last not much more than a day or two before, thanks to Vetala's aforesaid Soldier, who still had hold of OMP-Akbar's Homeworld Sceptre at the time.

Wasn't visibly wearing him (it?) now, though he was probably not far away between-space. The general public found dead, if remarkably none too smelly, rays – Ronnie Raybum, after the no longer president-elect of the United States, Ronald Reagan, was her preferred name for him – even more difficult to deal with than her famous fishisms.

"Not dead, grandmother," said Balkis-Sheba, who had spent a considerable amount of time on the Outer Earth, most recently as the willing shell of Faceless Strife (Fitna Marutia, Maruta Kanin, Kore-Eris, Discord, Kore-Concord's breed sis-ter, after whom both the ill-favoured month of Maruta, November, when the winter season began in most of the northern hemisphere, either side of it, and the vast plains of Marutia, Sedon's Cheek, were named).

Their other breed-sister was Belialma, the onetime – or, more accurately, twice-time – Prime Sinistral (Lust) of Satanwyck, hence also Hell's Belle, whose star still shone in the night's sky. Beguiling Belialma was the devil who kept the balls roll-ing by body-bouncing between supranormals and their spouses or mates, many of whom were also supras, as they bed-bounced away the night of the autumnal equinox in Vancouver back in '53. As the stars themselves laughed afterwards, Lady Lust swept through the city leaving Mama Maternity in her wake.

One of the end-results of all those pregnancies were the events on Salvation Island of Christmas Day 1953. That was where and when Blind Sundown and Raven's Head dropped the Soviet-built Hydrogen Bomb atop not just Jesus Mandam, Solomon and Sheba's father, crucified as he was, and the remains of The Rache, an Outer Earth, mostly European, Axis Revenge Squad. They also dropped it atop Dark Sedon himself.

In addition to killing, never to rise anew, all the mortals below them, the explosion thereof caused the Moloch Sedon's star, the brightest star shining above his Headworld for nearly six thousand years, to dim to the point of invisibility for the better part of the ensuing quarter century.

(If Jesus Mandam rose, yet again, he didn't last long. Was never seen again; at least no one ever heard of him being seen again out there. The same held true for in here. The Boulder-Brain Conqueror Raven's Head overcame on the 1st of Yamana in Cabalarkon City, the same fellow Fisherwoman and Pusan Wanderlust saw with Aortic Amphitrite in replicated Versailles, the capital of Temporis, not long thereafter, was a Mantel reactivated specifically for taking Raven out while Master Saladin sought to slay her fellow Wakinyah Creature of the Cosmos, John Sundown.)

Discord, Concord and Concupiscence, to call them by their attributes, as their fellow often devils did, were the Bad Apple Goddesses, the ones that spoiled the barrel. The term had next-to-nothing to do with Ap Isle. They earned it due to the fact they each had an apple for a power focus. Discord's was the Golden Apple of same; made infamous for its role in provoking the Judgement of Paris, a prelude to the Trojan War, as recounted in Homer's Iliad most notably. Concord's was the Little Green Apple of Eternal Youth, so-called because it never ripened, while Lady Lust's was the Ruby Red Apple of … what else? Concupiscence!

They were born simultaneously, as all Master Devas were to the Trigregos Sisters, only one litter of three below that of Thrygragos Varuna Mithras's firstborn: Tantal Thanatos, the Frozen Isle of Lathakra's Death King; sister-wife Methandra, Heat to his Cold, the Scarlet Empress of Lathakra as well as the Crimson Queen of Mythland in the Mystic Mountains; and Phantast the Dreamweaver, whom Jordan Tethys blamed for his first death, had been deathly afraid of ever since.

(The star of this last had also disappeared from the Sedon Sphere on the 30th of Maruta. As far as anyone knew, Phantast had yet to reappear on either side of the Dome. Not that that meant he wasn't around, somewhere. Mel-Illuminatus, before she vanished with her children, blamed Phantast for the terrible dreams the Witch complained of having since becoming pregnant back in Tantalar. Then again that somewhere could be light-years away from the planet. As for the Pauper Priestess, she was from Mithras's Ninth.)

"Not yet anyhow," Sheba Faerieflight added, referring to George-Jordy. "Might be soon. Not sure about the fin-caustic carp-crap either, but Fish's right about the fucking. That's what he was doing when he had his aneurysm. The skilled, but untrained Afrite of his, Cosmicompanion Carmine Carmichael, must have put a some sort of wicked whacking whammy on him."

"So much for done deals with the Devil," said her grandmother, Miracle-Cybele, who had more than a few trysts with the Legendarian over the years, hence their son. "I'm out of here."

"Wait," commanded Miracle-Pyrame. "Maybe it was a natural occurrence, a stroke or some such. Jordan Tethys has always been a heavy drinker. Every Jordy I've ever come across, even the women, has been. You can't run out on us now that we're so close to success, Cybele." That said, she was suddenly out of there herself.

Those remaining, who for the moment were all of them, could not believe their eyes, any of their eyes — and some of them had three of the sighted things. One of these last, Irisiel Mercherm (Lazareme's Heliodromus, their intermediary to the stars, only one of which mattered, the one who promised to turn off Trinondev prison pods such that they – the devils on board the Valprey – couldn't be captured once they entered Cabalarkon's territory), began to blur.

"Could Freespirit Wilderwitch have done it already ... killed her father?" she, also both Speedy and Angelus, wondered aloud, her voice utterly unwavering for clarity's sake.

Fish whirled. Was so agitated she could barely spout any of her famous 'fish-isms'. "Freespirit who? What the fucking hell are you angling at, Angelfish?"

"I'll find out," the devic messenger responded. Then she did run out on them, quite literally. Taking her lead, the other Master Devas on the Valprey took their leave. Were gone, complete with their shells, those that bothered to occupy shells. Only Irisiel bothered to run. Even if they were Panharmonium zealots, most were hardly fitness fanatics.

Whether she was a shell or altogether her own self, Miracle the Maenad – not the humanized Memory so-named – stepped on a Korant Kernel, as the Corn Queens' version of witch-stones were known. As she faded from sight she had a parting word to the wise for her grandson. "Give them what-for, Sol."

"Oh, I will. Be assured of that. All Sed-sons must die!"

The anticipation of finally being given a chance to fulfill his father's lifelong ambition was such he couldn't completely quell his sudden glow.

And Glows blow.

========

He didn't. Did, instead, manage to quell his excitement.
A few minutes later the tidal wave struck.
****

Eleven-Demon: **Quaking Cabalarkon**

========

The Summer Solstice 5981

That Saladin Devason, the Weirdom's black god, was sitting in the Master's throne, his white goddess, six months pregnant, sitting in a slightly lesser-sized one of her own beside him, was not what he found immediately unsettling. Nor was where he was: the Master's throne room in Skyrise. Or who else was there: a number of Trinondevs, most of whom had their veils drawn such that even their eyes were obscured.

No, what was immediately unsettling, Master's Mace in lap, Sal was tauntingly waving about his Brainrock quill as he spoke. At the same time Cynthia Masterwife, who still hadn't said a thing, was flipping through his pad of otherwise ordinary paper upon which he'd made a number of potentially compromising drawings. Whatever happened next, Jordan 'Q for (ordinarily) Quill' Tethys consoled himself, it'd make for quite the tale.

Too bad it was beginning to look like he wouldn't get around to telling it until his next 30-year lifespan. Which could be a long way off. While perhaps not all there mentally, due to suffering from foetal alcohol syndrome all her life, his likeliest next stop, Ukemoshi's daughter Kirin, was physically very healthy. So were her triplet sisters' children, albeit not their mothers, neither of whom survived last Tantalar in Hadd, now Haas. At least not alive they didn't.

Why couldn't one of them have had the common courtesy to have a boy?

========

The Panharmonium Project pushers wanted to proclaim the name of the newly illuminated Headworld's capital city with a minimum of fuss and bother.

Since the putative Metropolis of Panharmonium had been, as it as yet still was, the Weirdom of Cabalarkon, certain preconditions had to be met prior to Dark Sedon approving of the howsoever nominal transfer of authority from one master to another. One of those preconditions was securing the blessing of call-me-Cabby. That was his task. Had been his task, rather. Now, simply staying alive struck him as more important.

"I just wanted to interview him," protested Tethys, thankfully not under the influence of Saladin's Speaking Stick, his Master's Mace, as yet. "Get Cabby's perspective on tomorrow's union of so many of the Head's Hate-Sedon factions right here in what amounts to Sedon's own protectorate. I mean, when you think about it, it's like the cat inviting the rats to a party and the rats coming."

"Sedon doesn't kill," Saladin reminded him. "In fact he cathonitizes devils who do. Besides, this isn't his protectorate. If it's anyone's, and it isn't, it's mine."

"So you say, Sal," 30-Beers challenged the Master. "Personally I find hubris too much like humus for my taste. They're both rotten."

"I thought it was made of chickpeas."

"That's hummus."

"Thought they were sodomites."

"You're enjoying this far too much."

"And you're conspiring against me; you and your sister in recurring deviancy, Pusan Wanderlust, the so-called trail-blazing Traveller. You were both in some of the pictures the High Illuminary – my wife, the High Illuminary – had processed today. You, her, what's left of the Zerosses and what's left of the Sarpedons."

"Including my niece, Witch Isle's non-Lemurian Aortic – former Aortic, the High Illuminary tells me – the one who doesn't look at all like her mother, my sister, anyways. Or her faerie fart of a father, for that matter. How do you combine white skin with blue skin and get reddish-brown skin?"

"How do you combine a black-as-midnight Utopian father with a white-as-light witch-mother and get a black-skinned, as well as black-hearted, Devason with a beard?" countered Tethys. When Saladin looked entirely displeased with that response the Legendarian tried a less confrontational, less signing-your-own-death-warrant, approach. "Answer is: You'd have to ask her that. Or hasn't she become quite that illuminated as yet?"

The Sed-son didn't look very happy with that, either. 'Ah well', 30-Years comforted himself, hardly for the first time, 'Maybe Sal'll sign it, the death warrant, with my quill. Then at least I'll know where to come when it's time to get it back' Had another thought, as well, not a very nice one. 'Although I'd hate to have screw Sal to get it.'

Then again – yet another thought, this one even nastier – maybe Ukemoshi's daughter, or one of her cousins, will be dying of a highly contagious sexually transmitted disease when she screws him. Before he, Tethys, got a chance to altogether come back and thereby rehabilitate her body. If not, aside from exceedingly rare Quit-Quills, she herself.

He had an image of Sal, corrupted through and through, and not because of his innate humus-rottenness; hopeless, pleading, dying of incurable STDs in his-her arms. What'd he-she say then? Had to be something cruder and ruder than 'I told you to give me the quill, not your dick.' Maybe something along the lines of 'but you were so hard, Sal, I thought you were already using a stone gnome condom'. He'd work on it in Limbo.

"Has to be a glamour," finally spoke Sal's High Illuminary, Cynthia Masterwife. Then, presumably just to show off, she made herself go from Sal's White Goddess version of herself to the fit and healthy looking, albeit ex, Anthean Aortic, Tsishah called Thrae but better known as Twilight, as she appeared in the today-just-reprinted photos.

"Better than looking like this," she added, showing off her face-dancing expertise again. This time she seemingly went from a six months' pregnant Irache-type in her mid-to-late thirties to a rapidly aging, sickly and possibly dying dryad somewhere in her fifties who nonetheless still had a baby-bellyful.

Suchlike toad-greenish tree nymphs, albeit rarely pregnant, but virtually always young, coquettish, were sometimes seen in Djerridam, Goatwood, Sedon's Goatee; in time-retarded Dukkha, the easternmost tip of Sedon's Moustache or Upper Lip, which stood on the outskirts the Forbidden Forest of Kala Tal; and in the Forbidden Forest itself, where mostly dwelled madness, especially for anyone already foolish enough to enter it.

They were far more common in Crepuscule, the sadly – as in also SAD: Seasonally Affective Disorder – seldom sun-dappled land of Twilight, where niece Tsishah spent years being possessed by Krepusyl Evenstar, Wilderwitch's putative devic half-mother, and thereby ruling as Faerie Queen Godda. That was also where Tethys himself once married one, Sylvia; their daughter being the aptly named Wooden Tethys.

(It was the mother, not the daughter, who killed him that lifetime; one of a dazzling number of deaths he experience on the same day, Thrygragon, the 25th of Tantalar 4376 Year of the Dome. His deaths – not all of which were caused by jilted or abandoned wives – barely rippled the fabric of legend. For that was the day, his feast day, that Thrygragos Varuna Mithras died for the first and, thus far, last time in the Great God's until then multiple millennia of existence.)

Saladin had visited Goatwood with the Zerosses when they were looking for remnant Weirdoms in the early Seventies. Had also been in Dukkha more than three decades before that. The Duchy, Cynthia must have learned from her studies – the same studies whereby she learned the rote she was to recite at tomorrow's wedding ceremony – was the birthplace of Tammuz Rhymer, become Tom-Tiddly Taddletale, Tsishah's father.

As for Twilight itself, well, Tsishah would never have become Witch Isle's now ex-Aortic if Fish, dragging him along against his will, hadn't gone there in the very early Sixties in search of newborn, mutual son Salmon (as in Sal-son) Capputis, who'd been kidnapped by Godda's faeries. That was when they realized whom Krepusyl Evenstar was possessing in order to become this Queen Godda (God-Devil, Godiva — and, yes, she did enjoy riding around the countryside naked, particularly in the summertime when the Seelie Court was running things there).

For a number of reasons Sal found that little excursion very embarrassing, though not so much so as his sojourn to Shenon, Witch Isle, where Tsishah was already ensconced as a Quarter Queen, did a dozen years later. Caught in a lie – he'd sold Cappy to the faeries as part of a deal he'd made with Fish's endlessly estranged, yet forever smitten husband, Achigan Auranja, the by then ex-King of Godbad – was infinitely preferable to being caught and boiled alive in a Lemurian soup pot.

"Do try to restrain yourself, Cynthia," Saladin cautioned her. "We have a guest." He also had many a veiled Trinondev in the room, but they'd become accustomed to her sheer witchiness – not to be confused with 'wickedness' – since her recent return from the coast. At least she was no longer seen accompanied by a ghastly spook.

"Whose sister's fauna-the-sauna?" she put to him, once again reverting to her white goddess semblance.

"So my never-wife, my onetime High Illuminary, once told me," Saladin put to her, querulously. Even if it was only a figurative relationship, surely Wilderwitch would know that.

Yet …

========

In the days since her return with Grudal from the depraved dynasty of Zeross-es' left-hardly-at-all-guarded coastal hideaway, Cynthia hadn't seemed herself. While it could be the Tinkerbells she'd been swallowing like so many oysters, pickles and other foodstuffs – can't say food goods; food goo, maybe – were highly inappropriate for a Mama Maternity Masterwife's digestive system, Saladin was beginning to wonder if there wasn't something else going on.

He had heard of postpartum depression. His former High Illuminary had often lectured him on 'do try being nicer to your exes' after they'd had his child. He wasn't so sure about ante-partum, as in 'pre-birth', excesses. Was Cynthia Master-wife no longer sleeping with him because she'd convinced herself that avoiding sex would result in her having a healthier baby? Wasn't anyone he could ask, was there?

Utopian doctors, such as they were, weren't psychiatrists, whereas his superbly well-educated sister-in-law, whom he relied upon far, far too much, was three months gone. He couldn't have private intercourse, make that discourse, with the Demon Queen Lilith because when Cynthia Masterwife was avoiding him, so too was her much more attractive – when it wasn't reptilian – half-self.

If he had a friend, Thobruk Grudal, Jordan Tethys, even Harry Zeross, which he no longer did, lack-of-friendship being the curse of authority, he might have asked them for their opinions. As for his devic half-father, the Mighty Mooch had gone so silent of late, Sal wondered if the Outer Earthlings had finally unleashed the ultimate nuclear warhead.

And, if so, whether his Mace could manufacture an adequate umbrella.

========

"Hot stuff, isn't she?" Tethys commented, referring to Pusan, who, though female, had the same inexhaustible proclivities as any male satyr. "Course she isn't my sister, except to the degree we've bonded over the centuries. Since the Attis vanished on Thrygragon, no one else recurs like us. Even our half-parents are only cousins."

(Pusan only had one recognized devic half-parent: Goatfish, Deneb Makara, one of Byron's three Winter Zodiacals, hence her pedam power focus, the equivalent of his quill. Her prohibitive father, the aforementioned Chrysaor Attis, gave it to her as a birthday gift after he'd disposed of her Capricorn of a half-mother in All of Incain, where she apparently got thoroughly, as in irretrievably, digested many centuries before Jordan Tethys came along for the first time.)

"Can I have my quill back?"

"We are not speaking as friends, Jordan," Devason told him, perhaps necessarily. "Forget that not." Tethys had just accused him of having too much fun; making the too often cocksure Legendarian squirm even more just added to his enjoyment of the moment, to rhyme some. "Nor are we speaking about your options, which aren't many. You will do as I say or you will stay here indefinitely until you do."

"I can think of worse fates."

"Offer him a beer," Cynthia suggested. Then she burped, very unladylike.

"All right," yielded Tethys, without a fight.

He'd had the (both cloned) Naurozes' homebrew before. The thought of having it again was almost as repulsive as the thought of having to come back as one of a previous self's daughter or granddaughter. Even worse, not thinking he'd be here long, let alone lose hold of his quill, he hadn't secreted any of the DDD's wonderful pilsners in a cooler between-space like he often did when travelling.

"Just beer in mind I can't draw anyone anywhere against their will."

"Beer in mind really isn't funny, Jordy, given your present circumstances. Or am I repeating myself? Besides, it isn't anyone I had in mind. It's an any thing; three of them. in fact. Draw the Three Sacred Objects and, once we discover where they are, we'll figure out who's going to go get them."

"And play a Trigregos Gambit all over again. Are you nuts? No one wins a Trigregos Gambit. Playing one's as close to fulfilling your own Immediate-Death-wish as you can get."

"Our guest looks even thirstier than I thought," observed Cynthia. "Perhaps you can send one of these gentlemen out to fetch him a pitcher of Golgotha's Best Bitterness." By gentlemen she was referring to the Trinondevs perched, in their all-covering robes, various unpleasant-looking gargoyles or grotesques manifested, around the throne room like so many vultures waiting to be fed.

(Tethys had seen what certainly looked like Reilly Haddeus playing Pied Piper – with rats, not children – in Godbad's new Headworld museum back in late Maruta. Had also seen what Janna Fangfingers did to real Reilly years earlier: namely, feed his gory, still dripping shreds to her vultures' chicks; the very same creatures that made up the 500-years' persistent, altogether alive, Cloud of Hadd. Had probably told the Master both stories; sincerely hoped he hadn't given him any ideas.)

Which of course meant someone had to die first. 30-Years realized who that would be .. and it wasn't either Saladin Devason or Cynthia Masterwife. "I'll need my quill to do that."

"You won't draw yourself away?"

"And miss the wedding, not a chance. The quill, Sal."

Devason hesitated. He really hadn't thought that through very well. Were oaths made by devic suicides – which, despite their interminable, never very convincing denials, Jordy and Pusan likely were – inviolable? Giving Tethys back his Brainrock quill would be like giving Cynthia back her witch-stones and the rest of her enchantments. Wasn't anything else for it. As far as he knew, no one except 30-Beers could make like a magic wand with his pen.

Hoping Tethys was as good as his word, he signalled Grudal, who was one of the veiled Trinondevs attending them; had him bring Tethys his regular old quill as well as passing on, from Cynthia, the pad of ordinary paper he was using to draw Cabalarkon in his between-space tub of Cathonic Fluid when he instead, no doubt much to his amazement and subsequent regret, ended up drawing himself to Devason's throne room.

Once back in his hand the pen – which manufactured its own ink out of the Brainrock it took in as if a syringe – immediately began to Gypsium-glow. The Legendarian set to work. He had no problem drawing the Amateramirror, the Susasword and the Crimson Corona. Had the models right there in front of him,

above the Master's throne. As he did so he felt the familiar state of blissful unaware-
ness he needed to be at his most effective kick in.

That should have worried him. It indicated there was something out there –
some things out there – to draw. Which there shouldn't have been if, as he'd heard,
D-Brig's Untouchable Diver, whom he'd met lifetimes before Hadd last Tantalar,
had indeed destroyed them in the lava lake of their origin on Sedon's Peak. He
nevertheless dutifully kept drawing, if only to find out what had actually become of
them. Had, for example, Tvasitar Smithmonger remade them?

The background filled in, as it should. It was … what else? Where they were
— right here, where they were. Sal was outraged.

"Not the fakes, damn you. The real ones." Tethys snapped with it. Shook his
head, flipped the page, drew anew, this time from memory. With his eyes closed.

He had seen the Trigregos Talismans before; far too often for his taste. Last
Tantalar he'd even come across Amateram, Susal and Crinsom in person, as it were.
They were the Master Deva cousins who absconded with the originals just after
Anvil the Artificer, as devils called Tvasitar Smithmonger, fashioned them slightly
over 4,000 years ago.

The three guinea pigs fluff, as he thought of the lightweight, lowborn devils,
had been decathonitized. Had in fact been occupying Cosmicompanions A, B and
C, Carmine Carmichael, who quickly became his latest lover — and it had to be
said one of his most enthusiastic. He drew them recathonitized and, by gosh and by
golly – more like by Sedon – they were, much to his surprise.

So now he drew the mirror; as the background filled in it melted. Same thing
happened to the sword. Finally he drew the corona, panned way back as it liquefied.
The background was of a blown-out mountaintop, a caldera, a lava lake, a bubbling,
veritable sea of molten Brainrock far below a semi-circle of three cliffs. Vaguely different, yet no less distinct faces glared out of each of these last.

And there, on a ledge some ways down slope from his cyclopean Prometheum
(after the Grecian Titan Prometheus, bringer of fire) at the summit of the middle
one, Demeter, stood … what? A crudely shaped obelisk? Not really. An actual Titan
somehow turned to stone by a Medusa or a gorgon? Not exactly. Although comparatively small, it was the monolithic form of Tvasitar, the devic Smithy, at rest.

Tethys opened his eyes; regarded the drawing his quill – more so than he – had
just done. He scratched the scar in the centre of his forehead with apparent be-
musement. Something didn't sit right. And it probably wasn't Tavy, as Tethys called
Tvasitar when they were having beers at the DDD.

Which had been there next door to forever, as far he knew; certainly for many
hundreds, if not thousands of years. What – and this he did know for sure – had
once been 'owned' by the incomparably Harmony, the Unity of both Balance and
(her version of) Panharmonium. And which their father and his grandfather, on
both sides of the bed, Thrygragos Lazareme, also sometimes frequented, albeit always in disguise. Knew this because they drank together there; perhaps not so much
recently, but fairly often in his previous lifetimes.

(Jordy's devic half-father was Rumour of Lazareme, who'd been eaten by fucking faeries shortly after his birth, around 4000 YD, in what was then the Land of
Daybreak on the far eastern coast of the Head. His devic half-mother was Meti-

sophia, Titanic Metis, Wisdom of same, who for the longest time dwelled in the upper part of the Cattail Peninsula not far from Sedon's Peak, which his quill had just drawn.

(Metis had lost her power focus, a Brainrock cauldron that among many another thing granted viewers of its revelatory steam far-sight, to Methandra Thanatos – her rival both in terms of beauty as well as Sedon's lustful affection back then, near the end of the Zodiacal Age of Aries – during the expansion of the latter's co-Empire during the Dome's 48th Century. Was, consequently, back to being a Spirit Being to this day. Claimed she preferred it that way.)

Saladin and Cynthia Masterwife had come down from their thrones to watch him work; Grudal was there as well. The four of them exchanged glances.

"That'd be a bird's eye view of Sedon's Peak," Tethys explained, just in case they hadn't figured it out for themselves.

"So the Diver did destroy them after all," understood Devason.

Cynthia licked out her tongue lickety-split. It, the tongue, was Lemurian in length and extensibility; was also forked, which was a demonic, not a Lemurian, trait. It, the Legendarian could see, if not yet tell, went between-space and sticky-snagged something. Retracting it, she swallowed that same something.

It was the third time she'd done so since his interview began. Given how difficult it was trying not to over-the-edge-offend Saladin Devason, Tethys found it very distracting. She'd probably been doing so since her going to, then returning from, the depraved dynasty of Zerosses' coastal hideaway. Had been vomiting up a lot of it as well, in her daily converse with the bottom of a toilet bowl, he did not doubt.

Then she proceeded to spit up; all over his hand, quill and paper. Grommets of consequential chthonic sputum thereupon took wing and flew away.

"Sorry," she said, with a feeble grin, dabbing her mouth with the edge of her expansive, and expensive-looking, robe. Tethys reflexively laid his pen down on the tabletop, began to wipe his hand off on his shirt. As if they'd silently planned it, Saladin seized the opportunity; snapped it up, in a Masterly Mace thought-bubble.

"Nicely timed, Cynthia," Devason congratulated her.

"The quill, Sal," required Tethys, reaching out for it.

Saladin stepped farther way from him. Grudal stepped the opposite way, between them, eye-stave at the ready. The occasionally fuzzy seal, the lookalike of Silkie the Selkie, Tina Zeross's favourite dolly, manifesting off its top, was having a non-cuteness day. Wasn't quite a walrus yet, but its front teeth were longer and sharper than usual.

"I think not, Jordy," said Saladin. "Could be you've somehow been preconditioned to draw the talismans melting in Sedon's Peak. Not quite sure of the how, but there are enough witches in those photos to make me pretty certain of the generic who. We'll talk about it tomorrow. After the wedding. Talk about it under the influence. And this time I'm not referring to beer." He waggled his Masterly Mace indicatively.

"In the meantime why don't you head off to the old Masters' Palace and reacquaint yourself with that charming outsider you've drawn on at least three sheets of that pad. Grudal, you may escort our guest there. Just avoid the temptation to visit your own darling family. Instead, see he isn't disturbed. You others," he said, turning to the remaining Trinondevs in the throne room, "See if you can swat down a few of these flying fucking faeries. They clearly don't agree with my wife. Come, Cynthia. You need a bath. I'll do your back."

Looking resigned to her fate, she took Sal's hand; allowed herself to be walked to the Matter Transducer behind the rebuilt throne room's curtains.

'Just close your eyes and think of Panharmonium,' she was no doubt thinking.

========

Feeling disgruntled, yet nevertheless comparatively pleased he had the opportunity to feel disgruntled, Tethys gathered up his pad and walked with Grudal to the Masters Palace. Cosmicompanion Carmine Carmichael was happy to see him. Needless to say, said disgruntlement didn't last long – although something else did, something attached to him. Did so without using a stone gnome condom.

They were well on their way to renewing their acquaintanceship, with great grunting gusto, when he stopped mid-thrust and simply slumped atop her.

Coitus thus so shockingly interrupted for both of them, it took Carmichael a couple of seconds before she caught her breath and realized he was no longer conscious. Worse, he was having trouble catching his breath; was in actuality breathing only in gulps and gasps. She shoved him off her, started screaming for help.

None of the Tinkerbells who stayed behind were big enough to provide any.

========

Saladin Devason left Cynthia Masterwife to have a shower before running her own bath.

While she did so he went to his off-limits quarters and, eyeorb atop his Master's Mace open and extended, did a scan of the room. Satisfied none of the Faerie Flight Tinkerbells were lurking in either regular or between-space, he shone his orb's kaleidoscopic light on a spot on the wall. His Solidium safe consequently revealed, he proceeded to unlock it.

He intended to secure Tethys's Brainrock pen inside it, along with Wilderwitch's enchantments and the Stopstone box wherein he kept the solitary witchstone his sister, Morgianna, had given him years ago, just in case he wanted to get in touch with her; perchance to rescind her exile. The safe was empty. Well, not quite empty. There was a scrap of paper inside it. Then the quill vanished out of his grip. Then, from down the hallway, he heard Cynthia shriek and then Grudal's voice came out of his eyeorb.

"Sir, something's happened to Jordy. He might be dying."

"Attend to it," he shouted back.

He whirled, already surrounded by a theoretically at least externally impervious force shield generated by his mace. Someone was in the room with him; someone extremely familiar, albeit not from here, between-space atop Skyrise. It wasn't a Tinkerbell; rather it wasn't just a Tinkerbell. It was the ghost of Cabalarkon, swatting at Tinkerbells. "What the fuck are you doing here?"

"Miserable creatures. Did you know we've a infestation of fucking faeries? If I were you I'd fire a few junior members of your stone gnome extermination unit."

"I said …"

"I know what you said, Sal. I just came by to say goodbye."

"What?"

"My Sedon of a thought-son has ever-so-thoughtfully decided to relocate my sepulchre."

"What? Where? Why?"

"You forgot the who and the when?" Despite the pestiferous, yet seemingly sentient gnats afflicting him, call-me-Cabby was grinning. Saladin wasn't.

"You already told me the who, damn you."

"So I did. The when is … Oops."

Cynthia Masterwife, buck naked and covered with brownish sludge, smearing the goop off her baby-bellyful with an already filthy towel, strode right through Cabalarkon. "What the faerie-fucking hell," she swore. Then she shuddered. "Bloody Mary, Mother of Blob, Sal, that was cold."

"Spooks are like that," half-apologized call-me-Cabby's ghost. Whereupon, the 'when' clearly having arrived, he disappeared.

"Christ," again cursed Cynthia Masterwife. "I must really be losing it. I thought I heard someone say …"

"Someone did," said Saladin. "What happened to you?" he asked her as he pulled the sheet of paper out of the otherwise empty safe. Then he did grin.

"What's it say?" she asked rather than answered him.

"'On strike for less work and higher appreciation.'"

"That explains that then."

"Appears it does."

"Didn't think stone gnomes could go on strike."

"Neither did I. Probably can't; probably it's just Sedon showing me who's boss again. Come on, let's get you cleaned up."

"How, if there's no clean water?"

"There's clean sheets. Unless you'd prefer to indulge in some mud-wrestling."

Cynthia Masterwife laughed at that. "You know, Sal, sometimes you're not half-bad."

"No, I'm all bad." She laughed at that as well. Now he knew for sure something was wrong with her. No one ever laughed at his jokes.

"That's what I meant."

Then the earthquake stuck.

========

"Wipe that stupid grin off your face, Mel."

"First my brother and now you. What's the matter, Witch? Never had a 6-year old before, one you didn't think of as a baby sister?"

"You're so muffled I can barely hear you."

========

"She's right, mom," said Persephone, called Percy, who'd run off to get Melina nee Sarpedon Zeross not long after dawn broke over Tempestuous Psychron.

"And Tina's seven," said Helen, called Paree (after Helen of Paris's Troy), who'd stayed behind. "Today's her birthday."

"Oh, fuck!" exclaimed Mel-Illuminatus, after ripping the happy face sticker off her face. She wasn't in 'call-me-Cabby's-Caddy' mode. Was carrying it, though, her caduceus. Wasn't all in white either. Was wearing jeans and a sweater. Even at this time of year, when the sky was overcast it was cool up here in the not so holy heights of the Whiplash Range. Hadn't had time to put on socks and shoes, however.

"Mom," gasped Helen, unused to her mother's propensity for profanities.

"Mom," echoed Percy.

"Mel," chastened the Witch.

"Sorry," she said. "What do you make of this, Witch?"

"Which-witch, that or this?" Wilderwitch was chained to her cot.

Melina took her eyes off the pad of paper on the table behind which Helen was sitting. It wasn't an easy thing to do. Jordan Tethys's Brainrock quill, its sudden appearance being what had provoked Percy into running out of the cabin to get her in the first place, was still ghost-writing something on it. Was doing so, painstakingly for a pen, minus anyone holding onto it. She turned her attention to the Witch, on her cot.

"Well, at least something's finally working out according to theory."

"It's stopped," said Helen. And so it had, the Brainrock quill: stopped and flopped atop the pad.

"What's it say?" had to ask the Witch.

"'Help me'," read, then said, Persephone.

A gust of wind blew in from the Head's eastern ocean. It blew the pen off the pad, blew the sheet of paper with the 'Help me' writing on it over onto a fresh sheet of same.

"Looks like we're in for some nasty weather," said Paree.

"Let's hope it's not a hurricane," said Percy.

"He was cathonitized, still is," said their mother. "Besides, it's too early in the season for a hurricane."

(She was referring to Vayu Maelstrom, Devil Wind, one of the Byronic Nucleoids cathonitized on the 6th of Tantalar last. Pre-Vetala, which was to say pre-Expansion of the Lathakran Empire, circa the 48th and 49th Centuries of the Dome, Iraches native to old Iraxas – nowadays renamed Haas, instead of Hadd – worshipped him as 'Huracan', which was generally pronounced with a soft 'a'. Mayans on the Outer Earth around the same time had a god of the same name.)

The quill reared onto its nib, pogo-stick-hopped onto the new sheet of paper. Whereupon it, somehow refilled with Brainrock ink, began not writing anew, but drawing anew.

"What's it doing?" asked the Witch, craning her neck in a futile effort to answer herself.

She was still 6-months pregnant. Her soul-self wasn't anymore. And, yes, she was chained to her cot by the regenerating Gypsium chains that had grown out of the torc around her neck. The wraparound, hula-hoop-necklace, her Tvasitar-crafted Brainrock talisman, was all that was left of Freespirit Nihila; all that was left of her after she ever so head-strongly got involved in something – even if it did mean standing back and watching the destruction of her half-daughter – she would have been far smarter to avoid.

Hell's Teeth, it wasn't as if Janna Somata hadn't already been dead for centuries.

Melina held up her caduceus, as if requesting patience until it was done. Finally, once again, the Brainrock quill stopped: flopped atop the pad.

"Holy fuck!" this time exclaimed Mel-Illuminatus.

"Mom," gasped Percy, just as unused to her uttering swear words.

"Mom," echoed Paree.

"Oh, come on, Mel," said the Witch. "The only Holy Fuck I've ever heard of was the Immaculate Conception."

"Unholy fuck then," said Mel. "How else do you explain that?"

"Show me."

Mel obliged. Picked up the pad and brought it over to the cot.

"Fucking Hell," said the Witch.

The drawing was undeniably brilliant, quite literally. Was of the father of Gloriella nee D'Angelo's only child, Estrella 'Star' Dark. Was of Mr Brilliant, not Doc Dark; not of the crippled, long-time wheelchair-dependent, if not chained, Summoning Child born Immanuel Dark. (Who was still alive in December 1980 on the Outer Earth, probably at the Houston Academy of Man where he generally hung his hat.)

Was of Lucifer, Domdaniel, Sinistral Pride of Satanwyck. Only it wasn't. Not quite. Even without the third eye there were subtle differences in the ambiguously brilliant ghost-drawing.

"Saul Ryne," concurred the former High Illuminary of Weir.

"Psycho!"

Whereupon the pad of paper burst into flame.

========

As irreducibly devastating as they were, earthquakes, tidal waves, hurricanes, all were natural calamities. The eighth-born Mithradite Master Deva referred to as Catastrophe (Nakba Ramazar, the Headless Apocalyptic of Disaster, of Sudden Destruction) was expert at instigating, if not necessarily inspiring, suchlike terrible events.

'Neutrally', he'd say, somehow making himself heard without a mouth out of which to speak. (If the devic Vultyrie was around, which she generally was when he was, he'd claim she was a ventriloquist.) 'Just doing my job', he'd assert, similarly so. 'Now if you'll excuse me, I've some hats to try on. Mind if I borrow your head to do so?'

Laugh a minute guys, Primary Apocalyptics.

========

Ramazar's star was back in the night's sky, the former High Illuminary of Weir assured Capputis Masterson sometime ago. Had been since the 6th of Tantalar last.

Nonetheless, as he rapid-fire-revealed to his father that morning, he in his anticipatory, now become tatterdemalion wedding finery, having spent an exhausting, no-sleep-night heroically helping to clear rubble and rescue imbeciles of Weir, there was an Apocalypse. It marked the end of his world if not, as yet, the Headworld.

"And why's that, boy?" queried Saladin Devason.

He'd just finished lowering himself and his woman, Cynthia Masterwife, via a thought-balloon emitted from his Master's Mace, down from the generally unseen, as yet not-overly-damaged top floors of Skyrise, and over to the great central square of Cabalarkon. To not very many cheers, it had to be said. It had been hours since the earthquake struck. What were they doing all that time?

"The Matter Transducers between Cabalarkon and Temporis, sir. They're ruined. My bride can't get here. It's a complete disaster. Who'll marry me now?"

"Cappy," said Cynthia Masterwife, pleasantly and altogether unusually familiarly for her, "This is Cabby's Weirdom. I've come to consider it a good place, with a good Master. All things come to he, or she, who waits. Don't waste your time being afraid. It isn't worth the worry. We'll see you married yet."

"Sir?" wondered Capputis, Cabby's Cappy.

"Fish ahoy!" came a voice from on high, transmitted through myriad eye-staves in their proximity.

"Fish?" said Saladin Devason, disbelieving his ears. "I thought it was supposed to be a ship, the Valprey."

"Whale ahoy!" cried another Trinondev's voice, this from one of the pupil-port's outskirt lighthouses.

"Fish it is then," appreciated Devason. "Your mother has always known how to make an entrance, Cappy. Let's go greet her."

========

"Sir," repeated Capputis Masterson, respectfully, to his father, Saladin Devason. "I'd really prefer it if you didn't call me Cappy."

****

Twelve-Demon: **Morgianna's Statuary Remains**

========

The Summer Solstice 5981

"That's not just any old whale. That's my Alma Mater. That's Island Leviathan." So said Saladin Devason the day he discovered he was no longer the Master of Weir.

Not that he discovered it in time to do anything about it. He was also wrong. If Island Leviathan, the impressively, if not – by the mere fact of his existence – impossibly, huge whale that swallowed Pyrame Silverstar when she was trapped in Aortic Amphitrite's mandroid guard-body the previous Tantalar, could be considered a school he was an Alma Pater.

Of course humour was only one of many things lost on the Summer Solstice of 5981 in Devic Eye-Land.

========

Aortic Merthetis, Amphitrite's mother, had known of him most of her life.

As one might expect he, likely the biggest and conceivably the most long-lived cetacean still alive, on either side of the Dome – but who probably wasn't the same Leviathan mentioned several times in the Outer Earth's Bible – had a voracious appetite. Lemurian frogmen and frogwomen were among his favourite delicacies. In 5918, so goes the story, Merthetis was merely a light snack.

She managed to make it through to the belly of the beast without being terminally masticated. There she found a Piscine baby — Piscines being slime-green and somewhat scaly-skinned humanoid amphibians. Many, including many an Illuminary of Weir, held Piscines were genetically designed by ancient Atlanteans. At least hypothetically, they knew their continent was sinking, yet no more wanted to leave it than they did to turn themselves into dolphins.

Might well have been right about that as well, these Illuminaries. Usually were; wouldn't be so much so illuminated if they weren't.

The newborn was miraculously breathing, albeit like all such amphibious humanoids through the gills behind her ears rather than her nose. (By contrast Lemurian men, who weren't amphibious, had them in the regular place, in their neck. So did their womenfolk, among them Merthetis, though they could breath through their mouths and nostrils too. At least they could for their first sixty-odd years. At which time, they had to move underwater permanently, the same as their men.)

Miraculously – as she later discovered, as in Miracle Memory, the name the Female Entity used when humanized – being the operative word. She had a waxy, gem-like lump of Brainrock, a Vesica Piscis she came to call it, attached to her baby-bellybutton. (Gave her a bilge bucketful of unnatural abilities, too. None of which manifested themselves until puberty.) It grew as she did. And she did because Aortic Merthetis rescued her from that selfsame belly of a beast.

She was wrapped in a fishnet blanket, what was keeping her warm, and had beside her a oversized fishhook or landing gaffe that glowed brighter than most torches. Which was what attracted Merthetis to her in the first place. All three, the bellybutton bauble, the net and the fishhook, were not only devic power foci, they were known devic power foci. Their proper owners' stars, that of Mandorla Auricaura, Pyçonja Volant and Diluvia Ran, had only then recently appeared in the night's sky above the Hidden Headworld.

As for how Merthetis rescued her, assuming she didn't try to make one of them work for her, well, she was a witch, a Hellion, had Hellstones.

Just like Cynthia-Tsishah Masterwife did.

========

"Your alma mater, Sal?" his White Goddess asked of her Black God.

"Shush, Tsishah. I asked you not to display your ignorance in public."

"Tsishah?" required Capputis Masterson, he in his tattered tux, wedding truss and minus the mental tranquillity he'd been concentrating so hard on self-instilling, having overheard his father call her other than Cynthia. He'd met Tsishah Thrae, perhaps better known as Twilight, a few times. This didn't look anything like her; looked everything like Cynthia Masterwife.

"Do me a favour, Cappy, and have your ears syringed out. The gills behind them have impacted your hearing negatively. I said Cynthia."

"As you say, sir. If..."

"Do me a favour and have your ears syringed out, Capputis."

"Thank you, sir."

========

While altogether extraordinary, and extraordinarily enormous, no one, not even Master Kyprian, in those days also the High Illuminary of Weir, could ever determine if Island Leviathan – and he was as big as a small atoll at the very least – was an altogether natural being. Might he be an eldritch elemental of the Deep? A shape-shifting demon? A size-shifting faerie? A state-shifting psychopomp?

Fish, for one, insisted he was none of the above. He had, however, omnivorous sort of natural being that she supposed he was, once ate a Brainrock asteroid, one possibly aimed at Incain, but one that had fallen short of the Prison Beach sometime in the late 59th Century of the Dome, when he was just a calf – or, as his feeorin friends might put it, a wee whelp of a whale – and thus gained an affinity for the Weird. (Leviathan was often seen off the coast of Crepuscule-Twilight. Indeed, he was one of the most common ways for faeries to get through the Dome.)

Why Saladin Devason told Cynthia Masterwife not to display her ignorance in public was because a certain maybe 10-year old wild child, a wolfish girl-child, a certain sister of a certain wolf-eel of a Fisherwoman in not just Flowery Anthea, once went for a swim off Twilight's shore. Whereupon she ended up in a certain Sal's dinner plate at the first Amsterdam Academy of Man not just on the other side of the Dome, but on the other side of the planet.

Wilderwitch would have remembered that. Probably. The year was 5938; make that 1938, since most of what transpired immediately thereafter occurred in Amsterdam. Fish was there. Amphitrite might have been too – disguised as she was in those days as a nice-looking, wholly human teenager by her shape-shifting, face-dancing mandroid guard-body – since both attended the Amsterdam Academy.

(So did a number of other Inner Earthlings: the Sarpedon twins, then best pal Thobruk Grudal, and his still-in-the-future wife Nephthys, among them. Many of them stayed in liminal dorms built into Island Leviathan, hence Saladin howsoever erroneously calling the whale his Alma Mater. All were there under Master Kyprian's sponsorship. Not that anyone out there would have been aware of that; rather, would have been allowed to remember she was sponsoring them.)

Tsishah wouldn't want to blow her cover by making silly statements Wilder-witch never would have made. That Demon Queen Lilith wouldn't have made either. That, therefore, those who were there when it happened would immediately appreciate meant Cynthia Masterwife was no longer the Witch.

Was no longer that witch, make it.

========

The early morning earthquake wasn't centred in Cabalarkon. It was centred in Fearsome Fobbiat, well off its coast, beyond its twenty-mile, effectively non-Masterly, Sedon-enforced sea-limit. Island Leviathan, surfing the resultant tidal wave, swallowed the Pani Merchant vessel just as it, the wave, hit the ship.

Hours later, bashed and battered as he was, Leviathan nevertheless managed to swim up the barely wide-enough channel to the pupil-port of Cabalarkon City and disgorge it. The Valprey made it to dock under its own steam – even if it was fossil-fuelled – after that. Lines were tossed off it; lines were secured. Pale-skinned Pani crew members extended the gangplank. The first person to walk off it, ever so regally, was …

"Mommy," cried Capputis, rushing up to embrace her.

========

The name then-Aortic Merthetis gave the newborn Piscine she found in the belly of the beast, Island Leviathan, in 5918 was Scylla Nereid. In so naming her, the Hecate-Hellion was mixing mythologies in the same way, thousands of years earlier, widely travelled Illuminaries of Weir on Earth named devils.

Scylla was a six-headed, folkloric sea monster who dwelt in a cave on the Italian coast, opposite the whirlpool Charybdis. A Nereid was a titillation-prone sea nymph akin to a siren or Richard Wagner's Ringmaidens. (Having been shipped from the site of ancient Xanthos, Turkey, in the mid 1800s, sadly damaged, but nevertheless splendid statues of three nereids, presumably none of them named Scylla, had been standing in London's British Museum for many years.)

Regardless of all the other names she'd accumulated over an exceedingly busy 62, almost 63, years of subsequent life, Scylla Nereid fit as well as any. However, most folks called her Fish; Fisherwoman being the codename she'd been given by none other than Master Kyprian before she, Fish, even started going to the Outer Earth when still a teenager, and already a mother, back in the early Thirties.

She didn't use All or the Stationary SAG Gap. Like her (usually) faerie friends often as not used Island Leviathan, but also used Kore's Hell, which in the Thirties emerged in, yes, the Sedoni Cave of Central Crete. Didn't go there alone either, not at first; was accompanied by her teacher, Ubris's sister, Kanin Nauroz. (Who was named after a different Weirdom, that of Kanin City, which was ruined during – unless it was immediately after – the 1000 Days of Disbelief.)

Aka Granny Garuda, she moved onto Fish's forever friend Solace Sunrise, Sorciere, acting as her tutor and sometimes protector, a few years later. By then though, January 1938, Granny could no longer remove her feathers. (Was, like many of them there then – like many still were – quite the her-story, was Granny Garuda.)

In most respects Fish was a typical Piscine. Had slippery, greenish, borderline scaly skin. Her eyes were ovular, slightly too wide apart; her lips thin, almost non-existent. She tended to pout in order to make them seem comparatively full. Often described as having seaweed hair, rather than a rat or mare's nest head of same, she did. Or looked like she did.

It probably was hair. If hair could be slime green. And, yes again, she did have a double-row of shark-sharp teeth. Was undeniably an exotic. Usually didn't wear too many clothes either — and what little of them there was could well have been thin strips of blubber sliced off a willing whale or walrus who needed to lose weight.

Despite her years on this or any other planet, and in spite of how many fish-spawn she'd had over those years – six or seven, depending on who was doing the counting – she had held together rather well, most would agree. Was today elegantly exotic, as befit a mother of the groom. Was hardly underdressed at all.

Wore a hooded cloak that didn't just look fishy. It was fishy. Yuck. Was in fact the demonized skin of an actual batoid — an eagle ray, to be specific. Although not as yet formally introduced, it was her latest psychopomp, Eagle Ray Revenant. At least it didn't smell dead fishy; hood had eyes, however. Very disturbing. Capputis hoped it didn't blink, especially not after everyone had finished eating.

Assuming the wedding got that far, that is. Which, given today's dire circumstances, didn't seem very likely.

Underneath said fishy accoutrement, Fish had on a midriff-barring slip beneath a fishnet gown that glowed like the ornament in her navel and the landing gaffe she held. Which could have been considered a weapon, and therefore inappropriate to bring to a wedding, especially one secured by Trinondevs, but she was using it like a cane, as if she had a shrimp-limp. A very mutable cane, no one doubted.

Was the underclothing she wore beneath the fishnet, presumably for modesty's sake, thin strips of reversed and, therefore, whitish blubber? Had to be. Or something similar. She kept her bellybutton bared, however. Always did. Enjoyed the notion of her Brainrock-pearly, navel accessory, which she'd had since birth, being akin to a lower level third eye.

One that, should she will it, projected an impenetrable golden shield about her being. Which of course made it less of a third eye than very nearly identical to the sort that poked out of every Trinondev's eyeorb when it was looking to spot, then activate and imprison, a Master Deva or any number of azuras.

Carried with her, in her left hand, said nevertheless wicked-looking gaffe. Being a materialist, like so many witches, could have kept it hidden between-space, but she liked being open about most things, including her ability to kill quickly, if not necessarily cleanly. Wore no shoes nor gloves. Seldom did. Welcomed others taking notice of her webbed toes and fingers. Might save them from impalement on their selfsame, toe-tip and fingertip, cuticle claws. Unless they were talons.

"Watch it, Cappy," Saladin Devason cried out, just as his son, by her, discovered why he was shouting.

She, Fish, caught him as he slid off her, toward a dunking in the drink — and him in his not-quite-so-fine-anymore finery. Caught him in the mesh of her gown. She was that slimy. Her fishnet gown was that transmutable, that stretchable, at her command. Her underclothing did appear to be reversed blubber.

Fishnet gown did look less elegant with a fully grown, big-headed, jet-skinned Utopian-hybrid-Piscine flipping about in it, like a gigantic mutated salmon in a torn tux. Which, not intentionally ironically, was the name she gave him at birth … Salmon, also spelled Salman, as in Sal's (little) man.

With not much more than a shrug she hauled him out of the air inches away from the pupil-port's aqueous channel and released him on the dry dock-top.

His pride wasn't the only thing ruffled. His 'do' had finally become all unstuck.

"Where's my 'Mommy!'?" gurgled one of the two female bipeds coming down the gangplank behind codenamed Fisherwoman (Fish informally, Lady Achigan officially, Scylla Nereid nominally). As a Piscine, Fish was munch of a bunch, as she might put it, a whole buffet, more humanoid than either of these two.

One, the one who asked the question, with reference to the whereabouts of her daughter, Lakshmi Arthadot, she also of Lemuria, who should have been there to greet her, to call her 'Mommy' as she ran to embrace her, was Aortic Amphitrite, she of Shenon, Witch Isle. The other had dainty, goatish horns; a face covered with silken hair; and a thin, next to translucent, goatee. This was Pusan Wanderlust, the trail-blazing Traveller almost as often addressed as 'Goat', an appellation of which she actually approved.

She dressed in hides, not many of them, carried a shepherd's crook akin to a bishop's crosier or pedum. Unless it was the other way around.

Said: "Where's my brother?"

========

One of the reasons even Fish herself couldn't be sure whether or not she'd had six or seven Fish-spawn was because she could never be sure if the one she had around this time of year, albeit in 5953, was a stillborn-girl or a replicate of one. Could have been a stillborn-boy for all she knew or cared. It was dead or, if it was a replicate, the fucking faeries who – hardly for the first time for her – stole the live whichever covered their tracks really swell in the well.

Mind you, as Fish sometimes suspected because she knew what had become of Granny's final apprentice, her onetime close friend Sorciere (Solace Sunrise become, once legally, in the eyes of the State(s), Sundown), it could have been the Conquering Christ who covered his tracks really well. The real Conquering Christ, that is, Jesus Mandam, not the Boulder Brain, Mantel facsimile of same she and Pusan first encountered in Temporis last Yamana; the one Tsishah insisted could be put to good use.

Moray fool she. (More fool, Sea-saw?)

========

If Fish was exotic and Pusan goatish, hircine, capric, both of which they were, Amphitrite was a frogwoman straight out of the Roman myth of Latona, mother of Apollo and Diana. Younger by a couple of years than Fish, she was a Summoning Child, the same as Sorciere and Granny's grandniece Morgianna (born Nauroz become Somata, then Sarpedon). Which meant she was born in late Tantalar or early Yamana 5920 in here; late December 1920, early January 1921 out there.

At sixty and, like Fish, having endured no intervening quarter century in Limbo, nor having any Utopian blood to slow the normal aging process, she was fast approaching the time female Lemurians lost their amphibious abilities; had to take to the underwater world permanently. That explained the bizarre contraption carrying her. It was a mandroid guard-body, one specially adapted to her needs, though not the one that, encasing Pyrame Silverstar, Island Leviathan ate back in the first of week of last Tantalar.

The way to think of her these days, Tsishah-Cynthia advised Saladin Devason the night before whilst most local Utopians were dusting themselves off after the earthquake, is of a humanoid frog squished into a soft blob of clay. Except the clay was ambulatory, like a Jewish Golem; had arms, legs and a slab for a head, all of which Treat fit into like an animate fossil.

She wore something very similar to mask her decidedly unearthly, Creature from the Black Lagoon appearance, when they both attended the first Amsterdam Academy of Man beginning in September 1938 out there. (At Master Kyprian insistence, all the Inner Earthlings slept between-space. In Island Leviathan, as it happened, hence why Sal called him, incorrectly, his Alma Mater, meaning benevolent mother.)

While he may not know it, it was her guard-body more so than her normal, as opposed to supranormal, amphibious self that earned Treat a place in SOS: the Society of Saints during the war years. After all, real Lemurians couldn't grow extendable tentacles like she (as Lady Lemurian) could thanks to said highly pliable golem.

Today's guard-body wasn't the same as the one she wore as a teenager in the late Thirties during the first period of time she was out there. For one thing it was no longer soft. Also had a water tank, like a different kind of frogwoman's air tank – a scuba diver's air tank – on its back. The water from it went into blood-vessel-like tubes running through to the Golem's front side, the moulded area wherein Aortic Amphitrite was impressed.

Some of the tubing simply kept Treat's area, and hence Treat herself, not so much soaked as moist. A few, though, came out as thin nozzles around her head and face. They intermittently spritzed more so than sprayed water on her. She'd probably never admit it – though it was pretty obvious to anyone who knew much about Lemurian females – but this setup was likely all that was keeping her from submerging herself permanently.

Oh, the lengths a mother would go to attend her daughter's wedding.

Whereas most not yet moist eyes were on the three uniquely distinctive women who'd emerged from the surprisingly intact Valprey, Saladin Devason's pair were looking upward, towards its hippocampus-carved prow or figurehead and beyond, to its masthead or crow's-nest, atop of the ship's main mast. Was something not quite right about it, he somehow sensed.

Reflexively, protectively, he cast an impenetrable, as well as imperceptible, thought-bubble about himself and Cynthia-Tsishah.

A thought-impenetrable thought-bubble, rather.

========

As the High Illuminary of Weir, it should have fallen to Cynthia Masterwife to greet and respond to the newcomers. Capputis, though, was too full of energy to shut up.

"I'm sorry, your Ladyship," he said to Amphitrite, after doing his best to brush off his clothing and straighten his hairdo, both of which were wasted efforts. "The Matter Transducers between here and Temporis ceased working as a result of last night's temblor. Unless we can get them going again – and our scientocrats are working hard at doing just that – the wedding will have to be postponed."

"And my brother?" repeated Pusan.

Capputis was at a loss. "I'm sorry, your, um, Goatishness. I'm unaware of what's become of any brother you may have. Does he have a name? Billy, perhaps?" The hydrocephalic non-clone looked across the dock for assistance; looked toward where the Master his father and the latest High Illuminary were standing with their own honour guard. Looked at them desperately so; Pan-panicky, as a fay might say.

"I assume you are referring to Jordan Tethys, Traveller," Cynthia obliged. If she sounded uncertain it wasn't because she didn't know of the purported, more assumptive than actual, relationship between Pusan and the Legendarian. She was uncertain as to why Saladin cast an invisible force shield about the pair of them, her and him.

"I know what happened to Jordy," said the fauna. "I'm referring to my brother faun, the satyr, Dervish Furie." It was her turn, Cynthia Masterwife's turn, to look for assistance. She looked for it from Saladin Devason. He, Master's Mace in hand, looked dumbfounded. Then he began to colour, anger growing.

"I have no idea," she said, hoping to forestall the inevitable.

"No, but he does." Pusan waved her shepherd's crook in Saladin's direction.

Cynthia, metallic marigold in her hand, linked arms with Saladin. It was a somewhat unexpected show of solidarity. Fish picked up on it immediately. Her grinning no matter how knowingly, how understandingly even, was never a pleasant sight. With double row of shark-sharp toothiness it was akin to a gourmand doing so, lick-lips-smilingly-so, in anticipation of digging into a superlative feast.

"Let's skipjack the informalities," she suggested, purposefully (almost) dispensing with the Fishisms. (A skipjack was a kind of tuna. It was also sometimes used to refer to fish that leapt out of the water like a bluefish or, perhaps, an eagle ray. The word also meant a form of fisher's sloop with a v-shaped bottom and vertical sides.)

"If there's to be no fish-bed-wetting wedding, then we'd best get on with the other formaldehyde formalities." Like Trinondevs with their veils drawn, her non-fishifying – even if she could never quite eliminate it completely – was never a good sign. Neither was her striding more so than walking toward them, her oft-times lover and his, as of last night, thus far only one-night-stand one, they together so charmingly arm-in-arm.

Perhaps misinterpreting her body language, not to mention her always off-putting smile, Cynthia Masterwife reinforced Sal's shield with one of her own, making it both double-layered and, consequently, more noticeable. Fish paused, waved her howsoever reduced, yet still oversized fishhook, which she really didn't need as a cane – really didn't need out in the open either – as if a signal of some sort.

Smiled if possible even more menacingly: "I am trying to be fish-lice-nice, Sal."

"I beat you once, Fish. I won 50's Challenge of Weir."

"Only in so far as I neither could nor would champion a dead person."

"And what's my sister, if not dead?"

"Cocooned, Sal. Like a caterpillar pre-butter-flying onto toasty tidbits. Recall cocoons, recall Mariamnic training, recall Eden Nightingale, Master Kyprian's successor as the Whole Earth's genuine Anthean Mother Superior. Morg didn't cocoon herself to prevent her corpse being animated by an azura. She cocooned herself to prevent becoming a corpse."

"So I've been informed. I've yet to see any proof of it."

"Dugong-dignity or digging-clams-indignity?"

"Formality, Fish. Let's get on with it."

"Geoduck-good," she said, continuing to revert to non-menacing form presumably in an effort to defuse tensions, to thereby get on with the official transfer of power that Tsishah had come here to arrange. In bed as well as baby-belly-beckoning should it be required. "My fishy feelings prehensory-precisely. We're both a mighty bite long in the narwhal-tooth to get seriously squid-squiggly. At our sages it wouldn't be a tentacle-spectacle; it'd be more a matter of splatter."

"Awfully cocky, aren't you?"

"I'd have said awfully Cockle-Shelly."

"I know you would have. The guy with the gun, up there in the crow's-nest?"

"He doesn't have crow's wings. Besides, I wasn't signalling him not to shoot, I was signalling Sheba not to shove him off the mast. No need to shoot an ex-Master, is there?"

"Thought it was something like that. Otherwise I'd have thought-lanced him off it already. Sheba would be …"

"Me, Devason. We've already met. Rather, you've already met parts of me." She, Sheba Faerieflight, birth name Balkis Mandam, the Fifties-born Korant Ventricular of Witch Isle, began to coalesce in front of them: Fish, Amphitrite, the Traveller, Capputis Masterson, Cynthia Masterwife, their guards, the Valprey's Pani crew members, intrigued bystanders, and he, Saladin surname Nauroz, who had already resigned himself to no longer being the Master of Weir.

She, Sheba, was sprites, dryads, naiads, garden gnomes, trolls, ogres, Leprechauns, fucking faeries of all sorts of pixilated allsorts. Every one of them had to be a self-psychopomp since none of them had been there a second ago. Been there visibly, that is, since they'd all come as if out of nowhere between-space. Most were wearing clothes. So too was she, after a fashion, the same clothes: particoloured, tatterdemalion patches of this, that and them.

Then they, the clothes, started coalescing as well. Not just self-psychopomps then; shape-shifting self-psychopomps. Faerieflight finished coming altogether herself, altogether her non-liminal Norma Normalman self again. Make that Norma Normalcy self. Like using Mankind instead of Humanity, both Normalman and Normalwoman had the taint of patriarchy about them. Reduced to its instigating kernel, the Panharmonium Project had almost everything to do with equality.

(She and her twin brother – members of the Family Ryne seemed to have a propensity for having twins – had been taken over by Strife and Daemonicus on the Outer Earth sometime ago. Dispossessed and fleeing WORLD's fishing trawler, in the company of its deposed chief operations officer, Salvatore Dis L'Orca – whose dead sister Garcia was still traipsing about the Hidden Headworld somewhere, animated by a Sangazur – in mid-December, they'd managed to avoid being destroyed with it by Crystallion {a cousin of theirs born Crystal St Synne}, Hell's Horsemen and their Nuclear Dragons.)

Sheba, born Balkis Mandam (father: Jesus; nominal-mother: Cybele-Miracle's daughter, Meroudys Maenad, nowadays masquerading as Ramona Avar, Lady Guillotine, beyond the Dome), wasn't an altogether bad-looking Normal-Woman in her late-twenties. Had on a dress, a toga actually, one no doubt inspired by fashions popularized in Imperial Rome, since most everything about the Korant Sisterhood and the Mithrant Brotherhood was Roman in origin. Did have reddish-blonde hair, though. At least it wasn't silver.

Once she did so, come together altogether, Sheba-Balkis eyed Fisherwoman quizzically. In the absence of her grandmother Miracle Maenad (born Cybele St Synne), and her nominal sovereign Queen Godda (whomsoever Krepusyl Evenstar was currently occupying), she had little choice except to defer to Fish.

It wasn't so much she, Faerieflight, the latest in a long line of the Faerie Flight type or variety of feeorin, was afraid of currently also Lady Achigan as they – her mortal grandmother and Twilight's immortal devic Dand – were wary of her. Had been for decades, with good reason. Some things needed changing. Now just wasn't the time.

(Krepusyl Evenstar was a second born Lazaremist. Conceivably, hah-hah, Wilderwitch's half-mother, she'd had hold of Tsishah Thrae, making her that era's Queen Godda, for a good percentage of her life; until 5960, to be absolutely accurate. Equally arguably Sheba's grandmother Cybele, whose hair was two tones of red, had hold of Divine Coueranna, a second-born Mithradite Apple Goddess, Strife's brood sister, to this day. Unless, as was often the case, it was the other way around.)

"It'll be non-Fish, non-disputatiously-dignified, Sheba-Sea-Bass," Aka Scylla Nereid, once also the marital queen of Greater Godbad, instructed her.

"And?" One had to be precise with Fish. Enough of her composite faeries had told her, Sheba-Balkis, of their kin comprising her, Fish's, compote over the decades.

"Formally, dogfish-dot-ditto."

Becoming Fish's soup, her uncooked bouillabaisse, did not immediately appeal so, not wanting to become faerie-soup either, Faerieflight returned hers and her ingredients' attention to the not-as-yet formally resigned Master of Weir here on the Whole Earth. "Then allow me, Saladin Devason, to introduce to you my brother, Solomon Taurson."

"You've been practising that, haven't you, Ventricular?" stated Cynthia Masterwife. Although prone to alliterative fay-saying herself, she – like her faerie fart of an underlying father, this despite his last name – wasn't very good at rhyming. She did, however, appreciate someone who could rhyme at any given time.

"Precious little else to do on Shenon, is there, ex-Aortic?"

Could rhyme occasionally anyhow.

========

Were Fisherwoman to see her sister in Miracle Memory, as well as Flowery Anthea, right that moment they would have agreed on one thing for sure.

A fishnet gown wasn't all that different from a chain-mail same. Well, maybe there was one essential difference. While both glowed with golden Gypsium brilliancy, Wilder-witch's chain-mail gown was knit so tightly she, the Witch, didn't need to wear under-clothes underneath it. Not even for modesty's sake. It was knit that tight.

Fish, though, would have wondered why it had knit her to a cot.

========

The vimana Golgotha Nauroz flew to the outskirts of the Zebranid Leper Colony a few days earlier had been moved to the colony's upper meadow. Golgo-tha, Black Skull-Face as members of D-Brig sometimes recalled him – recalled his codename during the Secret Wars of the Supranormals – and the three elite warriors of Weir he brought with him had been captured.

No matter how elite you were, no matter how well your vimana was equipped, what good were four Trinondevs armed with eye-staves against dozens of exiles from Cabalarkon and their descendants armed identically? Answer was, all the more so since the Zebranids were also armed with Godbadian guns, not much good at all.

Golgotha wasn't in the leper colony anymore. They, the Zebranids, knew where he'd gone, he and one other, Andaemyn Sarpedon's new boyfriend. Were where Jor-dan Tethys had drawn them before he drew himself to the Weirdom. Weren't too sure where on the Hidden Headworld that was, however. Wasn't too likely they'd find out anytime soon, either.

The pad the recurring Legendarian left behind – the one with a failsafe draw-ing of him sitting behind the table where Helen, Persephone and their mother, along with a few medically trained Zebranids, had been sitting at playing cards during their nightlong vigil over Wilderwitch – had gone up in flames.

Fortunately, when it did, Melina nee Sarpedon Zeross, who'd been holding it, hadn't dropped it on top of the Witch, lying helplessly as she was chained to the cot by Nihila's somehow finally regenerating power focus, her Brainrock torc. (Which Mel-Illuminatus had fastened around Wilderwitch's neck after she abducted, and Cabby's Caddy-carried, the Witch to the Whiplash colony from her family's now swamped hideaway a couple of days earlier.)

At the cost of some burned fingertips Mel was quick thinking enough to toss it to one corner of the shed. Unfortunately, where she threw it, there were some curtains skirting the picture window. Zebranids didn't have any firestones-topped obelisks to generate electricity. Lived a pretty basic life up here in the (very) high woods. Which of course was the other part of the problem. Their cabins – very nice-ly built they were too – were made of wood; worse, were preserved with creosote.

Paper-pad afire, curtains, wooden cabins covered with much the same, highly combustible creosote, an oddly dry spring, the rain when it came was very welcome. As for why it never seemed to stop, well, that was another matter. Forty days and forty nights had to start – restart – sometime.

Why not Midsummer?

========

If one can call a vimana a casualty, Broom was a casualty. Thirty storeys is a long way for a no matter how well-shielded extraterrestrial shuttlecraft to fall. Yet that's how far it fell when the quake's vibrations shook it off Skyrise's roof. Could be it was hopelessly damaged. Not that, if the Witch lasted long enough to successfully assimilate Nihila –

integrate her, more like – with her pregnant body beautiful, she'd need a vimana to come for her.

She'd become a self-psychopomp. Just like her first and thus far only born, Fey Woman; like Raven's Head after Limbo, if not consciously beforehand; like the Diver, after consuming Fish's agates, and some of her Vesica Piscis, on Sraddha Isle; like Mel-Illuminatus, when she assumed the form of Cabby's Caddy; like Sheba Faerieflight's semi-sentient component-selves. Indeed, just like Tsishah's eldest son, Toothy Teoti, did for awhile.

And not just when he was acting as the then still Aortic's self-made pet-pomp.

========

As for the other twenty vimanas still in Cabalarkon, with the stone gnomes shut down – they couldn't be on strike, didn't have that level of intelligence; that had to be Sedon's idea of a joke – they never got off the ground. Neither did the Weirdom's Warrior Elite form a winged-globe along the lines of the symbol seen on so many ancient Assyrian cylinder seals; the same as they had when many of them went out to the Slopes of the Sleepers in mid-Tantalar last year.

Nor a Wyvern of Weir formation like they had a few days earlier when they took out Mars Bellona, as motivated by Guardian Angel Tyrtod on Drenched Dust-mound. Not even Golgotha's personal favourite from their first arrival in Hadd, their Batty Battalion. Indeed, understandably – due to the chaos still reigning after last night's earthquake – the Trinondevs didn't form anything at all.

Formed nothing to either greet or confront the Pegasus-creature that had flown in from the tidal-wave-decimated coast of Fearsome Fobbiat; was now soaring in ever lowering circles overtop Cabalarkon's great central square. Didn't do anything, either; other than to use their eyeorb-projected thought-bubbles to push the masses out of the way such that it could land without squishing anyone. Which it did, land, the Pegasus-creature, though in truth it was more of a Night Mare creature.

Those who revealed themselves after they dissolved the collectively mani-fested gargoyle were armed with eye-staves at the very least. Some were armed with enough other varieties of firepower they could topple firestone-topped obelisks sin-gle-handedly. While they might call themselves Warriors of Weir, they, men and among them a significant, though smaller, percentage of women, weren't proper Trinondevs. Couldn't be.

Of the younger ones, many were striped. Of the others, all the men weren't necessarily black-as-midnight any more than all the women were necessarily white-as-light. That may have made them hybrids, but not necessarily. While some may well have been mixed bloods, as few or as many more of them may have been from other onetime Weirdoms. And there were a few of them: Shenon, Manoa, Sraddha Isle, Godbad City, Kanin City, Corona City, The Argent, to name seven of the doz-en or so thus far discovered. Either/or their ancestors had been.

As for the older ones, amongst them a few Summoning Children or close to it, Saladin had stripped them of their rank when he exiled them thirty years earli-er. Didn't confiscate their eye-staves; that would have approximated murder. How could they survive in the wide, vicious world, not all of which was radioactive, after a certain distance away from Cabalarkon, without them? Answer to that was not for very long.

Not a one of them was in Arabic or Middle Eastern garb. Were, if anything, dressed casually; like any ordinary Norma and Norman Normalman on any street in Greater Godbad. Mostly that was because they didn't have anything to wear except store bought or traded for clothes. And then only clothes commonly sold in Greater Godbad, which extended to the southern city states of the Cattail Peninsula and high into Bandrad proper and the Whiplash Range.

They definitely didn't have any uniforms. Not even their leader. Or his daughter. She was striped, however.

========

Irisiel Mercherm, Lazareme's female Heliodromus or Sun-Runner, aka Speedy for reasons obvious, recognized something had to be wrong in Trans-Time Trigon the moment Pyrame Silverstar, humanizing Miracle Memory as she was at the time, vanished from the Valprey. She suspected it had gone back into the time stream; in other words, that someone had found a way to kill the Male Entity.

Had a fair idea who as well: the same formidable fellow Sal had tried to do away with last Yamana. Who had a habit of turning the tables; of killing those who sought to kill him or his.

========

The Moloch Sedon wanted the Dual Entities eliminated, or at the very least neutralized, as part of his compensation for allowing the capitalization of Pan-harmonium to go ahead. Probably would have been satisfied if Harmony – in her harmonious, as opposed to her recently nihilistic aspect – had managed to hold onto Machine-Memory last Tantalar. That hadn't happened; was unlikely it could now. Especially if someone had indeed managed to kill Heliosophos.

Since Helios was a bifurcated being possessed, both halves of him, head and body, by Lord Yajur, both halves of him, the devil's head and his body, an obvious suspect was Datong Harmonia herself, as Nihila, Balance in her non-Nemesis, nihil-istic aspect. Belatedly postmortem, and revival, she had grown to hate her fellow Unities, Order as much the third one, Chaos: albeit him, Unholy Abaddon, likely more so than Yajur-Order.

It was Young Death's Uncle Abe Chaos – Young Death, Auguste Moirnoir be-yond the Dome, (ostensibly) being born Augustus Nauroz in here and, as such, the fairified father of both Sal and year younger sister Morg – who had left her pinned to a slab of Brainrock with the Susasword for something like 500 years after all.

However, after what happened to Freespirit Nihila during the latest battle of bats, it was a bit early for that. Before she could have a chance to kill Helios-Yajur she'd have to be alive, or at least functional. And the last Irisiel had seen of her, all that was left of Nihila was her Brainrock torc, her Tvasitar-crafted power focus. Even if Wilderwitch, who apparently was the ex-Unity's incarnation and definitely was still six months pregnant, with a solitary girl-child, could revivify her, which aspect of her would come back dominant, Harmony or Nihila?

More importantly, would either of them be sane?

========

Irisiel Mercherm ran through between-space to Absudyl-Minius.

For a devil irreverently named Speedy, it took far longer than she figured it would or should. Machine-Memory had set up some formidable fortifications, not least of which was the mostly mindlesss-molasses' under-footing that marked the demon-like Godcrud making up so much of the Upper Head's subcranial Hell-Well of the World regaining some semblance of what, for them, passed as cognition. Which should have twigged her it was still there. And, yes, altogether visibly now, there it was, Trans-Time Trigon.

The devic messenger was so startled by its hulking presence – it, by all accounts up until a dozen years ago, a three-peaked Aegean Island, in the midst of a flat sea of veritable asphalt – she made the mistake of stopping her motion forward. Just stood there gawping at it. Whereupon Absudyl's mandroid mush rose up, sought to solidify her within itself.

She hot-footed it inside.

========

Simultaneously, approaching the great central square of the Weirdom far above Absudyl on the Head's surface, different Trinondevs than those then landing in it, official Trinondevs, were using thought-bubbles manifested from the tips of their eye-staves to part the masses along the boulevard leading from the port to the plaza.

Weren't bowling them over, fortunately. That would have been rude; occasionally fatal even. Would be no way to make an impression; especially not in the stonework.

Were more like gently beach-balling them to either side of the road.

========

Led by the Master of Weir – rather, led by Saladin Devason, though he still held his Master's Mace in one hand – it was quite the procession.

If the Trojan Horse had just landed in Cabalarkon's plaza, no Greeks hidden within it came out to ransack Sedon's Devic Eye-Land. There was a statue of a solitary, figurative Greek rumbling up the boulevard akin to the Trojan Horse; a Morrigan Night Mare of a horse, more precisely. What, who, it contained wouldn't be doing any ransacking, Tsishah-Cynthia had assured Sal; neither of the city itself, nor of the surrounding countryside right up to the Slopes of the Sleepers themselves. No one would.

Who it contained would be ruling it, the Weirdom of Cabalarkon; ruling – make that, albeit also as its Master – the Weirdom of Panharmonium.

There was something to be said for the size of the thing. Something to be said for the size of the thing carrying it as well. This last wasn't an armoured tank. Sal had seen tanks before, in Godbadian lowlands, on the Cattail, which along its long, bountiful, west coast wasn't quite as mountainous as the subcontinent, in the Bloodlands (New Valhalla), and throughout the vast plains of Marutia, Sedon's Cheeklands, also its Breadbasket, before the Time Quakes returned a couple of years back.

There had even been tanks – Nazi panzers, leftovers from World War II – on the flats below Dustmound last Tantalar. (He hadn't seen them then; had to take the word of Golgotha and surviving members of his Batty Battalion for it. Did recognize the marking they described: From the Outer Earth during the War and, more than just remarkably, absolutely stunningly, the so-called Lost Legion that reassembled outside the Gates of Cabalarkon back in 5950. Were reputedly led by the same field marshal, Tyrtod von Blut, though he must have been a Dead Thing Walking by the time he and his tanks got to Hadd thirty years later.)

It did have tank treads. The cab, its tinted glass windscreen hiding the identity of its driver (one Cromwell Necator by name, whom Sal would have met in Godbad and, chances were, elsewhere over the years), was armoured. It wasn't a flatbed truck, though it did have a flatbed. It was an all-terrain military vehicle, the kind used for transporting helicopters and missile batteries in the Middle East and elsewhere beyond the Dome.

Interestingly, the heavily armed soldiers on said flatbed, hanging onto the guy-lines keeping Morg's statue in place, and those who were marching, as separate units, behind and to either side of it, were wearing different uniforms. Since both sets of guys on the guy-lines, without a woman among them, were heavily armed with Godbadian-made, or Outer-Earth-imported, automatic weaponry, one group, not surprisingly, was from Godbad.

As if to confirm that, they were dressed in Godbadian uniforms; New God-badian uniforms, Sal reminded himself, blues instead of greys. The other group, though, was dressed in uniforms that were not so much a throwback to Imperial Roman times on the Outer Earth as were the current version of the uniform worn by Ap Isle's Mithrant Legionnaires; the uniform that had been current for something like 2000 years, likely more.

Legionary Mithrants, ditto their Korant womenfolk, and indeed Trinondevs of Weir, were firm believers in non-evolving traditions.

Now there, thought Sal, when he first saw them march out of the somehow sealed-against-the-sea, industrial-strength gates at the Valprey's prow, beneath its seahorse (hippocampus) figurehead, was an alliance made anywhere except heaven. Not in, or under, Sedon's heavenly hotel for star-stuck devils anyhow.

Weren't they enemies? They were ... they, fronted by General Quentin Anvil, the never-conscripted, professional soldiers of Godbad; and they, fronted by Solo-mon Taurson, the born-to-the-blade – a 'gladius' naturally – legionnaires of Apple Isle, even if it'd been more born-to-the-barrel-of-a-gun for the last few hundred years. What kind of deal had Morg and her mostly witch-proxies made ... and not just with the Devil?

Were the two biggest military forces on the Western Headworld, that of God-bad and that of Apple Isle, jointly going to invade the Outer Earth? Were they, on the obverse side of the same coin, preparing to jointly defend the Head from invading Outer Earthlings in case the Dome collapsed, as it may soon be doing if those beyond it didn't stop developing Atomics?

For Saladin Devason neither scenario held any validity. As far as he was concerned both militaries were here for one purpose, and one purpose alone. It wasn't to celebrate the spirit of how the Weirdom was going to be renamed. They weren't here to ensure both sides gained equal access to Cabalarkon's extraterrestrial doo-dads and gewgaws, no matter how non-functional all of the ones that were working had become overnight.

They were here to ensure neither side gained access to them exclusively.

Sal foresaw three options: one would, both would, neither would. Then again, if he was still Master of Weir; if he hadn't supposedly lost the confidence of the people, they who afforded him his Masterly Might; if the stone gnomes hadn't gone on strike; and if, most importantly, his Sed-son's Sed-father hadn't left him in the lurch; there'd be a fourth option. They all would. Get it, albeit mostly the nether-regions of the equation. Would get it in the face, too.

As for the statue itself, he had to admit the quality of the workmanship that went into it was first class. It was much better than anything produced by stone gnomes. Might even have been faerie-struck, as in faerie-forged. Hard to understand why the sculptor or sculptors didn't put her on a Night Mare, or find a place to put the Night Mare insignia – the Valprey got itself a hippocampus prow it wouldn't have had all that long ago – but it was nevertheless a fine likeness of his unlamented sister.

Not surprisingly. Morg was about to come out of it; once she, the statue containing her cocoon, was driven to Cabalarkon's central plaza. His sister always enjoyed playing to a crowd. Sal knew that. Tsishah had only reminded him of it. Last night, when he fell in love with Cynthia Master's Daughter.

His own niece!

========

Other than their own honour guard of Trinondevs and Illuminaries, virtually everyone in the procession led by Saladin Devason and Cynthia Masterwife were outlanders. As it happened there was a fair smattering of outlanders in the crowd already gathered in the square. Most had come in via Matter Transducers from Temporis over the previous few days, before the teleportation devices went down.

Most were sick from eating the dubiously-guaranteed-edible sludge that passed for food in Cabalarkon, what of it that still dribbled out of the Stone Gnome processors. Most were tired, physically drained. Were nervous wrecks, prone to shuddering and shivering involuntarily. And shaking their heads in amazement every time they realized they were still alive.

An earthquake in Temporis invariably resulted in a landfall. As one might imagine if one lived in a howsoever night-and-day cavern, landfalls were about the worst thing any of these presumably fully alive Temporites could imagine. As a consequence of the Matter Transducers going down, not only would there be no wedding to attend, most weren't sure how they were going to get home.

The rest weren't sure they had a home left to go home to now – Temporis mostly lay under Sisert, the Mystic Mountains and the Ghostlands, not the Weirdom, not even its farthest out borders, the Slopes of the Sleepers, pocked with millennia-abandoned millennial ships that they were – but, still, it was an appreciable concern. Not a one had brought a shovel to dig his or herself back home, as required.

About all any of them were grateful for was that the cyclopean stonework that made up most of the city was built to withstand earthquakes. Stonework so finely formed, so tightly chiselled, so hence perfectly fitted, there was no need for mortar: that did the trick. Regardless of stone gnomes, it had to have for the city's structures to have lasted for so many thousands of years in such tremendous condition.

What none of them knew, or professed not to know, was that well beneath Cabalarkon lay Absudyl, Minius, the Subterranean Land of the Mandroids. The Dual Entities had deliberately taken Trans-Time Trigon there once they tumbled out of the time stream to the Whole Earth for the start of his, the Male Entity's, hundredth lifetime in 5975.

They reckoned it was safe there, as it had been on previous occasions, because the Moloch Sedon was as afraid of going to Absudyl-Minius as he was of going too near All the Invincible and the mostly between-space She-Sphinx's Prison Beach of Incain. And so it was; appearances, or lack thereof, sometimes to the contrary.

Had been for over five years — just not for any more.

========

There was a struggle going on inside it, in the tip-top hollow of one of its three peaks. It was a struggle for Trans-Time Trigon, its soul, its innards, its controlling mind. It was a struggle for nothing, no one, less than the Mnemosyne Machine. Was a lot more going on there than just that, too.

'Oh,' Irisiel flashed to herself, 'That's where they got to.'

Then, her with it, them all with it, Trans-Time Trigon did depart Absudyl. Though not back into the time stream. Not yet.

Someone had won. And it wasn't any of them.

****

Thirteen-Demon: **Skyrise Kills**

========

The Summer Solstice 5981

Saladin Devason had been waiting for this moment since the night before; since Cynthia Masterwife revealed herself to be his niece, Tsishah Twilight, half his niece anyhow, and they had made love anyway. It wasn't like she was going to get pregnant. She already was, six months so. Or Demon Queen Lilith was; he still wasn't quite sure how that worked.

Wasn't elementary birds and bees stuff, that was for sure.

========

The Trinondevs, his and Sarpedon's, working together, levitated Morgianna's statue in thought-balloons off the flatbed military vehicle then, without incident, lowered it into the middle of the central square. That done, everyone stepped back; looked to him for the next move. He hesitated, contemplated trying for a lightning bolt effect of his own. If Cynthia had been Wilderwitch she'd have insisted on it.

But Cynthia was Tsishah; had quite rightly told him that if Morg wanted a lightning bolt, to mark her emergence by shattering her out into the open arms of her adoring public, she could provide it. All he had to do was whack her statuesque grotesquery with his, her, mace and she'd do the rest.

She, Cynthia Masterwife, gave him an impatient nudge. Clearly, it was time for him to decide how to play out this fiasco.

Was he going to go with dugong-dignity, as Fish put it, or risk digging-clams-in-dignity, as she also put it, in her inimitable manner? Was he going to just accept what was apparently inevitable; to meekly give over Cabalarkon to Morgianna and her hated cadre without a fight? Or was he going to risk a whole lot more than just indignity, risk his very life, and strive to hold onto power?

To hold onto, besides (maybe) his clothes, what the people, its source, and the evidently duplicitous Moloch Sedon, the people's unwanted backup – unless the All-Father of All-Devils was the Weirdom's real power, which he might be – had seemingly already determined he didn't deserve to hold onto anymore?

He, Saladin born Nauroz, stepped out of their jointly mind-made, and reinforced, much more than merely mental shield. Maintained his own, its imperviousness, with his Masterly Mace. Didn't doubt he was the only one. Trinondevs on both sides would have already had theirs up.

The same with Fish, via her Vesica Piscis, which could do all sorts of things. As could her other two power foci – the three supposedly being gifts from her Miracle Memory of a thought mother, having disposed of their devic owners God – though possibly not the Devil – knew how.

There were various theories re that. Fish came along after Sal's half-mother, Pyrame Silverstar, lost control of Machine-Memory, due to cathonitization, but before Hot Stuff, Methandra Thanatos, got hold of her again. Most believed Pyçonja Volant, one of Byron's Winter Zodiacals – that of Pisces, duh-the-dogfish that – was her devic half-mom. However, Pyçonja's power focus was a fisher's gaffe.

By contrast Fish's bellybutton bauble had belonged to a Lazaremist extremist, Mandorla Auricaura, whereas her soul-net belonged to cloud-headed Diluvia Ran, she being one of Mithras's Lesser Apocalyptics, that of Flood. So, was Miracle Memory playing at approximating the Trigregos Sisters by possessing all three simultaneously when she conceived and bore Fisherwoman? He could ask her, if she showed up. She might even answer, as a personal favour, assuming Pyrame still had her.

Cynthia nudged him again, knocking him out of his reverie and into motion.

This was it. He didn't have what protection his Masterly Mace afforded him, he could be about to die. Could, equally so, be killed the moment he gave it up. Today did not feel like a good day to die, as Crazy Horse reputedly said just before the Battle of Little Big Horn, during the aftermath of which the Cheyenne Medicine Man Manitoulin found, and thereafter helped raise, the infant Sedon St Synne. (Although history books on the subject never made clear whether, back in 1876, on the Outer Earth, he was referring to General Yellowhair, George Armstrong Custer, or to himself.)

No matter. What did matter was that he didn't feel like dying. Therefore, God and the Devil willing, he wouldn't. Probably.

The fellow stepping out of the flatbed-bulldozer's armoured cab, he recognized. Was Cromwell Necator, the Fatman's protector, Greater Godbad's most notorious, state-appointed assassin; its most effective executioner. The guy over there was Solomon Taurson, also Mandam. He blew. And it wasn't a party trick. The boy was a deviant; his ability truly daemonic.

Fortunately, as his grandmother, the other Miracle (the Korants' long-serving Miracle Maenad), boasted most recently on the Valprey (before she buggered off between-space), he glowed before he 'blowed'. Unfortunately he also came back together, ready to do it again almost immediately. The overweight – though some called her voluptuous – septuagenarian supposedly so thoroughly imbued with a highborn Apple Goddess (Divine Coueranna) eyeorbs couldn't extract her, not even in Cabalarkon, was invited but wasn't there. Not in the (ample) flesh at any rate.

The same held true for Amal-Althea Brand, Lazareme's Female Healer, out of Melina Sarpedon, who many believed was born with her inside her; born here as well. Did a ditto for Wilderwitch – who may not have been born here, but spent a lot of time here, both before and after her quarter century doing the legless Limbo – when it came to Datong Harmonia.

Also applied to Barsine Mandam, who was born with Nergal Vetala inside herself. It didn't then Golgotha's Batty Battalion should have been able to take her out in Hadd with their prison pods. It wasn't like it was her protectorate. Vetala, especially in her Fecundity days, which lasted hundreds of years, supposedly didn't have a protectorate exclusively her own.

Not in Hadd anyhow, which was Byronic territory; hence unaffected by the Thrygragon Compact of 4376 Year of the Dome., Even though, as Fecundity, she may well have had one in what became the Ghostlands in 4825, she'd been in Hadd since the year before, so it couldn't have been very important to her.

Talk about weirdness in the Weirdom – even if it was more like 'muse about' – Solomon's twin, that Miracle's granddaughter, Sheba Faerieflight, born Balkis Mandam, stood within easy podding distance. Most of her did anyhow. Couldn't be sure she was all there because she fractured, too. Only she didn't call it that. She called it pixilating. Had nothing to do with computer graphics or holograms; had everything to do with pixies, fucking faeries. Deviancies, especially in here, were so, well, strange.

Over there the hated Sarpedon Summoning Child, also one of twins, non-verbally daring him to try something stupid had the oldest eye-stave on either side of the Dome; what should have been his, had his own grandfather Ubris Nauroz chosen him instead of Demios. Granny's brother hadn't been malevolent or even precognitive, she used to console him. Upstanding Utopian that he was even after he became a vampire during the Simultaneous Summonings, he just hated devils and their spawn; including, perhaps even especially, Sed-spawned deviants.

Dem-Wit's dangerous daughter Andaemyn – Sal's other niece besides Tsishah-Cynthia, whose 28th birthday it was today, he recalled, and whom he should have put permanent paid to on Haunted Dustmound last year – had enough firepower about her she wouldn't just topple firestone-topped obelisks. She'd holler timber before she did so.

Why was Aortic Amphitrite's mandroid guard-body hardening in front of her as quickly as it was already hardened behind her? He knew the answer to that. Solidarity, as in solidity, as in invulnerability. Would it be strong enough? Was everything about Fish, her bellybutton accessory, her fishnet gown, so recently shed of son Cappy, her fishhook, glowing so brightly because she was about to get away? Or was it because she was hungry?

Fish was always hungry. Which-witch was why he'd never yet seen her far from water: a dip away from a quick catch and snack. Saladin rarely was; not just because he slurped slime out of stone gnome food processors. Food-approximating replicators, make that. He was a satisfied guy. Why shouldn't he be? Rather, why shouldn't he have been?

He stepped forward. Raised his formerly Masterly Mace high; didn't repeat, didn't recite, the rote with which the latest High Illuminary of Weir had provided him. Didn't say what he was supposed to say. Said instead: "By this Mace I hereby proclaim …" Not you, Morgianna, not you as the new Master of Weir: "A new Challenge of Weir."

The lightning bolt came from below Cabalarkon.

========

All the Invincible (self-proclaimed), in her mobile form of an eagle or garuda-winged She-Sphinx, flew out of between-space high above the wildfires raging on the mountain meadows and woodlands overlooking her Prison Beach of Incain. She'd been under instructions from her mistresses, primarily Pyrame-Memory, to pick up the remaining Zerosses and whomever else Melina nee Sarpedon chose to bring with them. That done, she was to transport them, in her, to what was today to be proclaimed the Weirdom of Panharmonium.

Her joint mistresses loved to put on a good show. As for All herself, she-it always enjoyed being as awe-inspiring as she was purely awesome.

========

Saladin Devason also looked up. His sister looked down upon him.

Correction, Morgianna, the Morrigan, the White Witch, Superior Sarpedon, her statue's suddenly manifestly open eyes did. Then she, her statuesque grotesquery, started wobbling. Wasn't the only thing wobbling either. That there, that was a firestone-topped obelisk. So was that. Was a whole forest of the phallic pinnacles wobbling. Then they looked to start toppling.

Morg could have had the common decency to shout 'Timber'. Everyone there could have shouted 'Timber'. Some might have as well. It was hard to hear anything amidst all the rumbling and grumbling, its shaking and quaking. So he hollered it. Seemed the proper thing to do, given the circumstances.

Yelled 'TIMBER!' at the top of his lungs just as the ground, the plaza's over-catacombs-ground, began cracking beneath his feet.

He, had he had time to think of it, could have yelled 'TEMBLOR' or, just as accurately, 'LANDFALL!' Both had two syllables, the same as 'timber'. Plus, both would have been sandbags more appropriate. Couldn't very well yell **'Catacombs collapsing in on themselves!'**. Not even at the bottom of his lungs. It had far too many syllables. But that was what was happening.

Until, of course, it had happened.

========

The smoke from the fires was so thick, she (resolutely not it; let alone, except to some of the devils still stuck inside her, she-it) couldn't spot anyone down below; let alone anyone to pick up. Then she looked up; knew right away she was in big trouble. Blazing out of the sky toward her, toward her beach, was … what?

All did not have much of a vocabulary. Wasn't one for grammar either. Was she really invincible? She was about to find out.

========

This time the earthquake, unless it was an even worse aftershock, was centred on Cabalarkon City, well up the comparatively wide, navigable Cabalarkon River from, yes, Cabalarkon Delta.

Was centred, better make that, beneath it, in Absudyl-Minius, the Subterranean Land of the Mandroids. Perhaps it shouldn't have – never had in the past – Trans-Time Trigon uprooting itself, even if it didn't immediately go back into the time stream, had to have some effect on the Weirdom above it.

Regardless of should have, never had, the effect was collapsing catacombs.

========

All the Invincible wasn't.

The She-Sphinx still didn't have much in the way of grammar. Had, however, come up with some degree of vocabulary. The word she'd been searching her synapses for was 'asteroid'. That was what coming out of the sky, the Sedon Sphere, an island out of the sky, the night's sky, when it wasn't the day's sky. Was an asteroid.

Was coming at her Prison Beach. Wasn't just blazing. Was Gypsium-glowing. Definitely had three peaks. She could tell because they all pointed at her; at All.

========

For every horror story there was a corresponding hero story. Was also more than a few heroine stories. Together therefore, hero and heroine stories outnumbered horror stories by a margin of two-to-one. As the day progressed on both ends of the Headworld – the Weirdom at the top of its forehead and the Zebranid Leper Colony at the tip of the Cattail Peninsula – the hero and heroine stories, Utopian and human, steadily increased their margin until they declared victory.

Then the burying began. Just not in the Slopes of the Sleepers. Those buried weren't sleeping.

One horror was almost impossible to forget. It involved Skyrise, the Saladin Master's Outer Earth modern, architectural eyesore, coming alive. Becoming a chthonic monstrosity, bending over the plaza, picking up a toppled obelisk and hurling it, like a stake or spear, albeit not Blind Sundown's, thereby securing the Mastery of Weir for, well, not itself. For who was animating it.

There would be no need for a Challenge of Weir.

========

The reason All of Incain hadn't seen anyone in the mountain meadows or adjacent woods was because, besides the smoke, everyone who hadn't altogether got away had sensibly fled as far away from the colony as they could. Had sought higher ground, or lower ground, or anywhere elsewhere so long as it was nowhere near the wildfires. They – the heavy-lifting capabilities of their eye-staves proving invaluable – included the three Trinondevs of Weir that 'Black Skull' Golgotha left behind when the Legendarian drew him, and one other, elsewhere.

Wasn't much else to do. Even on a Hidden Headworld, even if Mother Earth hadn't started the conflagration, just took over once it began – to multiply its munificence, as it were – Nature had to take its course. As for All, the She-Sphinx had to take her explosions. Both in the Weird and beyond it.

Except, Brainrock exploding, along with the last Atomic Twin, be it Osiraq or Tammuz, was the last thing All needed. Other than to prove she wasn't invincible.

========

Someone once said that, when it came to witches, it was always best to let them make their own bed of straw before setting it alight. Panic set in at the Zebranids' colony the moment the fire in the Witch's cabin got out of control, outside it as well as inside it. Whereupon, once it got outside, it spread like, well, wildfire.

Mel's first thought was the same as that of her daughters. As for her effectively adopted, medically and non-medically trained Illuminaries, their first thoughts were for their own behinds. They gave up fighting the cabin fire as it reached the ceiling; fled through every available orifice. Couldn't very well help save anyone else if they hadn't saved themselves first.

"Tina," cried Mel-Illuminatus, going call-me-Cabby's Caddy all of a sudden.

Was getting easier and easier the more she did it. Had to be careful. She'd known Barsine, Jesse's supposed twin sister, quite well, especially since she moved indoors, as it were; under the Dome, as it really was. And look what became of her, become Vetala, once she started letting out the devil she was born with too often.

Mel hadn't necessarily been born with Amal-Althea Brand after the Summoning. Had more like brought her out, of necessity, some thirty-five years earlier when she first acquired her even then caduceus-shaped power focus. Which, as she always claimed, came out of the Olympian Tantalus Agenor Heliopolis, Kadmon and Europa's father, by different mothers, got hold of in the late Thirties beyond the Dome.

Be that as it may, caduceus-like self-psychopomp that she thus became, she was through the Weird to the big cabin wherein she'd left her youngest, on her seventh birthday, finally sleeping after a restless night. Tina wasn't there. Her other two daughters were, however, having used their father's Gypsium rings to port themselves to the same place, for the same purpose.

Tina didn't need rescuing. The excellent, if at times excessively energetic, youngster had a set of daddy's rings, too. A teleportal formed in the air about two feet off the floor. Tina was standing, self-suspended, in its opening. Her night clothes were neither soiled nor singed. She had favourite dolly, Silkie the baby Selkie, in one hand; was pointing the other, with Gypsium rings on every finger, including her thumb, at her family.

Mel, Helen and Percy didn't have time to call her name before she expanded the portal and, as if the hose of a vacuum cleaner, sucked them through it, through between-space, all the way across the Hidden Continent, about as far as one can go without running out of Headworld. The terrified birthday girl, at such a young and vulnerable age, could have no way of knowing what, let alone how, she was doing what she was doing. Just knew she and her family were in danger; that she had to get them out of it as quickly as her still developing mind could fathom.

Speaking of which – fathoms – she had no way of knowing her family's coastal hideaway had been inundated by an overnight tidal wave. That it had been smashed, pulverized, into so much fractured stonework and toothpick-timber, then mostly swept out to sea. For her it was the safest place in the Headworld, either side of it, either side of the Dome as well.

At least the headland above it was still there, as were some of the sturdier outbuildings, where they could find shelter from the storm as required. That's where Percy and Helen got them, Tina and her mother, their mother, and themselves, after the youngster faltered as if an unsupported dolly herself.

Tina couldn't do it all herself. Mel wouldn't let go of her. Her littlest one had taken them that far; might not have done so consciously. Or, if she had learned the tricks of using her father's rings, certainly wasn't conscious anymore. She'd swooned, lost it, said consciousness, the moment she realized her anticipated haven was effectively no more.

"The Witch!" cried Helen, finally remembering whom they'd left, power-focus-pinned to a cot in the blazing cabin, when they went to rescue Tina.

"I'll go back," said Percy, as the rain started. As if they weren't wet already.

"Fuck the Witch," yelled Mel-Illuminatus, still in Cabby's Caddy mode, though the serpents entwining her arms looked terribly dead. Which only made them look more terrible than usual. "We don't want Tina becoming another Child Harry. Percy, find the Traveller. She's supposed to be with Fish-Treat in the city. Bring her here; give her no choice. Helen, you stay with us."

(Fish-Treat referred to the amphibious, unrelated, but brought up together, hence sisterly twosome, Scylla Nereid and Amphitrite of Lemuria. It wasn't too clear who coined the term – their 'mother' Merthetis maybe; possibly Granny Garuda,

Kanin Nauroz, who'd known Merthetis most of her life; or, at least conceivably, the Celestial Superior sometime shortly after Treat's birth ca Mithramas 5920.

(Which of course came as a result of the Simultaneous Summonings she – either Celeste Mannering or Celestine D'Angelo, dependent on which side of Cathonia you were on – and Ubris Nauroz, her Nubian, called in February 1920 out there, Balek 5919 in most of in here. Whosoever started it wherever, they'd endured the joint diminutive virtually all their lives. Hadn't complained about it too much. Apparently they liked each other.)

Percy obeyed. Helen didn't. They both went away, in teleportals of their own; Helen after Percy, though not after her in the sense of following her.

Her last words to her mother? "I'll go get Daddy Harry."

========

Lakshmi Arthadot, the Kronokronos Supreme of Temporis, was another disobedient child. It was her big day, not her atrocious mother's, so she'd scrapped the porcelain pretty, even lustrous look Amphitrite favoured; had her guard-body go with the jade-green and texturally scaly look she personally preferred. Had opted for tinsel-white hair rather than tinsel-silvery. Which, silver, Fish had told her was an unlucky colour in the Weirdom.

And, regardless of recent differences, she was still her hero; consequently paid more attention to Fish than Treat, her very own mom. (She whose own mom had fostered Fish in the first place, decades before her birth.) She wasn't going to let any otherwise brainless stone gnome, or whomever-whatever had shut down the Matter Transducers between Centurium and Cabalarkon, spoil her wedding.

If her purloined approximation of half-daddy the Dand's Tvasitar Talisman couldn't do the job beyond Temporis, she had witch stepping stones; knew how to use them too. This last due to the Athenan War Witch training she'd taken at Fish-Treat's insistence as soon as she reached puberty; was therefore deemed eligible to receive it. Even if the previous Master had blocked access to Cabalarkon via that method, it wasn't his Weirdom anymore. Make that shouldn't be his Weirdom, all going well. Which it should be.

Fish, her mother, their exceedingly resourceful mainstay in the Panharmonium Project, Tsishah Twilight, even Pusan Wanderlust – who could get around the Grey by herself, courtesy of her shepherd's crook; hence probably only used the things to cast glamours about herself – would have brought witch-stones with them.

Mel-Illuminatus, if she was back from Tsishah's perch above Incain, and her Althean healers – the ones she'd left behind in the Weirdom, not the ones who'd set up in the Zebranid Leper Colony her twin and his Hecate-Hellion of a cocooning wife founded high up in the Cattail's Whiplash Range a decade before her birth, in accordance with said project – would have as well. Surely that self-same mightily impressive Morrigan, Morgianna Sarpedon, would have lifted the liminal blockage on their teleportive workings by now.

So, dressed to the nines, in virginal white over jaded guard-body, she set out to stepping-stone-step her way, by herself, to Cabalarkon.

Unless it was already Panharmonium.

========

Ask any demon how many angels could fit on the head of a pin and the demon – if it had any wit about it, which wasn't too likely – would reply something like: 'As many as we leave room for'. The same could be said for devils since Master Devas gained self-contained solidity by possessing debrained demons. Notwithstanding whether or whether not Celestial Angels existed, the Hidden Headworld's monstrous multitude of demonic denominations were composed of subtle matter; were size- and shape-shifters.

So were faeries. Which of course meant so too was Sheba Faerieflight. Many faeries had birdlike qualities. Many of those ones had birdlike appetites. Ogres would eat anything. Then again, though they had nothing against fish, their personal favourite foodstuffs were birds. And, yes, ogres were a form of faerie; ergo of demons, spelled without the 'a'. In other words, of the man-eating variety.

When the earthquake struck, Balkis Mandam reflexively went from being a nicely dressed, relatively attractive Shenon Ventricular, in a formal, as in not too revealing, Imperial Roman outfit, to Sheba Faerieflight: a variegated, motley, tatterdemalion if ever there was one. Whereupon she fragmented. One of her fragments was an obese, quadruped ogre.

Ogres always had trouble deciding on what they should look like. This one was fat, yes, but there was something of the pantomime horse about it. Except, its midsection seemed filled with hot air instead of intestines, and such like viscera, let alone two clowns. Its particoloured skin looked more cloth-like than hide-like. It had done 'commedia dell'arte' puppets at the ends of its four appendages.

There was the head of a punchinello, a pantaloon, a harlequin, a columbine, unless it was some other character, at the end of its hooves. The puppet-heads yelped and cried out, in perceptible pain, as the ogre walked on them. Walked with them, as hooves, better put. Hadn't done its own head very well either. Had started out with, and still had, the back of a horse's skull, ears, mane but, instead of a snout et al of a horse at its front, it opted for a 'you-are-what-you-eat' bird's head, beak et al.

It was as if during her time on the Outer Earth, probably but not necessarily when she wasn't possessed by Faceless Strife, Balkis had spent too much time studying surrealists such as Max Ernst. Of course it could be Max Ernst had spent sometime in here, using Faerie Flight type ogres as models for his peculiar paintings. (Her particular inspiration looked to be his 1937 'L'Ange de Foyer', 'The Angel of the Hearth', aka 'The Triumph of Surrealism'.)

Before the danger passed – the quaking abating its shaking, as her constituents would have it – and she could recall all her fragments, it had swallowed something small and pearly. It wasn't a birdie, wasn't even a fishy, though it was more akin to the latter than the former. Was most akin to a clamshell without a clam. Had something else inside it. Besides between-space.

Capputis Masterson knew what it was. He'd been standing beside her when the quake began to bake and shake, which was when parts of the plaza began collapsing into the catacombs below. More than a decade too young to become a properly trained and invested Trinondev, he wasn't very good with eyeorbs, but he could project a passable thought-balloon. Which he did, around the obese puppetry-ogre. Could constrict it as well. Which he also did.

"That's my mom," he shouted. "Cough her up, damn you, whatever you are."
That shouted, he was promptly attacked by bumble-bums.

Although bumble-bums had humanoid faces, they most resembled orange and
yellow striped bee-creatures. Equally so these fairy sorts were similar to flying dartboards, albeit with the dart-tips, their stingers, sticking out of their bottoms rather
than into them, as if they were actual dartboards. They hurt like the proverbial
dickens; as in stick'ems, also as they'd have it.

Seems Cabby's Cappy, as he'd been dubbed by whomever, had forgotten one of
the primary drawbacks to Trinondev force shields, something true Warriors of Weir
seldom did. Never did, make them, when dealing with guys with guns, archers with
arrows, spear-casters with missiles, and bee-men with bumble bums. The farther
and thicker you thought-projected them in front of you the thinner, more easily
penetrable, they became in back of you.

Was no blunder their instructors reminded them to 'buttress your behinds'.

========

Saladin Devason hadn't forgotten that deficiency.

========

While keeping himself covered every which way, he concentrated on projecting
a thought-bubble upwards and sideways. He didn't want to create an absorbent
cushion between himself and Morg's falling statue. He wanted to shove it away such
that it wouldn't fall on him. Whereupon, for him, two things happened.

First the ground beneath him gave away and he tumbled through the resultant
pit into the catacombs. That would have been fine; he could levitate. Except, at that
very second, he couldn't. His command of the Master's Mace had transferred to his
sister. As did the mace itself, physically; though, she having no manipulative hands
to catch and hold onto it as yet, it bounced off her, it, her statuary remains, and
came to rest at her (its) feet. The mace's masterly powers were hers, however; must
have used them to keep herself, the statue containing her cocoon, herself cracking
out of it, from falling any farther.

It was selfish of her; wasn't even necessary. Her husband, himself levitated into
the air, had already caught her, it, in a mental mind-grid. Demios Sarpedon was
very good with eye-staves. His was the oldest still extant; the orbs it produced as
good as or better than anything that came out of Weir's erstwhile Mother Machine
replicators for the past hundreds, even thousands, of years. She wasn't going anywhere other than safely down to the ground once the plaza finally stopped playing
at percolating plasma.

Cynthia Masterwife, having absolutely no training whatsoever, was even worse
at using eye-staves than 'don't call-me Cappy'. Also, her truncated version of an
eye-stave, the Witch's metallic marigold, was likely the most recent one the stone
gnomes had manufactured to order. Which, perhaps, made it even less effective than
that of the sadly far too inexperienced 'please-call-me-Capputis'.

Gifted since birth with formidable willpower – likely what attracted Miss Mist,
Krepusyl Evenstar, to her when she needed a new Queen Godda of Crepuscule – she
nevertheless managed to project a thought-bubble of her own; one that caught Saladin before he could fall any farther. She was, however, another who'd forgotten the

problem with Trinondev force shields; might not have even known of it. Thinking bubble forward left her backward bits too thinly protected.

Cromwell Necator didn't shoot her. He had no instructions to shoot her; just the Master, if he refused to give up his authority. Saladin wasn't the Master anymore. Consequently, while Tsishah-Cynthia may be in the process of saving Sal's life, or at least preventing him from having a really bad fall, Crom felt no need to stop her doing so. Someone else did; someone creeping up behind her, between her and him. He was glowing.

Amphitrite of Lemuria, encased as she was within her mandroid guard-body, with only her eyes showing – and they shielded by her Golem's Solidium substance gone transparent – apprehended what was happening even before Necator opened up. She was of two minds as to whether it was a good or bad thing, but shouted a warning anyways.

"Tsishah, behind you!"

It was all so loud her onetime fellow Aortic may or may not have heard her. Crom didn't miss; he rarely did. Was a true professional. Was also lethally accurate; hit Solomon Mandam in the back, spinning him around. The deviant son of Jesse-Wiccan and Meroudys Maenad, ultimately Ramona-Guillotine, blew anyhow; reflexively blowing the bullet out of him as he did. Tsishah didn't so much lose her concentration as had no concentration left to lose.

She plummeted into the pit, Sal finished his fall on top of a Sleeper's sepulchre, damaging it slightly. Tsishah's body landed on top of him. That's how he lost his left eye; the butt-end of her metallic marigold – marigolds being the Mexican flower of death – doing the damage; fortunately for his immediate longevity only glancingly sideways-so. Otherwise it could have rammed straight through his eye into his brain, slaying him instantly.

The Traveller, Pusan Wanderlust, moved very quickly; almost as quickly as her fellow, howsoever brief-time faun of a generic brother, Dervish Furie, could when he put his mind to it. Unless it was the Furie's mind, assuming he had one. She didn't have his next-to-impervious, armadillo-armoured hide. Nor did she have his steel-girder bone structure. She broke both her legs landing awkwardly to one side of the nevertheless already dribbling sepulchre. Healed herself immediately, stood up, then had a mind of her own to make up.

She couldn't save both of them simultaneously. That was beyond her healing talents, especially given she'd just used some of them to next-to-instantly re-knit her legs. Was beyond the abilities of Amal-Althea (Althea Brand), Lazareme's devic healer, whom she'd reacquired from Telepassa of Godbad sometime ago, as well. And there was no one else around to provide trauma first aid in order to keep one or the other breathing until she could get to him or her.

(Regardless of whether Mel-Illuminatus was born with the Lazaremist inside her, it didn't follow that that was all of her. Wilderwitch, for example, could have been born with Datong Harmonia, but that didn't mean Freespirit Nihila couldn't separately exist. She did; they'd first met in the Faerie Garden of Temporis.

(Also didn't mean Nihila wasn't simultaneously Harmony, the selfsame Unity of Balance; she was once … for thousand of years, up until roughly five hundred years ago, once. It therefore followed that the devic Althea could have been around as a Spirit Being at the same time Melina born Sarpedon was muddling through thus far merely sixty years of her life as a potential incarnation of her.)

Managed to hoist them off the sepulchre, to lay them on the ground beside each other, but still had to decide who it was to be: Cynthia-Tsishah, one arm already blown off, bleeding profusely from its stump, but with an unborn Sed-son demon-deposited inside her? Or former Master Saladin Devason, one eye gone the route of Cynthia's arm, but with the potential for breeding many more Sed-sons inside him? Turned out she didn't have any choice in the matter.

There was suddenly this teleport-hole right there in front of her. Someone looked out of it. She wasn't a faun, but she was nice-looking; most Utopian-human hybrids were nice-looking, for such an unattractive combination of species. It was Persephone Zeross. Who didn't give her the chance to decide who to save. Her talents were needed elsewhere immediately.

It was better that way anyways. What better birthday present was there for a just-today-turned seven-year old than a chance to turn eight?

========

The Witch didn't burn to death in the Whiplash Range. Her no longer pregnant soul-self got her out of there. Soul-selves were very useful things.

Even if they were chained.

========

Cromwell Necator could multi-task.

He was moving while he was shooting. Having watched an American Western brought in from the Outer Earth by his patron, Alpha Centauri, a movie that wasn't called 'Solace Sunrise and the Blind Sundown Kid', he reckoned he was a better shot that way. Using it for cover he squirmed under the front end of the all-terrain military vehicle, the flatbed with tank treads.

When he reemerged he was fully reloaded. Good thing too. The near-by Mithrants had seen him blow away Solomon Mandam-slash-Taurson, the odds-on-favourite to become their new Taurus. Needs be he'd take a few of them with him. Except they hesitated. He reciprocated.

What made them hesitate was that they, the Mithrants, knew that when true blue Outer Earth Glows blew, they blew themselves apart, spraying anyone too close to them with not just fleshy bits, pointy bone-shards and pieces of themselves, but what they were wearing as well.

When Taurson blew he vapourized concussively, albeit only temporarily. So it wasn't as if Necator had killed him just by shooting him. Chances were the bullet or bullets that should have killed him would be lying in the dirt by the time he did re-form, clothes and all.

Why he – Cromwell Necator – hesitated, why he had no choice in the matter and what saved his life, this time, was Demios Sarpedon could multi-task as well or better than he could. Plus, Demios really was good with eye-staves. And, encased as Crom suddenly found himself, in a Dem-cast, Trinondev force field, he would truly hate to die of his own bullets ricocheting.

What would his already dead, but Sangazur-reanimated, father Godfrey say?

========

Although nicknamed Dem-Wit, he was no fool.

Lifting and therefore perceptible thought-bubble-surrounding her statuary remains – as the Fatman, Godbad's Alpha Centauri, had once ever so callously referred to what wasn't exactly all that was left of her – indicated his wife had usurped control of the Master's Mace. It was lying there, on the cracked and cracking plaza in front of her, if further proof of her fait-accompli-Mastery was required.

Consequently, even if she hadn't as yet broken all the way out into the open in order to greet her adoring public – almost all of those who could, almost of all of those who hadn't died or weren't quite dead yet, had already run off – Morgianna had no more need of anyone's help. Thus freed up, Demios had gone off to attend to the business of being a hero. Which, since she couldn't, included rallying the troops.

Besides being the right thing to do, he reckoned Morg would never have a chance to amount to much of a Master if he didn't make the effort on her behalf.

Hundreds of her new subjects dying in the earthquake or aftershock was one thing. Not much anyone could do about that. However, should a significant percentage of the many thousands of commonsense-lacking idiots that made up the majority of her not-yet-adoring public die in the quake's aftermath, she would be starting her reign with a severe image problem. Would likely only be accepted long enough to be rejected.

Fires, for example, even in a largely stone megalopolis, would end more lives than falls did. Ceilings-and-floors-crashing down in damaged buildings crushed a lot more people than heart attacks killed them. Things like huge blocks of the plaza collapsing into the catacombs, or any number of other apocalyptic tragedies that invariably followed such a howsoever natural disaster, were far more deadly than the instigating event.

Keeping Necator covered with his force shield in case the Mithrants changed their minds, decided just to shoot him on general principals, he used his ever-so-antique eye-stave in its mike-on-a-spike mode. Bespoke loudly, for everyone about to start blasting everyone else, the Godbadians at the Mithrants, and vice versa, to hear: "Any of you devil-loving vermin want a piece of any of our extraterrestrial crap, you better start earning your hero-badges right now. We've a Weirdom to preserve."

The ensuing gunfire, explosions and suchlike erupting virtually the moment he finished his mike-on-a-spike exhortation came from the other end of the plaza; the much larger section that hadn't collapsed into the catacombs. For the most part it was coming, emitting, from the stripe-skinned Zebranids and the rest of those Demios brought to the Weirdom not via between-space, though both All and the Zeross girls were available, but by a Godbadian submarine.

The Fatman, Alpha Centauri, authorized the submarine in early Antheal, April on the Outer Earth. It was heading up north anyhow, to finish what amounted to a circumpolar expedition to map the Headworld's seas all the way out to where the Cathonic Zone began. He authorized it after both Sarpedon and Tethys returned from the Weirdom to report Saladin Devason was at best a paper-pope, a Master in name only. Of course he didn't do so just on the strength of their observations. He had other influences, did Centauri.

Without Byronics around to safeguard him; to preserve his place on the top of the Godbadian heap; to keep CE, Centauri Enterprises, his corporate empire, expanding even at a fraction of its previous pace; to keep his heart ticking, thank you whatever little was left of APM; the Fatman – born Alfredo Sentalli in the Outer Earth's Toronto, Canada, in 19/5927, the same year as Wilderwitch, Meroudys Maenad and the real, but long dead, Ramona Avar – was feeling positively insecure.

He could no longer afford to scoff at threats from witches, at least one of whom was related to him by marriage (Janna St Peche-Montressor, she being the source of Aphropsyche Morningstar and her nonetheless welcome, heart-soothing assuagements), Dead Things Walking, Undead Things Flying (and biting), fucking faeries, boys, girls, and Celestial God knew what else, they with their Gypsium rings, plus any number of other Panharmonium-pushing, fine finny friends of seemingly everyone except he himself and his pride and joy Centauri Enterprises. Accommodations were duly made.

Demios saw what they were shooting at; so did everyone else. Which was why those that had guns and mortars and bazookas and even radios, to call for missiles to be launched from that self-same Godbadian submarine, which had somehow weathered the tidal wave, had opened up. Skyrise did seem to have a one-armed Sed-shape by then.

(In his fifth lifetime Heliosophos – along with Machine-Memory and the as yet not Undying Utopian, Cabalarkon himself, Sedon's co-creator – used his sunray sword, his version of Lord Order's lightning blade, to slice off the devic All-Father's right arm at the elbow. Although the mighty Moloch typically in the sky could and often did re-grow it, he liked to appear in public as if a war-amp.)

It did seem to step into the plaza and did – not seem – reach down to pick up a toppled-over obelisk, stellar-powered firestone no longer atop it. This it hurled at Morg's oversized statuary remains. Master's Mace or no Master's Mace, it, the obelisk, got through not just her force shield. It got through her oversized back. Had the Mighty Mooch of a Moloch Sedon finally killed someone? And if he had, wouldn't he have to cathonitize himself as a consequence?

A highly silly notion that. Cathonia, the Inner Earth's Night's Sky, its Day Sky as well, was him, Dark Sedon, his essence. So what then? Repeat the question please. Question was: Had Sedon killed Morgianna born Nauroz become Somata, at Master Kyprian's insistence, decades ago, and then become Sarpedon, after Kyprian-Copperhead's death? The answer was no.

Who had then? The answer was obvious.

========

Who had ever heard of, let alone seen, either an All-Father of Devazurkind or a king of All-Demons, even before they were one and the same, being a 30-storey high, ambulant abomination? No one, that's who. No one who lived to tell the tale anyhow. It was, however, at least conceivable.

What, knowing Dark Sedon was resolutely male, wasn't conceivable was seeing him as a walking, glass and metal architectural monstrosity six months pregnant. Ergo it wasn't him.

Ergo it was the new Master of Weir on Earth!
****

FOURTEEN-DEMON: **Freespirit Wilderwitch**

========

The Summer Solstice 5981

Tsishah Thrae, called Twilight, was born on or about the Autumnal Equinox of 5934, Year of the Dome. Although often seen afterwards, she died on the Summer Solstice of 5981. In time many mourned her. At least, some consoled themselves, she died in love. Too bad, a few of her nastier mourners added, the person she was in love with hadn't been the one who died.

Came close, though.

========

He opened his eyes. Tried to, rather. Was covered in a thickening crust of dust. Finally succeeded. Too bad only one, the right one, was still there to open. What he saw out of it was this teleport-hole right there in front of him. Someone looked out of it. She was nice-looking for her age, which was borderline teenage; call her cute, then. Had Gypsium rings on all ten of her fingers.

"Paree?"

"Uncle Master," she acknowledged.

"Get me out of here."

"First things first. You broke Daddy's sepulchre landing on it. It's leaking."

"Come back for me, then."

"I'll have to think about that."

That said, that thought, Helen Zeross rang herself away; Daddy's sepulchre almost weightlessly lassoed behind her in one of said Daddy's ring-things.

She didn't ring herself back to the coast; she rang herself upstairs. To what hadn't as yet, which was most of it, collapsed on the great central plaza. No dummy Helen – even if she was technically not yet a teenager; wouldn't turn 13 until the coming Autumnal Equinox, what would have marked Tsishah's 47th birthday – she rang herself to Aortic Amphitrite.

She of Shenon was good with mandroids. Ergo, once also the Outer Earth supra known as Lady Lemurian was good with Stopstone-Solidium.

"Gross," she exclaimed upon arriving at the Lemurian Aortic's side; her mandroid guard-body's side.

Helen was comprehensibly, not just understandably, grossed-out. Which was why she said 'Gross'. Something was growing out of Treat's belly. Something had grown sideways out of the Aortic's belly. It not only looked like, it was: Lakshmi Arthadot, she also of Lemuria, evidently back in the belly whence she came.

"Help us," they both cried out.

"I'll have to think about that. Can you seal Daddy's sepulchre?"

They could. They did. Rather, they had she of Witch Isle's guard-body give up some of its substance to seal it.

Helen, feeling herself too young and far too healthy to get Gypsium sick, took them to Subcranial Temporis. Left them there, along with said Daddy's resealed sepulchre, which they claimed to have the wherewithal to replenish, in one of the once Thousand Caverns of Dand Tariqartha; its main one, both before and after the Time-Space Displacer self-cathonitized on the 6th of Tantalar last year; a day, one of a few, Wilderwitch almost died.

Left them in Centurium, replicated Versailles. Went back to her mother, Mel-Illuminatus, her two sisters – perky anew Athena and pretty, probably perpetually perky Percy – and the Traveller, Pusan Wanderlust, they in a make-do shelter on the coast of Fearsome Fobbiat. The fauna hadn't been needed to save Tina's life such that she had a chance of reaching eight.

Had, however, livened her up nice and smartly. (Thank you, Goat.) The moment Paree returned, Percy went off in search of Wilderwitch. To no avail. When they returned to Cabalarkon City some time later, it was to witness the swearing in of a new Master of Weir. It wasn't Saladin Devason.

Was arguable he was even there.

========

As much as she may have appreciated son Cappy's borderline-bumbling efforts to contain the 'Puppetry-Ogre of Surrealism' after it swallowed her – she reflexively protected between-space inside her Vesica Piscis – Fish didn't need his help. Rarely needed anyone's aid; had made it through over sixty years mostly self-assisted. What clammed up,shrunkenly so, could and did ram-clam out, expansively so. Was just as well.

Absolved of his filial duties, Capputis Masterson, bum-stung (bumble-bummed?) as he was, could finally concentrate on what he really wanted to do.

Scream, long and loudly.

========

"Sal, you there?"

He opened his eyes. Tried to, rather. Only one, the right one, was still there to open. What it saw, down in the tomb with him and Tsishah's corpse, he didn't like. It was Solomon Taurson.

"Thus die all Sed-sons." Taurson – Sol, not Sal; Solomon born Mandam – was a Gloman. Glows blow. He blew.

Despite being in a Weirdom not only teeming with eye-staves, but maybe one of only two places on the Head outside of Trans-Time Trigon where they were made (Temporis being the other), he was also, in all likelihood, animated by a Sangazur. In all likelihood, but not necessarily.

While Sangs, and indeed any variety of azura, could be taken out with prison pods – so could daemonic bodies, according to Illuminary traditions – the Trinon-dev wielding the eye-stave had to will it. And, especially now that Saladin was no longer the Master of Weir on Earth – a living eye-stave up here – there were none so armed in the immediate vicinity. Not as such; not one fully grown, as it were. Was a stunted one, though. He'd lay beside its (late) owner.

Sangazurs kept Dead Things alive, sort of, as well as compos mentis, mostly. However, as the son of Wiccan Warlock, Jesus Mandam, the Conquering Christ, he who kept on rising from the dead, until the day he didn't, on Salvation Island in late December 1953, Taurson had inherited an even more amazing ability. He rose from the dead, reincarnated, re-formed rather, wholly flesh and blood again, wholly clothed as well (very daemonic that), the merest of moments after (not really) dying.

Which is what he did now. Rose ready to blow anew, a (super) human bomb, a living, breathing, perpetually blowing machine. Was suddenly ravelled in Gypsium chains, hauled out of the pit. Blew anyhow. Without any measurable effect. Other than he combusted completely, vapourized. So he formed anew. And blew anew. Same effect. Nil. Pun intended.

Formed yet again. This time he regarded the person from whom the chains extended. Hence said pun.

"You done blowing off steam yet, blowhard? You are Taurson Solomon Mandam, aren't you? Fart son of a turd father."

The person – and he believed it was a person, a different kind of person; a deviant like he was, albeit one more devic than daemonic – was female. That much he could be sure of because her shape had all the right curves for being female, including a pronounced baby-belly bulge in the appropriate position.

She glowed, like he did before he blew; only it wasn't her face or body that glowed. It was all of her, especially her clothing – what there was of it, call it raiment – which consisted of nothing but tightly-knit chainmail. Unless that was her body. In which case her entirety consisted of chainmail.

Then her head didn't. Neither did her neck, though it consisted entirely of a hoop or torc from which her chainmail extremities depended. There was something about her face and olive eyes, two of them, that reminded him of someone. Something about the massive tangle of hair, too. Both her face, ruddy, and said hair, dark, had something of a gypsy quality. Her aurous-golden glow, that of her chains and neck-hoop, had everything of a Gypsium quality to it.

"Not going to answer?"

"I can blow forever, Brainrock babe. Can you hold onto me forever?"

"Brainrock babe?"

"Well, you're too old to be a Gypsium gal. Besides, you've a bun in the oven. Wait … don't tell me. That's your Brainrock Babe, not you." (Sol, who could only have been a matter of a few months old when his father died on Salvation Island, had clearly inherited Jesse's acidulous tongue to go along with his cocksureness.)

"Smart ass."

"Hey, I'm smart all over." Wrong response. He gasped; gagged, more like. She – whoever, whatever, she was – was done talking; was instead tightening the chains holding him in place. Was doing so like something out of a pirate movie just before he, the guy thus trussed up, got tossed overboard.

He blew, re-formed, the chains were still tightening. He had never felt pain like that before. Didn't think he could. Blowing up never hurt so much. "Stop it!"

Saladin Devason, left eye no longer there, left side of his face consequentially a dust-encrusted, bloody mess, was tingling all over. Wasn't on his feet; was levitating into an upright position. Had shaking hands-hold of what was once Wilderwitch's metallic marigold. Was his now; was making it work, too.

Had activated it a split-second before Sol blew down below. Had saved his life then; was using it now to regain the surface.

"Kill him if you can, Witch. Look what he did to your surrogate, my niece."

Not even Pusan Wanderlust – had Persephone given her the opportunity, which she hadn't – could have done anything for Tsishah Twilight. Just as much so, neither could equally-goatish Althea Brand (Amal-Althea), whom Pusan had, yet again, goat-got hold of that day in mid-Tantalar last.

Which was when Pyrame Silverstar displaced her, Althea, by taking over her previous host, Telepassa of not just Godbad, whose life she'd saved twenty years earlier. (In the absence of her Tvasitar Talisman, the devic Althea could only remain a howsoever mobile Spirit Being. Might well have been brain-damaged so severely by then, she may not have realized whom she'd been; let alone who she was or what she could do … seemingly effortlessly heal people. And not just people.)

As for what became of Telepassa and her four daughters, three of whom could well prove to be Trigregos Incarnate, that Pusan didn't know. Did know the Pauper Priestess, once also called Providence, must have ditched her somewhere because she, Pyrame, also formerly known as the Perpetual Presence, adult, female, had been inside Machine-Memory, humanizing her, rendering her Miracle Memory, ever since. Which in turn suggested they were safe somewhere, probably on the Outer Earth.

"Witch," hissed Sol, hearing Sal. "Wilderwitch, Fey's mom. How many times can you rise from the dead?"

"Haven't died yet. Haven't ever been cathonitized either, so I couldn't tell you. I'm not Wilderwitch. Wilderwitch is the one pregnant. I'm just carrying her with me on account of, well, it's too early to say if we can ever altogether separate again. I was pregnant for awhile too, while she revivified me. Not anymore; it got away. From her as well, it seems," she added, indicating Tsishah Twilight's finally bled-out remains down in the hole.

Whatever glamour Tsishah may have been wearing dispelled with her death. Rather, from the looks of her now, had gone when her soul-self tore tangibly out of her body. For that must have been what happened. Morg's firstborn left a very sorry-looking carcass behind. It wasn't just missing part of an arm; it had been rent asunder, split open (brain) stem to stern, tip of head to tip of tiptoes, shoulders to fingertips, dot-ditto.

It was as if whatever was inside her body had literally torn itself free, exposing her innards, leaving nothing but bone, blood, skin and already putrefying entrails behind. As badly damaged as he was – covered as he also was, had to be, with de-sensitizing Solidium, the stuff of not just Stone Gnomes, but of the millennia-ancient metropolis itself – Sal didn't need to guess who that might have been. Couldn't be anyone else.

He ascended fully out of the pit; hovered there, in the almost as dusty, but open air. If such a man as he could be revolted, as terrifying as he must have looked himself, with one eye working and a gore-hole where the other one had been seconds earlier, he was horrified by everything he beheld.

Over there, through the rising smoke and settling dust, very close to where he came out of the catacombs, on a part of the plaza that hadn't completely collapsed, he made out what had become of his sister. It was a nauseating, threefold shish kebab of sheer dreadfulness.

An obelisk, the shish, the skewer, had gone all the way through the statue's back, one kebab. Had also gone most of the way through Morg's cocoon, two kebab. She herself, her physical self, was the third kebab. Had almost got out in time, hadn't she? 'Almost' explained 'hadn't'.

The still sparking wires at the obelisk's tiptop, where its now missing firestone shone for quite conceivably thousands of years, was providing the necessary heat to finish roasting her alive. It wasn't complete combustion. Not like Nihila had been. Nonetheless, more than six months after she should have been, Morgianna was a certifiable corpse.

Her as yet minutely hovering husband, her very nearly life-long companion, Demios Sarpedon, was among the first to spot him, Saladin always Nauroz. He, Dem-wit, looked stricken, shocked, disbelieving. What he didn't look was angry. They'd come so far, he must have been thinking, done so much, only for this unmitigated ... whatever it was ... to happen. Had in one hand his ages-old eye-stave; in the other the Master's Mace.

Just as the rain intensified he pointed his eye-stave at the moments ago deposed Master, drew him wilfully – albeit against Sal's will – toward him, toward them, him and War Witch daughter Andaemyn, inextricably. It wasn't just rain splotching Andy's cheeks, who was next to him, albeit not hovering due to an absence of eye-stave. Was very much also tears: for her mother, for her father, for all they'd planned together. But she still had her guns.

Was going to shoot him; shoot Sal. Who hadn't been covered in quite enough Stopstone-Solidium to become bulletproof. Cromwell Necator was going to shoot him. Probably everyone with a gun on the plaza was going to shoot him. Well, had he a gun – which he didn't, though there were plenty of them lying around, in the grips of dead men, one or two dead women as well, some of whom were striped – Capputis likely wouldn't shoot him.

He was standing, unsteadily to Sal's remaining eye, beside his mother, who wasn't going to shoot him either. Fish had someone else not quite entirely herself yet, entwined in her fishnet. Was, from the looks of it, about to go all electric eel on her, Balkis Mandam, she of Shenon's Korant Ventricle, her Quarter Queendom on Witch Isle.

Fish could do that sort of thing: channel the attributes of aquatic creatures through her net, her oversized fishhook or even her bellybutton accessory. That was probably why, back in late Tantalar, Wilderwitch – her permeating over-coating rather, Primeval Lilith – had striven so strenuously against allowing Fish in the Weirdom to bear witness to the various necessarily aborted announcements they'd had then scheduled.

(Fish and the Witch only exchanged glances when they did see each other, on the 1st of Yamana still 5980. Had a proper reunion later — just before the latter made the mistake of putting on Nihila's oddly hardly even tarnished golden torc. Was an eventful time for a few folks; a climactic one, again, for Janna Fangfingers, if apparently not her devic half-mother from her Datong Harmonia days.)

Electrification had a proven capacity to de-demonize – de-fay, in Balkis's case – otherwise normal folks, even Faerie Flights. Sal had seen her do it; had seen Electrocretan, the startling beautiful (literally) Laodice born Atreides, become Hent, yet another supranormal Summoning Child from years, and supra-groups, gone by, do it, too. But Fish wouldn't shoot him. Nope. She'd gaffe him. Guess it was time to die after all.

Demios Sarpedon brought him down; dissolving the thought-bubble that had been holding him up with the merest wave of his antique eye-stave. Sal found he had a great deal of difficulty standing. Dizziness swept over him like a carpet cleaner. Sarpedon tossed something at him. At the wrong side of him, his eyeless left side. (Sal's depth perception wasn't what it had been.) Whatever it was plunked against his increasingly encrusted chest; dropped to his feet. Was the Master's Mace.

"You wanted a Challenge of Weir, Devason. Pick it up. Let's get to it."

"Don't think that'd be fair, Dem," said the strange entity that claimed she wasn't Wilderwitch, but looked a lot like her, from the neck up.

Looked a lot like a two-eyed Freespirit Nihila, minus the thatch of butterscotch hair, from a similar vantage point. Except, with or without a devic eye, and a replacement thatch – make that a rat's, if not a mare's, nest – of dark hair, it couldn't be her, Nihila, ex-Harmony. Not in what had been, and maybe still was, the Weirdom of Cabalarkon.

Trinondev prison pods, the usually uncracked eggs atop their eye-staves, would have instantly snapped open, activated, sucked her totally into them: torc, chains, daemonic body (had she had one, were she not just substantively Godstuff) and all. Which also explained why no one dead could clamber to his or her feet, Sangazur-mindfully or otherwise. Not today, not here anyway.

Warriors of Weir eyeorbs, once open, were even better with azuras than they were with their just as immortal parents. Could only hold onto one devil at a time, for example, whereas dozens of azuras fit inside a prison pod. Besides, in Morg's case, even if Demios was tempted, there wouldn't be much point.

She was so thoroughly crisped she'd fall apart the moment anyone tried to move her. (That was why the shaven-headed, brown-robed priests and priestesses of Sraddha Isle, in what was then Hadd, but was now Haas, carried fire-boxes strapped to their back; had done since the time of Sraddha Somata himself. No matter how badly dismembered they were, you don't burn them nigh onto ash, Dead Things could – and would – still find a way to kill, thereby conscript, you.)

This entity, with the curves of a woman made up from the neck down of Brainrock chains, was evidently a self-psychopomp since her voice preceded her materializing as if out of the air itself. Still had Solomon Mandam-slash-Taurson in an extrusion of her chains as well. He looked very uncomfortable. Looked about to expire, sooth said.

Also looked to be in a very nearly identical situation to his twin, who seemed to have a few patches of herself yet missing from when Fish expanded her Vesica Piscis so inside-out forcefully, end-game Pantomime Ogre of Surrealism. Which wasn't good for either of them, Sol or Sheba. Was a state of affairs not lost on Fish.

"What fay-say, Sis-Witch … on the count of three we snap-zap-crackle them together?"

(Young Life, Hush Mannering – presumed to have been born Pandora, but lately best known on the Head as Dory the Dolly – had last been seen on Apple Isle in Tantalar being 'toyed' with by Tralalorn. That'd be the perpetually seven year old demon-devil who fairified her in the first place. Fairified her, in fact, just after she gave birth to Morgianna at that time also Nauroz on the 25ᵗʰ of Tantalar 5920.

(More than forty years earlier in Rome – early January 1938, to be precise – Hush, who loved playing, albeit not as one of Trala's playthings, her living dolls, led SOS: The Sorority of Sausages as General 'Huff 'n' Puff' Jollity. Fish was around then, so obviously recalled Hush dubbing Electric Lady Lao then still Atreides 'Snap-Zap, the Boltwhip Babe', hence her 'snap-zap-crackle' inducement.)

"I'm not the Witch, Fish-witch. I'm her soul-self."

"The devilfish-sandwich you didn't fay-say. Soul-selves can't talk."

========

"And this witch can't walk," responded another voice.

========

This one came as much from between-space as from the ground below the Weirdom; perhaps from as deep as Absudyl-Minius (after Magnus Minus, its 'Mighty Minotaurus', who was a total sot), the westernmost terminus of the Hell-Well of the World. (The Head's brainy grey cells, according to some.)

"But she is. Kill them or let them go, be my guest. Then don't be my guests. Go away yourselves, those of you that can, while I'm feeling generous."

That witch, the one that could talk, but shouldn't be able to walk, was another seeming self-psychopomp. Her voice preceded her. Except, she didn't so much materialize out of the Weird as stepped up, from the earth itself. Which shouldn't really have surprised anyone given that, along with her still absent, much missed but, for her, next-door-to-forever lost mate, Daemonicus to her Lilith, Daemon King to Daemon Queen, she was the early-on definition of eldritch earthborn.

Somnambulated out it, rather. Her eyes were closed.

(Interestingly, when he was around – which he wasn't always, not consciously – Magnus Minus fancied himself less the new, than the rightful King Daemonicus. That belief brought him into conflict with Judge Warlock, who wore the Daemonicus husk when he was on the Hidden Headworld, a number of times in the past.

(Equally interestingly, the Judge's 'son' Wiccan, Jesus Mandam beyond the Dome, actually befriended said Mighty Minotaurus in the late Forties. Then again Wiccan – who probably wasn't the Boulder-Brain Conqueror, but probably was both the King Conqueror and the Conquering Christ – was just as buddy-buddy with Saladin Nauroz, whom he first met in the late Thirties, prior to both attending, howsoever briefly, the Amsterdam Academy of Man.)

"Cynthia?" said Saladin.

"Haven't got that far yet," she admitted. Then she, this chalky white-skinned, babies-belly-protrusive sleepwalker dressed in a widow's black, enlarged to accommodate a double-pregnancy, opened her eyes, reached out her left hand. From the former Master's feet to said outstretched hand came the Master's Mace.

With it – all this in the pouring rain that for some reason wasn't washing the Stopstone crud off Saladin, though it was off everyone else still standing outside –

she raised from the pit below the ravaged corpse of Tsishah Twilight. That'd be the actual witch who couldn't walk; couldn't breathe either, due to death.

After visibly expanding it, her most recent undercoating, skin-wise, for purposes of globular protrusiveness, Diminished Dustmound's Black Widow (briefly, last Tantalar, when Demios Sarpedon first encountered her, aka – according to her – Olivia Tenebrous, searching for shards of a broken mirror) in effect stepped into it.

Stepped into, merged with, what had been, and conceivably still was, after a fashion, a definite her, the mother of four, now with at least one more seemingly on the way; a potential postmortem postpartum, to fay-say some.

"Yes, this feels much better," she announced, after what amounted to zipping it up from the inside. "Tsishah was right about being good with daemons. Sal, you can keep the metallic marigold."

With an exterior wiggle to correct her looks – and an additional shake to make sure her daemonic, replacement arm looked human – Cynthia Masterwife was back in the business flesh, if not necessarily the blood.

=========

Other than exchanging glances, her veritable Challenge of Weir got no response from either the Sarpedons or their supporters. Whereupon, evidently having silently agreed amongst themselves that they weren't about to become either her guests or next victims, Demios floated more so than stepped tentatively forward.

Making sure Master and ex-Master, not to mention the two extraordinary deviants holding onto the bordering on slightly less impressive Mandam twins, realized he wasn't threatening any of them, he pulverized what was left of Morg's corpse with a thought-sledgehammer projected from his ancient eye-stave,

Further showing off his psychokinetic prowess, he next reformed the end of said stave into a monstrous gravy-whisk, whipped it around in a circular motion. Thereby gathered up the by now sooty fragments of his wife in a resultant whirlwind, like something the cathonitized Byronic Vayu Maelstrom, Devil Wind, might do. Raised the splintered flakes into the sky; propelled them over the river and sea westward.

Turned his attention to the four that mattered, particularly Saladin; as good as challenged them to stop him: "Urn that, Sally Devason."

=========

Sally Devason was a decades-unheard insult leftover from the few months they attended the Amsterdam Academy of Man before the Outer Earth's Second World War began in earnest. The urn-reference was to the dispute, thirty plus years ago, over what to do with Master Kyprian's body after she finally succumbed to the never-determined illness that had been plaguing her for years by the time she died.

As the then newly anointed Master of Weir on Earth, Saladin ordered her cremated; her ashes and bony bits put into an urn then deposited it in the Catacombs of the Sleepers beneath the citadel of same. It wasn't a popular move. Nor should it be, argued – among others – Morg herself, before following Demios into exile. After all, Kyprian wasn't sleeping. Was genuinely, irrevocably, dead. Note the urn and what filled it, if you needed proof of that.

Sal wouldn't hear of moving it elsewhere; especially not anywhere the idiots of Weir could make a shrine of it. Such remained the situation until none other than the Ghost of Cabalarkon, the Undying Utopian, complained that the ashes were giving him hay fever. Hearing predictably restored, Saladin relented; placed the urn in a locked, but otherwise unmarked closet within the Masters Palace. In apparent disgust Morg left to join Demios in exile.

Some months later, Melina a decade still Sarpedon discovered the urn had vanished. No one came forward to acknowledge responsibility for the theft. Without any evidence, let alone any chance to exact consequences for it, Sal blamed Morg. The controversy took years to – as it were – die down.

What Cabby wants, Cabby gets, being the moral of that story. Mostly because what Daddy Psychic Vampire desires, Satanic Sonny Sedon provides.

========

Receiving no response, Demios formed anew his Nightmare Grotesquery. Joined by what was left of the same Zebranid or Utopian klatch that came in with them earlier that day – except with Andaemyn, whose name meant 'without a demon', hopping onto its back – the Pegasus reared up, leapt into the sky and rode off westward, in the same direction as the dispersal.

How did they know to emulate Blind Sundown and Raven's Head from last year after such a short stint in the Weirdom? Sundown had told Andy of their legends-leaving departure from Cabalarkon at the beginning of Yamana one night in the bed they shared.

Then something even more disturbing to many left behind occurred.

With barely a nod to new Master Cynthia, she by now standing beside old Master Saladin, Thobruk Grudal, wife Nephthys and their adult children with them, rose into the air with perhaps another dozen Utopian Trinondevs of Weir; used their eye-staves to form their own collective. Wasn't of a winged globe or eyeball; was of a winged, fuzzy-looking baby seal, an simulacrum of Tina Zeross's dolly, Silkie the Selkie.

Mel's men and women, thus united, seemingly went in pursuit of the Sarpedon contingent's Nightmare. Theirs wasn't a chase. Neither did either Master seek to recall them. Was a good reason for that. The Sarpedons slowed down, waited for them to catch up, then both airborne behemoths continued flying westward together.

"You're not Scup-4-Supper surprised?" Fisherwoman queried Sal; Balkis-Sheba gone calm, no longer struggling, in her net.

No fool she, the Mandam-Faerieflight must have decided to stick close to Fish, who at least had Mariamnic training, rather than submit to the new Master's tender mercies. Which – as was now apparent, her being a chthonic concretion – may well be nonexistent. Given that her Tsishah aspect, while alive, had been a Queen Godda up until a couple of decades previously, this may seem counterintuitive.

Still, she must have felt, better the (non) devil you know, even if she wasn't always a fan of fucking faeries, than the demon you don't anymore.

"Grudal's my friend," the ex-Master answered, "But he was always Mel's man."

"Doesn't that make him a traitor, dad?" wondered Capputis, unsure as to whether he should even be addressing his father so familiarly; let alone at all.

The Solidium encrustation seemed to be twisting him, not so much disfiguring as refiguring him. Into what, he couldn't be sure, but he'd heard stories; including those of the Death's Head Hellion and whose control she fell under after dispossessing herself of Pyrame Silverstar, hence the Ghostlands, back in 4825.

"Only if he'd done it while I was still Master, son."

"Guests," repeated Cynthia no longer Masterwife (Master Woman?).

"You'll kill them if we let them go," countered the wafting form of bodily Nihila; hair, face and under-chains-pregnancy Wilderwitch.

"Then take them with you," Cynthia put to her.

"Where?"

"I've an ocean of a notion," said Fish. "What about you, Cappy?"

"Mom," he started to protest. Solomon blew, as if to remind everyone he was still there.

"Salmon will be fine here," Saladin reassured her. "Just get rid of those two."

"He better be-the-sea bream," said Fish, finally deciding it past time to do something about the Mandam twins.

She extended her net, Balkis in it, to her devilishly sisterly comrade, who in effect clipped her onto her chainmail body like an ornament. The ex-Queen of Godbad then materialized Eagle Ray Revenant (whom she still wanted to call Ronnie Ray-Bum, after the by now presiding POTUS on the Outer Earth). Rather than wrapping her up as he would if he was going to take her through the Weird, he flapped her up, up and away, also westward.

With the Mandam twins ravelled in her chains, Freespirit Wilderwitch flew off beside her. Taking their dead with them the Godbadians, led by Quentin Anvil and Cromwell Necator, who obviously felt it wise to let the dust settle quite literally before seeking to deal with Cabalarkon's newest set of prevailing powers, were swift to follow, albeit to the Valprey and away thereafter.

The pale-skinned Pani merchantmen and crew, they with their dead, who weren't as numerous, were just as grateful to be heading out of Cabalarkon. So were the Temporites, those who dared go with them, and the Mithrant legionnaires, who didn't have much choice in the matter. Didn't have much choice in locking up their weaponry in the ship's hold before leaving, either.

At the Panis' insistence, with Anvil's howsoever reluctant concurrence, the Godbadians who wouldn't fit in their off the coast waiting submarine did a ditto. As the Panis put to Anvil and Necator, it wouldn't do for them to have to helm a ghost ship if Godbadians and Mithrants went at each other while en route to Apple Isle.

Island Leviathan happily led them back into Fearsome Fobbiat, Fish's ocean of a notion.

=========

Last Tantalar, Primeval Lilith seeping into her so beneficially was most of the reason Wilderwitch survived her ordeals in Subcranial Temporis. In many respects Sal owed his survival today, the Summer Solstice of 5981, to her mutated male counterpart. Magnus Minus, the Mighty Minotaurus of Minius, may not precisely be King Daemonicus, but he was over-coating Saladin.

Together on the quayside, the reunited, parlous pair watched the Valprey until it chugged out of sight.

"Gods, I'm thirsty. Wonder if there's any beer left in the Masters Palace?"

"If there isn't," promised presumptive Master Cynthia, months of depression and NDEs (near-death experiences) vanquished by his presence, and doubly-delighted to hear

he'd remembered her king's voice, "I'll get the stone gnomes onto it directly. As soon as they finish subsuming Weir's dead, that is."

In the city proper Skyrise – already back in place and almost back to its regular shape – seemed to smile.

****

Epilogue 1

It was still raining days later when the remaining members of the Family Zeross – dead and buried Child Harry being, as Sal and Mel knew all along, only a Mantel replica of Kid Ringo from a cavern in Temporis chrono-collected by its Dand (Tariqartha), said Chronocollector, circa Midsummer 1953 – finally returned to Cabalarkon City.

=========

The Traveller, Pusan Wanderlust, possessed as she was (again) by Amal-Althea, Lazareme's female healer, carried a still fragile though, as ever, exceedingly enthusiastic Athena. Helen wasn't doing all that well herself, not after her Brainrock exertions on her baby sister's birthday – Gypsium Sickness had claimed the Mantel Child Harry weeks earlier, but being a Temporis half-life he'd never been as vigorous as his template's daughters – so Mel was propping her up.

Even though she'd failed to find Wilderwitch amongst the Zebranid evacuees in the Holy Heights townships of Bandradin Orange-Skins, where most were taking refuge until the wildfires up in the Whiplash Range died down, the eldest, Persephone, was holding up best, so she performed the necessary ring-work.

Was Salmon Capputis Nauroz, the former Master's son who greeted them upon their prearranged arrival inside the portico on the upper steps of the Grand Cathedral's entrance. No surprise there. He'd been the middle man Mel used when she clandestinely returned, as Cabby's Caddy, to surveil the scene before deciding whether to bring her family home.

Was Capputis, as he preferred, who confirmed with the old and new Master – Magnus Minus, staying carefully under the surface, as it were, thereby allowing Saladin to use his regular voice when speaking to anyone but Cynthia-Lilith in private – that they'd be welcome. Taking them at their word Mel thereupon determined it'd be safe to not just return, but to resume the position they not-so-unexpectedly proffered as the Weirdom's High Illuminary.

Pusan didn't disagree with her decision. Except for who ended up Master – should have been the Morrigan, Morgianna long Sarpedon – that'd been the original plan: to substitute the Witch for Tsishah Twilight such that the former could perchance revitalize Freespirit Nihila whereas Primeval Lilith could have the opportunity to deliver her Sed-son (via Tsishah) here, in what amounted to Dark Sedon's private protectorate.

Dead as she was, Tsishah was looking awfully good; emphasis on 'awfully'. Awfully pregnant, too. Which was as it should be, though she needed to work on the smell. Goat could do something about that; had plenty of perfumery-medicaments back at her base in the Dinq Doinq Danq Cavern Tavern. (Faunas like her smelled of sex, so some select scents were advisable if she didn't want to put up with any unwelcome attention.)

Of course Mel-Illuminatus could probably whip up a few of her own, should not yet Lactating Lily, or anyone else, choose to confide Tsishah's terminated condition to her. Which neither Lil nor Sal desired to do quite yet. That being the case Pusan decided not to hang around. What was the point?

Everyone knew they could reach her through the DDD if they changed their mind. Went to Temporis first, in order to see what, if anything, she could do for Aortic Amphitrite and her equally stricken daughter Lakshmi Arthadot. (Whom Capputis was still in love with; hence him being desperate for news re her.)

After Pusan left, promising to return with an update as soon as possible, the Family Zeross performed their inaugural act post-reconciliation. They, Tina's sisters more so than Tina herself, were allowed to retrieve and redeposit their father's again refilled (with Cathonic Fluid), and Solidium-sealed, sepulchre within a largely-intact crypt beneath the remarkably undamaged Grand Cathedral.

The Hate-Sedon-Sphere having not been stone-gnome-rebuilt – not yet rebuilt anyway – and reverted-Skyrise being used up to the 25th of its 30-storeys as a hospital, one of much too large a number of repurposed buildings in the decimated conurbation, they then moved into the Masters Palace.

A few days after their return, the disturbingly unrelenting but, equally so, rinsing rain forcing the ceremony inside the selfsame tri-towered, hence Trigon-like, edifice, they witnessed the swearing-in of a new Master of Weir. It wasn't Saladin Nauroz, still never called either Sally or Devason; certainly not officially.

He was there, however, as lacking in depth-perception as he (presumably) would be forever thereafter. So was his eldest acknowledged son, Capputis also exclusively Nauroz since the Solstice. (Rarely called himself Salmon. For one thing, it sounded too much like Saladin. For another, guys his age would undoubtedly start calling him Sally – a girl's, therefore a sissy's name – once they discovered it.)

Mother Scylla, Lady Achigan, was already back on the scene, though not Nihila-Witch, nor either of the Mandam Twins. (They'd marooned them on Whaledreck Island, about as far out to sea as you could get without hitting the Cathonic Dome, the transdimensional barrier between the Hidden Headworld and the Outer Earth's North Pacific Ocean.)

Thobruk Grudal, the Sarpedons and their followers, Zebranid and Utopian, were among the uninvited missing. The Legendarian (Jordan Tethys), together with Cosmicompanions A, B and C (Carmine Carmichael and the Zerosses' cousins, Angelica and Baalbek), were ostensibly invited no-shows.

Along with the still inexplicably absent members of the Damnation Brigade (Raven's Head, John Sundown, Dervish Furie, Gloriel D'Angelo, ex-Kronokronos Akbarartha, the Untouchable Diver and honourary brigadier, the eighty year old clone, Golgotha 'Black Skull' Nauroz), what had become of them remained mysteries to resolve, if possible, in the future.

Wilderwitch's whereabouts was known in general terms. The Gypsium Wall separated the occipital region of the Upper Head and the Cattail Peninsula, Sedon's Ponytail. Up until her disappearance – read immobilization, in the comparatively close-by Crystal Mountains of renamed Samarand (once the Land of Daybreak) – five hundred years ago, it had often been referred to as Harmony's Hairband.

Might soon have to start calling it Nihila's Ditto. But that too was for the future file.

General Quentin Anvil and Ambassador-at-large Gomez Niarchos, his head solidly stitched onto his shoulders, were among the Cabalarkon-returnees. They were there to represent the Sovereign State of Greater Godbad. Call-me-Cabby's ghost was present, insubstantial but oddly perceptible.

Was, perhaps not so strangely, visibly happy. And not just because there remained thousands of inbred imbeciles he could siphon off of psychically.

(The Fatman, Alpha Centauri, had not abandoned his aspirations to tap into the Weirdom's extraterrestrial technology. Just hadn't made up his mind as to whether there was any point in continuing to rely on diplomacy or whether it was time to test the new, reportedly – by Anvil and Cromwell Necator, who'd been under fire so hadn't seen as much as they could have – daemonic, Master militarily.)

They, the powers that then were, in late Azky (in honour of Lazareme's male healer, Azkeecyoos, himself named after the Classical Greeks' Asclepius), the Outer Earth's June, were equally happy. They'd finally agreed on something. The realm would remain the Weirdom of Cabalarkon.

The only other realistic choice was to christen it (ha, ha) the Weirdom of Lily Master-Daemon. Which-witch would never do.

Not in the long term, that was for sure.

========

Epilogue 2
The rain stopped in early Kamor, July on the Outer Earth, well short of the forty days and forty nights those on the Head with a biblical bent had begun to fear it would last until. As the clouds lifted, summer reasserted itself. So too the despair that had seemingly set in over the Weirdom of Cabalarkon since at least the Solstice dissipated.

Miraculously – more like demonically – everything was working again.

========

For days and endless days, become weeks and seemingly endless weeks, Mel-Il-luminatus had little opportunity to perform the duties of the High Illuminary. Had – so many of her people, idiots of Weir for the most part, having been severely injured during the short, but deadly cataclysms of midsummer – little choice except to be Dr Melina nee Sarpedon Zeross.

As undeniably bright, superbly well-educated, on both sides of the Dome, hence medically knowledgeable and, equally so, surgically adroit as she was, she nonetheless managed to find enough time to postulate a feasible explanation for all that had taken place on and around her (thankfully) trying-as-ever, youngest daughter's seventh birthday.

The earthquakes, aftershocks and deluge – perhaps even the Whiplash wild-fires – that bracketed the solstice had to be Dark Sedon having a temper tantrum. This after reportedly (by Irisiel Mercherm on the Valprey, just before the tidal wave hit and Island Leviathan swallowed it) agreeing, perhaps against his better judgement, to leave the Inner Earth to the altruistic ambitions of those behind not just the Witches of Weir's Panharmonium Project.

Except, after getting what he wanted: namely, the destruction of All on Incain, and the Dual Entities (presumably) slipping back into the time stream; it became more a matter of a quickly improvised Sedonplay. That being the case, he – the long-ago-latter-day Demon as well as forever Devil King – must have felt unbound by any oaths he may have made. Had seized opportunities presented to him. Had, as usual, won the game.

For the nonce anyhow. But, if he had, which he had, so too had Lively Lilith, even if she was just a Demon Queen; albeit the first and hopefully the last such.

Damn that Nihila to a smelly hell. How could she, a firstborn Lazaremist, a devil wearing an ostensibly debrained demon's body in order to keep herself solid, have so turned against her own unkind kind come endgame? Or had she? Had the endgame yet to come? Would Wilderwitch, wherever she – not her soul-self – was, had been since the Solstice, have a girl?

Could, would, she have three of them?

========

Epilogue 3

Back in the late Sixties, early Seventies, long after she and her bass-ass of an orange-skinned husband, deposed King Achigan Auranja, made their peace with Alpha Centauri (born Alfredo Sentalli on the Outer Earth, whom Bodiless Byron possessed as he then was, bodily), Centauri Enterprises and the resultant Corporate State of Greater Godbad, she (born Scylla Nereid, myrionymous Fisherwoman, the She-Fish of so many names) participated in a map-making expedition of the Hidden Continent's lands.

She'd always promised herself to lead a map-making expedition of the Headworld's seas. Finally, all these years later, that was precisely what she was doing.

========

The Fatman's roving ambassador to the Upper Head, Godfrey Necator, became Sangazur-possessed as a direct consequence of said mid-Sixties expedition; his precipitously fired bullets ricocheting into his own stupid skull, killing him on the spot. His mission to Sanguerre, capital of the Bloodlands, Sedon's Inner Nose, recently concluded, howsoever successfully, he was there for this one, too.

So was his trigger-talented, non-stupidly, non-trigger-happy, and as yet non-Sangazur-possessed son, very much alive Cromwell. The Necators weren't the only family affair aboard the Godbadian submarine when they spotted the fabled island in the Head's northern ocean. Capputis formerly Masterson, bum-numbed as he still somewhat was, disconsolate as well after Pusan Wanderlust told him to forget about marrying Lakshmi of Lemuria, was there too.

"Mom", said bum-numbed. "What's the name of that island?"

"Whaledreck. I tunny-told you about leaving the malevolent Mandams there in Azky."

"As in an Island Leviathan turd."

"As in all of Island Leviathan's turds, yes. They're as smelt-smellily-suffused with Brainrock as they have been for deep-diving-duck decades, ever since he swan-swallowed that Allegheny asteroid." A small part of Whaledreck Island promptly blew up as if in confirmation. Then it began to reform.

"I've a better name for it."

"What's that, Cappy?"

"Mom!"

"What's that, Capputis?"

"Take a look through these binoculars. Aren't those statues?"

"Oh deer in the beer, dear," she confirmed.

"Hadn't we better start calling it Damnation Isle then?"

========

Epilogue 4
Mel managed to wangle a day off in order to celebrate Helen's 13th. As if.

========

On the autumnal equinox of 5981, Master Lily began giving birth. Didn't stop with one either. Well, actually she did. It was Wilderwitch who couldn't.

"Where's my baby?" she kept repeating, screeching all the louder every time.

"Still scum-coming, Witch," kept responding Fisherwoman, her nine years' older sister in more than just Flowery Anthea.

"Not her, Fucking Fish-face," the Witch spat anew. "Fucking him!"

"Fucking Hell," exclaimed Mel-Illuminatus, realizing what had happened. There'd been two after all.

========

And the firstborn, a boy and already missing, was Satan Incarnate.

****

Next ...

Phantacea Phase Two continues with 'Wilderwitch's Babies 3'

"DESTINATION DAMNATION"

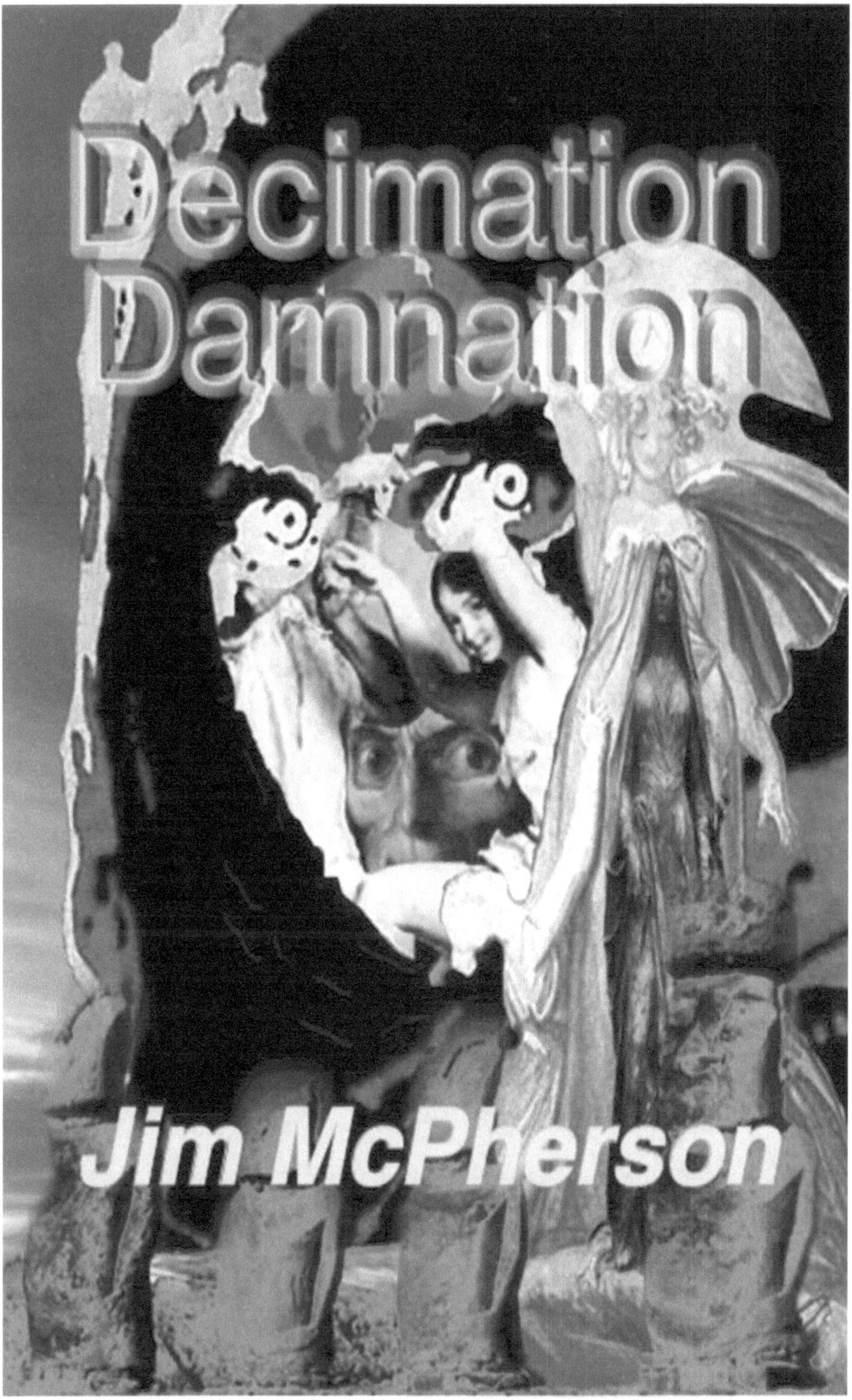
Decimation
Damnation
Jim McPherson

The Creator of the **PHANTACEA** Mythos presents
three intertwined novellas leading up and in to
the open-ended saga of **"Wilderwitch's Babies"**

Hidden Headgames

Jim McPherson

Daemonic Desperation

Jim McPherson

Destination Damnation

And then there were none ... in the Weirdom of Cabalarkon

ABANDON ALL HOPE Ye Who Enter HERE

So where did they go? Precisely!

Phantacea Publications

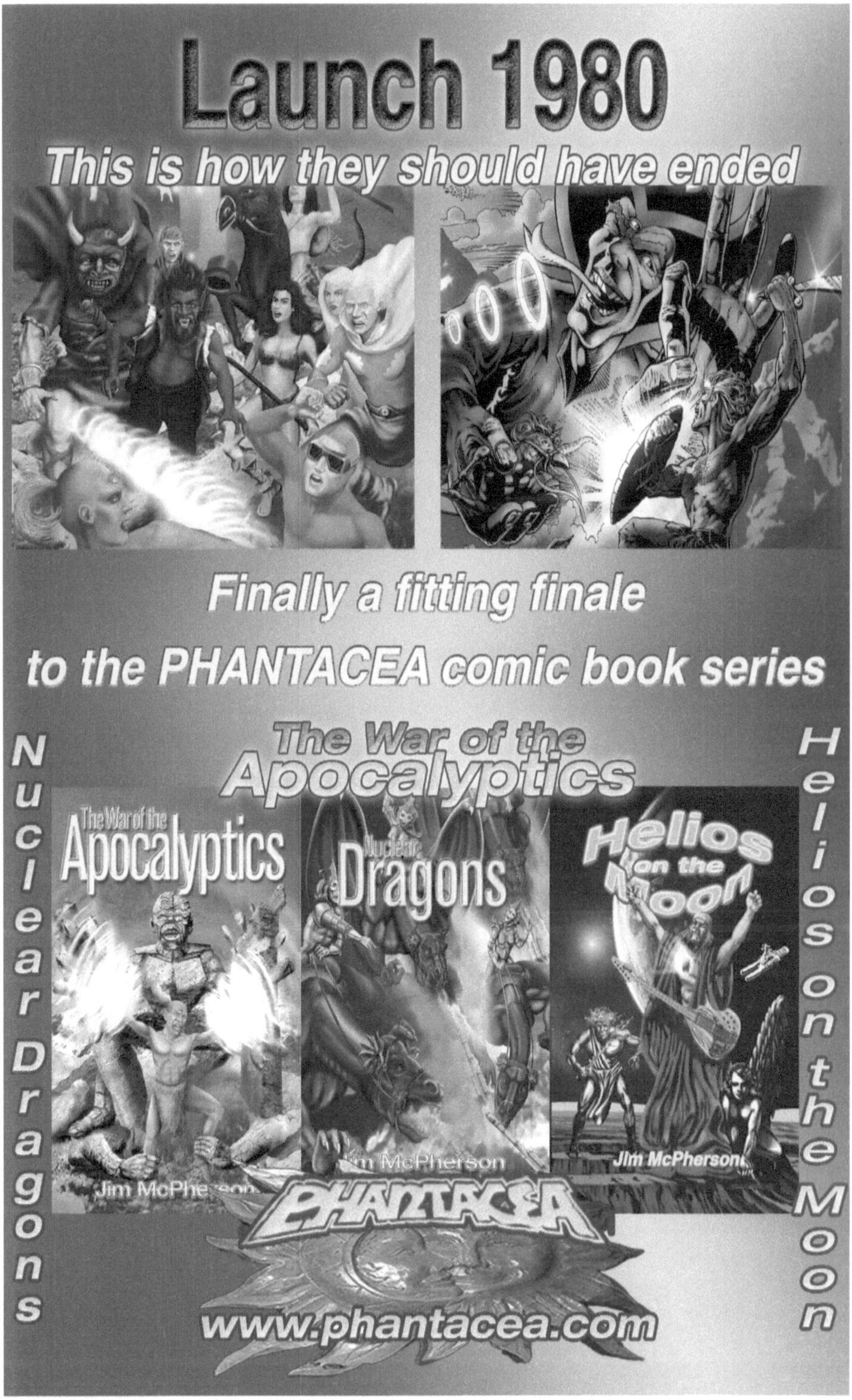
Launch 1980
This is how they should have ended
Finally a fitting finale
to the PHANTACEA comic book series
The War of the Apocalyptics
Nuclear Dragons
Helios on the Moon
The War of the Apocalyptics
Jim McPherson
Nuclear Dragons
Jim McPherson
Helios on the Moon
Jim McPherson
PHANTACEA
www.phantacea.com

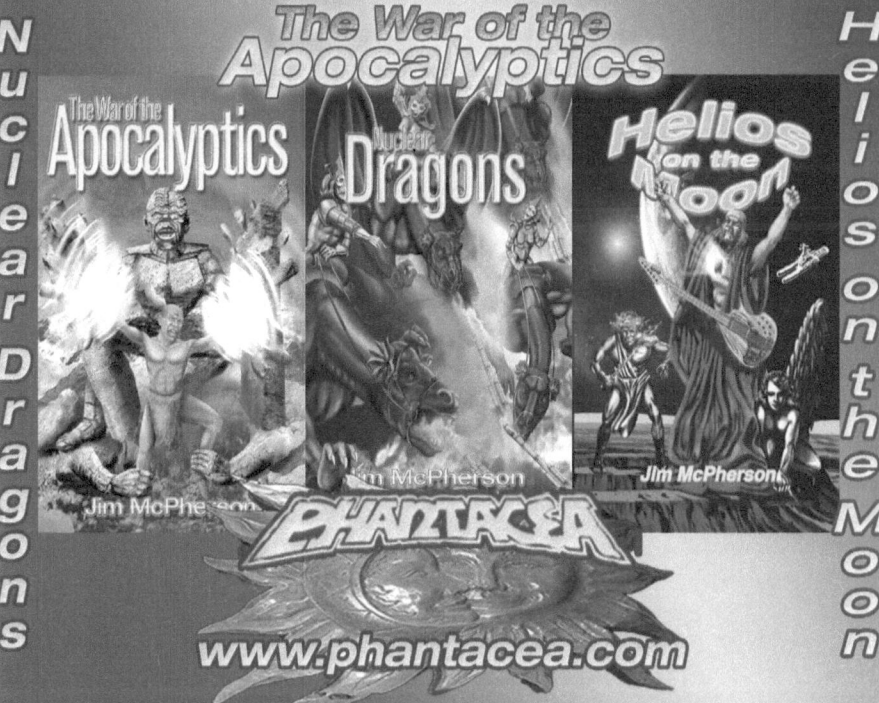